THE GRAVE IN THE ICE

Satu Rämö is a bestselling Finnish-born crime author who has lived in Iceland for the past twenty years. Her Nordic crime *Hildur* series has sold over one million copies worldwide and has been a bestseller in Finland, Iceland, Sweden and Germany. A TV adaptation will premiere in 2026 and the series has also been adapted for the stage. Satu has also published numerous bestselling, prizewinning non-fiction titles in her native Finland.

She lives with her Icelandic husband and two children in the small town of Ísafjörður in northwest Iceland.

THE GRAVE IN THE ICE

Some bodies don't stay buried

SATU RÄMÖ

Translated by Kristian London

ZAFFRE

First published as Rósa & Björk by Werner Söderström Ltd in 2023
Published in the English language by arrangement with
Bonnier Rights Finland, Helsinki, Finland

First published in the UK in 2025 by
ZAFFRE
An imprint of Bonnier Books UK
5th Floor, HYLO, 103-105 Bunhill Row,
London, EC1Y 8LZ

Copyright © Satu Rämö, 2023
English language translation © by Kristian London, 2024

All rights reserved.
No part of this publication may be reproduced,
stored or transmitted in any form by any means, electronic,
mechanical, photocopying or otherwise, without the
prior written permission of the publisher.

The right of Satu Rämö to be identified as Author of this
work has been asserted by her in accordance with the
Copyright, Designs and Patents Act, 1988.

This is a work of fiction. Names, places, events and
incidents are either the products of the author's
imagination or used fictitiously. Any resemblance to
actual persons, living or dead, or actual
events is purely coincidental.

A CIP catalogue record for this book is
available from the British Library.

ISBN: 978-1-80418-847-7

Also available as an ebook and an audiobook

3 5 7 9 10 8 6 4 2

Typeset by IDSUK (Data Connection) Ltd
Printed and bound in Great Britain by Clays Ltd, Elcograf S.p.A.

The authorised representative in the EEA is Bonnier Books
UK (Ireland) Limited.
Registered office address: Floor 3, Block 3, Miesian Plaza,
Dublin 2, D02 Y754, Ireland
compliance@bonnierbooks.ie
www.bonnierbooks.co.uk

At my journey's end I find you
welcoming me with open arms
I've come home,
yes, I've come home.
'Ég er kominn heim,' lyrics Jón Sigurðsson (1960)

(p. 200) Excerpt from the *Laxdoela Saga* translated by
Margaret Arent,
1964. University of Washington Press.

BEFORE

Chapter 1

1994, Ísafjörður

Big, wet snowflakes hit the glass faster and faster, like fat flies smearing against the windscreen. It was November, early winter. The days were dark on the way in to work, dark on the way home. The sun rose in the northern sky for a few hours but remained behind the mountains encircling the town. The locals spent the whole winter in shadow.

The man's jaw was twitching, and his hands clenched the wheel. He knew he was late, badly so. An hour earlier, his car had got stuck in the snow, and freeing it had consumed precious time. He was behind schedule.

The car was moving too slowly, but he didn't dare drive any faster: he hadn't switched to winter tyres yet, and the road was slick. If he accelerated, he might drive off the road, and everything would be ruined.

He shouldn't be here anyway, shouldn't have let himself get caught up in this. He cursed himself for having agreed to it. But it wasn't as if he'd had a choice. No one was going to hire a lonely, uneducated man like himself. His dead gran's favourite phrase had been, *Once you start playing you can't reshuffle the deck*. You had to work with the cards you were dealt. His grandmother had been widowed young and looked after her brood of children on her own, milked the cows and salted the cod. Earning a livelihood had meant a lot of hard work. It still did. It was his lot to take whatever grunt jobs he could get, legal or not. He made more money from the latter, and money was what he needed. This was the sort of job that provided it.

The man hiked up the sleeve of his off-white sweater and glanced at his watch. Four o'clock. Somehow the snowstorm had already moved in from the sea. Goddammit. The weather forecast had said it wouldn't snow until evening.

Past the roundabout the road appeared to have been ploughed. He decided to take a risk and give it more gas. The snow kept coming down harder, but the lamp posts standing sentry on the roadside helped him navigate.

Then he saw something that extinguished his spark of hope. The school bus. The vehicle carrying children drove past in the opposite direction. The disappointment stung. He was too late.

At the next intersection, he took a left onto the street. He pulled up in front of his building, turned off the ignition, and pondered.

He rubbed his forehead, where beads of sweat had formed. The scar itched. Anytime he was agitated, it started to itch. He scratched at it a couple of times with the thick nail of his forefinger. Pure pleasure. The nail sank into the pitted, pimpled skin and moved back and forth. He let out a deep sigh and kept scratching. He knew picking at the scar was stupid, but the momentary relief was so gratifying he found the temptation impossible to resist.

Now he knew what he needed to do. The school bus would make several stops. He could pass it and drive to the right stop to wait. That's what he'd do. Of course.

He was just twisting the key in the ignition when he spotted movement to his left. The front door opened. He turned that way and saw two little girls had stepped out. They stopped at the corner of the building, apparently to discuss something. They were hunched over to shield themselves from the swirling snow.

What were the girls still doing here? The school bus was gone. He rubbed his scar again and thought. Maybe they'd missed it. He sat up straighter but didn't start up the car. Not yet. He didn't want to draw attention to himself.

He took a closer look at the girls. Their appearance matched his client's description.

His client. That's what he called anyone who asked for any variety of services in exchange for payment. Today's job had seemed bizarre, but the amount offered had been so substantial that he'd stifled his doubts and accepted the commission.

There were supposed to be three girls, but he only saw two. Where was the third one? He observed his surroundings for a moment but didn't see anyone. So be it. He'd do as promised regardless.

Two little girls with a slight difference in height. Lambskin winter hats, the younger in a fur-trimmed winter coat. The taller had a red backpack with a pony on it. They were still deep in conversation. The smaller one was pointing at her shoes and crying. The bigger girl took the little one by the shoulders and whispered something in her ear.

Then the girls set out walking. On small, cautious steps they headed for the main road, using their hands to shield their faces from the lashing snow.

The main road only led in one direction, away from the centre of town. He kept his eyes on the two hunched figures. He waited until he decided they were far enough before starting up the car. The girls didn't look back once. They were walking single file along the shoulder. He pulled out when they'd reached the church and the bend in the road.

The storm had driven everyone indoors. When the weather was this bad, no one was out and about unless absolutely necessary.

There was very little traffic. He saw a grey car pass the girls on its way into town, but it didn't even slow down.

Fantastic. This is fantastic, he thought to himself. His client would be happy; he'd be happy. He'd finish the job, and everyone would win.

Well, he wasn't sure about the girls. He didn't know exactly what to make of them. He didn't really know them and didn't understand his client's thinking. He drummed the steering wheel erratically. Understanding wasn't part of the job. That was why he had no intention of beginning to wonder why the girls needed to be picked up or where they'd end up. He'd carry out the assignment and collect the second half of his commission. After that, he'd forget everything, as if none of it had ever happened.

A few minutes passed and the snow eased. He flicked off his windscreen wipers in satisfaction. He let his thoughts wander to the money that would soon be coming his way. To all the wonderful things it would make possible. He'd have a deposit for a place of his own. He could take a break from mind-numbing outdoor labour, leave the grunt work to others, and focus on enjoying life for a change. His pockmarked face broke out in a smug smile.

He steered to the side of the road and stopped. He wanted to wait for the girls to get a little further on.

The bigger girl took the smaller one by the hand and they walked faster.

The man smiled to himself when he realised where they were headed. They weren't going to take the highland road home; they were going to enter the new tunnel that linked three villages. It wasn't open to vehicular traffic yet, but almost all the locals knew it was finished. The tunnel ran all the way through the mountain now.

The snow started picking up again. The afternoon light was fading. Before long it would be as dark outside as it was in the tunnel. The man smirked and scratched at his scar again. The girls' plan suited him to a T. There would be no one else in the tunnel, no witnesses to what was about to happen.

The man maintained a couple of hundred metres' distance between himself and the girls, monitoring their progress through the windscreen. Step by step, the girls advanced into the tunnel. The last glimpse he saw was of the red backpack. And then the girls were gone.

He quickly glanced around again. He saw no movement anywhere. No people, no cars. He was enveloped in a late-afternoon gloom that was growing thicker with every passing moment. The yellow plastic bags in the back seat contained the clothes the client had insisted on and a few stuffed animals. He scratched his forefinger across the scar one last, long time, relishing every moment.

Then he stepped on the accelerator, and the car vanished into the mouth of the tunnel.

Chapter 2

Summer 2008, Ísafjörður

The suit jacket fitted impeccably, even though the low chair forced the tall man into an awkward forward tilt. He tried to straighten his legs under the table. He couldn't fathom why anyone would want these uncomfortable Danish designer chairs in their home. He didn't find the cognac-coloured furniture particularly beautiful, but he supposed it suited the understated Scandinavian décor. A single chair probably cost more than a month's rent for a studio apartment in downtown Reykjavík. You would think for money like that you would get a seat that was comfortable. Apparently not. He nudged his chair back from the dining table, sat up straighter, and crossed his right leg over his left.

'These chairs are a nightmare,' the man in glasses said, filling the tall man's cup with steaming coffee. He explained he didn't care for his wife's taste but had come to tolerate it. 'We get along better when she can do whatever she wants with the house. And when she's happy, it's easier for me to take special privileges.' He gave a conspiratorial wink and returned the chrome coffee pot to its stand.

The tall man chuckled and reached for the carton of cream. The nurses at work always packed the break-room fridge with foul-smelling skim milk. He swirled a silver spoon around his cup, took a sip, and shut his eyes. The rich cream accentuated the deep flavour of the dark roast. Just now life felt perfect.

Life seemed to have treated his old friend well too. The house was stunning: light-filled and large, at least two hundred square metres. The garden was gorgeously maintained, and there appeared to be a fountain burbling in the backyard. Contemporary Nordic art hung on the walls. The gleaming new kitchen appliances replicated the meticulously curated images from the latest interior design magazines.

'Beautiful house,' he offered. 'I haven't been here before.'

'We moved here a few years ago. We needed more space,' the man in glasses said, seating himself across the table.

He pushed an assortment of chocolates toward his friend. 'Have some Belgian chocolate. I found this amazing shop in Bruges when I was there on business. We have them delivered from time to time.' An enigmatic smile spread across his face as he savoured his confection. 'Not to mention, the woman who makes them is really something else.' His hands made a gesture suggesting curves. 'The loyal customer benefits are so good I've got in the habit of stopping by in person to pick up gifts to bring home.'

The tall man burst into laughter and shook his head. 'You haven't changed a bit.'

'Why would I? If it's not broken, don't fix it,' the man in glasses said, helping himself to a second truffle from the tray.

They took a moment to appreciate the chocolates' flavour. Then the tall man shifted in his seat again. He didn't have much time. He was supposed to be on duty in thirty minutes, ready to receive patients. The deadly dull evening shift had fallen to him this week. Children with earaches, farmers kicked by horses, blood pressure checks, prescription renewals. His private practice in Reykjavík was his bread and butter, but he had to take the occasional on-call shift in the public sector to maintain his medical licence. He preferred to do so in rural areas, where the pay was better.

'So why did you ask me over for coffee on a busy weekday afternoon?'

The man sitting across the table removed his round glasses, rubbed his eyelids between his forefinger and thumb, and put the glasses back on. He reached over to a nearby shelf, retrieved a blue folder, and laid it on the table in front of him.

'Inside this folder, there's a piece of paper with a name on it. You treated this individual. Now her paperwork has mysteriously disappeared.' He pushed the folder across the table and looked his friend keenly in the eye. He stressed his words by tapping his forefinger on the folder three times: 'Do you understand? Disappeared. It's unfortunate, but these things happen sometimes.'

The tall man hesitated. Then he picked up the folder, slipped off the elastic straps, and opened it. When he saw the name printed on the piece of paper he flinched. Of course he remembered the patient. It had been an exceptionally ugly case. What was being asked of him felt impossible. There was no way he could—

The man in glasses cleared his throat and raised his voice the tiniest amount. 'I can see your reluctance. There's no need for it. It's not as bad as it seems at first glance. Ultimately we're talking about minutiae. It will be over before you know it.'

The folder felt clammy in the tall man's hand. He set it down. His gut lurched, and he felt nauseous. The creamy coffee was churning in his stomach.

'It's simple! The paperwork disappears, and you get that piece of land you've been eyeing all these years. I'll get the council to vote on the matter next week,' the man in glasses continued, interlacing his fingers under his chin.

The piece of land. The tall man had been trying to buy the plot of county-owned land for ages. He had an idea for a very profitable business. The international investors were all lined up, and the groundwork had been laid. All he needed now was the land. Once he had it, there would be no stopping the money from flowing in.

The fish-processing plant would be his road to riches. He had no intention of spending the rest of his life prodding strangers' bodies and listening to their complaints. He had a nice salary, he wasn't denying that, but practising medicine wouldn't ever bring real wealth. A facility for processing farmed salmon was a totally different matter. It would make him a lot of money. He would initiate operations and sell to Norwegian investors after a couple of years. The preliminary agreements had already been signed. His long-term plan was to leave doctoring behind and switch wholly to business. He wanted to make his way into bigger circles, to get away from this miserable island. And the fish-processing plant played a critical role in his plans.

The tall man reached for the pitcher on the table and poured himself a glass of cold water. He forced himself to think logically. The situation called for nerves of steel. Plan well, execute fearlessly. Don't waffle. Attack when your opponent is unprepared. He'd read that in his favourite book, Sun Tzu's *The Art of War*. That's exactly what he would do; there was no alternative.

He set down his empty glass, stood, pushed the uncomfortable chair back under the table, and took the folder. Then he held out his hand, sealing the deal.

NOW

Chapter 3

Reykjavík, February 2020

A mild early spring breeze tousled Detective Hildur Rúnarsdóttir's long hair, fluttering the tips northward. She folded her towel and set it on the bench next to her backpack, then slipped into her cheap white sandals. Sandals were a must, as the shoreline could be littered with shards of glass and other rubbish. She crossed the pale sand and passed the pier. The lagoon excavated to its right was heated; a hot spring pumped into the water kept it at over fifteen degrees Celsius. Hildur ignored the warm water and made for the unheated sea. She kicked off her sandals and stepped into the cold water.

The chill first hit her ankles, then her knees. The sandy bottom pleasantly massaged the soles of her feet. The waterfront homes of Kópavogur rose across the bay. When the eight-degree water rose above her abdominal muscles, she threw herself in and began to swim.

She was irritated she had to share the beach. The sea had always been her place to enjoy peace and quiet and do without the presence of others. Although it was early in the year, Reykjavík's public beach was surprisingly busy. Cold-water swimming had exploded in popularity in recent years, and it showed. The shore was packed with swimmers in neoprene suits and gloves, chattering loudly with each other.

Hildur never used gear when she swam in cold water. She wore a wetsuit when she surfed, but swimming was a different matter. You were supposed to feel the cold on your skin. She wanted to cool off properly now and again. As the chill surged from the soles of her feet to her core and torso, her heart slowed. That soothed her.

After swimming a good two hundred metres, she heard someone on shore yelling at her. A stout older man in a white terry-cloth robe had formed his hands into a trumpet and was shouting at the top of his lungs:

'You shouldn't go out that far!'

Hildur was annoyed at having to stop. She waved at the man and gave him the thumbs up to let him know she had things under control.

The sea meant everything to Hildur. It medicated her grief and helped her find joy. It gave her solitude and the chance to wrestle with something she could never best. She loved surfing. But it was hard in Reykjavík, because there weren't the waves or empty beaches she was used to back home in the Westfjords.

Hildur knew the city well from her student days: she'd attended the police academy in the capital and stayed on for a few years to work. When the police station in her hometown had advertised it was looking for a detective and someone to head up the rural missing children's unit, Hildur had applied for the job and got it.

The return to Ísafjörður had gone well. For the last ten years, her life had been relatively stable. Hildur felt at home between the steep mountains and the surging sea. Many found the forces of nature and dark winters as oppressive, but not Hildur. For her, the restless wind and huge waves that lashed the shores of the small town brought clarity and calm. They formed limits that forced her to stay put.

Existence could be unbearable at times. When the angst struck, Hildur would retreat into her own bubble. She'd feel isolated from the rest of the world. The heaviness in her chest and stomach would swell, constrict her breathing. When that happened, all Hildur wanted to do was hide in the chill of the stormy sea.

She'd only had a couple of chances to go surfing over the past two months, which was no doubt why she'd been so tense lately.

Hildur had been compelled to temporarily return to the capital the month before. Tumi Einarsson, a friend and colleague from her Reykjavík days, had tripped on the job and banged up his knee. The resulting sick leave had been estimated at two months. Hildur had promised to substitute for Tumi, because his friendship meant so much to her and because he'd asked for her specifically. He led the national missing children's unit. But Hildur didn't care for the city life. Sitting in traffic, construction noise, and the non-stop flow of cases exhausted her. She longed to get back to Ísafjordur. Luckily Tumi only had a couple of weeks of sick leave left.

She'd soon make her escape. Maybe that would alleviate the unease that had nagged at her for the past few days. The feeling was a familiar visitor and had been since her childhood. Hildur knew her grandmother had once been one of Iceland's best-known seers; Hrafntinna had predicted the future and offered advice to those who sought it. According to folk tradition, seeing was a hereditary gift but not passed down to all. Tinna, the aunt Hildur had lived with as a young woman, thought Hrafntinna's gift of foresight had skipped a generation and been transmitted to Hildur. Hildur wasn't so sure. When it came down to it, she had little use for fortune tellers and fairy tales. She did sometimes predict accidents and acts of violence just before they happened. But there was nothing she could do about them.

A couple of weeks before, Iceland had witnessed a tragic air accident. A small aircraft had plummeted into the sea right after take-off, killing the pilot. A few days prior to the accident, Hildur had been unusually restless, so she hadn't been surprised when she heard about the plane dropping into the water. She'd been expecting something of the sort.

When younger, Hildur had nursed a fervent hope that her premonitions would convey practical information. At least they'd be of some use, then. But she simply had to tolerate the knowledge that something bad was about to occur, with no idea what or to whom. Her powerlessness in the face of approaching devastation was something she couldn't evade. She'd just tried to learn to accept it over the years.

Hildur took a few more strokes, slicing through the icy sea. When the expensive-looking terrace houses on the Kópavogur waterfront drew near, she turned around. She inhaled, dived, and kicked. The water's rush filled her ears, and a trail of tiny bubbles erupted from her mouth. She felt the familiar burn in her lungs. She gave a few more kicks before letting her body rise. When her head broke the surface, she greedily gobbled air.

Hildur emerged from the sea and made her way to the sand, wrung most of the saltwater from her long hair, and slipped into her old sandals.

The arms of the man in the terry-cloth robe were folded demonstratively across his chest. He glared reproachfully at her. 'Diving like that in the winter is risky for your health.'

Hildur hopped on her right foot to drain the water from her right ear. The guy's supposed concern rubbed her the wrong way: she knew if she were a middle-aged man, no one would be trying to baby her by offering swimming advice.

'I'm used to cold water,' she said simply as she passed him. 'I'm from the Westfjords.'

Her blood was surging through her veins. The cooling sensation was followed by a safe warmth. The swim had taken away some of the swelling heaviness inside her. She folded the towel, set it on the wooden bench, and sat in the cold air for a moment. The wind felt delicious on her sea-chilled skin.

Hildur pondered. The oppressive feeling generally passed after the misfortune occurred but the plane crash hadn't dispelled it. She still felt a little uneasy. She remembered experiencing the sensation for the first time the morning of the day her sisters Rósa and Björk disappeared. They vanished on their way home from school, never to be seen again.

The lack of progress in the case galled Hildur. When she'd stumbled across new information about her long-lost sisters during a convoluted murder investigation last autumn, a wisp of hope had kindled inside her. The clothes her sisters had been wearing when they disappeared had turned up buried with a pile of bones. But Axlar-Hákon had analyzed the clothes and bones in Reykjavík and was sure they weren't human.

The pathologist Hákon Bjarnason had been bequeathed a memorable nickname during his student years, when he'd played the lead in a student production about the sixteenth-century Icelandic serial killer Axlar-Björn. He'd thrown himself into the role with such gusto that he'd been called Axlar-Hákon ever since, in honour of the axe murderer's weapon of choice.

Hildur was grateful to her friend for analyzing the bones. She'd hoped the newly discovered belongings would provide fresh clues as to her sisters' fate, but her hope had proved in vain. The tracks had come to an end, and she hadn't managed to decipher anything new.

As Hildur observed the chatting crowd, she sensed the onset of spring's brightness. Before long the days would lengthen and then summer would arrive. But she needed something to snap herself out of this feeling. Today's feeble waves hadn't provided sufficient relief after all; she'd have to think of something else. She stood and walked to the dressing room. Once clothed, she reached into the side pocket of her bag for her phone and brought up the relevant app.

Chapter 4

Westfjords, February 2020

The wood floor creaked underfoot as the hunter crouched to peer out the window. A pair of birds arced above the snow; otherwise all was still. It was early evening. The sun would soon set behind the mountains, but for now it continued to bathe the surroundings in a soft light. The sole sound was the wheeze of the hunter's breathing. A whiff of oil and metal tinged the air.

The little wooden hut stood in the middle of an open expanse. It was as cold inside as it was out, but the walls offered protection from the wind sweeping across the uplands.

The hunter stroked the warm barrel of the Sako 85 rifle and grunted in satisfaction. The stock was oiled walnut. It felt good against the hunter's bare hands.

The hunter took the black cylinder from the ledge running along the longest wall. The hunter's fingers curled lightly around it. The silencer would muffle the report. The accessory had other good qualities too: it dampened the muzzle flash and improved the firearm's precision.

When the magazine was in place, the hunter loaded the chamber, pulled back the safety, and sat down, steadying the barrel against the windowsill. A standing position would have been too awkward for such a shot.

The moment would soon arrive. The hunter bent down to peer through the scope and waited. A moment passed, another. Eventually the anticipated target appeared in the sights.

Remove the safety, check the target, hold the breath, purse the lips. Slide the finger to the trigger. A second later, pull it.

A look through the binoculars confirmed it was a bullseye. The shot had found its mark exactly as intended.

Chapter 5

Reykjavík, Summer 2016

Dísa

'A crowd of up to thirty thousand is expected in downtown Reykjavík today. Those arriving from elsewhere should note the city centre is closed to vehicular traffic. Buses will be driving alternate routes until 11 p.m. Up next, we have the weather . . .'

The radio was blaring from the speaker at a nearby hot dog stand. Dísa lowered her hands to her legs and dug her fingers into her skinny thighs. She was trying to calm herself. The buses that had been diverted earlier that day had complicated her commute. The food bank was located at the outskirts of a large shopping centre a few kilometres east of the old centre. Dísa had taken the bus out and filled her backpack with bread and tinned food, but on its way back into town the bus had turned away from the centre instead of driving to the station. She'd had to walk over half an hour from the stop where she got off to her basement flat on Nönnugata.

Things had gone to hell at the apartment. If she'd made it home earlier, she wouldn't have run into her landlords, Palli and Eiríkur. The men had said she could stay with them for a modest rent until the end of summer, when Hilmar would be released from prison and need his room back.

Dísa's ten-metre-square room was a former storage space at the back of the flat. There were no windows, and she couldn't lock the door from the inside. She'd harboured no illusions about what pricks Eiríkur and Palli were. But she'd had no choice. She was tired of living on the streets.

Dísa had decided, come what may, she would never be homeless again. It was too unsafe. Besides, she couldn't stand the stares of passersby. Hauling her belongings around day in, day out, filled her with shame.

She'd been kicked out of her previous home that spring because the entire building was being converted into Airbnb rentals for tourists. The house before that, where she'd been lucky enough to live for almost two months with a few other quiet homeless people, had been damaged in a fire.

After getting evicted, she'd bumped into Palli and Eiríkur. They all hung around the same crowd at the Hlemmur bus station, self-medicating. Whoever had the funds bought. If you bought on credit, you paid on time or you had real problems. And women always paid a heavier price than men; Dísa knew that from personal experience.

Today had been another example of this. She'd owed Eiríkur some money for a fix from a few weeks back. She was supposed to pay by yesterday but couldn't. She had no money. The day before yesterday, she'd snatched a couple of purses from a tourist café, but it hadn't done any good. Neither had contained cash or anything she could quickly exchange for it.

When Dísa had returned to the flat with her food, Palli and Eiríkur had been waiting for her in the kitchen. Eiríkur had been furious, justifiably so. Dísa owed him, and debts had to be paid on the agreed date. The rules were clear.

Even though she knew it was pointless, Dísa had asked for more time. This had simply fed Eiríkur's rage, and he'd slapped her across the face. After the slap, Dísa had decided she'd stop begging. She'd accept the consequences and take what was coming to her. After pushing her around and rifling through her pockets, Eiríkur had dragged Dísa into his room and torn the clothes from her body.

Palli had brayed and locked the door from the outside. The assault had lasted ages. Dísa couldn't say exactly how long, but it didn't matter. She hadn't said a word the whole time, just waited in silence for it to be over. As Eiríkur yanked his trousers back on, he mentioned – as casually as if talking about the weather – that she'd just covered the interest. She still had to repay the loan.

The early evening sun was shining right into Dísa's eyes. She stared at her feet and focused on breathing calmly. Her long-sleeved hoodie concealed the bruises on her arms. She'd pulled up the hood to hide her swollen cheek. The last thing she needed was people staring at her. But she hadn't wanted to stay in her gloomy room, either; she'd had to get out. Maybe the fresh air would clear her mind, and she'd think of a way to pay her debt. She'd grabbed the backpack with the food in it just in case. She wasn't sure when she'd be able to return to her lodgings.

Crowds began to fill the city centre. The narrow pedestrian street was packed with people waving Icelandic flags; they moved in a single wave toward the hill next to the concert hall, where the celebrations would soon begin.

The city was seething like an anthill. Dísa experienced the human swarm as tiny electric shocks on her skin. She pulled her sleeves down over her hands and clenched her fists. The unsettling tingle reached all the way to her fingertips, and her head ached. If she didn't get something soon, she'd crumble. She had to get her next fix; it was the only way she'd be able to stand this shit.

Her feet struck the backpack under the bench. The cans from the food bank were still in it. Maybe she'd be lucky and someone at Hlemmur would want to exchange the food for a single pill. It was the first good idea she'd had all day, and it improved her mood a little.

Dísa became aware of a swelling roar. The blast of horns that just a moment ago had been far away was drawing close. The crowd on the street kept growing. The thunderous cries of support and applause were repeating rhythmically: *Hú! Hú! Hú!* The celebrating mass of humanity was coming down the street, and the victory cries got louder. Someone was leaning on a car horn.

Suddenly the hard bench felt revolting against her broken skin. The surrounding intensity was making her more and more anxious. Dísa decided to head to the bus station then and there. She was most likely to run into someone she knew around this time anyway, before the homeless shelters opened their doors.

Then Dísa spotted the approaching vehicle. The only one allowed to drive along the streets of downtown Reykjavík today. The vehicle was the reason all of them were there.

The big black truck gleamed in the rays of the evening sun. It turned downhill at the church and descended the street lined by handcraft stores and goldsmiths' shops. It crawled along at a slow, dignified pace as the driver sounded the horn.

Iceland's soccer team had returned from France. Dísa couldn't care less about soccer, but even she couldn't ignore the soccer madness billowing around her. Over the past few weeks, the Icelandic national men's soccer team had beat first Austria and then England in the European Championships. After every game, the streets of downtown Reykjavík had filled with cheering crowds. Today was the day the players had come home.

The black truck slid down the street toward Dísa. There they were, standing proudly in the bed, the players making their way to the stage set up downtown, where tens of thousands of fans were waiting.

Dísa had no interest in joining the crowd. She set out in the opposite direction. The Hlemmur bus station was located at the other end of the city centre.

When the truck reached Dísa, it turned left toward the concert hall. And at that moment, she made the mistake of looking up.

One glance was all it took. Dísa felt the wind being knocked out of her. The world started spinning. She had to steady herself against the bench.

She recognised him. He was standing in the second row, behind the team captain. Dísa couldn't get a clear view of him, but seeing his face was enough. She would never forget it. His eyes were scouring the sea of people, greedy for admiration, and then she saw them linger on her for a fraction of a second. Dísa wasn't sure if she was imagining it, or if the terror of recognition had actually flashed across his face when their eyes met. The stony expression vanished from his face as abruptly as it had appeared, and now he was smiling broadly again and waving at the worshipful crowd, like a king sitting on his throne.

Still steadying herself against the bench, Dísa watched him raise his fists in the air and whip up the fans walking alongside the truck in a cheer: *Hú! Hú! Hú!*

The players' gestures were raucous and their faces radiated joy. They knew they were being worshipped. *Unbelievable talents.* That's what all the newspapers in the world had been writing about them over the past few days. *Miraculous Icelanders. Gifted players. Huge heroes from a tiny country.*

A bitter taste filled Dísa's mouth. She turned her back on the crowd, grabbed her backpack, and began slowly making her way in the opposite direction.

She was glad she had the food. All those cans of different sizes and colours knocking around in her backpack in time to her footfalls. Tuna, beans, corn. If she was fortunate the flat tin might contain meat. That would be a lucky break. Tinned meat was a valuable commodity.

She imagined the feeling of the pill on her tongue just before she swallowed it. And then she started walking faster and forgot about the man standing tall and smug in the bed of the truck.

Chapter 6

Reykjavík, February 2020

Hildur took a sip of the triple-shot latte she'd ordered. It tasted superb. She did a few shoulder rolls and the pleasant, familiar burn permeated her arms. The strength training at the Reykjavík MMA gym had sapped her upper body, and it felt great.

The warm sun shone into the coffee shop. It was located at a prime spot on Laugavegur between a couple of hotels and an Icelandic streetwear store. People strolled down the pedestrian street more slowly than usual. They weren't hurrying out of the rain or snow; they were luxuriating. The surprisingly bright sunshine brought smiles to their faces. It wasn't as if winter had completely retreated. Even down south here in Reykjavík, it continued to breathe down Icelanders' necks. But today it felt almost like spring.

Cheerful chatter carried from the back of the coffee shop. The baristas were steaming oat milk for speciality drinks. The place smelled of fresh-baked pastries. A mood of light-hearted giddiness and anticipation filled the venue. It was Friday, after all.

Superficially Reykjavík seemed lovely, but Hildur knew that wasn't the whole truth. Work had been unusually heavy today. She'd had a particularly depressing case to deal with. A seventeen-year-old boy had been the victim of sexual assault. The interview had been conducted at the Children's House, which was located at a secret address on the outskirts of Reykjavík. All interviews with underage victims, perpetrators, and witnesses of crimes took place at the house, where police and prosecutors could talk to the children with the support of trained trauma therapists and psychologists.

Helping children and adolescents made Hildur feel like she was doing something important. Maybe she was trying to compensate for what had happened to her family so long ago. She'd probably felt that by helping children she could help herself.

After work, Hildur had had to get her mind off things. What she really wanted to do was go surfing, but the waves weren't cooperating. Yesterday's swim in the sea had done her good, but on Fridays the beach was far too crowded. So she'd hit the gym instead.

Hildur didn't spend time on social media. She had a Facebook profile, but only for work. She didn't use her full name and didn't give away any details about herself. The profile was merely a tool for her to acquire information. People shared surprising amounts about themselves on social media, and a lot of people's profiles were completely public. Friends, trips and interests were just a couple of clicks away. And that was useful when doing detective work.

She only installed Tinder when she wanted company. After a date, she'd shut down the account and delete the app from her phone. She had other rules she adhered to as well. To keep things simple, she only went on dates with foreigners and only in Reykjavík. There was no question of hook-ups back home in Ísafjörður, and it would have felt awkward to open the app and see a bunch of faces she knew, from a neighbour to the librarian. Everyone in Ísafjörður – population two thousand, give or take – knew each other, and forming new acquaintances was hard without the whole town finding out. Hildur didn't usually care what others said, but just now she wasn't in a place where she wanted to be the subject of any gossip.

It had been a hard winter. She'd lost someone important to her: her next-door neighbour Freysi. The two of them had been seeing each other for some time and gradually grown close. And then Freysi was murdered.

It had been a massive shock.

But now, a few months after Freysi's death, Hildur was beginning to feel the impulse to date again. Some might consider four months a short mourning period, but Hildur didn't see it that way. She still thought of Freysi all the time. Despite her sorrow, she had no trouble reminiscing about her good memories of him. And the day would no doubt come when enough time had passed that she'd no longer be savaged by grief.

Hildur had no interest in a life partner, let alone a husband. She was pretty sure there was no one she'd be able to stand that much shared time with, in the long run. No way could she assume responsibility for someone else's happiness or constantly take their needs into consideration. Before long, someone would get bored, and then at least one of them would get frustrated. Why make things complicated if there was a simpler option?

Hildur stood at the bar table in the front window, swirling the teaspoon around her latte. The foam had spilled over the edges of the light-brown mug. She scooped some foam into her spoon and took a bite of her cookie.

She'd come across a good-looking guy on Tinder who, after a brief exchange of private messages, turned out to be a Finnish fireman. His name was Jari, and he'd said he was in town for a training course. The two of them had agreed to meet at this coffee shop. He said he'd be coming straight from his class.

Just then the door opened, and a short-haired man in a black tracksuit stepped in. He had a brown leather satchel slung casually over one shoulder, and he eyed the place one table at a time. Hildur liked what she was seeing. He was at least as handsome in the flesh as in his photos, and she could read from his demeanour he was sure he'd come to the right place.

When he turned toward the window table, a look of delight spread across his face. He walked straight up to Hildur.

Hildur took a sip of her latte and nodded at the barista toiling at the espresso machine: 'You want a coffee?'

Jari didn't say anything; he just stood there. Hildur found the situation amusing. She thought about her partner, the Finnish police intern Jakob, who wasn't one for small talk either. *Are all Finnish men so stingy with their words?* she wondered.

Jari adjusted the bag that had slipped from his shoulder and kept smiling. 'We can get coffee later, can't we?'

Hildur nodded and pushed away her empty mug. She reached down to grab her gym bag from under the table and swung her braid over her shoulder to the back of her neck.

'Sure. My hotel is right nearby.'

Hildur was feeling frisky. The late-February sun was making her squint, and she was overcome by a momentary lightness.

Life can be like this sometimes too, she reflected.

And she meant to make the most of it, at least for the next few hours.

Chapter 7

Westfjords, February 2020

Hermann Hermannsson stepped lightly out of his SUV and allowed his sinewy body to rise to its full height. He inhaled, filling his lungs with the fresh February mountain air.

He would be turning sixty-five this summer, and he still felt like he was in the prime of his life. Lean and lithe, no paunch. When it came down to it, many things in life depended solely on one's personal choices.

Hermann pulled his black windproof gloves from the pocket of his ski jacket and slipped on his lightweight beanie. The ski box attached to the roof of his SUV opened effortlessly with a click. He pulled out the skis and poles, slipped them under his arm, and walked over to the little lodge housing the café and information desk.

The cross-country skiing area looked empty. The lodge was dark, and there were no other vehicles in the car park. Hermann pressed the switch on the exterior wall to turn on the trail lights. It wasn't dark yet, but if he took the longer route, darkness would fall before he returned. Of course he had a headlamp, but it only illuminated a short, narrow sliver of track.

Orange cones and blue ropes marked the start of the track. They'd been set up for tomorrow's fifty k. Hermann knew his fitness would have easily put him among the top ten. But he didn't have time to participate; he had other plans for the weekend. This time a Friday excursion would have to suffice.

Hermann jammed his poles into the snow and left them there as he skied off for his one k warm-up. He found it easiest to get in the rhythm of classic cross-country skiing by relying exclusively on the power of his legs and core. Skiing went more smoothly if you took a moment to find the right rhythm with your lower body before you began.

Once he was warm, he grabbed his poles and pushed himself toward the first climb. It was a beautiful evening. The sunset sky was stained lilac, and the horizon blazed orange. The terrain was dominated by a flat-topped mountain nearly a thousand metres tall. The track to the mountain's base was stunning, and at the turnaround you felt like you were above everyone. Hermann chuckled at the thought. And so he was! He was a man who made things happen.

He glanced over his left shoulder at the vista. More and more sea filled the view. The town on the fjord looked tiny from his bird's-eye perspective. The snow down in Ísafjörður had already melted away, but up here in the mountains there would be snow late into the spring.

Hermann's bright orange ski jacket stood out like an exclamation mark in the white landscape. He was a glowing smudge advancing steadily across the terrain.

Kick, glide. Kick, glide. At the beginning of the gentle descent, he pushed off with both poles and dropped into a squat. As he made his way downhill, his thoughts wandered to the upcoming weekend. He had much to do.

He would have to spend all day tomorrow at the office, preparing for next week's county council meeting. He had to convince one of the members to vote for his project. If he didn't get a majority to back his superb proposal, a lot of people would lose a lot of money – including himself. If, on the other hand, construction began in the autumn, by the end of next year he would be a wealthy man. He smiled to himself. It wasn't as if he were short of money now, but he wasn't about to let a rolling stone stop. Growth had to be constant, and money had to be kept circulating.

The plan was in place. Hermann would persuade that one ninny to vote the way Hermann wanted. He just had to send a curt, well-considered email. The plan brought together profit and pleasure in a novel way. From Hermann's perspective, the situation was downright fantastic.

He glanced at his sports watch and was pleased by the reading: well under five minutes a kilometre. At this rate, he'd ski a full twenty k before dark.

Hermann picked up the pace. Just a couple of more kilometres and he could take a break, drink something, turn around, and backtrack the way he'd come.

He abruptly glanced to the side. It was almost as if his eye had caught movement, someone or something out there. An Arctic fox? He slowed and stopped in the middle of the track. No. It couldn't have been a fox. None had been seen in the area for years. They preferred to live far from human habitation and the noise of ski lifts. A small maintenance shed, a few square metres in size, stood a couple of hundred metres up the hill. The movement might have come from that direction. Someone had opened the shed's little window. The organising committee for tomorrow's race must be getting the tables and dishes ready to take to the water stations. But why at this hour? What were they doing clattering around up there in the dusk?

Hermann thought it was a minor miracle the decision had been made to hold the race. There had been news of a coronavirus spreading abroad. The health authorities said it was likely just a matter of time before the virus arrived in Iceland. One of them, the tall guy with grey hair, had flashed the notion of prohibiting large public events and establishing limits on crowd size.

Regardless of what happens, things will fall into place, Hermann thought to himself as he kicked off again. Sweat was making his glasses slip. He would have to remember to visit the optician when he was in Reykjavík next week and have the arms tightened.

It wasn't so late yet. He decided to circle past the maintenance shed and say hello to the active members of the local skiing association. A politician had to maintain good relations in every direction. He raised a hand in greeting, angled his body toward the shed, and started pushing his way steadily over to it. There was a soft swoosh as the skis slid across the snow's surface.

Suddenly he heard a dull pop. His poles had just hit the snow when a searing pain flared up at the left side of his chest. Red splattered to the white ground. Tiny drops spread into broad blemishes as the warm blood ate into the cold snow.

Hermann looked at his chest in disbelief. A dark splotch had appeared on his orange jacket and was growing. Everything had happened instantaneously, and yet time seemed to have slowed. A powerful rattle rose from somewhere deep within him. As he coughed, more blood burbled from his mouth to his torso. Then he fell to his side on the snow and lay there, skis still on his feet. One of the poles was trapped in an uncomfortable position beneath him. The hard metal tip dug painfully into his leg, protected only by the thin high-performance fabric. But from Hermann's perspective, it no longer mattered.

An hour passed, and a shadow shivered next to the exterior wall of the lodge. A hand encased in a leather glove reached toward the light switch. The finger stopped at the red button and pressed. There was a sigh as the lights went out one row at a time. The lights of the nearby practice track died first. Then the spotlights further up the slope went dark. Last of all, the lights at the top of the area were extinguished. The mountains were cast in blackness.

Snow began to drift down from the sky. And before long, a white sheet covered the bloody corpse of one of the Westfjords' most influential politicians, Hermann Hermannsson.

Chapter 8

Westfjords, 1986

Eight years before Rósa and Björk's disappearance

A keen shriek from the sea roused Rakel. She must have drifted off, but not much time could have passed; it was still light out. She heard the loud noise again. It carried in through the barely open window. A second voice joined in the shriek, and then a third.

Rakel gingerly rose to a sitting position on the bed. She craned her neck and looked out the window. She did so warily, avoiding rapid movements. She didn't want to wake the baby sleeping at her side.

Rakel's eyes swept across the farm. Everything looked so brutally ugly in the spring. The melt revealed a bleak, lumpy yard, and the surrounding fields weren't green yet. The hard-crusted snow dotting the muddy terrain clung to winter's memory. Rakel knew from experience it wouldn't melt for some time yet. The year before last, the snow hadn't disappeared until early June.

The breeze set the grey-dotted curtains fluttering, and fresh air filled the room. She wished she could keep the window open a bit longer, but the penetrating cry troubled her. How had they come so soon?

The Arctic terns had arrived unusually early this year. They shouldn't have made it this far yet. The little white birds usually landed on the beach in May and started nesting in June. It was only the beginning of April.

Every summer, some of those small, swift-winged creatures that wintered in southern Africa overran the fjord where she and her family lived. After their arrival, no one had any business going down to the water. The raucous birds dive-bombed aggressively in defence of their territory.

Rakel turned toward her baby, who was resting her tiny fist in front of her sleeping face. Rakel was filled with warmth as she gazed upon the wheezing infant. She'd long hoped for a second child, and she'd finally got pregnant and carried to term. It had been a protracted, painful labour, but ultimately things had gone well enough that there'd been no need to travel to Reykjavík. The baby had been able to enter the world at the local hospital. A couple of days later, the doctor had given mother and child permission to go home. Rakel had the urge to run her forefinger across her dozing infant's cheek but resisted it. Instead, she reached over and pulled the window shut. She couldn't stand the shrieking another minute. It made her splitting headache worse.

As she shut the window, Rakel spotted movement down at the water. The birds were shrieking because someone was walking along the shore. A little figure in a white beanie moved across the dark sand on short, fast steps, unzipped coat flapping in the wind. The figure's back was tilted forward in a determined hunch. A red plastic bucket dangled from one of its hands; it held a long, thick stick in the other. Hildur! How had the child made it so far so fast? Playing on the shore when terns were around was forbidden; she'd been told so time and time again. But the child didn't always obey Rakel. Hildur never argued. She'd look you in the eye and nod in agreement, but as soon as she stepped out the door she'd forget whatever promises she'd made. Rakel could have opened the window and shouted for Hildur to come in but decided not to. She wanted to observe from a distance.

Hildur was advancing across the shore, making for the waterline. Rakel noticed the birds move in. They gathered a few metres above the child and got into attack formation. The terns defended their territory by pecking at an intruder's head and shrieking in that shrill tone reminiscent of a human scream.

But nothing about Hildur's movements suggested fear or uncertainty. She just kept walking despite the chaos the birds were creating. She bent down to pick something up off the ground and dropped it in her pail. The sea had swept treasures ashore during the night, and the low morning tide was revealing them. Hildur had gone out to collect seashells.

And then Rakel saw her firstborn child focus all her will at the sky and start shouting. She raised the stick over her head and swatted at the birds. She shouted again.

The birds retreated. They flitted upward and seemed somehow confused. Hildur stopped shouting, knelt back down on the sand, and continued her concentrated digging. She dropped the seashells into her red pail.

The terns flapped their wings. Gathered into attack formation again and tried a second time. A shriek and a dive, but once more, Hildur held her ground.

Rakel watched Hildur play: her hand movements, expressive face, headstrong being. When the pail was full, Hildur left the beach and tromped home. As she walked, she held the stick over her head to ward off any attacks from the terns. That child handled herself well in any and all circumstances. She wasn't afraid of the birds or the sea, helped with the sheep at the neighbouring farm, and already knew how to ride their gentlest horse.

Rakel pressed her hand to the windowpane and watched her daughter approach. She saw Hildur climb to sit on the broad stone wall encircling the house and start counting her seashells in satisfaction.

Then Hildur spied her mother, and her smile died. Rakel started and pulled back from the window. She returned to her baby's side in the bed. Rakel knew Hildur could sense her moods, even share in them. It was unnerving.

Rakel heard a rustling just outside the house. It was as if a door had creaked too loudly somewhere. She'd heard the sound many times before. Someone was approaching. Someone who'd disturb their peace. It felt as if an oppressive chill had settled over the windswept valley.

Rakel tried to stay as quiet as possible and relax. The springs of the old mattress dug nastily into her left side. As she gingerly adjusted her position, her headache intensified, and milk spilled from her taut, swollen breasts. The warm liquid formed a deep splotch like a big bloodstain on the Christmas-red sheet.

Rakel wanted to feed her baby, but she didn't dare touch her. Not just yet.

Chapter 9

Reykjavík, February 2020

Hildur reached over to the nightstand to check the time on her phone. Only six thirty. No new messages. She'd promised to go for a run with an old police colleague around noon but didn't have anything else planned. A full day off stretched out before her. She could easily sleep for another hour or two.

Or could she? Hildur knew it would be pointless to try. She wouldn't be able to fall back asleep now. Once her brain started up in the morning, it was hard to shut down.

But she didn't want to get out of bed yet, so as not to wake her guest. The fireman appeared to be slumbering peacefully, which was perfect. Hildur didn't have the heart to wake him. A faint smile spread across her face as she thought back to the night before. She and Jari had come straight from the coffee shop to the hotel that served as her temporary home. It had been impossible to find a rental in Reykjavík; the city's population was growing faster than its housing stock. Besides, most downtown flats were listed on Airbnb these days, and there was no way a long-term renter could afford those prices. So her employer had put her up at a hotel with a government contract. Hildur had no complaints: breakfast was laid out every morning, and someone cleaned her room while she was at work.

Jari had been her second successful date since Freysi's death. The first had been a German tourist who happened to be ordering a drink at Dillon's at the same time as her. Hildur couldn't remember his name, but she remembered they'd had a good time. They'd sampled various whiskies at the rock-and-roll bar before ending up at his Airbnb at the west of the centre in a state of rising intoxication. When she complained of a headache the next morning, he had massaged her arms and shoulders, explaining he was a physiotherapist. The two of them had chatted about workouts for another couple hours, then said their goodbyes.

Hildur looked at the man in her bed. The hotel's sumptuous duvet revealed a muscular upper back. They hadn't had much time to talk, but he'd struck Hildur as a considerate, decent guy.

In the end, surprisingly many people are nice, she reflected as she rolled onto her back.

The city lights slinking through the cracks in the drapes cast pale stripes across the ceiling. It had been painted darker than the walls. Apparently that lent a space a soothing ambiance. But it wasn't working on Hildur.

Something was bothering her. Her restlessness could be because of the man sleeping at her side. It was odd spending the night next to a stranger. But waves of the unsettling sensation had been troubling her for a few days now, so it couldn't be all be Jari.

Hildur watched the light play on the ceiling. It quivered and made tiny back-and-forth movements. She was used to her mind reacting readily to her surroundings. The instant she felt anticipation spark within her, it meant unpleasantness would follow. For her, anticipation meant something bad was coming, not something good. Maybe that was why she was happiest when her mind and body were occupied with things that demanded her complete attention. While surfing, she had to dedicate every ounce of focus to the waves, the sea and her board. There was no room to think about the past or the future as she adjusted to the movement of the waves. Not being able to surf for the past couple of months had been frustrating. She wanted to get home.

The thought of home made her a little wistful. Hildur's life had changed when her little sisters disappeared. Her mother had grown distant and her father spoke even less. Then they both died in a car crash, and Hildur had been taken in by her mother's sister Tinna.

Hildur was grateful she had Tinna. The two of them remained close. Tinna had eventually lost her eyesight, but Hildur still went over for dinner every Monday, and the two of them talked about anything and everything. As soon as Hildur got back to Ísafjörður, she'd drop by her aunt's to say hello.

Hildur felt a touch on her shoulder and jumped. She'd been so lost in her own world.

'Sorry, I didn't mean to startle you,' said a soft, morning-sticky voice at her side.

Jari was awake. His eyes weren't more than halfway open, and he smiled drowsily. Hildur rolled onto her side and looked at him.

'What are you thinking about?' Jari asked, gently pinching Hildur's cheek between his forefinger and thumb.

Hildur grabbed Jari's hand and inched it toward her sleep-warmed body in response.

'I'm guessing you have quite a few secrets,' he continued.

'And I'm guessing you do too,' Hildur replied, parrying his questions. 'Tell me something about you.'

Jari grunted in surrender. 'I work out four times a week and play chess in the evenings. I'm here for pan-Nordic security training. I didn't know anyone who lived here until yesterday afternoon, when I happened to log on to Tinder and ended up at a hotel with this intriguing woman whose biceps are bigger than mine.'

Hildur's phone rang. She reached for it, shooting an apologetic look at the man stretching at her side. The caller was Elísabet Baldursdóttir, or Beta, Hildur's boss from the Westfjords police.

Beta wouldn't call on a weekend morning without good cause. Hildur's mind was overcome by unpleasant premonitions. She pressed the green receiver icon and lifted the phone to her ear, gripping it tightly as she listened in silence. Once again, Hildur's subconscious had been correct. Her sense of discomfort had already told her the news was bad.

'OK. I'll head straight to the airport,' she said. She hung up and turned to her companion, a thoughtful look on her face. 'That was work. There's been a change of plan. I have to get going.'

They dressed in silence. Hildur noticed Jari's wallet sticking out from under the bed. She bent down to pick up the leather billfold and handed it to him.

'I'm not sure I know what to say . . .' Jari said, hesitantly. He slipped the wallet into the front pocket of his shoulder bag and grabbed his coat from the back of the chair.

Hildur leaned casually against the doorjamb and tucked a fugitive strand of hair behind her ear. 'Thanks. And goodbye.'

She pressed herself against Jari, and they hugged. He opened the door and disappeared into the dim hotel corridor, winter coat under his arm.

Hildur glanced at her wristwatch and started throwing her clothes into her suitcase. Tumi's sick leave would be ending sooner than expected; Hildur had to get back to the Westfjords immediately. A helicopter would be waiting at the airport. She'd be hitching a ride to Ísafjörður with the forensic investigators.

Beta had just informed her over the phone that the individual who groomed the cross-country tracks had come across a body showing signs of a violent death. The victim wasn't just anyone, either: it was Hermann Hermannsson, a long-term local politician whose actions over the years had earned him the unofficial title of Sheriff.

And now the Sheriff had taken a bullet to the chest.

Chapter 10

Reykjavík, February 2020

Dísa

A horrific stench wafted from the rubbish. Dísa lifted the lid and turned her face away.

She felt a stabbing pain in her neck. Her body ached, especially in the wintertime. Summers were easier. She ignored the pain and steadied her right hand against the edge of the bin so she could sink in her gloved left hand. This bin should have just contained paper and cardboard, but now and again some lazy, inconsiderate individual shoved their trash in the first receptacle they came across.

At the bottom, her fingers struck the thick slabs that were hard at the edges and soft in the middle. Dísa recognised the shape and yanked out her hand. Used diapers, left unwrapped in the recycling. A week rarely went by without her coming across some.

Dísa had no intention of separating other people's refuse after the fact. In one swift movement, she lifted the lining out of the bin and tossed it and its contents into the big bag of mixed trash hanging from the rim of her cleaning cart.

She pushed the cart to the far side of the hall, where she emptied the receptacles at the main doors. The ceiling lights gave the terminal a pallid ambiance. The wall-high windows gave onto the quiet car park. The lone driver at the taxi stand leaned against her car, smoking a cigarette. Other than that, the lot was deserted. Most of the passengers for the morning flights had come and gone. A pair of tourists stood at the car rental counter in the middle of the airport, gawking around and looking lost.

The next flights wouldn't be taking off for another couple of hours, which made mornings the best time to clean. Dísa had a flexible schedule. The terminal floors needed mopping and the rubbish bins needed emptying once a day. The restrooms were cleaned twice a day. Dísa usually got to work at eight, but today she hadn't come in until ten. Her day off yesterday had stretched past midnight. She'd been incredibly tired that morning and augmented her sleep with an hour or two of dozing.

Dísa was hunched over her cleaning cart when she felt something crash against her ankle, hard. She straightened up – too fast. Her lower back didn't like sudden movements and immediately punished her with a piercing pain. She swore under her breath and turned around.

A man in a red waterproof coat had knocked his suitcase into her, and the jerk didn't even apologise. It appeared he'd been absorbed in the piece of paper in his hand and hadn't watched where he was going. Dísa noted the blue sweatshirt visible under his unzipped coat. The front was emblazoned with the words 'Iceland Football' in the colours of the Icelandic flag and an image of a man in a Viking hat. The petite woman standing behind him wore a matching sweatshirt in a different colour. She stared at Dísa's cleaning cart curiously. Dísa was annoyed.

'Excuse me, could you help us?' the man began in broad English, looking back at the printout in his hand. 'We rented a car, but there's no one at the counter. We've been waiting a while now. There's a phone number here, but calling foreign numbers with our phones is so expensive. Could I borrow your phone?'

He held out the printout toward Dísa. He had an expectant look on his face and shifted his weight to his other leg. The woman behind him had a small leather bag dangling from her arm. As she stared at Dísa, the curiosity in her eyes turned to insistence.

Dísa let her eyes glance off the paper, but she didn't take it. She noticed it was a printout of the email from the rental agency. There was a photo of the car they'd reserved: a silver-grey Land Rover Discovery. That would have cost at least fifty thousand krónur a day. Dísa found herself seething. *Too expensive to call, huh?* They'd flown here across the Atlantic and rented a car for a daily fee that equalled what Dísa was left with after a week of cleaning.

'No.'

The man looked at Dísa in disbelief. His eyebrows rose and his jaw dropped slightly. 'Hey, come on. I'm just asking to borrow your phone so I can call the rental agency.'

Dísa shook her head. The woman took her husband's arm and stepped up at his side.

'No. I'm not a telephone operator,' Dísa said, turning back to her cart.

The man's jaw began to twitch. He waved the piece of paper, so flustered he didn't know what to say. 'What the hell? Shouldn't you be happy to have tourists here?'

'I couldn't care less,' Dísa said, pushing her cart toward the windows facing the runway. They needed washing from the inside at least twice a week. Children watching the aeroplanes take off and land would press their hands against the glass. Dísa could see the window was covered in palm-shaped smears today too. She clenched the cart handle, knuckles white.

She hadn't had an easy life. Dísa had been to the bottom, and the journey from where she'd been to where she was now hadn't been accompanied by any fanfares. After many stumbles, she'd succeeded in making her life manageable again. Getting a permanent job as a cleaner had been a major achievement.

Dísa reached for the bottle of cleaning solution. In the minds of other Icelanders, a job cleaning Reykjavík Airport was only suitable for immigrants who didn't speak Icelandic and those whose employment was subsidised by the government. The pay was ridiculously low, and the job offered no challenges or bonuses, but Dísa was satisfied at having made it this far. The airport had become an important place for her.

Dísa glanced back at the couple who'd asked to borrow her phone. She was irked. Tourists wore sweatshirts celebrating Icelandic soccer and thought everyone else should react to their childish enthusiasm with gratitude. Dísa pinched her lips into a firm line and gritted her teeth. Spoiled schmucks like that would never understand what she'd been through.

Dísa spotted movement on the runway. But according to the screen on the wall, the next flight wouldn't be leaving for hours. She walked up to the window and focused her eyes between the greasy smears. A helicopter stood, door open, in the middle of the airfield. Two people wearing jackets marked with police insignia were walking toward it. A pair of agents at the departures desk were doing paperwork and chatting. Dísa heard them mention a helicopter about to take off for Ísafjörður.

When Dísa heard the name, a sudden nausea struck her. Ísafjörður was a place she'd never forget.

They look like they're in a hurry, Dísa thought to herself, squeezing the bottle in her fist. Blue-green liquid spurted onto the glass. Yes, they were in a hurry. Damn it. After applying the glass cleaner, you were supposed to wait a minute. Dísa tapped the edges of the cart with her latex-gloved fingers and watched the police officers disappear inside the chopper. A crooked, barely perceptible smile spread across her face.

And then she reached for a rag and vigorously scrubbed the smears out of existence.

Chapter 11

Ísafjörður, February 2020

Hildur put on her headset and looked out the window at Reykjavík's deserted airport. To the south, the airfield was bounded by the sea, to the north by the old centre of town, and fences to the east and west bounded single-home residential areas for upper-income brackets. Hildur could have flown commercial to her home fjord, but the flight wouldn't have left until late that afternoon and she didn't want to waste time waiting. The only thing in the world you can't get more of is time. And so she'd insisted on hitching a ride to Ísafjörður with the crime scene investigators, who already had a helicopter waiting at the airport.

The Westfjords didn't have the resources to hire technical investigators of their own. When a forensic investigation was required, experts had to be flown in from the capital. Luckily the flight conditions were favourable today; they'd be able to take off without any delays. The sooner Hildur arrived at the crime scene, the better. She wanted to see it before the technical investigators started examining and moving the body.

Hildur was the only detective in the sparsely inhabited Westfjords. Most of the work occupying their little police force was basic stuff: investigating traffic accidents, pulling over drunk drivers, destroying cannabis plantations. Plenty of cases involving domestic violence and child neglect came across Hildur's desk, too, and those were the ones that got under her skin the most.

Two men with gear bags strode across the airfield toward the helicopter. Hildur immediately recognised the pair: Sveinn Þórsson and Hörður Arnarsson worked in forensics at the Reykjavík police. The pair had visited the Westfjords the previous autumn, examining the victims of a serial killer.

Sveinn and Hörður were surprised to find Hildur sitting in the helicopter.

'I've been on assignment down here,' she explained.

Hörður climbed in next to Hildur and started looking around for his headset. Sveinn turned around in the front seat so he could see Hildur. 'One person's death is another person's paycheck. Do you know what we have waiting for us this time?'

Hildur shrugged. 'A hell of a circus, at least. A local politician was shot skiing the cross-country track. His skis were still attached to his boots. That's all Beta could tell me when she called.'

'Hmm. Sounds pretty weird to me,' Sveinn said, stretching out his words. 'We're not in the habit of killing our politicians.'

Hildur found it all weird too. Had the victim been killed because of his work in politics? In the past, political violence in Iceland had consisted of egging the Parliament building and scratching ministers' cars. Homicides in general were rare and usually the result of a drunken fight or payback among criminals. Although it was true that last autumn Hildur had investigated a complex string of homicides.

The pilot flipped a few switches on the control panel and gave the thumbs up. A moment later, the helicopter rose into the air, rocking lightly from side to side.

Seen from above, the island resembled a huge white snow pile, its black outline drawn by the dark, roiling sea washing the beaches of volcanic sand. The rivers carrying meltwater from the big glaciers never froze, even in winter. From above they looked like fast-flowing veins.

Buildings became matchboxes. The wind had blown the snow from the roofs, exposing their redness. The roof of just about every farmhouse was red and had been since corrugated metal replaced peat and grass as a roofing material in the late 1800s. The metal had originally been rust-proofed with a lead mixture that was red in hue. Paints had improved over time, but the colour had remained the same. The roofs turned the houses into tiny blood spatters in the snowy terrain.

Hildur kept her eyes on Route 1, which followed the shoreline as it circled the country. As they gained altitude, Iceland's most important roadway turned into a thin, slithering ribbon. The sight was simultaneously ugly and beautiful. They were too high up to make out any cars.

Hildur's thoughts wandered to her own vehicle, good old Brenda. Brenda had been left in Reykjavík. Before leaving for the airport, Hildur had spoken with an acquaintance who worked as a manager at a car rental agency, who'd said she'd be happy to drive Brenda to Ísafjörður. The manager was going to have to go out to the fjords anyway to pick up a car and drive it back to the capital before the weekend. Driving Hildur's Land Cruiser to the Westfjords would save her from having to fly, which she truly hated.

The helicopter dropped altitude after they crossed the final peak before the fjord. They could now spy the familiar seashore town between the mountains, awaiting their arrival. The lights were still on at the shrimp-processing plant that was on the verge of bankruptcy. The shrimp population had moved on, and the massive investments in the plant had proven unprofitable. It was only a matter of time before it closed its doors for good.

Hildur's eyes swept across the little town. Two fire engines were parked outside the fire station. Fishing vessels bobbed in a straight line in the harbour. The sight was somehow touching. Hildur had only been gone a few weeks, but it had felt like an eternity.

Hildur was standing on solid ground, but even so she felt unsteady on her feet. Her body would continue to experience the helicopter's rocking motion for some time.

She heard someone shout her name. Jakob was leaning casually against the side of a Škoda Octavia, waving at her. Hildur took a couple of brisk strides toward him and greeted her colleague. He smelled of a new cologne and lambswool. A bit of grey sweater peered out from under his parka.

'It's so nice to be home,' Hildur whispered. She uttered the words so softly that she figured Jakob hadn't heard. Then she added in a louder voice: 'You shaved off your beard!'

Jakob stroked his chin in satisfaction, perhaps not quite sure what to say. 'Guðrún wanted me to. It doesn't look too bad, does it?'

Guðrún had been the flight attendant on duty the first time Jakob had flown to Ísafjörður and had immediately set her sights on the newcomer. Aside from her airline work, Guðrún ran a yarn shop in town, which was perfect for Jakob, who liked to knit. Hildur knew the two of them still lived at different addresses, but apparently the relationship had taken swift strides forward, what with the beard having been given the heave-ho.

Hildur opened the boot and tossed in her bag. Sveinn and Hörður added their gear and climbed in the back seat. Hildur sat next to Jakob who confidently steered the car out of the car park and onto the shoreline road. At the turn-off to the ski area, he flicked his left indicator. Hildur gave her partner a questioning look. She knew the body was at the top of the cross-country track. It wouldn't be possible to get to it by car.

'The ski area's closed, and the lifts aren't running. We'll take snowmobiles to the top.'

Hildur nodded. Jakob had come to Iceland to complete the necessary internship for his police degree. He'd quickly got a handle on day-to-day police work. He was of more use than many of Hildur's permanently employed colleagues. Besides, over the past few months the two of them had become fast friends, which Hildur appreciated.

Jakob parked next to the ski rental. The place looked strangely abandoned. The slopes of the little resort were generally buzzing on late-winter weekends. Kids always made the most noise. They gathered several times a week under the guidance of their skiing instructors to practise using the lifts and their stopping techniques. Now there was no one around. A soft breeze blew across the valley, kicking up the powder that had fallen overnight into puffs of white clouds.

Two resort employees waiting off to the side waved the forensic investigators over to their snowmobiles. Jakob started up a third, and Hildur climbed on behind him. She let Jakob drive because he was better at it. He'd told her stories about his youthful years spent in Finnish Lapland.

After reaching the top of the slope, the convoy of snowmobiles continued south. Hildur knew the area. She occasionally came up into the mountains to ski. She wasn't a fan of classic cross-country, but she enjoyed gliding on the freestyle course groomed between the tracks. Hildur gazed at her surroundings from behind her tinted visor. The snow looked smooth. Apparently enough had fallen overnight to cover the tracks.

A small group of people had clustered a little further off. Petite, curly-haired Beta was easy to spot. Two tall men stood next to her. Hildur greeted her boss with a quick hug; a wave was enough for the patrol officers.

Beta nodded at a white mound a few metres away. If Hildur hadn't known better, she wouldn't have necessarily guessed it was a body. The fresh blanket of snow had melded the corpse with the white landscape.

'The track groomer found him this morning,' Beta said, then explained there was to have been a cross-country race today. Because of the race, the groomers had headed out to the tracks at six that morning.

Hildur glanced at her watch. 'That was four hours ago. How long has the body been lying here?'

Beta frowned. She didn't know. 'I just spoke with Hermann's secretary. According to her, Hermann had something on his calendar for this afternoon, but he was free last night. We haven't had a chance to talk to anyone else yet.'

Hildur peppered Beta with questions: 'Has the doctor been here? What about a dog?'

Beta nodded. The doctor had come and pronounced Hermann dead. The search-and-rescue dog's handler had the flu, so there would be no canine team today.

'I wonder if he has Covid,' one of the police officers said, shaking his arms to stay warm. The tip of his nose had turned white, and the look in his eyes revealed how tired he was. No wonder. He and his partner had been posted on this windswept slope for hours, keeping an eye on the body.

Beta freed the frozen officers and told them to go back to the station to warm up. She, Hildur, Jakob, and the team from Reykjavík would take it from here.

The forensic investigators had pulled protective suits over their winter clothes. First they photographed the spot the body was found in and the body itself. Then they gingerly approached it from different angles, taking more photos and collecting samples in baggies.

'Stiff as a spear,' said Sveinn, who was bent over the corpse.

Hildur knew what that meant: at least four hours but fewer than forty-eight had passed since the death. When a person died, calcium flooded the muscle cells, causing the muscles to contract and stiffen. A body was most rigid about twelve hours after death, and the stiffness disappeared after a couple of days.

That aligns with the time the body was discovered, Hildur thought to herself. 'What did you say about the secretary again?'

'She'd spoken with Hermann around five yesterday afternoon. He'd mentioned he was heading out to ski,' Beta replied.

Hildur, Jakob and Beta looked around in silence. A local politician had been shot on a ski track and his sprawling body left there to be discovered. Such things didn't usually happen in Iceland. Homicides were rare in the island nation of just under four hundred thousand inhabitants, at most one or two a year.

Hildur shook her head. Just last autumn they'd had a complicated string of murders to untangle, and now this. She shivered. The cold seemed to be snaking its way through her clothes.

'Yup, we have a clear bullet wound here in the chest. The bullet exited from the back,' Sveinn said, stating his observations. He stood up and looked at Beta and Hildur. 'When you consider the position of the body, it looks like the bullet came from that direction, a little higher and to the side.' He pointed at the small grey structure in the snow.

Hildur knew the shack was used to store track markers. 'Do you think the shooter was waiting there?'

Sveinn exhaled through his nose and gave a couple of thoughtful nods. His breath was steaming. The temperature was dropping again. 'Maybe. We'll have to take a closer look at the shed. But we'll finish with the body first and pack it up for transport.'

Hildur set her hands on her hips and took in the surroundings. A few grey peaks stood out against the whiteness; the wind had blown away the snow. Their craggy faces looked like fortresses of darkness in a white world. Also grim was the little corrugated metal building where the shooter might have been lurking.

'I'm just thinking whoever it was must have been quite the shot if they were waiting up there. That's at least a hundred metres away,' she said.

Beta pulled down her beanie, flipping up the tips of her curly hair. 'Hermann was an avid skier. The perp must have known he skied here all the time. No one brings a rifle to a cold, windy ski slope by accident.'

Hildur kicked at the snow with the toe of her boot. 'There are a lot of stories going around about the victim. If even half of them are true, he had plenty of enemies.'

Beta nodded and turned back toward the body. 'No doubt about it. Now we just have to grit our teeth and wrap this up as fast as possible. Let's start combing through those closest to him; we need to talk to the secretary again right away too. Hildur, you handle that.'

Just then a fresh gust of wind blew in from the sea, sending the surface powder swirling. All outlines were momentarily blurred by the puff of white. Spring had definitely not arrived in the Westfjords yet. Cold weather continued to maintain a firm grip on the area.

'Someone must have got really upset with Hermann this time,' Hildur said. 'Once and for all.'

Chapter 12

Hildur poured coffee into mugs bearing the logo of a local athletic club. They were part of the large collection Beta had accumulated over the course of her career as police chief. Hildur left both herself and Beta room for milk; she added four teaspoons of sugar to Jakob's coffee and smiled as she swirled the little spoon around his mug.

'That was a speedy homecoming. A helicopter ride and all,' Beta remarked. She'd claimed a seat for herself in the corner of the conference room, near the window.

'Life is full of surprises,' Hildur replied as she set the mugs down on the table and freed a package of chocolate cookies from under her arm.

Jakob sat, knitting, at his now-usual seat next to the wall. He'd hung a bag from the back of the chair; heavyweight unbleached yarn snaked out of it. He pulled his circular needles closer and quipped: 'Death is full of surprises...'

Hildur couldn't help smiling. The better she'd come to know Jakob, the funnier he'd become.

'I just spoke with Sveinn on the phone,' she continued. 'The boys have completed the on-scene investigation and bagged the body.' The technical investigators would be flying back to Reykjavík that evening. The body would undergo a more thorough examination at the forensic pathologist's office. The results probably wouldn't be available until after the weekend, Monday or Tuesday.

They'd been frustrated that they hadn't found the bullet that had passed through Hermann's body. 'They spent quite a bit of time searching for it in the snow,' Hildur reported.

A shooter in the maintenance shed would have been uphill from the victim. Because the bullet was fired at an angle from above, it presumably struck the ground soon after hitting its target. So it wasn't necessarily very far. Sveinn had performed a superficial examination of the bullet wound. Apparently it couldn't have resulted from some small firearm; it had looked too big.

After concluding this summary, Hildur paused to take a sip of coffee.

Jakob looked up from his knitting: 'Are you saying it was a hunting rifle?'

Hildur nodded and took another sip before continuing: 'They're going to have a look at that old maintenance shed as soon as the canine team has had a chance to search the area. They don't want to contaminate any scent trails.'

The Westfjords were home to about ten villages. Some had no more than a couple of hundred inhabitants, but each had its own search-and-rescue dog trained to find people who'd gone missing or been buried under an avalanche. A free dog had turned up in Hólmavík, about a two-hour drive away. The handler had set out with the dog as soon as he got the call and had just arrived in Ísafjordur.

Jakob took a closer look at his needles and counted loops. When he reached the end of the row, he glanced at Hildur. 'So what kind of guy was this Hermann Hermannsson?'

Jakob had only lived in Ísafjörður for about six months. Unofficial information hadn't made its way to him yet. Hildur let Beta explain.

'Small towns, and even slightly bigger ones, usually have two centres of power: the official one and the unofficial one. Hermann was the latter. He was on the county council for years representing the conservative party, but he never ran for mayor or even council chair. He played a role in official decision-making bodies, but he often turned to unofficial mechanisms to wield power. He was a schemer of the worst kind. Exploited information he'd heard in official contexts to his advantage as a businessman.'

Beta gave an example: a few years ago, the council had decided to improve local care for the elderly. The population was ageing, and within the next few years the county would run short of beds. Hermann had immediately purchased a lot next to the existing nursing home in his company's name. Because staff needed to be able to move easily between all parts of the facility, it was plain any extension would be built next door to the original nursing home.

'Hermann bought the property for peanuts, and once the details of the decision to expand the nursing home were finalised by the council, the rent had risen to triple the original estimate. Hermann made a nice profit for himself, but the county lost money.'

The nursing home incident wasn't an outlier. Hermann had slipped taxpayer money in his own pockets in numerous other projects too.

'But would some angry taxpayer actually have resorted to shooting him?' Jakob asked.

A lot of people expressed their rage on social media, some aggressively so, but it was a totally different matter to reach for a rifle as opposed to a smartphone. Killing another human being was no small thing. Even if the perpetrator were capable of pulling a trigger, the potential of a life sentence would have been a high price to pay. Or life sentence of a sort. Icelandic law recognised life sentences, but no one had received one yet. There were a few instances of judges in lower courts handing down life sentences for murder, but in each case an appeal to a higher court had commuted the sentence, usually to about sixteen years.

The three of them pondered in silence. Hermann had spoken with someone yesterday at 5 p.m. He'd been on his way to ski, but because the resort didn't have any security cameras, any later timelines were impossible to verify. Snow had covered the body during the night and rigor mortis had set in, so the death had to have taken place at some point between 5 p.m. and 5 a.m. An accurate cause of death would be included in the pathologist's report, but the gunshot wound made it pretty apparent.

Beta's phone rang. She swiped the screen, tucked a curl behind her ear, and answered. She listened attentively and managed to squeeze in a couple of responses through the flood of speech. Hildur sat quietly during the call, entranced by the whisking motion of the needles in Jakob's hands. They moved so fast it was hard to see them individually.

A few minutes later, Beta ended the call and lowered her phone to the table.

'The dog picked up a scent. The trail ran from the maintenance shed straight down to the car park, where it disappeared. Apparently the perpetrator left the scene by car.'

'And last night's snow covered all the tyre tracks,' Hildur groaned in disappointment. She intended to talk to the people who lived in the area next. Maybe someone had seen a car leaving the area. She also wanted to talk to Hermann's secretary face to face. She would be sure to pay the secretary a visit today too.

'There's one more thing, and it's not great,' Beta said, looking first at Hildur and then Jakob. 'A shell was found on the floor of the shed. Sveinn identified it immediately. A Sako .308 caliber cartridge.'

Hildur twirled her near-empty coffee mug in her hands and sighed deeply. 'Goddammit. You'll find those bigger rifles in every second gun locker in the country. They're used for reindeer hunting.'

Jakob shot Hildur a puzzled glance. 'Reindeer? You shoot reindeer here?'

Hildur explained that reindeer hunting was a popular national pastime. Every autumn, the government issued a few dozen reindeer-kill permits. Because there were more hunters than permits, a lottery was held. If you happened to get lucky, you were allowed to hunt a reindeer under the watchful eye of a licensed guide. Reindeer meat was a delicacy. It was put in the freezer in the autumn and pulled out for Christmas dinner or a New Year's Eve celebration. Domestic reindeer meat wasn't available from the store; in order to get your hands on some, you had to know someone who'd been issued a permit.

Iceland had never been home to any wild mammals larger than an Arctic fox. Reindeer had been brought to the island to correct the situation. According to Hildur's recollection, the first reindeer had arrived in the 1700s from Norway. Miraculously enough, the animals had survived from winter to winter, decade to decade. 'The descendants of those imported reindeer still live in eastern Iceland.'

Jakob rubbed his forehead in amusement. 'Hell, what passes for entertainment here?'

Hildur shrugged and tilted the last drops of coffee down her throat: 'I guess shooting little birds isn't motivating enough. The hunters want to bring down something bigger.'

Chapter 13

Hildur parked at the side of the road. She'd driven to a terraced development a couple of kilometres from downtown Ísafjörður. During the drive, she'd realised she was hungry: evidently the boiled egg and bowl of hot cereal she'd gobbled down for breakfast at the hotel hadn't sufficed. Luckily she'd found a chocolate bar in the glove box. It was smushed at one corner but otherwise looked edible. Hildur ripped the yellow wrapper from the licorice-chocolate bar and devoured it in two bites. She shoved the empty wrapper in her coat pocket and grinned broadly in the rearview mirror. She had nothing in her teeth.

The terrace house was newish. Its wood exterior was painted black, the windows were big, and a six-person hot tub stood in a prime location in the sheltered front yard.

Hildur strode up to the entrance and looked for the doorbell. She ran her fingers over the gold-painted dog's head next to the door and found it between the ears. A deep chime echoed inside, and the door opened immediately. Hildur had been expected.

Agnes Axelsdóttir was about sixty; she was wearing a heavy, calf-length plaid skirt, a grey rollneck, and a red cardigan. She waved Hildur in, then lowered her glasses from her forehead to her eyes and studied her visitor. 'I assume you drink coffee?'

Hildur removed her shoes in the entryway and followed her hostess into the kitchen. An old-fashioned coffee pot was already percolating on the stove. Agnes set two decorative coffee cups and silver spoons on the kitchen island. *The good china*, Hildur noted.

'Condolences on the loss of your boss,' she said.

Hildur had called Agnes that morning and explained she was investigating Hermann's death. The media hadn't been informed of its criminal nature yet. Hildur had wanted to talk to Agnes first, because she presumed as Hermann's secretary, Agnes had been the person closest to him. Or at least the person who'd seen him most often. Hermann's former wife had moved abroad with her new spouse years before, and Hermann had lived alone since. Their only child lived abroad too. As soon as news of the death had been delivered to the family, Beta could send out a release announcing the homicide.

Agnes filled her own cup now and seated herself across from Hildur.

'I can't believe it's real,' Agnes said quietly, looking out the window at the street.

Hildur wanted to start gently. She was curious as to how long Agnes had worked for Hermann.

Agnes nodded thoughtfully. 'It's been about twenty years.'

She added that the secretarial position had been her first job. She'd been a housewife, and her husband, who'd died of a heart attack a couple of years ago, had worked as a teacher in town. 'Staying home isn't very common these days, but for me it was a matter of values. I didn't start working until my youngest went off to study in Reykjavík.'

Remaining a stay-at-home mother to children coming up on twenty was an unusual choice, but Hildur didn't comment. She hadn't come to ask how Agnes and her deceased husband had divided up their parental duties.

Agnes explained she hadn't had a stitch of work experience when she applied for the job, but evidently Hermann had appreciated her traditional values. He'd found her dedication to her family admirable.

'He later admitted my years as a housewife were the reason he hired me.' Agnes smiled, seemingly lost in old memories.

Hildur wanted to move the conversation forward. 'When did you last see Hermann?'

Agnes adjusted her glasses and thought. Hermann had dropped by the office on Friday morning. 'I called him yesterday evening just after five to let him know the documents he'd wanted were on his desk. After that I left for dinner at my friends', as I explained over the phone.'

Agnes spoke quickly, and her eyes wandered. She was visibly agitated. Hildur suspected it was because of the interrogational nature of the conversation.

Agnes's alibi had already been confirmed with the hostess of the dinner party and two other guests. Hildur was sure the phone lines between the women were blazing hot. No doubt they were all curious as to why the police had called and asked about Agnes. It wouldn't be long before they had a lot more to talk about, when word of Hermann's death made it into the news.

Next Hildur probed Agnes about the contents of the documents, provoking a disconcerted response: the documents were private business. Agnes raised her hands in protest as if to underscore her answer.

'Under the circumstances, you can tell us,' Hildur assured her. 'All information might be of use in our investigation.'

Agnes turned back to the window. The wind was gently tossing the bare bushes outside. She took a couple of deep breaths before replying.

'They were building committee documents. Hermann mentioned something in passing about a meeting he'd scheduled for the weekend; he said he had to do some arm-twisting. It was related to the harbour expansion project.'

Hildur's interest was piqued. She wanted to know more about project and why it might require a weekend meeting.

Agnes's guarded demeanour instantly sharpened: 'Listen here, miss. I worked for Hermann for over twenty years. One reason for my long employment was I never asked too many questions.'

Hildur didn't care for being called 'miss', but she let it go in one ear and out the other.

Agnes interlaced her fingers under her chin and looked sternly at Hildur. 'Do you have children?'

Hildur started and shook her head. No, she didn't have children. She enjoyed the company of children but had never wanted her own.

Agnes's stony gaze was penetrating. 'Children come first, and work comes second. One's personal whims come third. Even though I didn't understand all of Hermann's preoccupations, I always did what I was asked, because it was my job. It was my responsibility to serve him. I don't know a fig about Hermann's projects.'

Hildur set down her coffee cup. She looked the older woman dead in the eye and lowered her voice. 'Did he have enemies? Had he had many visitors lately?'

Agnes laughed drily. 'The Sheriff wasn't a very well-liked person. At least not among those who got in his way. His no-nonsense methods could sometimes cause bad blood.' She paused, then added with a deliberate slowness: 'He was a driven man. I respect that kind of dedication.'

Hildur noted Agnes used the same nickname for her dead boss that critical locals did: *the Sheriff*.

'He always paid me on time and treated me well. I did what was asked and could be out of the office whenever the situation demanded.'

'The situation?' Hildur immediately interjected.

Agnes's aged, furrowed face had taken on a faint flush. She rolled her eyes and shook her head. After a brief pause, she pulled her cardigan more tightly around her and clicked her tongue against the roof of her mouth. 'Well, the women.'

Hildur sensed Agnes had little interest in delving any more deeply into the subject. But over her years on the force, Hildur had learned the things people didn't want to talk about were usually the things that mattered most. She gave Agnes an empathetic look and asked her to continue. Tiny details that seemed trivial might be of use.

Agnes loosened her grip and let the cardigan fall open. 'Now and again Hermann would have visitors – women, I mean – who weren't to be marked in the calendar.' She lowered her hands to the island top and shut her eyes. 'Hermann would give me a certain look, and I'd hear the door to his office lock from the inside. Over time, an unspoken agreement formed between us. On such occasions, I would step out to run errands or have a long lunch.'

A readiness now tinged Agnes's voice. Her right hand whisked on the island top in time to her words.

'Do you have any idea what was going on?'

Agnes shook her head and smiled. 'I didn't get involved in things that weren't my business.'

Hildur asked Agnes to think back over recent weeks. Had Hermann had any unfamiliar visitors? Had he been acting strangely?

'Are you saying I ought to be able to recognise all those women?' Agnes snapped.

Hildur stressed that any and all information might be of use. They were trying to get to the bottom of Hermann's murder.

Agnes would be showing loyalty to her dead boss if she shared everything she knew.

'Well, there was one familiar face . . . Linda. Linda Jónsdóttir. Married to Björn Ísaksson.'

Hildur knew Björn. He was a powerful figure in the local progressive party, in other words, a political rival of the influential Hermann. Hildur wrote down the name. She would have to talk to Linda as soon as possible. She asked a few more detailed questions and jotted down the answers in her notebook. Then she stood and put her coffee cup in the sink. She left her business card on the island.

'Thank you for the coffee. You'll call if anything else comes to mind, won't you?'

Agnes, who was still seated at the island, murmured in the affirmative and turned back to the window.

Hildur shut the front door behind her and stepped out onto the street. Next door, two little girls in snowsuits were rolling balls from what remained of the slushy snow. Hildur passed them on the way to her car. The girls smiled at her, and she smiled back. She saw a private, shared world there in their eyes.

She thought back to what Rósa and Björk had been like at that age. On winter days, the three of them would play in the snow until their clothes were soaked. Her little sisters had always teamed up against her during snowball fights. When they came in and took off their coats, they'd whisper and giggle at Hildur, who'd got the most snow down her collar. But Hildur had never experienced it as cruelty; just the opposite. A demonstration of trust.

As she walked up to her car, Hildur had to close her eyes for a moment. An uncomfortable tightness had formed in her chest while thinking about her sisters. She'd been their big sister. They had trusted her. And yet she hadn't been able to do anything. She hadn't been able to stave off catastrophe.

Hildur kicked her tyre with the tip of her trainer. The slight pain in her toe brought her back to the present moment. She reached into her pocket and pulled out her car keys.

Then she started. What was it Agnes had just said about Hermann's weekend meeting? *Arm-twisting*. What exactly had he been up to?

Chapter 14

There was a sharp hiss as Jakob cracked his bottle open. The first bite of cold beer felt amazing. He stood in his unlit kitchen, gazing out into the dark evening. There wasn't much snow in the centre of town; patches of brown grass poked through the thin, broken crust. The windows at the house opposite were still dark. Jakob remembered the family who lived there had left for Reykjavík a week ago to visit relatives. They must still be out of town.

Extended visits to extended family. Whenever people mentioned travelling to see family members, Jakob's mood darkened. When it came down to it, his family consisted of one person, his soon-to-be six-year-old son Matias. Jakob's ex-wife Lena had taken Matias to Norway and convinced the Norwegian social workers to side with her. She had been granted sole custody and did everything in her power to hinder contact between Jakob and his son.

Jakob had spent a lot of time lately reading up on the experiences of parents who'd encountered similar problems. He'd read accounts on anonymous blogs and online forums about other fathers and mothers who'd found themselves in international custody battles, lost their children and money on court costs. He'd entered into a private correspondence with several parents, and that had been a big help.

He'd also come up with a plan for addressing his situation. He wasn't sure it would work, but he meant to try.

The twinkling stars stood out against the midnight blue sky. He wouldn't be able to enjoy them from his kitchen window much longer; the days were lengthening. Spring was approaching, and the nights were growing shorter.

Jakob was pleased with his new home. When he'd moved to Ísafjörður the previous autumn, he'd found a studio apartment just outside the centre. It had been in a shabby shape but passable for the first few months. With time, the place had started to feel needlessly small, especially as he and Guðrún spent more time together. But there were so few rental units available in town that he hadn't found anything better.

Then something horrible happened that led him to this unit in an old duplex: Hildur's friend Freysi had died. When his estate was distributed, Hildur learned Freysi had left all his property to her, including this two-bedroom home. Hildur owned the duplex's other unit. She hadn't wanted to sell Freysi's half, so she rented it to Jakob. *It's nicer to have someone you know clattering around on the other side of the wall*, she'd said, slapping the keys in Jakob's fist.

Jakob heard footfalls outside. A moment later, the front door opened. Jakob hurried to turn on the lights, but it was too late.

'What are you doing here in the dark?'

Jakob tried to explain something about stargazing, but his words drowned in a belch. Hildur clicked on the lights in the entryway.

'Want a beer?' Jakob asked and, without waiting for an answer, cracked a second bottle and passed it to Hildur. They settled onto the couch side by side.

Jakob noticed his colleague staring at the wooden coffee table. He knew Freysi had built it. 'I've been meaning to change the furniture,' he said.

Hildur turned her keen eyes to Jakob. 'Stop.' She took a long swig, reached for the basket of coasters on the table, and set down her bottle. 'He's dead. These are just things. There's no way you're buying new furniture just because this stuff used to belong to Freysi.'

They sat in silence for a moment, drinking their beers. Jakob decided to change the subject and asked Hildur to pass him his knitting bag from the other side of the couch.

'I need a woman's opinion,' he said, pulling the beginnings of a sweater from the bag. The yarn was heavyweight Álafosslopi. He had about ten centimetres of the hem finished; the torso would be a paler wool.

Hildur eyed the heap of yarn as if it were an exotic snake.

Jakob spread the hem across his lap. 'Tell me honestly: do you think it's corny I'm knitting matching sweaters for me and Guðrún?'

Hildur chuckled. 'Couples start to look like each other over time. You've decided to accelerate the metamorphosis a little.'

Jakob threw one of the skeins of yarn at Hildur.

'No, it's not corny. It's cute.' She asked how things had been going with Guðrún.

Jakob said they'd been going better than well, aside from some gossips they'd run into. 'A couple of old women stopped me when Guðrún and I were at the supermarket the other day.' The women had taken it upon themselves to approach Jakob in the dairy section and warn him about his companion: apparently Guðrún was rather 'active' and enjoyed male company a little too much.

Hildur replied that was nothing but the envy of bitter people and lifted her feet onto the coffee table to underscore her message.

Jakob was well aware he wasn't Guðrún's first boyfriend. And to be perfectly frank, he couldn't care less how many had preceded him.

'I assume Guðrún didn't take it personally?' Hildur said, and in the same breath asked Jakob if he had another beer.

'Of course not,' Jakob chuckled, getting up to fetch two more lagers from the fridge. 'I told her we have this great saying in Finland: *A little rowing isn't going to drain the lake*. It's become our private joke.'

'How was Reykjavík?' he continued, handing a bottle to Hildur. The two of them had exchanged the occasional message during her absence, but it had been a while since they'd seen each other.

Hildur reported on her time there. The more she talked, the better Jakob understood how heavy the past few weeks had been. Social problems seemed to accumulate quickly in the capital. Young people who'd drifted onto the wrong path found illegal substances with a few clicks in private social media groups. After a few experiments, the price went up and their debts swelled. Theft entered the picture, as well as violent debt collection visits. And the problems weren't limited to any one social class. Those with more money were able to hide their problems for longer, but they always came out eventually. The ones who had it worst were those young people whose parents didn't care at all. Hildur also told Jakob about Tryggvi, the seventeen-year-old client of child protective services who'd been molested by a child protection services employee.

Jakob saw her struggling with the subject and listened without interrupting. This was par for the course since they'd become partners. There wasn't much in the way of crisis counselling or assistance at their tiny police station. The resources simply didn't exist. They both found these confidential one-to-one conversations critical in processing the pressures of the job.

Tryggvi had been running from the police for weeks. Hildur understood him: he didn't trust the authorities. Why would he, when his trust had been broken in the worst possible way by someone whose job it was to protect him?

'Your turn. Have you been in touch with Matias since Christmas?'

Jakob felt his body tense. Right, Christmas vacation ... The court's judgement granted Jakob the right to spend five consecutive days with Matias in December. In the presence of representatives of child protective services, but still: five days. The first day had gone well, as had the second. On the morning of the third day, Lena had informed Jakob Matias was sick and wouldn't be able to see him. Jakob had tried to argue back. He'd shown up at Lena's door to see his son. He'd known it was a mistake, but he hadn't been able to stop himself. He'd peered through the letterbox and heard Matias playing inside. The boy hadn't sounded the least bit sick, even though Lena had claimed she had a doctor's statement. Jakob had knocked on the door and tried to talk to Lena through the letterbox. Lena had called the police, and a patrol officer showed up to escort Jakob from the building. They'd threatened to arrest him if he didn't leave of his own accord. Jakob had given in and trudged wearily back to his hotel. The trip had come to a terrible end.

Just then, there was a knock at the door. Jakob glanced out the window. Seeing Guðrún always put a smile on his face.

He went to open the door, and he and Guðrún embraced in the cramped entryway.

'Hildur's here,' he whispered in her ear. She took a step backward. A mischievous smile had spread across her face. Her lips formed two soundless words: *OK. Later.*

Jakob fetched a third beer from the fridge. Hildur had moved to the armchair; Guðrún and Jakob sat side by side on the comfortable couch. They chatted about this and that, the weather and their plans for tomorrow.

After a short pause, Guðrún got down to business: 'Listen, I just read the news about that dead man.'

Not long before, the police had released a statement about the man found dead on the ski track and published the victim's name. The method of killing hadn't been made public, but the police had decided it would be best to release news of the suspected homicide as soon as possible, because rumours were bound to spread like wildfire anyway.

'Hermann Hermannsson was found dead this morning,' Jakob said. 'The investigation is still pending, so I can't—'

Guðrún tossed her thick blonde hair over her shoulder and put his mind at ease: 'I know, I know, honey. You guys can't tell me anything. But I will say this town is full of potential suspects.'

'What do you mean?' Hildur asked, intrigued.

Guðrún worked at the local daycare a few days a week. There were fewer domestic flights during the winter, and it didn't make sense for her to keep her shop open more than a couple of days a week, as most orders were placed online these days. And so she'd taken a job as a part-time daycare worker.

Guðrún took a sip of beer and belched. 'The daycare's where you hear all the best gossip.'

Children were known for telling the adults at the daycare everything they saw and heard at home. But the worst gossips were some of the daycare staff. For many, the highlight of the working day was the chance to share juicy stories in the break room. Jakob and Hildur waited.

'The cook's cousin was having an affair with Hermann. I heard he was also screwing the owner of the pizzeria, one of the managers from the shrimp-processing plant, and the girls' volleyball coach. When things are that messy, it doesn't take much for someone to lose it. I wouldn't be the least bit surprised if one of those women or their husbands had felt disrespected and set out to get revenge,' Guðrún reported.

Jakob listened to his girlfriend's chatter, fascinated. A crime of passion? A cold end to a hot relationship? It was possible, of course, although not particularly common in Iceland. When studying homicides at the police academy, he and his fellow students had reviewed the statistics: the most common homicides in Finland were stabbings that took place among groups of drunks who knew each other. Jakob had learned Icelandic statistics told the same story.

But in Hermann's case, the scenario was an impossibility. The location and long-distance shot spoke of forethought.

Jakob made a note of the details his girlfriend revealed. He and Hildur would circle back to them tomorrow when they paid a visit to Hermann's home and rummaged through his wardrobes. Based on what he was hearing, Jakob wouldn't be the least bit surprised if they found a few skeletons there.

Chapter 15

Hildur was feeling energetic. She'd already been for a morning run and fetched Brenda from the rental agency car park where her acquaintance had left her beloved Land Cruiser. After grabbing an early lunch at the pizzeria, she'd dropped by Hermann's office. The place had turned out to be a disappointment in terms of clues; she'd found almost nothing of interest. The shelves had primarily been filled with folders of bookkeeping records from over the years, and going through them would take time. But they didn't have the resources to start slogging through receipts just now. They'd only do it if no clues turned up elsewhere. They had to prioritise.

Hildur had also come across old issues of *The Economist* and a collection of wine glasses. Hermann's office had been surprisingly spacious but contained little in the way of material related to his business affairs. The big, solid wood desk, high-backed chair, bookshelf, pair of ottomans, and divan along one wall had given the impression of a living space as opposed to a workplace. It was plain Hermann entertained visitors in his office; Agnes had said as much. Hildur had found several unopened wine bottles in the massive cabinet behind the desk. Hermann didn't even have a desktop computer in his office.

The sole item that grabbed Hildur's attention was the tidy stack of building committee meeting minutes on the desk. Hildur had taken the papers and would look through them later. Before that, she and Jakob would search Hermann's house.

*

Hildur decided to try her luck and reached for the brass handle of the stout door. A small downward movement let her know the bunch of keys from the central console of Hermann's car wouldn't be necessary. The front door of the murdered man's home wasn't locked. There weren't many locals who locked their door for an absence of less than twenty-four hours. Typically a key was used only if the residents planned on being gone for multiple days.

The lights came on automatically as Hildur and Jakob stepped into the entryway, Hildur leading. The technical investigators had already been by to retrieve samples to compare to the fibres found on the victim and in the maintenance shed. But because this wasn't a crime scene, the decision had been made not to conduct a more thorough forensic investigation here.

Hildur and Jakob pulled blue plastic covers over their shoes, and she handed him a pair of disposable gloves. They meant to go through every corner and drawer in the hunt for clues about the previous days' events. If they found anything in the home that demanded closer analysis, they would call the tech team back in.

Jakob nodded and let the latex glove snap loudly against his wrist. He said he'd check the entryway and wardrobes, then move on to both bathrooms. Hildur would start from the rooms on the second floor. They would tackle the kitchen last.

It was Sunday, but that made no difference during a murder investigation. The results from the pathologist's autopsy and the lab tests in Reykjavík probably wouldn't arrive until early in the week. While waiting, Hildur and Jakob would scrape together as much relevant information as possible from other sources.

Jakob opened the shoe cupboard and started going through the footwear and storage baskets. He aimed his torch into every last corner.

'People's biggest secrets are usually found at home,' Jakob muttered to himself, squatting closer to the floor.

As she started up the stairs, Hildur felt her hand slip from the railing. She stopped on the bottom tread, suddenly nauseous. The acidic fluid burned her oesophagus as it rose from her stomach. Luckily it wasn't far to the front door. She rushed out. She had to get fresh air. She leaned against the house and gulped frantically to stop herself from vomiting.

'Everything OK?'

Jakob had appeared at door. Hildur didn't immediately respond. She kept her eyes on the waves and focused on breathing. Hermann's house stood at the edge of the neighbourhood and a stone's throw from the sea. The views from the sloping plot were stunning. The covered grill area was empty, aside from a few folded wooden chairs leaning against the structure's rear wall.

'I can't tell. All of a sudden I felt terrible. Maybe there was something in the pizza I had for lunch . . .'

Jakob rubbed his forehead with his wrist and said he'd keep working alone. 'Take it easy. This house isn't going anywhere.'

Hildur recognised the feeling. It was disgust. The first place one's body registered disgust was in the digestive organs. She had a tendency to get nauseous when she saw the body of someone who'd died a violent death or heard stories about those who'd experienced violence. What she didn't understand was why it had struck now. There wasn't anyone inside the house aside from Jakob.

Hildur kept leaning against the house and closed her eyes. She took a couple of deep breaths and pulled a red-and-white box of Opal Fruits from her pocket. The strong flavour of the licorice lozenge masked the bitter taste of the bile. *I can do this,* she decided, walked back inside, and pulled on a new disposable glove.

Jakob had already been through the cupboards and drawers in the entryway. Judging by the clatter, he'd moved on to the bathroom. Hildur stopped at the bathroom door: 'Find anything interesting?'

Jakob was bent over one of the vanity drawers. As he rifled through its contents, he gave a brief report: 'There are a lot of expensive-looking leather shoes and sport coats in the entryway, all the same size. I'm not finding anything out of the ordinary here in the bathroom either. Except Viagra. But I suppose that's not out of the ordinary.'

Hildur looked in the drawer and saw several empty blue-and-white boxes at the bottom. She took one and peered in. 'Someone has a busy social life . . .'

She returned the empty box to the drawer and told Jakob she was heading upstairs.

The carpeted stairs didn't make so much as a squeak underfoot. A few tacky landscape watercolours of Santorini hung in the stairwell. When she reached the second-storey landing, Hildur stopped. The light fell beautifully through a large skylight, lending a tranquility to the space. A black leather couch stood against the longer wall, paired with a white sheepskin footstool. Two red leather armchairs faced them, a small, slim table between. Hildur noticed a bunched bit of black cloth in one of the armchairs. She lifted it to eye level. A pair of lace panties, more hole than fabric. Hildur slipped them into a sealable plastic baggie.

There were three crumpled tissues on the side table. Hildur sealed them in separate bags too. They might contain DNA. *We can send them to Reykjavík for analysis if necessary*, she thought to herself, as she checked the rest of the landing.

She then stepped into a sparsely furnished home office. A big black desk and two high-backed leather chairs. A floor-to-ceiling bookcase along one wall. Hildur quickly scanned its contents. A box of chargers and cables. Icelandic sagas, biographies, bird guides, books of old maps. Nothing that immediately caught her interest.

A wireless printer stood at the edge of the desk, along with a box of pens. The item of most interest gleamed in the middle of the desk: a silver-grey Apple laptop. The charger indicator was glowing green and light was shining through the apple-shaped logo: the computer was on. Hildur lifted the lid, and the screen came to life. An exotic undersea scene appeared, along with a field for a four-character password.

She entered the first four-digit password to pop into her head: 1234. The screen shuddered as the password was rejected. She tried again: 1111. The laptop thought for a moment, but then the screen shuddered again. Incorrect password. Then 0000. Wrong again. As far as she could recall, Apple laptops had no limit to the number of incorrect password attempts allowed.

The password field stared insistently at her. The password could be anything. If it wasn't one of the most obvious alternatives, it would be impossible to guess the correct sequence of characters. Hildur pondered.

Hermann had influence. He'd been the magic lamp of Ísafjörður, the genie who could make people's dreams come true if so motivated. Maybe he thought he was invincible? The kind of person no one would dare defy? After all, he hadn't even locked his front door.

Hildur pressed the space bar and hit 'enter'. The screen vibrated again, indicating an incorrect password. 'Goddammit,' she hissed. She'd guessed wrong, that Hermann hadn't used a password at all.

The IT specialists in Reykjavík might be able to get into the computer, but that would take time. Hildur went through all the desk drawers, hoping to find a list of passwords. Surprising numbers of people wrote them down on paper and kept them within arm's reach. But there was no password booklet in any of the desk drawers. Not even a calendar or address book.

Hildur thought about her own passwords and had an idea. She checked her notes for Hermann's *kennitala*, the ten-digit number consisting of an individual's date of birth and a four-digit identifier.

Bingo! Hildur smiled broadly. The password was Hermann's birthday, the fourth of June.

Hildur would have a closer look at the computer's contents back at the station, but she couldn't help glancing at the windows that were open. The laptop appeared to have been shut in a hurry. Hermann had probably been intending to get back to it quickly, because he'd left a lot of programs up. His email was open, as was Facebook Messenger. The icon for Preview software was active. Hildur clicked the icon and gasped.

A series of photographs opened on the screen. This wasn't your average vacation photo album. Hildur quickly browsed through all twenty or so pictures. They'd all been taken in the same place and of the same person; only the angle changed.

Hildur recognised the woman in the photos from the running path. She remembered having bumped into the woman a few times, and they'd even exchanged a few words on occasion. The pictures were of Linda Jónsdóttir. There wasn't the slightest doubt. Hildur had looked her up on Facebook after talking with Agnes. In her profile picture, Linda had been smiling with her husband and child on the terrace of a summer cabin on the shores of some fjord. The sun had been shining from a cloudless sky.

But in these photos, Linda was posing lasciviously in a red leather chair, showing herself off. Hildur recognised the panties pulled to one side. They had the same lace flowers as the pair she'd just collected as evidence.

Chapter 16

Reykjavík, February 2020

Dísa

There was a whine as the supermarket's sliding doors pulled apart. Dísa dodged the puddle that had formed in the vestibule and headed straight for the row of refrigeration units at the back wall. A yellow clock was ticking behind the meat counter. The minute hand had just crawled past nine, and the store would be closing soon. She'd come at just the right time. Of course she had. She went to the supermarket every Sunday at the exact same time. The big deliveries were made on Monday morning. Before the new products were shelved, any products on the verge of expiring were sold at a steep discount. Red-sticker items were found in the left-hand refrigerator and the basket in front of it.

Dísa scanned the evening's selection. Skim milk at half price, vacuum-packed fishballs at 70 per cent off. The red sticker on the liverwurst said another 30 per cent would be taken off the price at the checkout. Dísa reached for a carton of milk. Then she checked the best-before date on the liverwurst: tomorrow. But best-before didn't matter much; the food would be edible for days, sometimes even weeks after the date printed on the package. She dropped the liverwurst in her shopping basket and calculated it was enough for four days of lunch sandwiches. Her money wouldn't stretch far enough for a fresh ciabatta. She took the cheapest package of crispbread from the shelf.

There were times she allowed herself to fantasise about sun-dried tomatoes, the delicious-smelling bread from the bakery, the selection at the cheese counter, and fresh juice with lots of pulp. But she'd gradually learned to shut her eyes to things she couldn't have. While at the supermarket, she didn't glance to the side or look at the enticing displays set up at the ends of the aisles.

When she got to the tills, Dísa handed the kid working it a thousand-krónur bill and a fistful of coins.

He sighed in frustration as he accepted her money. 'Don't you have anything bigger? It's going to take forever to count all these.'

Dísa stood there looking at the boy, a pang in her gut. She dug her nails into her palms and clenched her fists hard. There was no way she was going to start crying in front of this pimple-faced kid. She shook her head at him. He muttered something to himself that Dísa didn't even try to catch. She pulled a cotton tote from her coat pocket, loaded her modest purchases into it one at a time, and walked out of the store, heart pounding.

She felt the rage bubbling up inside her. Of course she would have loved to pull a smooth ten-thousand-krónur bill from her wallet! She would have handed it to the cashier with a smile and casually apologised she didn't have anything smaller this time. It would be even grander to own a credit card she could swipe across the terminal with a chic nonchalance. Silver-tone, with her name embossed on it. But there was no way she'd be able to get anything of the sort. During the worst times, she'd done stupid things and ruined her credit rating. It would be a while before any bank would grant her a credit card.

Dísa clenched the cotton tote against her body. She turned left at the corner, and the bus stop came into view. Her purchases were slim, but it was all she could afford right now. After paying her modest monthly expenses – the rent for her tiny basement studio, her bus pass, and her phone bill – she had very little left. She did everything she could to avoid the food bank, because it reminded her too much of the past. She'd decided to look after herself, and she knew she could do it.

Dísa kicked a rock. There was a sharp thunk as it hit the glass wall of the bus stop and bounced into the roadway.

That pimply kid could have been friendly to her; at the very least he could have chosen to give good customer service and accept a fistful of coins without protest. He needed to be taught a lesson he wouldn't forget. An idea began to take shape in Dísa's mind. She was pretty sure how she'd proceed. She'd take action the way she always did in such circumstances. First she'd make a plan, then she'd execute it step by step. The boy would come to regret what he'd done.

They all would, all those who had wronged her.

Chapter 17

Ísafjörður, February 2020

The next morning, Beta, Hildur and Jakob stepped onto the rickety metal stairs leading over the boulders to the beach. The rubble barrier had been built on the northern shore of Ísafjörður a couple of decades before to protect buildings and the pedestrian-and-cycle path from big waves. Today the sea was calm. It was such a gorgeous late-winter day that they'd decided to have their morning briefing outdoors.

'That way I can get some fresh air too,' Beta said. She had two preschoolers at home, a job as police chief, and a spouse who worked full time outside the house, so she had very little time for her own interests. Maybe someday, when the kids got a little older.

Beta was the first to step from the stairs to the strand. Tides were extreme in the fjords. At low tide, it was pleasant to walk along the two-hundred-metre-wide beach. Small waves swept across the white sand.

'I spoke with Axlar-Hákon. The results of the forensic analyses and the autopsy will be coming the day after tomorrow at the earliest.'

Hildur shot her boss a questioning look. 'At the earliest?'

'Yes. He had to examine the body of the man who died in that small aircraft accident first.'

The plane that had taken off from Reykjavík had headed west, toward Ríf county and the northern shore of the Snæfellsnes headland. It hadn't made it far at all when it suddenly lost altitude and dropped into the sea. Beta said the weather had been so bad after the accident that divers hadn't been able to approach the wreckage until a few days later.

'Axlar-Hákon said he'd never seen anything so gruesome in all his years as a forensic pathologist,' Beta said. 'In all likelihood the pilot was a man named Gullaugur Emilsson. The bad thing was his corpse had been chewed full of holes by fish. There was almost nothing left of his face.'

Nevertheless, the pilot's identity had to be definitively confirmed. He hadn't had any recognisable tattoos or sizeable moles, and his name didn't bring up any fingerprints or DNA samples in the police databases. It was Axlar-Hákon's responsibility to verify the identity of those who died of unnatural causes, and this time he would presumably have to use the teeth to do so. That would take some time.

Beta realised Hildur was lagging behind. She turned to check what had happened to her colleague. Hildur was just standing there, looking at her and Jakob in frustration.

The windless weather had suddenly changed. A brisk gust blew off the sea.

'So now we're even ranking the dead?' Hildur huffed.

Beta grunted. There simply weren't any other alternatives. They could make use of the wait to look into other things. 'You went by Hermann's place yesterday?'

Jakob reiterated the findings from the previous evening's search: Viagra and amateur pornography. Hildur then reported on her visit to Hermann's office and her attempts to talk to the residents of the homes on the road leading to the ski slopes.

'No one was able to provide any new information relevant to the case. No one saw any vehicles driving down from the mountain on Friday night.'

Beta pondered this information. On Fridays, people gathered at friends' homes for dinner parties. They might have a little wine with their meal and maybe even a drop of cognac afterward. It was possible to drive from the ski area to the main road without passing a single home that was in year-round use. It was not surprising no one had noticed anything.

Hermann's computer would be sent to the IT specialists in Reykjavík for closer analysis, but Jakob and Hildur had been able to take a superficial look through its contents earlier that morning. Aside from the photos, meeting minutes and notes made up most of the material on it.

'But we found one really interesting thing in his email,' Jakob said.

The three of them were now walking side by side so they could hear each other. For the moment the sea was calm, but even its slightest movement created a background slosh that drowned out all other sounds.

Jakob told Beta about the email Hermann had left unfinished. 'A message in the Drafts folder had been written on Friday morning. Those amateur porn shots had been attached to it, and it read – how did it go . . .'

His voice faded, and he shot Hildur a pleading look.

Hildur quoted the message word for word: '*Cooperation would be the best option for everyone's sake.*'

This news about the email struck Beta as incredibly significant. 'Who was the intended recipient?'

'The recipient hadn't been added yet, but our guess is it was meant for Björn Ísaksson, the husband of the Linda in the photos,' Hildur said.

Beta thought for a moment. The email was a blackmail note. Hermann's apparent lack of precautions when sending such a message was striking: from his normal Gmail account without any encryption.

Jakob nodded and said that, judging by his browsing history, Hermann hadn't even bothered to use an Incognito window to keep his browsing private. 'He'd done quite a bit of surfing on porn sites. But totally normal stuff.'

Nothing Beta was hearing came as a surprise. She'd lived in Ísafjörður long enough to know everyone in the public eye by face and name. Most of the local decision-makers, entrepreneurs, and Instagram celebrities were at least somewhat familiar to her. She'd got to know Hermann right after moving to town. Hermann had come by the police station to suck up to her, sent bouquets and invited her to lunch. But Beta had reacted with caution, because she'd been warned about Hermann before the move. Evidently it was easy to get caught in his net and drown. So she had politely but firmly declined all attempts at closer contact. She'd heard plenty of stories about how impossible it was to start a company in the area without discussing the matter with Hermann first. If he wanted, he could sweep from the market any companies he viewed as detrimental to his business, even if it required illegal means.

Beta began sharing more details about Hermann with her colleagues. As a local, Hildur no doubt knew all of this, but for the foreigner Jakob this was all new information.

Hermann had been born in Ísafjörður. He'd attended an elite high school in Reykjavík before moving to London to study business. Beta remembered having read in some old newspaper article that Hermann had spent a few years working for investment banks in the City before returning to his hometown with his earnings. Hermann had told the journalist he'd longed for the peace and quiet of the countryside and his majestic homeland.

Beta hadn't believed a word of his clichéd descriptions of nature. She was sure Hermann had moved back to Ísafjörður to be a big fish in a small pond. It was much harder to achieve prominent status in a metropolis than it was here.

The trio stopped at the far end of the beach and watched the fishing boats sail out to sea. Grey, low-hanging clouds had suddenly appeared in the blue sky, and Beta felt a breeze rising in the east. The mass of clouds wrung out a few raindrops.

'The woman in the photographs you found on Hermann's computer. Are you a hundred per cent sure?' Beta asked.

'Yes. It's Björn's wife.'

'What about the building committee minutes you found in Hermann's office?'

Beta listened as Hildur summarised the contents of the documents she'd reviewed that morning. The harbour expansion had been debated in multiple committee meetings. Several studies had been commissioned and costs compared. The latest minutes included a note from Björn: the amount of reclaimed land had been intentionally left at just under five hectares in the expansion plans to avoid the necessity of an environmental permit. Björn felt fudging decimals was a bad idea; he thought it would be wise to apply for the permit anyway. 'If Björn were a "yes", the committee could have voted on behalf of the project in its next meeting and passed the matter on to the council for approval.'

In light of the documents, it appeared Björn had put the brakes on the project. That no doubt frustrated Hermann. Beta reflected on this, nodding slowly. She asked Jakob what thoughts had occurred to him.

The wind was cooling the weather. Beta noticed Jakob pull up the collar of his rollneck sweater to keep his throat covered.

'Björn had adopted an oppositional stance to Hermann's preferences. And then nude photographs of Björn's wife turned up on Hermann's computer. That doesn't sound like a coincidence.'

Beta nodded in agreement. 'We're going to have to talk to both of them as soon as possible. Björn, of course, too, but first Linda.'

'It's already in hand. Linda's coming in,' Hildur glanced at her sports watch, 'in an hour.'

Beta gazed at the water. She had to remember to pick up the kids from daycare earlier than usual to get them to music on time. The music classes had been her husband's idea, yet here it was Beta who was driving the kids around. And the chauffeuring would only get worse. That she was sure of.

Hopefully the kids won't get interested in soccer, she thought to herself. It wasn't that Beta had anything against the sport per se, but the summer tournaments and travelling to and from gobbled up the lion's share of vacation time in families where soccer was played. If they lived in Reykjavík, all the important matches would have been nearby. But living in the countryside meant endless hours on the road. Beta thought about her neighbour, whose middle-school-aged children were serious about soccer. The neighbour had detailed all the driving she'd be doing during the upcoming summer. First to northern Iceland for a week in June, then eight hundred kilometres away to the east, a couple of tournaments in the Reykjavík area, and a week-long tournament a boat ride away in the Vestmannaeyjar archipelago. Beta had broken out in a sweat simply listening to her.

She stopped to take in the beach spreading out before her.

'What's on your mind?'

Beta had been lost in thought. She heard Hildur asking something but wasn't sure what it was in reference to. She gave Hildur an apologetic look. 'Nothing.'

Beta should have known Hildur would ask. Hildur was incredibly quick at reading situations. Within a few days of her return, she had guessed something was off.

The fact of the matter was major changes were taking place in Beta's private life. Her husband Óliver had to travel a lot for work, and in December Beta had begun suspecting his business trips to Reykjavík included activities other than meetings and development project pow-wows. Beta's suspicions were first roused when she was paying the bills from their joint bank account. Óliver's debit card had been used to pay for multiple meals at one and the same restaurant: Grill Market, a fancy steak joint in downtown Reykjavík. Beta had reviewed the substantial charges and, after comparing them to the prices on the online menu, concluded the totals corresponded to the cost of dinner for two. Beta hadn't wanted to confront her husband about it right away. At first she thought he'd maybe gone to eat with friends. But in January his business trips increased in length and frequency. He'd explained them away as necessitated by the final stages of the development project. But there were just too many coincidences. His phone was often off in the evening, allegedly because it had died. His wardrobe had been augmented by new clothes inconsistent with his usual style.

Beta and her husband had twin sons who were full of energy, while both parents were always working and had very little in the way of shared free time. Beta didn't find it particularly surprising that this had occurred. It was how things went in a lot of long-term relationships. Some couples divorced; others stuck together despite the affair. But raising the issue was hard. The moment it was spoken out loud was the moment it became more real. So she'd decided to take the easy road and let the whole issue lie for the time being.

At least she wouldn't be able to ruminate on it now, because she was feeling the pressure of the murder investigation. Journalists had been contacting her more or less non-stop since yesterday's press release. Calls had been coming in from abroad since first thing that morning. Judging by the questions she'd asked, the SVT correspondent from Sweden was working on a speculative story about political violence having raised its head in idyllic Iceland. The reporter's hardball questions had left Beta tongue-tied. She didn't want to add fuel to the fire, but lying wasn't an option. And the reporter hadn't accepted her vague answers.

Beta looked out to sea. A restless flock of gulls had gathered around the mouth of the sewer line. Ísafjörður's waste water was released directly into the sea, and the birds kept a vigilant watch, diving for the food scraps neglectful residents flushed down the toilet. The local waste management was nothing to write home about. 'When are we going to get a wastewater treatment plant here?'

Hildur took a few steps toward the waterline and glanced at the gulls: 'Never. No one cares about shit they can't smell in their own backyard.'

Beta shook her head. Despite her occasional lack of delicacy, Hildur was right: pushing for a new indoor athletic centre was more likely to get you voter support than pushing for wastewater treatment.

The drizzle was angling into their faces. In this part of the world, rain rarely fell vertically. The wind pushed any precipitation sideways.

A few employees in workwear stood outside the old shrimp-processing plant, taking shelter from the rain. They'd pulled down their white masks to puff on their cigarettes. Beta nodded in greeting.

It looked like the plant had ordered its employees to wear masks, despite the lack of any official decisions yet. Presumably one would be made soon. Beta predicted the coronavirus that had originated in China and spread across the world would cause a lot of damage. There were bound to be more cases than the few that had been mentioned on the news so far. The worsening contagion would presumably also mean a cutback in her husband's business trips. Beta wasn't sure if that was a good thing or a bad thing. She shook the thought from her mind.

She registered the sound of Hildur's footfalls behind her had suddenly stopped.

'Hey, wait a sec,' Hildur called out. She was standing still, staring intently at Beta and Jakob. 'Something just occurred to me.'

Beta glanced at the mountain rising behind Hildur. Down here in town, precipitation came in the form of rain, but up in the mountains it was no doubt colder. She'd been excited about the onset of spring, but maybe she'd celebrated too soon. She'd still have many occasions for disappointment.

Hildur looked Beta in the eye first, Jakob second. Then her gaze turned upward and fixed on something Beta couldn't see. 'That plane that fell into the sea. I have kind of a weird feeling about it. What if it wasn't an accident after all?'

Chapter 18

Westfjords, 1987

Seven years before Rósa and Björk's disappearance

There was a sharp hiss as Rakel dropped a dollop of room-temperature butter in the pan. She used the tip of the wooden spatula to steer it across the smooth metal surface. A mild fatty smell filled the kitchen.

Rakel poured the melted butter into a bowl to cool. Then she took the leftover oatmeal from breakfast and folded in a couple of fistfuls of flour spiked with baking powder and a dash of sugar. She bent over to take a spoon from the kitchen drawer.

The cat that had been purring at her feet instantly got out of the way. It was skilled at predicting its mistress's movements. There was a big white splotch around its black nose, which is why it was named Rjómi, *Cream*. Rjómi had come to them from the neighbouring farm. Helga had had her hands full with her sheep, and Rakel had walked over several days in a row to help out with the spring shearing. Rósa had napped in the back room of the sheep barn, and Hildur had helped bag the wool. When Hildur saw the black kitten with the white nose in the basket in the corner of the back room, it was love at first sight. Helga had suggested that if it were all right with Rakel, the kitten could go home with them. Rakel had smiled and stroked the cat under the chin. A mouse catcher was always welcome.

Rakel thrust the thin-handled wooden spoon into the dough and started mixing. Around, around, around. The rays of the late-summer sun warmed the kitchen counter. The room smelled of butter, the cat was purring; she was making pancakes. It had been ages since Rakel had felt so peaceful.

The back door opened, and Hildur ran in. With her shoes on, of course.

'Remember to take off your shoes.'

Hildur spread her arms and feigned confusion. 'But I'm only gonna be here five seconds; I'm not staying.'

'Even so. You'll track in dirt, and I just swept the floor.'

Hildur backed up a couple of steps and asked for something to drink.

Rakel took a small glass from the cupboard and filled it at the tap. Hildur had spent the whole morning outside. Her cheeks were red, and her hair was wind-tousled.

Hildur drank her water and was handing the glass back to her mother when she changed her mind. 'I want to collect worms in it.'

'As long as you don't bring them inside,' Rakel called out as her daughter made for the door.

Hildur turned to glower at her mother and shook her head like an adult. She took a deep breath to communicate how severely her patience was being tried. 'Of course not. I'm giving them to the birds.'

Rakel smiled. If Hildur wasn't down at the shore with the birds, she was in the pasture with the horses or digging up rocks in the backyard. Rakel sometimes wondered if it was good for a child to spend so much time playing alone. They lived on one of only two farms in the valley. It was a long way into town, and she only took the girls in for supermarket runs and occasional trips to the library. But things would be changing soon, when their third child arrived.

'I'm about to make pancakes, so don't go far. I'll call out when they're ready.'

A squeal of delight echoed from the doorway. Rakel knew Hildur loved *lummur*: small, thick pancakes served with syrup and sugar.

Rakel waited for the door to close. She mixed the dough, waited a moment, then another. There was no noise. Had Hildur left the door open?

Suddenly Rakel felt the familiar stabbing in her head. The pain had refused to leave her in peace today as well. It always found some way of slinking in, of reminding her of its existence.

Chapter 19

Ísafjörður, February 2020

Hildur sat at the front edge of her office chair and bit into her tuna-paste and mayo sandwich. She was waiting for someone to answer her call. She'd been forced to listen to the cheery but annoying 'on hold' music for a while now. She was almost finished with her lunch.

As she chewed the last mouthful, she finally heard someone pick up. A low voice growled: 'Róbert.'

'This is the Safety Investigation Authority, I assume?'

The Icelandic custom of answering the phone with nothing more than a first name sometimes caused confusion. After receiving an answer in the affirmative, Hildur explained why she was calling. She wanted more information on the small aircraft that had plunged into the sea two weeks previously.

Beta had reacted sceptically when Hildur began audibly pondering alternative scenarios leading to the plane's destruction. She'd reminded Hildur the accident hadn't taken place anywhere near the Westfjords, and there was no good reason for them to dedicate their energies to it. Hildur had decided to look into the matter on top of her regular duties. She'd be getting the autopsy report from Axlar-Hákon, but conditions at the time of the accident, potential problems with the aircraft, and other factors that may have played a role in the crash were the province of the Safety Investigation Authority. The authority investigated every fatal accident that occurred in Iceland.

'It's going to be a long time before we have any information on that, young lady. The guys didn't get the wreck to the surface until the day before yesterday.'

Hildur was having a hard time making out Róbert's words, because he kept mumbling. She pressed the phone to her ear and wished he'd open his mouth wider. Hildur knew the next question was pointless, but she asked it anyway: 'What caused the accident?'

Róbert laughed. His loud guffaws were punctuated by powerful coughs. Hildur pictured the spraying spittle so vividly that she pulled back from the phone. 'An unexpected gust of wind. Or maybe the pilot had a heart attack. I'm not going to start guessing.' Róbert paused before posing a clearly articulated question: 'Which police department did you say you were calling from?'

Hildur told him and continued in the same breath that she knew the matter was beyond her unit's jurisdiction – the aircraft had come down in Western Iceland, after all. But she had her reasons for asking. She strained to keep her voice steady and a mild smile on her face. 'I know you guys have your hands full and inquiries from curious policewomen don't make things any easier. But could you give me a call when you know more about the incident? I'd highly value the views of an experienced accident investigator.'

A few seconds' silence ended with a slimy cough. 'Sure, I'd be happy to. Was it Hildur? That's a pretty name. What's your mobile number?'

Hildur recited the number, politely bade Róbert goodbye, and wished him a pleasant day. When the call ended, she couldn't help smiling. Apparently playing the role of damsel in distress had produced the desired outcome.

There was a cough at the doorway.

Linda Jónsdóttir had shown up five minutes early. Her face was pale, and she was wearing a long-sleeved floral tunic. 'I'm not sure who I'm supposed to check in with,' she said in a thin voice.

Hildur scrambled to her feet, introduced herself, and led Linda into the conference room. The tiny station didn't have any dedicated interrogation rooms; all conversations took place at the round table in the conference room. If the individual being questioned was known to be violent or there was cause to believe they might try to escape, one of the basement cells was used instead.

Hildur thanked Linda for coming in and explained she wasn't suspected of having committed a crime. This would be less of an interrogation and more of a free-flowing conversation. Even so, Linda seemed extremely tense. She tugged at the hem of her tunic and took quick, shallow breaths.

'I could get us some coffee. Or would you prefer tea?' Hildur asked, gesturing for Linda to seat herself at the table.

'Could I have some herbal tea without any sugar, please?'

Hildur walked into the kitchen and saw Jakob had just made a fresh pot of coffee. They had decided Hildur would talk to Linda alone. In the meantime, Jakob could continue looking through the photo files on Hermann's laptop and conduct a more thorough review of his social media channels.

Dry goods and coffee filters were stored in the cupboard above the coffee machine. Hildur reached for the brown box containing teabags. A thin layer of dust had settled on it. Tea was rarely drunk at this station.

She pulled out a yellow bag and raised it to her eyes for a closer look. 'Is this herbal tea?'

Jakob laughed, took the box, and plucked out a bag in a red sleeve. 'No. But this is.'

Hildur thanked him, heated up a mugful of water in the microwave, and dunked the bag of rooibos. She walked back to the conference room with the hot beverages. Linda took hold of the teabag's tab and lazily swirled her tea around the mug. Her hands were trembling. It was hard squaring this quivering herbal-tea sipper with the bold woman in the photographs.

'I'd like to talk to you about the death of Hermann Hermannsson. I assume you've heard about it?'

Linda nodded and squeezed her eyes shut.

'Sad situation,' Hildur said. 'My condolences.'

Linda spoke softly, a little more than a whisper: 'What . . . but what does it have to do with me?'

Hildur slowly raised her coffee to her lips and took a long sip. She wanted to make Linda wait for an answer. Sometimes a brief, oppressive silence did more to get people to talk than direct, precisely framed questions.

Linda fiddled with her hands. The corners of her mouth were turned down in the faintest of frowns. She was clearly uncomfortable.

Hildur took another sip and felt the hot coffee warm her throat. When her mug thunked to the tabletop, she said: 'We understand you and Hermann were acquainted.'

Linda clenched her mug and answered a bit too readily: 'Everyone in Ísafjörður knew him.' Her chin rose slightly, and her eyes went wide. Hildur noted everything about the woman's manner signalled nervousness. Linda looked like a horse on the verge of bolting.

Hildur took a couple of deep breaths and assumed an empathetic but firm expression. She didn't want to ask direct yes or no questions; she wanted to lead Linda into speaking more expansively on the subject at hand.

'According to our information, the two of you were intimately involved. That's why we wanted to talk to you.'

When the shield Linda had been maintaining finally came down, it came down quickly. Hildur saw the woman sitting across the table crumple. Her shoulders slumped, and her jaw dropped. It gave the impression that her face had collapsed.

Then Linda started gasping for breath, raised her hands to her mouth, and bent forward.

Hildur realised what was happening. She grabbed the wastepaper basket from the floor and passed it across the table. Linda retched. The contents of her stomach splattered to the bottom of the wastebasket, and an acrid stink filled the room.

Hildur found a pack of tissues in her pocket. She took one, unfolded it, and handed it to Linda. After a pause, she asked Linda if she wanted to freshen up in the bathroom.

Linda nodded and glanced at her questioner as she exited the room. The look in her eyes made Hildur start. She'd just hurt this woman with her questions, and yet she read gratitude there as well as shame.

Five minutes later, Linda returned to the table, even paler and clutching a paper towel in her fist. 'Good God. I didn't think anyone knew about the affair,' she stammered.

Hildur looked encouragingly at her but didn't say anything. She guessed Linda was prepared to tell everything now without having to be prodded.

'We met a couple of months ago at the building committee Christmas dinner. It's an annual tradition for the committee members and their spouses to celebrate the year that's coming to an end with a nice meal. I was there with my husband. My husband and Hermann have been on the committee for years...'

Linda reported every detail she could remember about the evening. Hildur listened to her breakneck account without interrupting.

The group had eaten dinner at the hotel restaurant, then gone across the street to the bar to continue the evening. 'By that point, Björn was so drunk he decided to walk home. I wanted to stay a moment longer. The moment went on and on, and before I knew it, Hermann and I were the only ones left. Then one thing led to another . . .'

Linda looked simultaneously miserable and happy as she reminisced on the past. Hildur noticed a little colour had appeared in her pale cheeks. But there was also regret in her voice, maybe a hint of sadness too.

'Hermann was so different to other men. Well, I hadn't had anyone else but Björn, but maybe as a woman you understand what I'm talking about.'

Hildur wasn't completely sure what it was she was supposed to understand, but she refrained from commenting. She smiled to encourage Linda to continue.

'He was . . . so incredibly polite and charming. He sent me goodnight messages in the evening. Always opened the door, helped me take off my coat, and asked how I was doing, really asked me. He sent flowers to my workplace, anonymously, of course, but I guessed they were from him.' Linda fell silent, then began sobbing softly. 'He looked at me. He thought I was sexy.'

She tried to pull herself together. She took a couple of deep breaths and sipped her tea. The paper towel absorbed the tears that had streamed down her cheeks.

'When did you two see each other last?'

Linda thought. 'Tuesday. A few days before . . . before he died. Björn had a meeting in Reykjavík, so he was gone for the evening.'

'Where were you and Hermann?'

'We spent the evening and night at his place. He lived alone, and we could have privacy there. He promised me we'd see each other again over the next few days.' Linda appeared to sink into a reverie. A sliver of a smile spread across her face, then abruptly vanished. Something seemed to have occurred to her. 'How did you know we were seeing each other?'

Hildur decided to tell the truth. She hadn't printed out any of the photos, but she figured her word would suffice. She explained they'd searched Hermann's house after the murder. 'We came across some photographs of a, hmmm, personal nature. I imagine you know what I'm talking about.'

Linda went bright red, then burst into tears again. 'This can't be happening. It can't.'

Through her tears, Linda explained that Hermann had promised the pictures would be purely for his personal use. *For lonely nights*, he'd said, swearing they'd remain in a hidden folder on his phone. Hildur didn't reveal they'd found the photos attached to an email on Hermann's laptop.

Linda was weeping inconsolably. She blew her nose loudly into the paper towel and sobbed: 'What are people going to think... What must you think of me now?'

Hildur took her by the hand and said, in as decisive a voice as possible, 'I don't think anything of you, trust me. You see all sorts of things in this line of work, and some of it's truly awful. You had fun together; there's nothing wrong with that. No one has seen the photographs except me and my colleague. We're just trying to figure out what happened to Hermann on the skiing track.'

Linda nodded but kept her eyes firmly shut.

'What did the two of you usually talk about? Did Hermann ever ask you any questions that struck you as odd?'

Linda blew her nose again, sat up straighter in her chair, and thought for a moment before answering. They'd often talked about cooking and wine. Unlike Björn, Hermann had been capable of discussing such things. 'Maybe that's why I fell for him.'

'Did you ever talk about your spouse? The two of them were both in politics but from opposing parties.'

'He tried to talk about Björn sometimes, and I didn't like it.' Linda seemed to be overcome by uncertainty again. She squirmed nervously in her seat and her eyes were closed again. Her fists were clenched on the table. 'This is maybe a little embarrassing, but ... He often talked about Björn when we were in bed. Maybe he got some sort of kick out of my being Björn's wife. It was sort of unpleasant, but I never said anything because he was otherwise so kind and considerate.'

Hildur nodded and asked if Hermann spoke about Björn in other contexts.

'No, I don't think so. They knew each other from local politics, and I couldn't care less about politics. I don't think I know anything about Björn that would interest – or would have interested Hermann.'

Hildur thought. Linda seemed sincere and perhaps a little naïve. Her guess was Linda had unsuspectingly ended up a pawn in a conflict between the two men. It was unfortunate, of course, that the draft message in Hermann's email hadn't included a recipient, but even without one the situation seemed pretty clear. Hermann had been planning on blackmailing Björn.

'I'm sorry I have to ask this next question. We're asking everyone the slightest bit connected to the case. Where were you from Friday night to Saturday morning?'

Linda blinked and looked flustered. She smoothed her hair behind her ears and thought. 'I was at a friend's place for our sewing club. I came home sometime after one.'

She gave Hildur the names of the club's other members and said she'd belonged to the club for several years. The close-knit group of women met at one of their homes every couple of weeks. Hildur didn't belong to a sewing club but she knew how they worked. The name might have suggested otherwise, but the primary purpose of sewing clubs was to talk and exchange news: they were basically gossip clubs one could only join by invitation. Hildur wrote down the contact information for the other club members. She would verify Linda's alibi later.

'What about your husband, Björn?'

'What about him?'

'Do you know where he was?'

'He said he was going to the cinema – the eight o'clock screening.'

Hildur nodded, tapped the tabletop with the tip of her ballpoint pen and stared at the notes she'd taken. Suddenly a thought occurred to her. 'You said Björn was at the cinema last Friday?'

Linda looked straight at Hildur and nodded. 'That's what he told me, that he was planning on going to the eight o'clock screening.'

Hildur nodded but didn't comment.

She would have to talk to Björn as soon as possible. It had been years since the local cinema had shown an eight o'clock film on Fridays.

Chapter 20

After Linda left, Hildur had called Linda's husband Björn. He'd answered from Hólmavík, explaining he was at a meeting at the town hall there and wouldn't be home until late that night. The seaside village of a few hundred inhabitants was only about a hundred kilometres from Ísafjörður as the crow flies, but the winding road following the deep fjords was over twice as long. Hildur had driven it countless times. During the summer, the trip only took a couple of hours; in the winter gloom the icy roads made it wise to set aside three. And so they'd agreed to meet the next day. She was surprised Björn hadn't asked anything about the reason for the call. Generally people's guards shot up when the police called. Well, she'd be wiser tomorrow.

Hildur began working her feet into her new running shoes. She'd bought them on sale from an athletic goods store in downtown Reykjavík a couple of weeks before. Her old trainers had come to the end of their road. Thumb-sized holes had appeared on inner collars of both shoes. Today she'd have a chance to break in the new pair with a short, non-strenuous run. Jakob had promised to go with her. They were planning on running to Hildur's Aunt Tinna's place, a few kilometres from the heart of Ísafjörður.

Hildur loved a home-cooked meal but wasn't much of a chef herself. She could boil an egg and flip a cod fillet in a frying pan, but cooking rarely interested her enough to truly focus on it. Besides, cooking for one felt like too much effort. It was easier to heat up store-bought fishballs in the oven or grab something from the local pizzeria.

There were a couple of knocks at the front door. The handle turned down, and the door opened. In Iceland, one didn't stand outside the front doors of acquaintances waiting for them to answer; you crossed the threshold without permission. Jakob's broad shoulders nearly filled the doorway. His long hair was tied in a tight bun at his nape, and he'd pulled a down vest over his thin black running shirt.

It wasn't completely dark yet, but the street lamps had already come on. There were only a handful of cars on the road as they sat off. Most folks had already made it home from work and were busying themselves in the kitchen or checking on their kids' homework.

Hildur glanced at Jakob and began running a little faster.

'Has Axlar-Hákon called?' Jakob asked, picking up the pace to remain at Hildur's side.

Hildur didn't immediately respond. The plane crash a couple of weeks back was troubling her. She'd checked the Meteorological Office website for flight conditions on the day in question, and there'd been no precipitation at all. There hadn't even been any clouds. The weather that day could be best described as having been 'creamy', as Icelanders put it.

They were approaching the fish-drying shed. Its perforated wall looked like the skeleton of some large animal. A popular delicacy, dried fish was made from cod, haddock and ocean catfish. The drying took place in the cold months, when insects weren't a problem. The fish couldn't be dried out in the open, because birds would have milked the opportunity to gorge themselves. The most effective solution was a shed with gapped walls.

'I called him, but not about Hermann. I wanted to ask about that pilot who died.'

Jakob shot Hildur a questioning look but didn't say anything. Because the pilot had died in an accident, a forensic pathologist's examination into the cause of death had to be performed. Axlar-Hákon had told Hildur he hadn't seen any signs of violence. But the fish had bitten off chunks of flesh from all over the corpse, so he couldn't say anything very precise about surface damage to the skin.

'What did he say about Hermann?' Jakob asked, wiping the beads of sweat from his forehead before they could drip into his eyebrows.

'Nothing.'

Axlar-Hákon had figured he'd have something to report on Hermann by tomorrow. As long as the lab results came in. Hildur was frustrated.

'Darn it, we always have to wait so damn long. If this were a bigger country, one person wouldn't have to do everything.'

Axlar-Hákon was the only pathologist in Iceland who performed forensic autopsies on people who'd died as the result of a crime or in otherwise ambiguous conditions. If two bodies were wheeled in during a single week, one of them would have to wait its turn.

Hildur suggested ending the run with a short sprint. She didn't hang around for Jakob's response; she took off as fast as she could.

She began feeling the pleasurable pressure in her thigh muscles. The familiar burn felt delicious in her lungs. At the last bend before Tinna's neighbourhood, Jakob was still at her side. He had an agonised look on his face, but evidently he wasn't giving up. They reached their destination at the same time and stopped to let their breath steady. Hildur thanked Jakob for the final spurt.

'I went running every night when you were in Reykjavík,' Jakob said, unzipping his down vest and letting the cold air dry away the sweat.

'You want to run the Reykjavík marathon together next summer?'

Jakob laughed. 'I thought you hate big sporting events.'

Jakob was right. Hildur wasn't sure why she'd even suggested it. But a lot of things were more fun to do with Jakob than by herself. Maybe she could make an exception for marathons if they ran together.

She leaned against a lamp post and stretched her legs. She noticed something different about the way Jakob was looking at her. There was a tinge of discomfort in it.

'What's on your mind?'

Jakob didn't immediately reply. Hildur released her leg and stopped stretching as she waited for him to answer.

'How have you been managing with Freysi's death? We never really talked about it.'

Hildur stood there, arms at her sides, staring at Jakob. For a moment she didn't speak, just looked. 'I don't really have anything to say about it,' she eventually said, then paused before continuing: 'I just try to think about it every day: he died, he died, he died.'

Hildur noticed the mystified look on Jakob's face.

'The more I think about it, the more ordinary it becomes. When I think about it a lot, I get so bored of thinking about it that it doesn't hurt quite as much.'

Jakob nodded. He seemed to have understood. 'Just make sure it doesn't take up all the bandwidth.'

Hildur smiled and nodded back. They started walking toward Tinna's house. And then Jakob spoke again: 'There's something you should know before we go inside.'

Hildur stopped in her tracks.

'While you were in Reykjavík, I came here for dinner pretty often on your usual day.'

'I think that's great. But why do you feel the need to tell me?' Hildur twirled her ankles one by one and bounced on her feet so the frigid air wouldn't cool her exercise-warmed body too much.

'Tinna will probably say something about it, and I don't want you to hear it from her first. I'm not saying you'd be jealous, but ... Yeah, I just wanted to tell you,' Jakob said, mumbling something else to himself that Hildur couldn't make out. Jakob's consideration was touching. They both seemed to know what it was like to not have anyone around. It's easy to get fearful you'll lose the little you do have.

'Thank you. I appreciate you being so thoughtful,' Hildur said, giving Jakob a friendly slug in the shoulder. 'I'm just happy you came by to keep her company. There's one thing I don't understand, though.'

Jakob whipped his head around and looked queryingly at Hildur.

'Why would anyone want to wear a down vest? It's a coat without sleeves. It's such a weird in-between form for people who can't decide whether to put on a T-shirt or a parka.'

Jakob laughed all the way to the door.

As always, Tinna was standing in the entryway to greet them. The long red apron she'd slipped over her comfy clothes was knotted in a meticulous side-bow. Tinna spread her arms, snatched Hildur in an embrace, and squeezed hard.

'It's so lovely to have you home again,' Tinna said with a sigh. After hugging Hildur, she took her niece's face in her hands and gave her two kisses on the left cheek. 'You feel as thin as you did when you left. Didn't you have any time to eat in Reykjavík?' she fussed, touching Hildur's hair and back.

Then Tinna hugged Jakob and squeezed his shoulders. 'And you, my favourite young man of the moment.'

'Now, is that a nice thing to say?' Hildur asked, hanging her coat on the rack.

Tinna just laughed at her own joke.

Hildur and Jakob followed Tinna into the kitchen and seated themselves. Hildur noticed a folded tabloid on the table. The back-page crossword had been half filled in.

'Have you had other visitors? This crossword . . .'

Hildur saw Tinna's cheeks flush. Her bustling took on a fresh briskness. Cupboard doors opened and closed as she pulled out serving dishes. 'Well, hmm. There's a fellow who comes by sometimes in the morning and sits with me. Ívar brings the newspaper and reads it to me out loud.'

Judging by the look on Tinna's face, the visitor was a welcome one. The crossword puzzle had been filled out carefully. The person solving it had begun at the top corner and advanced systematically. Hildur read through it, looking for mistakes, but couldn't find any. Every letter was neatly in its own square, and every word connected with others. She was on the verge of asking more questions but was interrupted when Tinna set out the boiled potatoes.

For Tinna, cooking and serving food was a matter of honour, so Hildur and Jakob let her carry the serving dishes to the table. Potatoes, rhubarb jam, gravy and green peas. Last of all, Tinna reached into the still-warm oven and pulled out a lamb roast with a nice brown crust.

'Jakob's favourite,' she announced. Tinna explained how she'd called Jakob one day after the Christmas vacation and invited him for dinner. They'd enjoyed each other's company, and evidently Jakob had a lot of funny stories about Finland.

Hildur jammed a fork into the roast and started cutting thick slices. The knife sank effortlessly into the pale brown flesh.

Tinna pushed the jam jar and the peas toward them. They were to help themselves to everything and have plenty of it. Tinna loved cooking, and Hildur loved eating. It was the perfect equilibrium.

Tinna dipped a bite of lamb in her rhubarb jam. 'So tell me: how did things go down south?'

Hildur told her aunt about the capital's tiny waves and constant traffic. Tinna nodded and said with a pensioner's certainty that life here in the fjords was as good as it was likely to get.

Aunt Tinna was probably right. Hildur was happy. She looked at Jakob, who was focused on cutting the slice of lamb on his plate. She looked at her aunt, who had always been on her side. This was her family. Biology wasn't necessarily a prerequisite for family ties; shared activities and a sense of belonging to the same tribe was much more important.

In this particular tribe, there was no point trying to get up from the table until you'd taken a second helping, if not a third. Accordingly, Hildur sliced more lamb and served each of them another round.

Tinna shifted in her seat and set down her utensils. Hildur noticed her aunt was straining to keep her voice casual, but the hint of tension in it revealed anxiety welling up from lack of certainty. 'Did you find out anything about Rósa and Björk?'

Hildur finished chewing her food, then repeated what she'd already told Jakob. More analyses had been conducted on the articles of clothing that had been found, but those analyses hadn't produced anything.

They sat in silence for a moment. The blare of the television carried from the living room. News about Covid-19 cases in northern Italy, stock markets plummeting around the world, a storm front approaching from the north. They concentrated on finishing their meal while semi-listening to the safe, steady voice of the news anchor.

When they were done eating, Hildur started clearing the table. Tinna swatted at her and told her to sit back down, then stood to get the pie dish from the sideboard. 'I've still got dessert.'

Hildur recognised the dessert from the smell. Her aunt had baked *hjónabandssæla*, 'wedded bliss', a rhubarb pie with a crumbly crust. She set it down on the table and held out the cake server to Jakob.

'Would you like the recipe? You could make it for that flight attendant when the right moment arises,' Tinna teased.

'Don't be surprised, Jakob,' Hildur said. 'Everyone knows you and Guðrún are an item. What my aunt was trying to ask is whether you two have started talking marriage yet.'

Jakob held the dainty serving utensil in his big paw, cut a slice of pie, then snorted and shook his head in feigned shock. But Hildur noted he didn't seem to mind the topic.

'You don't have to answer right away. I'll go whip the cream first,' Tinna said and started clattering around the kitchen cupboards looking for the handheld whisk.

A few minutes later, each of them had a slice of rhubarb pie and a white mountain of whipped cream on their plate.

Jakob seemed to have sunk into his thoughts and ate his pie intently. 'Listen, Tinna. Now that you mentioned rhubarb, it reminded me of something that's been bothering me.'

Tinna turned her face toward him. When conversing with Tinna, you could get the impression she was looking right at you. But it was just an impression. Since Tinna had lost her vision at a relatively advanced age, she could still train her eyes on yours out of habit.

'Do you remember when we were looking at those old photographs last autumn?' he asked.

At the time, Tinna had shared details about the past that had helped Hildur and Jakob track down a murderer. They'd been sitting at this very table, perusing pictures from Hildur's youth.

Jakob continued: 'Everything was moving so fast and so many things were happening at once that I forgot to ask about something that's been nagging at me in one the pictures. It's the one where the two of you are chopping rhubarb with some other women.'

Tinna nodded.

'Could I take another look at it?' Jakob asked.

He began pushing back his seat to rise from the table. Tinna stopped him with a gesture and stood herself. She walked into the living room and over to the television. Some old adventure film was starting on Channel One. Tinna turned down the volume and opened the top drawer of the television stand. The photo album embossed with the year 2000 was right there on top.

Tinna handed the album to Jakob, who started flipping through it, one page at a time. Hildur ran her finger through the last dab of whipped cream on her plate and licked it clean.

Jakob let out a satisfied hiss between his teeth. 'I'll be damned, here it is!'

Hildur turned to look at the picture. Four women were sitting on a bench that had been carried outside a summer cabin. Big, thick green leaves were stacked in a tidy pile next to the bench. Colourful plastic buckets overflowed with chopped rhubarb.

Hildur didn't immediately understand what Jakob had spotted.

'Look at the clothes,' he said.

Hildur looked at a her twenty-year-younger self. She was wearing a plaid shirt with the sleeves rolled up and dark, well-worn jeans.

'That pastel plaid shirt, you mean? Those were all the rage back then.'

'No, no, no. The sweater Tinna's wearing,' Jakob clarified, tapping at the album with his forefinger.

The white sweater looked hand-knitted. It had a striking pattern: thin black lines topped by irregular dots like stars. Jakob described the sweater to Tinna and asked her if she remembered it.

Hildur noticed her aunt's demeanour soften. A smile rose to Tinna's face as she nodded. 'It was my favourite sweater. Lightweight and warm. Eventually it wore through in too many places to patch. I threw it out a few years ago.' Tinna seemed to sink into her memories, then turned to Hildur: 'That sweater was really special to me. Your mother knitted it. She knitted one for all three of us sisters: for herself, for me, and for Hulda.'

Hildur sensed Jakob tense at her side.

'This is really crazy, but you know what? I've seen this sweater before.'

Hildur knew Jakob knew Icelandic sweaters like the back of his hand. She'd only seen a few books on Jakob's meagre bookshelf: military titles and guides to knitting Icelandic patterns.

'Jón's death last autumn...'

Hildur remembered the incident: how could she have forgotten the death of the disgusting paedophile? And then later finding items belonging to her little sisters buried on his former property.

Jakob coughed to clear his throat and drew a deep breath. 'Jón was wearing a sweater like this when he died.'

Hildur didn't respond, just kept staring ahead in silence. Her mind was piecing bits of information together. 'Are you absolutely sure?'

'Really damn sure. It was exactly the same pattern.'

The teaspoon clinked as it dropped from Tinna's hands to her dessert plate. 'What did you say?'

The softness had vanished from her face. Her voice sounded startled, and her lips had pinched into a firm line.

It was left to Hildur to state what seemed both utterly incomprehensible and yet the only possible explanation: 'My mother knew Jón.'

Chapter 21

The cold saltwater stung her hands. Hildur had intentionally left her neoprene gloves in Brenda's cargo space. She finally had a chance to go surfing after the extended hiatus. She wanted to feel the cold water on her skin.

The air smelled of salt. The surface of the water was moving. The pitch-black ravens wheeling over the sea croaked loudly at the dark figure on a green surfboard, paddling out to sea in a full bodysuit.

An intense exchange of information appeared to be underway among the birds. They were talking to each other. A strange clanking sound emerged from their throats. It was due to the nearby fish-processing plant. A hammering noise often carried from the facility as boats unloaded their cargo and forklifts hoisted big crates into the trucks waiting in the parking area. Ravens were masters at adapting to their environment. They knew where to find lidless rubbish bins and could mimic repetitive sounds from their environment.

The salt stung Hildur's knuckles where the thin skin had split. Lotion would have helped, but she hadn't found any in her medicine cabinet. Hildur was a three-product woman: deodorant, toothpaste, and face cream were all she needed for daily enhancement.

Even they hadn't been any help that morning. Hildur had woken to the same unsettling feeling she'd fallen asleep to after the evening at Aunt Tinna's. She'd wanted to look through more of Tinna's old pictures. Hildur had almost no photographs of her childhood or youth. The one photo she had of her little sisters she'd hung on the wall at her office. All the pictures from Hildur's childhood had been left at Kotsdalur, the farm Hildur had inherited upon her parents' deaths. She hadn't wanted to return after her parents died and didn't know if Tinna had ever gone there to retrieve anything. She hadn't wanted to ask. The wound had scabbed over, and she had no interest in picking at it anymore.

But yesterday she'd found herself interested enough in Tinna's photographs to pack up every album from the drawer. She and Jakob had walked home with heavy cotton totes slung over their shoulders.

Hildur had looked through the photos that same night. Pictures of Tinna's old singing students, nature shots of erupting geysers and waterfalls. Photographs of the Christmas table after it had been set but before anyone was sitting at it. Hildur had also seen pictures of herself that Tinna had saved all these years. In her confirmation portrait, Hildur's round face was framed by a bob. By her high school graduation picture, the roundness was gone. Her dyed black hair had been pulled back into a tight bun, her sleeveless dress revealed muscular arms, and the look in her eyes was severe and apathetic. But nothing was further from the truth. It wasn't apathy; it was fear. Hildur hadn't known what she wanted to be or where she wanted to go after high school. She'd never thought particularly positively about her future. She'd just had to shoot for a spot at some university and hope for the best. After straying into the humanities department for a couple of years, she'd ended up at the police academy. The academy's physical training and the thought of helping others had lured her to the profession.

But sinking into old memories had left her even more exhausted. She'd browsed through a few albums without spotting any other pictures of the sweater. Eventually she'd decided she'd pull out the photos again when she felt fresher.

The morning wave forecast had promised such good surfing conditions that Hildur had had to get out on her board. She'd left the house before six and driven an hour southward. The forecast had indicated the waves today would be best a couple of fjords from Ísafjordur.

The symmetrical waves rolling into the black sand beach were about a metre high and deliciously long. That was typical of a falling tide. As the tide rose, the sea was often more restless and the waves choppier.

The further Hildur glided from land, the greater the wind's resistance grew. Her arms were starting to tire, but she kept paddling, She wanted to go a decent way out and catch a wave she could ride for a long time. Or maybe the waves rode her. The ravens in the sky suddenly arced sharply to the left and started back toward shore.

Thoughts somersaulted through Hildur's mind, despite her attempts to focus on the sea, the wind, and the direction of the waves. Jakob's observation about the sweater Jón had been wearing had tormented Hildur to the point that before going to bed, she'd walked over to the station and logged in to the police database, LÖKE. She went through the notes she'd recorded about Jón the previous winter and the photographs taken of his body when it was found.

Jakob had remembered correctly. The sweater worn by the man buried in the snow was exactly like the one Rakel had given Tinna back in the day.

This felt incomprehensible to Hildur. What could Jón the paedophile and her mother have had in common? Hildur had paid Jón many visits in her role as a police officer, but he'd never given any indication of having known Rakel. When Icelanders first met, they always started by looking for any possible existing connections. Kinship, the same daycare, studying at the same university ... There was always something. If Jón had known her parents well, he would have no doubt spoken up.

Suddenly Hildur heard a strange, loud noise. It sounded like a rushing rapids or the crackle of an old analogue television after broadcasting ended. The thought reminded Hildur that when she was a child, there'd been nothing on television on Thursdays. It had been a broadcast-free day across the country.

Hildur immediately paid the price for allowing her thoughts to wander. She saw an extra-tall wave bearing down on her. Its size caught her off guard, and it looked as if it might break at any moment. She couldn't let herself get sucked into the wave. Hildur tensed her core to inject more power into her movements. She shifted her body and pressed down on her surfboard as hard as she could. She took a deep breath and aimed into the water.

The attempt came a second too late. She didn't make it under the wave; she ended up in its dark, wet mouth. It all happened very fast. The board spun over from the force of the wave, and Hildur fell on her back. The roiling mass of water crashed down on her. She tried with all her might to flip onto her belly so she could swim, but it was in vain. The sea tossed her around like a rag doll. Hildur coughed water from her lungs and felt her ankle leash tighten to the extreme, then suddenly go slack. She knew what would happen next. The rampaging mass of water had ripped board and surfer in different directions. Out of the corner of her eye, Hildur saw the green polyurethane board fill her field of vision.

She didn't have time to react. She tasted the sea in her mouth and felt a blow to her forehead. Then everything went dark.

Chapter 22

Westfjords, 1988

Six years before Rósa and Björk's disappearance

The door to the school taxi opened, and Hildur climbed aboard in her red sweater and white beanie. It was her first day of school. She waved at her mother from the van's side window.

Despite the important day, Rakel felt chagrined. She'd spotted a run in Hildur's sweater. She'd just sent her firstborn child off to school in a top with a hole in it. What would the teacher think? She ought to have done a better job going through Hildur's clothes the night before. She ought to have been more attentive. She also felt bad she hadn't been able to take Hildur to school. But she didn't have the car today, because Rúnar had to pick up some spare parts for the tractor and run a few other errands.

Hildur would be fine on her own, and it would be best for her to learn to take the school taxi right away anyway, as Rúnar had said the night before. *You're right*, Rakel had conceded. Hildur didn't need her mum to hold her hand all the time.

Rakel watched the taxi drive off. Two-year-old Rósa stood at her side, waving at her big sister with a broad smile on her face. The girl's hand whisked the air until the van disappeared from view.

Rakel had promised Rósa that after Hildur got off to school, they'd go for a short morning walk. They'd check the crowberry patches to see if the wild berries were ripe. Both of Rakel's younger girls had woken at six that morning. Six-month-old Björk continued to wake up every couple of hours at night. Around seven, Rakel and Björk got up to start their day, and Rósa usually clambered out of her little bed at the same time. Hildur would have slept till midday if Rakel didn't wake her.

Björk was asleep in the stroller, under a knitted wool blanket. A few tufts of hair stole out from under the wool beanie pulled down over her head. Her tiny mouth had turned up in a satisfied smile. She slumbered as the stroller rocked slowly along the sandy road.

Rakel hadn't slept well. She'd woken up to a headache in the middle of the night, and the pain hadn't relented. Maybe a quiet walk in the fresh air would help.

The worst thing about the headache was it gave unpleasant thoughts too much room and the pain painted everything in sombre tones. One thing that had been troubling Rakel still wouldn't leave her in peace. During their last appointment with the nurse, the nurse had said Björk's eyes had a secretive look to them. The words had been spinning through Rakel's head for days. Had the nurse meant there was something wrong with Björk's eyes? Was there something in the baby's head that didn't belong there? After days of studying her youngest's eyes non-stop, Rakel had finally reached for the phone and called the nurse.

At first the nurse hadn't said anything. Rakel had clenched the receiver in her hand and asked again, in a slightly louder voice, if there was something wrong with her child's head. The nurse had assured her the child was perfectly fine. She had simply meant Björk had alert eyes and observed her surroundings closely. The nurse had urged Rakel to not stress herself and get some rest while the younger children were napping. Then the mild-voiced nurse had suggested Rakel stop by for a chat the next time she came into town. Rakel had thanked her for her time and ended the call. She didn't need anyone else watching over her.

Rakel lowered a hand to Björk's warm face and lightly pressed the baby's eyelids with her forefinger and thumb. They felt normal. She felt the slippery spheres beneath the thin skin. She brought her hands to her own eyes. They felt exactly the same, but that didn't mean anything. Björk was six months old. There was no way Rakel could know what sort of person the child would grow up to be. She would just have to keep monitoring her daughter's development.

Rósa tugged at the hem of Rakel's coat and looked questioningly at her. Rakel turned away; she couldn't look anyone in the eye just now.

'Mum?'

Rakel mumbled a response and pushed the stroller into motion again. She walked slowly so as not to tire herself. She and Rósa kept stopping to marvel at the ladybugs climbing the tall stalks of grass.

Suddenly Rósa spotted something on the side of the road that caught her attention. 'Mummy, Mummy, put it on my coat,' she cried, pointing a fat forefinger at some plants.

Rakel stepped on the stroller's brake and checked what Rósa had found.

Delicate purple flowers grew at the side of the road. Rósa had remembered! The name of the plant was *gleym-mér-ei*, forget-me-not. It got its name from the way its hairy stalk clung to clothing and hair. That past summer, Rakel had shown her girls how to attach the flowers to their coat lapels to make them pretty.

Rakel broke off a bloom and pressed it to the front of Rósa's sweater. Rósa eyed the flower in satisfaction.

They continued a few hundred metres to the crowberry patch, but the berries hadn't ripened yet. Their taut skins didn't give when Rakel and Rósa pressed them.

Rakel shook an unpleasant thought from her mind and turned the stroller around. 'We'll check again next week.'

They walked home. The gravel crunched under the stroller's tyres. The morning sun was shining, turning the mountains golden-brown. Rakel stopped to zip up her sweater. It was only eight, so it was no wonder the air still felt cool.

When they got back to the house, Rúnar was loading the car. He looked at Rakel and stopped what he was doing. 'Where were you?' he asked, shutting the boot.

'I walked Hildur to the taxi.' Rakel approached Rúnar and stopped a couple of feet away. She smelled coffee and cigarettes.

'I thought the taxi left a while ago.'

Rakel gripped the stroller handle and tried not to think about the eyes of the child lying within it. There was no way Rúnar could be allowed to catch wind of her suspicions. Rakel told Rósa to go inside and promised to be right in.

'We went for a little walk. We went to see if the crowberries were ripe yet.'

'Did you drop by the neighbours'? Hallgrímur is home alone this week, since Helga is in the hospital.'

Rakel focused on breathing deeply. She clenched the stroller handle twice as hard to make sure the tremble in her hands wasn't visible. She didn't want to show her fear. She didn't want her husband to look in the stroller.

'That would have taken longer than fifteen minutes.'

If only Rúnar didn't bend over the stroller and see the beanie framing the bulging eyes of the child lying there.

'You seem off somehow. What's wrong with you?' Rúnar asked, thrusting his head closer to his wife.

A big cloud slid in front of the sun, drawing a shadow across the valley. The temperature instantly dropped. Rakel's body stiffened in suspense. A single wish kept spinning through her head. *Please don't look in the stroller. Please don't look . . .*

Rúnar's dark eyes stared insistently at Rakel. His nostrils quivered as he tilted his head in front of his wife and evaluated her like a cat eyeing a mouse anticipating its death-bite.

Suddenly Rakel had to use the bathroom. She looked at her husband and settled for a wary nod.

'For God's sake, try and pull yourself together,' Rúnar said as he climbed in the car and drove off.

Chapter 23

Ísafjörður, February 2020

Hildur came to. She was icy cold. Her teeth were chattering; she tasted iron. She tried to spit to see if it was blood but couldn't pull herself up or open her eyes. Her right hand tingled like hell. It was pinned between her ribs and the wet, rocky ground. Her legs swayed slowly in the shallows, in time to the frigid waves. She heard a faint burble and hiss as the water sank into the gravel-dotted sand.

After a few attempts, Hildur managed to roll onto her back. She had no idea how long she'd been lying there. Her eyes were killing her. She forced them open and felt the sting of salt water. The sky was pale grey. It was lighter than it would have been in the early morning hours. Was the sun still rising or was it setting? Two ravens flew across her field of vision. They were flying out to sea. To where she'd just come from.

Supporting herself on her left arm, Hildur managed to haul herself to a sitting position. Her surfboard was still attached to her ankle. It bobbed in the shallows; the waves had stilled.

Hildur made out a yellow disc through the silver veil of clouds. The sun was in the east, so it still had to be morning. Her gut spasmed, and vomit gushed from her mouth. Seawater. Hildur spat until her mouth was empty. The red clumps of blood that came up last dribbled to the wet, black rocks and vanished inside the earth, carried off by the seawater. She gently probed her teeth with her tongue and uttered a silent thanks at each one.

She still had all of them. Dentists charged a fortune for implants. At least half a million krónur per tooth. Hildur started to laugh. Why on earth had that just occurred to her? Her laughter turned into a hacking cough, and she retched again.

Her limbs moved. Sensation was restored to her right arm. She felt a powerful, pounding ache at the left of her forehead. Hildur raised her hand and touched it. A big lump had formed there. It felt like the skin was split.

She pressed both icy white palms to her face and started to shake. She staggered to her feet, freed the surfboard from her ankle, and started climbing the path to the road. There had been something about the sea today she hadn't completely understood.

Hildur started up Brenda and turned the heat on full blast. Only afterward did she strap her board to the roof, rip off her neoprene suit with her frozen fingers, and slip into the dry clothes she had in the back. She saw her bloodied face in the side mirror. The sight didn't faze her; she was pretty sure the cut was a small one. Head wounds just bled a lot.

Hildur spat on the sleeve of her black fleece and used the damp fabric to wipe away the blood. She'd been right; it was a small cut, but the bruise would be big. She reached up and pulled her hair over the left side of her face; it would hide the cut and the lump that was gradually turning blue. No one would notice anything if she didn't want them to.

Hildur sat on her hands in the driver's seat, trying to get her fingers to work. Shivers racked her body. Brenda's windows fogged up, but Hildur didn't care. The scenery had been ugly, weighed down by heavy grey tones.

She was scared. For the first time, the sea had done her harm.

Chapter 24

'Two with the works,' Hildur said, placing her order at the grill next to the police station. She set the cans of orange soda she'd taken from the fridge on the counter. She and Jakob had decided to grab hot dogs before heading out to see Björn.

Jakob amended the order: 'No tartar sauce for me.'

Hildur grunted. 'Are you on a diet?'

'I just don't like mayonnaise,' Jakob said, exchanging one of the sodas for the light version.

Hildur shrugged and paid. She was a good hour late because of the surfing incident earlier that morning, but Jakob didn't seem upset. On the drive home, she'd pondered her mother and Jón. The more she thought about them, the more she felt the sea swelling inside her. There was something about this whole thing that frightened her. Deep down she knew the only way to conquer fear was to face it head-on. Even though confronting old memories felt uncomfortable, she had to have the courage to look backward. She had to keep digging into her mother's life, to unearth it.

There had to be some connection between Jón and her mother. Everyone had secrets. For some they were trivial. Blank rows on tax returns. Excuses to put off seeing an unpleasant relative. Feelings that couldn't be stated out loud. A long marriage that had never known love.

Hildur grasped she would never fully understand her younger sisters' fate if she didn't have the guts to move toward what she didn't yet know.

She accepted the hot dogs and thrust family matters from her mind. She and Jakob had a long, demanding working day ahead. Beta had been unusually uptight that morning. She'd snapped about the lack of progress in the case and complained about journalists calling her non-stop. Of course, Hildur understood Hermann's murder needed to be solved as fast as possible, but panicking and pointless fretting weren't going to do any good.

Hildur unlocked the car with a click, climbed in on the driver's side, and popped out the cupholder. 'Did you know driving teachers here in Iceland take their students to the grill, order hot dogs, then get back in the car and keep driving?'

Jakob had just crammed two big bites of hot dog in his mouth, so he just shook his head.

'It's better to learn driving one-handed under a watchful eye,' Hildur explained and started the engine.

The smell of the hot dogs filled the car. The maritime weather report was coming from the radio. Fog warning in the eastern seas. No wind from this afternoon until tomorrow morning. Hildur steered into the roundabout and out the other side.

Björn had driven back early this morning from Hólmavík and gone straight to his office. He had a one-man consultancy that calculated structural loads for the construction industry and provided assistance with legal matters relating to construction regulations.

Hildur pulled up in front of a solid white house with big windows.

Jakob eyed the place: 'Looks like the construction industry is going strong.'

'The office is in the back,' Hildur said, then started off down the flagstone path running along the side of the house. A former playhouse that now looked like a shed stood at the rear of the rectangular backyard. Its patio served as storage for folded garden furniture. The structure housing Björn's office was located on the long side of the yard.

Hildur knocked on the wooden door and pushed it open. The harsh weather in Iceland meant that, as a rule, exterior doors opened inward. But luckily it was spring, so the winter snows near buildings had, by and large, melted away.

A stout, dark-haired man was standing at an adjustable desk, observing his visitors over his large computer screen.

'Detective Hildur Rúnarsdóttir. This is my colleague, Jakob Johanson, a police intern from Finland.'

'I see, all the way from abroad,' Björn said, then switched from Icelandic to fluent English, which he spoke with a strong American accent. 'Well, what can I do for you?'

Hildur and Jakob stood in the middle of the room. She looked around. The desk was generously sized and contemporary; the office chair looked comfortable. The stone floor was accentuated with two round red rugs. A large, expensive lighting fixture hung from the ceiling. (Or maybe it was from IKEA, who could tell?) A golf bag filled with clubs leaned against a bookcase in the furthest corner.

'I'm usually here alone, so unfortunately I don't have anywhere we can all sit,' Björn said, stepping out from behind his desk. He was wearing neat black trousers and a flax-coloured dress shirt.

'No problem; we're happy to stand. We only have a few questions. We're investigating the death of Hermann Hermannsson. I assume you've heard about it?'

Björn gave a curt nod and ran a hand over his head of healthy-looking, well-groomed hair that was barely tinged with grey. *I wonder if he dyes it?* Hildur found herself musing. She shook the pointless thought from her mind and returned her focus to the moment at hand.

The walls were hung with hunting photographs. One of a broadly smiling Björn standing next to a reindeer carcass with a few other men caught Hildur's attention. 'So you hunt?'

Björn nodded again.

'What sort of gun do you use?' Hildur asked, even though she already knew which firearms Björn had permits for.

If Björn was thrown by the question, he did a masterful job of concealing it. 'I have two Sako rifles. They're the best.' He turned to Jakob: 'I bet you know that.'

Jakob didn't comment; he just let Hildur continue.

'Where were you on Friday night?'

Björn took off his glasses and set them on the desk. He rubbed his face. 'At home, as best as I can recall.'

He was answering Hildur's questions without being particularly forthcoming.

'According to your wife you'd said you were going to the cinema.' Hildur left it at that. She wanted to see how Björn would react.

He lowered a hand to the desk at his side and drummed his fingers against its hard surface. The vibrations prompted a paperclip to jump threateningly toward the edge. 'Yes, I guess that's what I told her.'

Björn's way of generating words without saying anything was getting on Hildur's nerves. She adopted a sterner tone. 'What film did you see?'

The paperclip fell to the stone floor, making an exaggerated noise. Björn bent down to pick it up and dropped it in a plastic organiser. He reached for a box of pastilles on the desk and didn't say anything, just popped one in his mouth and sucked it in concentration while staring at Hildur and Jakob.

'Listen. If you'd bothered checking, you'd know there haven't been Friday evening screenings at the Ísafjörður cinema for a long time. Your wife Linda was at her sewing club that night and your son Orri spent the night at a friend's. Linda said the house was empty when she left and empty when she came home. So where were you from Friday evening to early morning Saturday?'

Björn's shell began to crack. A faint flush rose to his neck, contrasting distinctly with the pale dress shirt. 'I had personal matters to attend to, and that's all I'm saying.'

And that's all I'm saying. What kind of answer was that? Hildur glanced at Jakob and read the same question on her colleague's face.

'When I ask a question, you need to answer it,' Hildur said sharply. 'We can go down to the station, if you'd prefer to continue this conversation there.'

Björn stared at them in silence. Eventually he said: 'I don't have anything else to say.'

Hildur drew a breath. Her patience was running thin. She assumed a wider stance and raised her voice. 'According to our information, your wife and Hermann were closely acquainted. I'm sure that wasn't pleasant, seeing as you were rivals politically too.'

Björn's throat turned crimson. Beads of sweat had formed above his lush eyebrows. But his voice remained steady. 'That's not news. Everyone in town was acquainted with that shithead.'

Hildur had had it with the engineer's contrary attitude. 'Listen. I know the relationship between Linda and Hermann wasn't just chit-chat across party lines; it was of a more physical nature. Do you want me to give you the details, or are you going to answer?'

This was too much for Björn. Without warning he took two swift steps toward Hildur and raised his right hand to strike a blow. 'You bloody bitch,' he grunted as his fist swung.

The punch took Hildur by surprise, but she managed to pull her head back in time. She adjusted her stance and attacked. Björn was off balance from his failed punch. Hildur grabbed his right arm and twisted it behind his back. Her sore forehead struck his shoulder, sending a sharp pain shooting through her head. Enraged, Hildur tightened her grip. She and Björn spun around a couple of times before Jakob kicked Björn's feet out from under him, knocking him to the soft rug.

Björn lay there face down. Hildur sat on him and pressed both his hands into his lower back. Jakob sat lightly on Björn's legs and pulled his handcuffs from his belt. Hildur silently thanked her colleague. She'd left all her gear at the station. *Stupid mistake*, she thought to herself. The morning's accident had thrown her off her game, and it had never occurred to her the interview could turn into a wrestling match.

Hildur clicked the handcuffs around Björn's wrists and helped him to his feet. 'OK, let's go down to the station to continue this conversation.'

She told Björn he was suspected of the murder of Hermann Hermannsson. She recited the legally mandated caution and led him out to the car.

Jakob sat next to Björn in the back and made sure both their seatbelts were fastened. Hildur buckled hers and started up the car. She glanced one last time in the rearview mirror to make sure they were ready to pull out. Jakob seemed to have things under control. Björn was staring her dead in the eye through the mirror. His gaze was penetrating but wary. He didn't look like he'd be giving in easily.

Well, I won't be either, Hildur thought to herself, taking a big swig of the orange soda she'd left in the cupholder.

Chapter 25

Beta ended the call and lowered her phone to the conference room table. She squinted, quickly eyed the notes she'd taken, then glanced at her colleagues. Jakob was focused on his knitting, running two different colours of yarn through his fingers. Hildur's semi-wet hair dripped to the table as she slurped her coffee. Beta knew Hildur didn't use a hair dryer; she said they made her scalp feel funny. Beta hadn't understood Hildur's sensitivity, but then again, she didn't have to. Everyone had their quirks.

'Come on, tell us what's going on,' Hildur said, drying the table with the elbow of her fleece.

Beta had two pieces of news: good and bad. The bad first. Beta sighed in disappointment. Axlar-Hákon had called from Reykjavík to confirm what they'd already deduced: Hermann had died of a gunshot wound. The entry wound was near his heart, the exit wound in his back. The bullet had pierced the heart; death had been more or less immediate. Hermann had died between 9 p.m. and midnight. The shot had been fired from a distance. The canines that had continued searching the vicinity after the forensic investigators left had retrieved the bullet that had pierced the body.

'The empty casing found on the floor of the shed is a match for the bullet.' Beta held a pause and glanced at her notebook. 'The good news involves the firearm too. We know more about it now. Axlar-Hákon said Hermann was shot with a .308 caliber Sako.'

Jakob stopped knitting and set his needles on the table. 'Björn has one.'

Beta nodded. Sakos were popular hunting rifles. 'My cousin who lives in the Eastfjords travels around Europe hunting big game. He sings the praises of Finnish moose-hunting rifles.'

She continued reading her notes. The shell was a 10.5-gram Sako Blade with an all-copper bullet. Nothing odd there, either: all-copper bullets had grown in popularity with hunters thanks to their unique characteristics.

Beta continued reporting what Axlar-Hákon had told her: 'The entry and exit wounds are exceptionally clean.'

Copper bullets didn't shatter like traditional semi-jacketed lead bullets when they struck bone. Less meat was lost. Plus, the bullets didn't release toxic traces the way lead did. Hunters were left with more game to eat.

'The choice of bullet is interesting,' Jakob pondered. 'Why waste money on expensive copper bullets? A lead bullet would have killed Hermann just as easily.'

'Maybe the perp is some sort of firearm nerd?' Hildur rose from her chair to get more coffee from the kitchen. 'We'll review all firearm sales and see if any light-bulbs come on. Anyone want a refill?'

Beta nodded gratefully.

Ammunition and firearms couldn't be bought through official channels without a valid permit. Before selling, dealers had to check the buyer's personal information and permits. But legal sales didn't cover all transactions: gun collectors could bring firearms to Iceland with a collectors' permit, and the police knew some of those firearms had slipped beyond the law's reach. A collector could have over a hundred firearms, from air rifles to automatic weapons. And some collectors modified firearms then sold them on the black market, making their origins impossible to trace.

The trade in black-market firearms drove Beta crazy. Their number was constantly growing. For years now, the police had been informing lawmakers about the problems with legislation pertaining to firearm collectors, but the laws never changed. The situation was intolerable. Even so, Beta asked Jakob to get in touch with all legal firearm dealers. Maybe they'd learn something that way.

Beta's mouth spread in a big yawn. She was tired. She'd got no more than four hours' sleep the night before. Coffee wouldn't do her any good, but she still decided to have another cup. Her younger boy had woken up in the middle of the night with a stomach-ache. Beta had served as bucket emptier and tried in vain to coax her older son back to sleep. Óliver's business trip to the capital had been extended by a night again. Beta had asked a neighbour to look after the boys until he returned from Reykjavík on the morning flight. She had to come in to work; the murder investigation demanded it.

Hildur returned to the conference room with two mugs filled to the brim. Beta gratefully accepted her refill.

'The post-mortem turn up anything else interesting?'

'No sign of alcohol or drugs. The stomach contents suggested Hermann's final meal consisted of fish and potatoes. Axlar-Hákon checked the menu at the town hall canteen: they served fish hash for lunch on Friday.'

A silence fell over the room. Beta took the scrunchie from her wrist and gathered her cloud of curls into a bun at the back of her head. 'The two of you could talk to Björn next. Maybe he had some time to cool down overnight.'

Hildur nodded. She'd conveyed the substance of the conversation she'd had with Björn's wife Linda to Beta and Jakob. Now she opened the folder sitting in front of her and spread the photos across the table, since Beta hadn't seen them yet.

'Hermann wanted to use these photographs to get something.'

Beta leaned in for a closer look, and a low whistle escaped her lips. She was surprised. She'd always thought of Linda as quiet and shy. A drab, well-meaning mouse who'd been crushed under her daily obligations. Beta felt a nasty pang inside and shut her eyes: that was exactly what had happened to her. That was why her husband preferred to go on business trips rather than stay home with her. Beta tried to dispel the intrusive thoughts. It was time to focus on the murder investigation, not her personal problems.

Beta took a second look at the photos. She couldn't get over the contrast between the demure, vaguely bland Linda and the glowing woman brazenly posing with her legs spread. She shook her head in amusement. 'It's pretty clear he got something. But why blackmail Björn? Wouldn't normal lobbying have worked, or promising to repay a favour with a favour?'

'I suppose it's our job to figure that out,' Hildur said, trying to attract Jakob's attention with her gaze.

It proved pointless. He'd turned to his smartphone and was staring intently at the screen. 'Wait a second. Let me just finish this article.'

Beta felt her alertness return as her headache-inducing exhaustion relented a little.

After finishing the article, Jakob turned toward his co-workers, an enthusiastic smirk on his face. 'I've followed news about firearms since I was a little boy.' He glanced at Beta: 'When you mentioned the lead-free Sako Blade cartridge, I remembered something. I just checked to confirm, and I remembered right.'

Jakob shoved his knitting out of the way and used his forefinger to draw a small circle on the table. 'I subscribe to the Sako newsletter, and one of their promotional emails earlier this year mentioned this new copper bullet. It's incredibly interesting that whoever shot Hermann used this specific cartridge.' He paused and glanced at his phone, as if to double check that he'd read correctly. 'The Sako Blade all-copper cartridge won't be on the market for another couple of weeks. It's not available from a single authorised gun dealer. The shooter must have unusually good connections to the gun manufacturer.'

Hildur looked thoughtful: 'A rare bullet, huh? That's weird. That means that for some reason the perp isn't bothering to cover their tracks.'

Chapter 26

'Did you get any sleep?' Hildur asked, offering coffee to the man across from her.

Björn was sitting on the bench in the cell: face pale, shoulders slumped, hair dishevelled. His gaze apathetically wandered the walls. His aloof demeanour radiated discomfort. Björn probably would have rather been anywhere else than here with them. Hildur offered the cup a second time.

'Not much,' he finally conceded and accepted the cup. Because the previous attempt at conversation with Björn had turned into a brawl, Hildur had decided to handle the interrogation in the basement cell at the station. She and Jakob had on their duty belts complete with batons and pepper spray. As she watched the trembling Björn, Hildur realised the gear was overkill. He wasn't likely to resist anymore; there wasn't a trace of yesterday's defiance left. The night in jail must have been rough on the first timer.

Hildur sat on a chair she'd brought into the cell and completed the required forms and formalities on her laptop. Jakob stood behind her, guarding the door.

'Murder. Violently resisting the authorities. It's a short list but all the more serious. What do you have to say about these suspected crimes?' Hildur asked, looking sternly at Björn. She decided she wouldn't speak again until he opened his mouth. She could sit here all day if necessary. The seconds passed. She continued to stare at Björn expectantly. A door closed somewhere in the building, followed by the sound of shuffling footsteps. Björn gazed at the coffee cup in his hand and breathed heavily. Hildur reached into the bag hanging over the back of her chair and pulled out a ripe banana. Her clipped thumbnail sank effortlessly into the neck of the fruit, splitting the peel. She skinned the banana with a deliberate slowness, eyes fixed on Björn the whole time.

Björn raised his head a little, and Hildur looked into his bloodshot eyes. 'I'm sorry about yesterday,' he said. 'I guess your questions pushed me over the edge.'

Hildur shrugged and kept staring. She and Jakob had agreed she'd handle the talking and Jakob would hang back and observe. Although he still spoke only a few words of Icelandic, he'd begun to understand more over the past couple of months.

'An apology isn't going to get you out of striking a police officer, and murder – well, that's a much more serious charge.'

Björn looked at Hildur, and she saw signs of fear had appeared on his serious face. His raised eyebrows had frozen in place, and his jaw hung, leaving his mouth half-open.

'Why did you kill Hermann?' Hildur demanded. 'What did he do to you?'

Björn's thick eyebrows rose even higher as he practically shouted: 'I didn't kill him. I swear it!' When he realised he'd raised his voice too much, he shut his mouth. He rubbed his hairline as he searched for the words: 'I thought Hermann was a total prick; I have no trouble admitting that. Shamelessly tried to further his own advantage.'

At first Björn spoke slowly and cautiously, but he gradually warmed up and spoke faster. Zoning was critical to Hermann's business interests. If it looked like the council wasn't going to vote the way he wanted, so he'd do what he could to convince his opponents to alter their stance.

'One time he bragged that all it took was one phone call and some guys from Reykjavík would come up and present the concluding arguments. He never went that far with me. But I've heard stories.'

Björn finished his coffee in silence. He placed the empty cup on the floor next to his feet, took a deep breath, and sighed. Then he returned to the topic of Hermann. Hildur noted that Björn cheered up with every minute that passed. He was feeling better, thanks either to the coffee or his decision to discuss matters more openly.

'Do you remember the salmon farm expansion a few months back?' Björn asked.

Hildur nodded. The project had divided the town, but ultimately the council had voted in favour of granting the expansion a construction permit.

'One of the dogs belonging to a council member who'd asked critical questions, a fireman, was found dead in his backyard.' A vet had determined poisoning as the cause of death. In the next council meeting, Hermann had commented to the dog's owner that hopefully his other dog wouldn't also end up eating something that didn't agree with it.

'It was obvious what had happened but, of course, there was no way of proving anything. Hermann was a master at getting his way.'

Björn fell silent again. He crossed one leg over the other and leaned his head back against the wall.

'What was the source of friction between you and Hermann?' Hildur asked.

Björn sighed deeply again.

Hildur now wasn't sure what to make of the guy sitting across from her. He seemed sincere and spoke effusively when he wanted to, but she still got the sense he was hiding something.

Björn said: 'He wanted to push through the harbour expansion so more cruise ships could visit Ísafjörður. The project would also give the harbour valuable reclaimed land.'

Like everyone else in Ísafjörður, Hildur was aware of the problems caused by the cruise ships. Pleasure boats carrying thousands of passengers sailed from harbour to harbour around the world. In recent years, interest had grown in northern itineraries, not just tropical ones. Ísafjörður had started to get its share of cruise ship tourism as a result. The vessels would pull into dock, and up to three thousand people would swarm Ísafjörður's narrow lanes for a day. Camera-toting passengers peered through people's windows into their homes and took pictures of everything they saw. But the cruise ships also brought in revenue for the harbour and bus companies selling day trips.

'Was Hermann involved in the cruise-ship business too?' Hildur asked.

Björn explained that Hermann had plans to sell land and had bought a stake in a big tour bus company. Doubling cruise-ship capacity would mint profits for the bus company.

Björn was also sure Hermann had had a construction company lined up to take him on as a minority shareholder for the project. 'They would have developed the harbour area together and sold the buildings for a nice sum. That was Hermann's usual MO. Find a way to buy cheap and flip the investment at a healthy profit margin.'

'Do you know Hermann's business associates by name?'

Björn shook his head.

Hildur considered what she'd just heard. Might Hermann have betrayed a business partner, who then took revenge in the worst possible way? She would talk to representatives from

Iceland's biggest construction companies, although she figured it was pointless. Such agreements were usually verbal in nature, with no written record of them kept anywhere.

'I don't have anything against people making money, but in my view the harbour expansion was poorly planned. An infrastructure project from hell. It should have been designed better. An environmental impact assessment absolutely should have been conducted,' Björn said. He said he voted to postpone the project.

'Hermann tried to lure me over to his side, promising me projects where I could charge a high hourly rate. When I refused, he threatened to take my current clients. Who knows what he would have come up with next?'

Hildur saw her opening: 'Listen. Did you know he and your wife—'

She didn't even make it to the end of the sentence before Björn raised a hand to cut her off. He brought his feet to the floor side by side and placed his hands on his knees. He leaned toward Hildur and lowered his voice: 'I knew Linda and Hermann were seeing each other. I didn't like it, but it was easier for everyone, especially our son, for me to pretend I didn't know.'

Hildur was startled by Björn's frank answer. She looked up from her laptop and studied his face. He didn't look angry or sad. He didn't look like a man who'd been betrayed.

'You're saying it didn't bother you at all?'

Björn snorted. 'The only thing that bothered me was she chose Hermann. If it had been anyone else ...' Björn's gaze sharpened. He realised what he'd said. 'I wouldn't kill anyone over something like that, for God's sake.'

Hildur continued taking notes. 'Do you want to know how many homicides are motivated by jealousy? Quite a few.'

Björn started. He looked embarrassed, as if he'd got caught doing something wrong, and hung his head.

'Your wife was fooling around with your enemy. He's found murdered on a ski track, and you don't have an alibi for the night of the murder. You don't have to be a very smart detective to realise things aren't looking very good for you. Besides' – Hildur held a pause before landing the killing blow – 'I checked your gun permit. You own a rifle that's the same model as the one used to shoot Hermann. We'll be sending it to Reykjavík for more detailed analysis.'

Björn sat up straighter and squeezed his eyes shut. He appeared to be wrestling with whether or not to give in to the inevitable. Eventually he said: 'If there's anyone in our marriage who ought to have been jealous, it was Linda.'

The response caught Hildur off guard. She leaned in to indicate she was listening. Björn was finally getting down to business. His marriage started to take on new tones.

'We have a child together, but . . .'

Hildur waited. The last thing she wanted to do now was interrupt Björn. He raised his hands to his eyes and stroked his eyebrows with his forefingers. He seemed to be searching for the words.

'. . . we don't have a traditional marriage. We never have, really. I'm not the kind of man Linda thought I was at first.'

His voice had softened; the final sentences came out as barely more than a whisper.

Björn said he'd tried to maintain an ordinary marriage, but over the years it had proven impossible. He wasn't interested in women. Life would have no doubt been easier for him in the city, but he'd made his choice years before and set up his company here.

'I have to consider my reputation. I don't want any gossip . . .'

Hildur gazed at the man sitting in front of her. Was it possible that for some people, homosexuality was still something that couldn't be spoken of openly? She didn't follow the line of questioning any further, because it had nothing to do with the investigation. For the first time, Hildur saw Björn as sincere. A weight seemed to have dropped from his shoulders.

'So where were you around midnight on Friday?'

Björn lowered his chin to his chest again and fingered the hem of his shirt. 'Can you please handle this with a low profile? I'm begging you.'

'We have a job to do,' Hildur said curtly. But in the same breath, she softened her words and promised that, of course, the police had no interest in making things difficult.

'Fine. I was at Hrafnadalur with Bjarni. I drove home in the middle of the night and filled up at the service station at Patreksfjörður. If I remember right, there are CCTV cameras there, so you can confirm I'm telling the truth.'

Hildur took in this information. Bjarni was a well-known local sheep farmer. He'd had a herd of over three hundred sheep and twenty horses for decades. Hildur remembered his sheep farm from her childhood. Bjarni had lived alone his entire life. Seasonal workers had come to help when the lambs were born in the spring and when the sheep were brought down from the mountains for slaughtering in the autumn. Other than that, he'd managed the farm on his own.

Hildur tapped at her laptop, then announced the interrogation was over. 'We'll go and talk to Bjarni.'

She closed the laptop and stood to leave. Jakob slipped the chair she'd been using under his arm.

Björn looked pleadingly at them. 'Bjarni's an old man, and he's never told anyone. Please be gentle with him. He probably wouldn't be able to take it if there started to be whispers going around town.'

'Not to worry. I know how to handle this,' Hildur said.

Chapter 27

Reykjavík, February 2020

Dísa

The red line spread across the pale skin with scalpel-like precision. Two passes, and the strip of skin was saturated. The woman parted her full, symmetrical lips and used a lipstick brush to press the colour within her lip lines.

Dísa poured cleaning solution in the toilet bowl. As she waited for it to take effect, she emptied the rubbish and filled the paper towel dispensers next to the sink. She had to stretch across the woman to reach the dispenser at the far end. The woman turned up her nose and stepped to the side. Dísa thanked her, but the woman didn't reply. Dísa turned back to the toilet that needed scrubbing and heard the woman loudly smack her lips as she spoke into her phone. Her voice was soft and persuasive. She smiled as she spoke.

'Invest ten grand. I know it's a smart bet. Because . . . Because I've seen the documents! The government's going to grant the project a subsidy next Tuesday. And the second that happens, the parent company's share price is going to shoot up like a teenager's dick.'

Dísa looked at the gleaming toilet. She flushed and closed the cubicle door behind her, then moved on to the next cubicle. Through the open door, she had an unobstructed view of the woman standing at the mirror.

The woman gave herself the once over and leaned in to check her eye make-up. Suddenly her tone turned demanding.

'I can't move a pinky finger until next week. The Financial Supervisory Authority would grab it and rip it off. But those monkeys working for the state can't connect you to this. Besides, you have relatives who live there near the river. You can always say you have a soft spot for the place and wanted to invest in an area you know.' The woman chuckled and said the decision was a good one and the matter perfectly clear. 'Of course you and I never had this conversation,' she concluded in a syrupy voice, then slipped her smartphone in the side pocket of her black leather purse.

Dísa lowered her hands to the handle of her cleaning cart and pushed it out of the ladies' bathroom. Over her years on the job, she'd come to learn janitorial staff were invisible to most people. The work she and her colleagues did was only seen when it was left undone. Cleaners pushed their carts through corporate offices, airports and the corridors of banks, and people said things in their presence they would never say in the presence of outsiders. It was as if cleaners didn't exist.

Dísa picked up a few scraps of paper from the floor in front of the Departures check-in counter and tossed them in the cart. Then she walked over to the big windows to watch the flight to Akureyri take off. The plane turned north in a beautiful arc, shrank as it receded, and soon disappeared from view.

Just like her.

When you were invisible, there were all sorts of things you could do.

Chapter 28

Ísafjörður, February 2020

Hildur ended the call with a quick movement and slammed the phone onto her desk, peeved. She did it with so much force Beta heard the noise all the way in the other room.

'Is something wrong?'

Raindrops pattered against the station window. It had been a beautiful morning, but the weather was turning grey again.

'Not something, everything.'

Hildur heard the floor creak as Beta stood. A moment later, her boss stood in the doorway of the office Hildur shared with Jakob.

'Everything's delayed because some kid has an earache.'

Hildur had just had a brief exchange with Róbert from the Safety Investigation Authority, and he informed her an investigator had stayed home to look after a sick child. The investigation into the small aircraft that dropped into the sea was still in process. *Jæjja*, Hildur sighed, silently cursing how small her homeland was. One primary-school-aged child has an earache, and all activity at a workplace came to a standstill.

Beta frowned. 'But you have no reason to be investigating that accident.'

Hildur was perfectly aware of that, but her instincts were telling her things weren't quite how they seemed on the surface.

Beta raised her voice a little. 'We have our own murder investigation to worry about. We don't have the resources to be looking into other criminal cases that aren't even criminal cases. I want you and Jakob to go and talk to that sheep farmer now. I'm going to continue reviewing Hermann's call data.'

Hildur was irritated. Beta usually let Hildur do her work as she saw fit, but her boss was coming off as atypically strict today. Hildur had the impulse to ask Beta what had put her knickers in a twist but decided it would be wisest to keep her mouth shut.

As she pulled on her coat, Hildur heard the landline ring down the corridor. Beta turned on her heel and returned to her office.

Jakob grabbed the car keys and said he'd drive. He and Hildur were on their way out the door when Beta called out to them. She looked serious.

'That was the daycare centre. Little Kata just showed up and said she was there to pick up her child. One of the workers saw a knife in her hand.'

Hildur knew who Little Kata was. Well under 160 centimetres tall and over thirty years old, Kata had been a regular law-enforcement customer for years. Wherever Little Kata went, problems weren't far behind.

Hildur had got to know Little Kata during her Reykjavík years. More than once, she'd brought Little Kata from a bus stop where she'd passed out to the station to sober up. She'd arrested and questioned Little Kata multiple times. Once, Little Kata had threatened the cashier at the supermarket with a knife, and Hildur had been the one who'd convinced her to hand over the blade and give herself up.

Little Kata had been convicted of countless assaults and frauds. She had two children, both of whom had been taken into state custody. The boy, now a teenager, had moved from Reykjavík to his aunt's in eastern Iceland about ten years before. Hildur had kept in loose contact with the aunt to make sure the boy was doing all right. Luckily the aunt was a totally different creature to her sister. She was a responsible adult who'd been able to offer the boy a safe, stable home.

After her son settled in the Eastfjords, Little Kata had left Reykjavík behind, moved briefly to Ísafjörður, and been impregnated once more, this time by a foreign temp worker who'd disappeared not long after. Little Kata hadn't managed to get her life in order during the second pregnancy either. Her daughter had been taken into custody a little under two years after being born. Little Kata had kept promising to mend her ways and swore she'd stop using, but nothing had come of it. The last straw had been when Little Kata left the girl sleeping in a stroller on the balcony. The toddler had woken up, and when no one heard her crying, she'd climbed out of the stroller and over the edge of the balcony. Luckily the apartment was only on the second floor. The girl's physical injuries had been minor: a sprained ankle and a mild concussion. The mother had been found passed out on the living-room couch with the door latched. The incident had prompted the courts to award the state custody of the child.

After that, Little Kata had moved away from the Westfjords. As far as Hildur knew, she'd been in the Reykjavík area.

Beta said the police patrols were a half-hour drive away. 'You and I need to handle this, now. You two will have to delay your visit with the sheep farmer a little.'

There were two daycare centres in Ísafjörður. The oldest children from both formed a separate group of five-year-olds who attended daycare behind the music school, a few hundred metres from the police station. Beta and Hildur decided to walk; it would be a lot faster than driving.

As she strode over, Hildur called Sara, the director of the daycare centre, whom all the local children worshipped, and all the local parents loved. Now coming up to sixty, Sara had worked at the daycare since she was twenty. In that time, she had taught hundreds of children how to tie their shoes and eat spaghetti bolognese with their mouths closed. She was also deputy chair of the local skiing association.

Hildur introduced herself and asked for details about the current stand-off. She listened attentively, then offered Sara some words of encouragement.

'Stay inside until the situation is resolved,' Hildur said, ending the call. She turned to Beta. 'Little Kata's in the backyard. She's pounding on the windows and doors and shouting.'

'What about the knife?' Beta asked.

'Apparently a switchblade.'

'OK. The patrol is on its way to provide back-up as soon as it can.'

There was no piano music coming from the music school the way there usually was. Two serious-looking teachers stood at the window, staring in the direction of the arriving police officers. Hildur and Beta circled around to the fenced backyard.

They immediately saw Kata. Her big green army coat hung open, and her grey sweats were covered in brown stains. Her legs in their sweats had been jammed into a pair of winter boots. Her thin body was hunched, and her face was shrunken.

When she was within twenty or so metres, Hildur called out: 'What's going on here, Little Kata?'

Little Kata turned toward Hildur and Beta. Focusing her unsteady gaze appeared to take effort.

Even though Beta was the boss, Hildur was taking charge in this instance because she knew Little Kata better. She spoke calmly and asked Little Kata to put down the knife.

Little Kata just hissed and started kicking the back door of the daycare centre. 'Open the door! I'm here to pick up Sigga. My little Sigga's coming home with her mum now.'

Hildur signalled to Beta to hang back while she approached Little Kata from the left. Hildur tried to talk sense to the screaming, knife-brandishing woman.

'Sigga's fine at daycare. You're scaring her, causing all this commotion out here.'

'Don't give me that bullshit. She's scared to be with strangers. She's my child and belongs to me. I'm going in, I'm going in now . . .'

And with that, Little Kata punched her clenched fist through the window. There was a crash and a tinkle as shards of glass scattered. Hildur saw her opportunity: she wrapped Little Kata in a bear hug and clamped down on her wrist. The wrist was so skinny there was a nasty crunch as Hildur squeezed. Little Kata shrieked, and Hildur saw the hand that had punched through the window was bleeding.

Hildur forced Little Kata to the ground face first and straddled her. She supported herself with her thighs so as not to put her full weight on the frail woman. She clicked the cuffs around Little Kata's wrists after checking the injuries to her hand: they looked like minor surface cuts that wouldn't bleed for long. After receiving medical attention, Little Kata would be taken to a cell to await further processing.

Once Hildur had Little Kata under control, Beta walked into the daycare centre to calm the staff and report that the situation was over.

'What the hell was going through your head?' Hildur asked Little Kata, lowering her voice.

The other woman continued to jerk beneath her as she wailed: 'I'm sober. I really am. This time it's for good. I've changed. If Sigga just lived with me, everything would be better. We'd manage fine. She's my child.'

Hildur held Little Kata in place and looked around. Sure, people could change. But judging by the smell, that day hadn't come for Little Kata yet.

'I even got clothes and toys for her,' she stammered, breaking into sobs.

Hildur was annoyed by the disturbance Little Kata had caused, but she also pitied the sad, gaunt woman. She found herself stroking Little Kata's head. Hildur let her saltwater-coarsened hands slide back across the other woman's scalp a few times.

'You have to try a little harder,' Hildur said softly.

Little Kata stopped twitching and listened. Hildur wasn't sure if the other woman heard her say that the only way to spend time with Sigga was to completely give up drugs and alcohol and seek help. Little Kata was the only one who could help herself. 'Causing trouble like this is only going to take you further away. Don't come here again, OK?'

Little Kata had stopped moving. She lay face down on the cold ground outside the daycare centre, breathing shallowly.

Before long, a car could be heard approaching. Two uniformed patrol officers climbed out of the vehicle and strode toward them. Hildur helped Little Kata to her feet and turned her over to the officers' care.

'First aid, then the detention cell. I'll question her tomorrow once she's sobered up.'

When the three of them had gone, Hildur turned and strode toward the back door of the daycare centre. She stopped a few metres before she reached it. A little girl was standing there at the shattered window, staring straight at her. The look in her eyes wasn't fearful, but it was full of questions. And Hildur didn't have any answers. She just looked back and tried to give a little smile.

The child held her gaze on Hildur a moment longer. Then she turned and joined the other children, braid swinging.

Chapter 29

Barðaströnd, February 2020

Jakob opened the boot of his car and pulled out his tall boots. The farmyard looked mucky. The approaching spring wasn't exactly flourishing here. Most of the snow had melted, but there wasn't any green yet. The ground was soggy; the smell of manure filled the air. In the rush, Hildur had forgotten to bring a second pair of footwear, so she was left dodging puddles in her trainers.

During the drive they'd decided Jakob would do most of the talking and question Bjarni. Jakob wasn't a local or even Icelandic, and his status as an outsider might make him easier to open up to. Although Bjarni was coming up on seventy, he was known to speak superb English. Nearly all Icelanders did. American soldiers had come to the island during the Second World War to secure the island's defences. Since then, North American culture had had a huge impact. Rock and roll, nylons, and the English language came to Iceland early.

Jakob and Hildur had driven to Hrafnadalur in a civilian vehicle so as not to draw needless attention to themselves. Björn had said he'd used a rental car when visiting Bjarni, and it had been easy to verify. Hildur had reviewed the information from the rental agency during the drive and noticed Björn was a regular customer. The most recent rental had been from Thursday to Saturday of the previous week. The Ísafjörður police station leased several cars of the same make from the local car rental agency. Nothing remained hidden from neighbours in the sparsely inhabited, treeless region.

The main farmhouse stood near the shore. The exterior paint was peeling, and it looked like it needed a new roof. A modern garage with a carport had been built next to the house. The rest of the buildings stood at the edge of a pasture: the barn, the stable and a third structure that looked like a shed for farm equipment.

Jakob spotted movement near the stable. He stopped at the pen, and Hildur hung back a little. A long-maned horse came over to say hello and nuzzle Jakob's hand. Its forelock was so thick and long the creature's eyes were hard to see.

Bjarni had driven a big round hay bale into the pen on a forklift and was presently tackling it with a knife. He was wearing blue outdoor coveralls and looked strong and healthy as he pulled back the plastic casing. The only signs of ageing were the silvery white hair and lush but equally silvery beard. Without them, Bjarni could have been mistaken for a man in his early fifties.

The horses at the bale were growing restless; they were eager to eat.

'Hello, Bjarni,' Jakob said. 'You speak English, don't you?' He explained he was from the Ísafjörður Police Department and wanted to ask a couple of questions. He then introduced his colleague Hildur.

Bjarni waved Jakob into the pen. 'From the police, huh? Well, come and give me a hand. Scatter the hay over that way,' he said, bunching up the plastic into a tight clump. 'The fence isn't electrified. It's there just for looks,' Bjarni continued, as he scratched the neck of a brown-and-white horse.

Jakob reached for the hay. The horses followed the trail of hay he dispersed and began to eat. The mood settled. A moment later, the only sounds were the rustle of hay and the animals' munching.

Bjarni shoved the plastic rubbish into the forklift's cab, then turned toward Jakob. 'Yes, so what was it you said you needed?'

'We're investigating the murder of Hermann Hermannsson.'

The smile on Bjarni's face froze. His mild expression hardened when he heard Hermann's name.

'He's one I hope won't rest in peace,' he said. To seal this declaration, he took a moment to hawk up a huge clump of phlegm and spit it to the ground.

'I'm not from the area myself, but I've noticed as I've chatted with people that he wasn't very popular in these parts,' Jakob said.

'Would you two care for coffee? I have some fresh in the pot,' Bjarni said, gesturing toward the main building. Without waiting for an answer, he jumped into the forklift and drove it out of the pen. Jakob started off toward the main house, with Hildur following.

They let their host enter first. A fat cat was purring on a bench against the kitchen wall. Jakob bent over to scratch the animal's cheek, then sat next to it. The cat took note of the scratcher's presence and climbed into his lap. Jakob looked around. A big iPad and an agricultural newspaper lay on the counter. The walls were hung with an old-fashioned, orangey floral wallpaper that set off framed photos of European capitals.

'I don't travel much anymore these days. It's so hard to get farm sitters,' Bjarni remarked as he set out coffee cups, milk, and sugar for himself and his guests.

Jakob reached for a couple of sugar cubes and dropped them in his piping-hot beverage. Bjarni laughed and said no one around here really put sugar in their coffee anymore.

'Well, I'm from Finland,' Jakob said. He gave a brief summary of his reason for being in Iceland and how he'd ended up as an intern in Ísafjörður. 'So we've been investigating Hermann's murder, and we've apprehended someone we have cause to suspect is the perpetrator of the crime.'

Bjarni's ears pricked up. He slurped his coffee loudly, then interlaced his fingers under his chin.

'Now, this man claims he was here at the time of the murder, on Friday night. He feels the matter is a little delicate and was reluctant to tell us at first.'

A faint smile played on Bjarni's lips. Jakob couldn't tell whether it was because he'd been caught off guard or for some other reason. He hurried to continue: 'There's nothing delicate about the matter in our view, but we respected his wishes and drove here in an unmarked car.'

Bjarni burst out laughing. He laughed so hard that at first Jakob couldn't understand what he was saying: 'And now Björn is sitting in a cell?'

Hildur conceded that that was the precise state of things.

The old man was still jiggling with laughter. 'Björn is a wonderful man, but he clearly has trouble accepting himself. Sitting in jail now, suspected of murder, if the alternative is to tell . . . Oh goodness.' When his laughter finally died, he continued: 'Yes. Yes, Björn was here. He came right after work that afternoon. We looked after the animals, cooked a nice meal together, went and did some shooting practice, and just spent time together. He left late; I think it was close to 2 a.m.'

Jakob jotted down a few notes. The account corresponded to Björn's in every respect.

Bjarni ran his powerful fingers through his white hair. 'Oh, it's easy to understand why he keeps quiet, since he has a wife and child and a very nice career. I don't think he has the courage to make a bigger change . . .'

He gazed into his coffee cup and sighed deeply. Then he changed the subject. 'Who's working at the police station these days?'

He seemed eager to continue the conversation. *Maybe he's lonely*, Jakob reflected.

'Beta is chief of police. Hildur here is our detective,' Jakob said, nodding at her at the far end of the table.

'Hildur?' Bjarni gestured toward the kitchen window, which faced the sea. 'You're the one I see out there on a surfboard from time to time?'

He stood and walked over to the coffee pot, raised it with a questioning look. Jakob agreed to a second cup, then gazed out at the sea. The curtains framing the window had green pears on them. Basil grew on the windowsill. It was a beautiful, nicely maintained home, but quiet.

Bjarni told them he'd been born in this very place seventy years before. An only child, he'd stayed on to run the farm when his parents' time came to an end.

'For understandable reasons, I never had children. I'll be the last one to live here. When I'm too tired to keep going, I'll sell the horses and have the sheep slaughtered for meat.'

Then he looked at Hildur and abruptly changed the subject again. 'I've known you since you were a child, by the way.'

Hildur had been born a few years after Bjarni had taken over the farm. It was almost eighty kilometres from Bjarni's to Hildur's family farm. 'But everyone here in the fjords knows each other. We did back then, too, even though there were far more of us than there are now. Every second farm stands abandoned these days.'

The countryside was emptying, and it was hard finding people to take over farms.

'Your mother . . . Rakel. Peace be upon her soul, but she was a bit of an odd duck.'

Jakob noticed Hildur tense and her mouth pinch into a firm line. She had almost never mentioned her parents in his presence.

Bjarni sighed deeply and shook his head. 'I apologise; I don't mean to pry. But I remember often wondering what exactly was going on at your place.' He paused to take a loud sip of his coffee. 'I'm used to observing people. When you live outside the ring, you quickly learn to read situations. To understand what's happening inside the ring. But I couldn't make head nor tail of your family.'

Jakob saw Hildur shift in her seat, as if it was getting to be time to leave. The clock on the wall ticked ahead and started donging. It struck four times.

Jakob thanked Bjarni for the coffee and stood. Hildur had already made her way to the door and was putting on her shoes.

Bjarni didn't appear to react to their departure in any way. He just sat there staring out the window, seemingly lost in thought. Jakob called out one final goodbye from the kitchen door. Just as Jakob was turning away, Bjarni's chair creaked, and he spun around to face Jakob and Hildur. His eyes were wide, and his voice sounded strangely calm. Spectral, somehow.

'There was definitely something odd about your mother.'

Chapter 30

Ísafjörður, February 2020

Hildur hadn't been able to get Bjarni's words out of her mind. What did he mean, her mother had been odd? Her mother had been a totally ordinary woman who'd looked after her children, cooked, been patient. She'd been quiet, it was true, and calm, maybe even distant, but so were a lot of people.

In addition to Bjarni's words, Hildur was frustrated by Little Kata's hijinks at the daycare. It had gobbled up a lot of the working day. The poor woman had been a mess. Substance abuse and homelessness. Her mind was already broken, and it wouldn't be long before her body gave out too. Nights in the lock-up and prison stints weren't going to heal her. She needed to get into treatment, but that was easier said than done. There were a limited number of beds for detoxing, and the waiting lists for accessing mental health care were incredibly long.

Little Kata had taken Björn's place in the cell. He could clearly be seen in the service station's CCTV footage filling his rental car at 2.35 a.m., Saturday morning. Bjarni's story held true, at least in terms of timing.

They were back to square one, or almost. Jakob had begun looking into how Sako shells that weren't on the market could have made their way to Iceland and who might be in possession of them. Beta was chipping away at the call data.

Hildur decided to go outside and soothe her nerves. She needed time to think.

She exited the police station, passed the pizzeria and cinema, and walked down to the water. There was almost no one on the paved pedestrian-and-cycle path, which was no wonder: it was raining, and a north wind chilled the air.

A crippled raven was hopping on a rock at the shore. Hildur recognised the bird: Hook. She often saw him alone down there. One of the locals had adopted Hook and fed him every day of the year. He could no longer fly, but for years now he'd been bouncing around the rocks near the water.

Nearly a week had passed since Hermann's murder, and they still had no real theories as to the perpetrator's identity. Almost all the victim's acquaintances and people he'd met through work had spent Friday night in the company of friends. More dinner parties than usual had been hosted in town. Maybe people were preparing for the rumoured restrictions on public gatherings Covid-19 would bring. Folks were getting together while they still could.

Half of Ísafjörður had an alibi. Maybe the killer wasn't a local? That was possible, too, of course. Hildur had reviewed the accounts of the companies Hermann owned and identified their major subcontractors, customers, and partners by sifting through receipts and invoices. A round of calls had turned up a big fat zilch. None of them were working with any of Hermann's companies just now. Hildur hadn't come across any unpaid invoices, and no one seemed to owe anyone anything. She'd spoken on the phone with several CEOs and CFOs, and no one had had a bad word to say about Hermann. His violent death appeared to have come as a shock to everyone.

It didn't look like the recent past was going to provide any breakthroughs, so Hildur and her colleagues would have to dig deeper. If necessary, she'd go all the way back to the hospital where Hermann was born to shed light on the case, turning over every stone she came across. *Keep pushing*, she huffed to herself. Her team needed to do something that would generate results!

Hair dripping from the rain, Hildur walked through the pizzeria's sliding doors and up to the counter, where she asked the kid with glasses to pack up some slices from the rotating case.

'Chicken or salami?' he asked, disinfecting his hands before grabbing the tongs.

'I'll take them all.'

She had a long afternoon and evening ahead of her. She'd reach out to the county archives and order all documents related to local decision-making involving Hermann. She'd also search the newspaper archives and download any articles mentioning him, starting from his birth to the present day. She wouldn't sleep until she'd read each and every one.

Something always turns up if you just look hard enough, she thought to herself as she approached the station doors, pizza box hand. *Always.*

Hildur was still at work when darkness fell. After hours of sitting at her computer, she'd finally succumbed to the ache in her shoulders and taken a short break. She leaned with her palms against the wall, hips wide, her body angled slightly, and let her shoulder blades sink and depress. Desk work stiffened the neck and upper back, and wall push-ups helped. Hildur counted to twenty and shook out her hands. She repeated the reps three more times.

Ordinarily such circumstances would have stirred the impulse to go surfing, but somehow the idea didn't spark excitement or any positive feelings. Simply the thought of her surfboard made a lump form in the pit of her stomach. Her reaction caught her off guard: had she begun to fear the sea?

Hildur shut out all unpleasant thoughts and returned to her computer. She'd only made it through about half the material so far. She'd begun by reviewing the minutes of county council and building committee meetings and organising the documents into folders based on agenda items. Then she'd gone through articles published in the press and divided them into the same folders graded by topic.

Hildur continued with the files she hadn't worked through yet. Interesting – scarily interesting, actually – timelines had begun to form in front of her. Whenever a decision was made in the county, you'd find Hermann or his companies there at the heart of it.

There'd been discussion on the county council about the need for a new daycare centre. At Hermann's suggestion, the county had considered renovating an empty retail space. Retro-fitting an existing building would be less expensive than building a new one. Hildur understood the need for more space: birth rates had risen and more families with children had moved to the area.

A couple of months later, an article published in the local paper reported the sale of said piece of real estate to a company owned by Hermann. The company had bought the old building at a remarkably low price.

Half a year later, the council decided in favour of expanding the daycare centre. The site chosen for the expansion – Hildur knew the answer before she even got to the end of the meeting minutes – was the former retail space now owned by Hermann's company. The contract with the county brought Hermann a profit of about twenty million krónur. Hildur shook her head and continued reading.

She came across several timelines. It was no wonder Hermann topped the list of the county's highest-income residents from one year to the next. Her review of the archives revealed how the people around Hermann had changed over the years while he remained.

Hildur shook her head in disappointment. Why hadn't anyone intervened in Hermann's shenanigans? For years he'd shamelessly exploited information he'd been made privy to in positions of public trust to advance his personal business interests.

Not that Hildur was surprised. Hermann had behaved the way Icelanders do. Things had always worked this way here. The influential scratched each other's backs without any fear of repercussions. The wall between them and the hoi polloi was so high it made it hard to dismantle structures favouring those who wielded the most economic and political power.

Hildur stood and stretched, again. She walked to the window and looked out at the street-lamp-illuminated scene. The police station was in the middle of a little peninsula that thrust into the fjord. This side of the building gave onto a view of the harbour and the fish-processing plants. The fishing industry. When Hildur was little, all Icelanders who could stay afloat fished. Folks fished and sold their catches, earned money and supported their families. In an attempt to limit fishing in the 1980s, the state had established a quota system; preventing illegal fishing and ensuring healthy stocks of fish were worthy aims. Unfortunately the quota system had proved to be incredibly unfair. In Hildur's view, the way the system had been structured was the biggest scam in Iceland's economic history. Those who'd fished in previous years were granted quotas that would allow them to continue fishing into the future. The fishing quotas became valuable commodities – whoever happened to come into possession of them could sell them or lease onward. Fishing became a billion-krónur money making machine that spat out profits into the pockets of a few dozen families. Quotas from small towns and villages were sold to bigger harbours, where foreign workers from Cuba and Poland were brought in to clean and process cod at starvation wages.

When the fishing billionaires sought more profitable places to park their money, they bought the state-owned banks. Hildur remembered the banking crisis of ten years earlier all too well. Some young banker with gelled hair had recommended she take out a mortgage in euros. The interest rate had been notably lower than that of an ordinary loan. Hildur had taken the young slickster's advice without – like many other Icelanders – fully grasping the risks involved in a foreign-currency loan. When the Icelandic economy tanked, Hildur's debt had doubled overnight. She was still paying it off. Inheriting Freysi's duplex had eased her financial situation a little, but nevertheless she had a mortgage on both units.

Since the collapse, Hildur hadn't trusted anyone who worked for a bank.

Hermann represented the Icelandic mentality. One link in the web of corruption that permeated all of society. And since the country was full of Hermanns, his actions hadn't drawn much attention.

A pair of small sailboats were pulling out of the harbour, and a few cars were driving along the shoreline road. Hildur glanced at her watch. Almost seven. She took the last pizza slice, which had been cold for hours, and sat back down at her monitor.

There was something about the newspaper articles that had begun to nag at Hildur. She'd come to learn her attention was almost never drawn to something without cause. When a wrinkle formed in a smooth surface, it was an exception, and exceptions were interesting. If multiple wrinkles formed, they formed a rule.

Hildur browsed through the clippings again, noting that a man visible in many photos accompanying articles about Hermann or Hermann's companies was never identified in the text or captions. The stories had been written under different bylines and published in a range of media, from agricultural weeklies to local papers. The tall, slim man in a dark dress shirt appeared regularly in the pictures. He'd be doing something in the background or standing near Hermann in a group photo. When Hermann was photographed in front of a big fishing boat, the taller, sinewy fellow stood off to the side, at the harbour's edge. At the mayor's invitation-only affair, Hermann posed with friends, a glass of beer in hand. The mystery man almost invariably appeared in these group photos. At the Independence Day celebration, at a construction site, at a charity gala. Hildur carefully read the articles, captions, and pull quotes, but the man's name was never mentioned. He was like a servant who was on hand when needed but never referred to by name.

Then he abruptly vanished. The mystery man hadn't appeared in a single picture since 2016.

What had happened? Hildur did a reverse image search for similar photos online. At first she tried the photos of construction sites. No results of interest. But she scored with a photo from the mayor's invitation-only event. She instantly zeroed in on it. A guest had posted the photo on their public Facebook wall under the following status:

Ah, summer! Thank you for a fantastic party, Selma Gunnarsdóttir. Getting lubricated with Hermann Hermannsson, Ben Bjarnason, and Gunnar Emilsson.

The person who'd uploaded the picture was apparently a secretary who worked for the county. Hildur recognised Hermann, of course. Selma was the mayor, and Ben was a deputy PM from the Independence Party. That left the tall man with the name Gunnar Emilsson.

Hildur googled the name. The first result made it plain why the man had vanished from all photos in 2016. Physician and ultramarathon runner Gunnar Emilsson had been named COO of a Cyprus-based subsidiary of Iceland's largest fishing company in August 2016. In the photo accompanying the article, Gunnar was smiling in the Limassol sun, hands casually resting in the pockets of his white linen trousers. The top two buttons of his dress shirt were unbuttoned.

Hildur rubbed her forehead. Hmm. A doctor heading up a corporation. Evidently Gunnar knew the right people.

Suddenly Hildur felt a tiny kick in the vicinity of her heart. *No way*, Hildur silently cried as she studied the photo of Gunnar. The familiar prickling appeared in her fingertips. She got the sense she'd just understood something significant. *Emilsson, Emilsson, Emilsson. Emil's son.* Emil was a pretty common name, so there were probably hundreds if not thousands of Emilssons in Iceland. She reached for her phone and brought up Axlar-Hákon's number.

He picked up after the third ring. Hildur thanked her luck at getting hold of the pathologist so fast. 'I'm sorry for calling so late, after working hours.'

Axlar-Hákon chuckled good-naturedly. 'I'm at work. I'm here playing with biopsies.'

The pathologist's day consisted not only of conducting post-mortems but analysing suspect tissue samples as well. He looked at biopsies taken from patients with tumours to identify the tumour type and any possible cancers.

'Listen, the pilot of that plane that crashed. As I understand, his name hasn't been made public yet. But last time you and I spoke, I think you mentioned it. It was Emil's son, wasn't it?'

The only response was the sound of steady breathing and footsteps. Then Axlar-Hákon said he was turning on his computer. 'Yup. It was Emilsson. Why do you ask?'

Hildur felt a tingle in her guts. She knew she was approaching something important. 'I'll tell you as soon as I can. What was his first name?'

Yet again, silence at the other end. Hildur heard a faint tapping in the background. Apparently Axlar-Hákon was typing something into the computer.

'Gullaugur. Gullaugur Emilsson.'

Dammit. I guess I was wrong, Hildur thought to herself. She felt her shoulders slump in disappointment. The shared patronym had been a coincidence. What had she been thinking?

She glanced at the blue folders on her desk. Maybe something else would turn up in the material, something that hadn't caught her attention yet. She still had a few dozen newspaper clippings to read. The work would last well into the night.

Hildur was on the verge of hanging up when Axlar-Hákon spoke again. 'Yes, so he had two first names. His whole name was Gullaugur Gunnar Emilsson.'

Hildur pulled herself up to her full height, and her grip on the phone tightened. Hallelujah! She felt like jumping for joy.

She'd been right: a link existed between the two deaths that had taken place in such rapid succession.

Chapter 31

Jakob heard the front doors of the station building thunk shut behind him as he stepped out into the gradually dimming evening. Hildur had stayed behind to go through old meeting minutes. Jakob had tried to get in touch with someone at Sako, but it was late in Finland and everyone had gone home for the day. He'd try again tomorrow.

Jakob decided to take the roundabout way home. He wanted fresh air and open space. He needed to clear his thoughts.

He started for the north shore of Ísafjörður. It was best to stay moving, as the damp, cold air quickly penetrated the bones to the marrow. A fog had rolled in from the sea. The light filtering through the soup faded all surrounding colours to tones of grey. The mist formed minuscule droplets on his skin.

Despite the cold, Jakob felt unusually good. The visit to Bjarni's farm had gone well, and he'd managed to extract information relevant to the murder investigation. He felt like he'd succeeded and achieved something significant. But it wasn't just that things had gone well today. Jakob felt like he was doing much better in general than when he'd arrived in Iceland a few months before.

Maybe it was due to the country's tranquil, mood-stabilising vistas. Or the fact that he'd immediately done something that made a difference in others' lives. He'd created a new space and a role for himself. He felt particularly grateful for Hildur's friendship. Jakob had immediately realised there was something special about her. His colleague was intelligent, fair-minded, and genuine. Hildur's struggles were hard for outsiders to see. After reflecting on the matter, Jakob had concluded that her tough shell prevented outsiders from immediately noticing anything was out of place. Maybe it took someone who'd had problems of their own to see such things. Either way, the two of them had quickly become fast friends.

Hildur had been so engrossed in her work that Jakob hadn't wanted to interrupt her before he left. He'd have time to tell her tomorrow: he'd received some really great news today.

The fog had formed such a dense layer over the water that it was impossible to distinguish between sea and sky. Jakob felt like he was standing at the edge of the world.

His thoughts turned to Matias. He and his son would be seeing each other in a few months. Jakob would have to buy his ticket to Oslo soon: flying anywhere from Iceland was expensive, and the closer to the day of travel you bought a flight, the more you had to shell out. Lena's stunts might have ruined Jakob's most recent visit, but there was no way he was going to let that hold him back. That would be giving up, and giving up was the one thing he didn't intend to do.

Since moving to Iceland, Jakob had regained his self-confidence. He'd decided to fight his ex-wife. For too many years, he'd let Lena walk all over him like an old doormat. She'd even succeeded in wheedling Matias's custody for herself. But the Norwegian courts had clearly awarded Jakob the right to see his son. And now Jakob had decided to fight for his rights and those of his child.

A few weeks ago, Jakob had met a woman in an online forum who'd had a similar experience with her ex-spouse. She had given Jakob the phone number for Pekka Jokinen, who worked in international judicial assistance at the Finnish Ministry of Justice's Department of Private Law and Administration of Justice, and urged Jakob to reach out.

Jakob had called Jokinen, and it had been worthwhile. Jokinen's calm voice and unhurried manner had motivated Jakob to tell the whole story from the beginning. After listening to Jakob's ten-minute monologue, Jokinen had noted such cases were unfortunately common. That was sad, of course, but it had given Jakob encouragement. He wasn't in this intolerable situation alone.

Jakob and Jokinen had spoken for over thirty minutes. Jakob had wanted to find out what he could do to force Lena to respect the court's decision and let him see his son. He had some familiarity with the Norwegian justice system and spoke Norwegian, but he'd always been at a disadvantage when it came to the language. That was why he'd wanted to get an understanding of how things stood in his native tongue.

Jokinen had summarised the main points of Jakob's story to ensure he'd understood correctly. The child's mother had custody, she lived in Norway with the child, and the court's judgement granted Jakob the right to meet his child at certain set times and maintain contact with him via videocall, but the mother continuously came up with reasons for limiting contact. Jokinen had then unambiguously stated that international agreements obligated the Finnish government to assist.

Jokinen's clear way of presenting things reassured Jakob. He felt like the amorphous burden that had troubled him for years had begun to take a firm shape.

Jakob needed to submit an application regarding his parental rights to the department where Jokinen worked. After it was received, the department would contact their Norwegian counterparts, whose job it was to mediate an agreement between Jakob and Lena.

Jokinen hadn't painted an overly rosy picture of the future for Jakob. Evidently mediation usually failed; Jakob would probably have to take the matter to the courts. And that would have to happen in Norway, where Matias lived. That meant Jakob would have to have legal representation in Norway. *So be it*, he thought, walking faster. He turned right at of the old captain's house and continued toward the centre of town.

If he had to get a lawyer to help him, he'd manage that too. He could take a second job on top of his police internship. A lot of people in Iceland seemed to work multiple jobs, so why shouldn't he? His internship would be ending within a few months anyway. After that he'd be re-entering the job market and earning a proper salary. Whether he'd work as a police officer in Iceland or Finland was still uncertain. He wanted to stay in Iceland. He had a work community and friends here. He wanted to live near Guðrún. But he tried to not let himself get carried away thinking too far ahead.

As he entered the square at the heart of town, he passed the liquor store and turned right at the cultural centre. When he reached the knitting shop, he peered in through the display window. Guðrún was arranging skeins of yarn on the shelves. He knocked on the window and mouthed: *See you tonight?*

Guðrún nodded with a broad smile and made a rowing motion with her hands. Jakob ran his hand across his forehead as if he were wiping away sweat and laughed.

He hurried home, half jogging. He still had time to go for a short run and make dinner before Guðrún arrived.

Jakob smiled. The day just kept getting better and better as it drew to a close.

Chapter 32

Westfjords, 1992

Two years before Rósa and Björk's disappearance

Rakel was hanging the Christmas lights in the windows. A glimmer of joy in the impenetrable December darkness. The hooks left in the window frames year-round made stringing up the lights a simple process. In summer, Rakel hung pots of herbs from the hooks. It was too windy and cold to grow basil and dill outside, but they thrived in the sunniest spot in the kitchen. That evening she and the children would set out her mother's old Christmas figurines. The aroma of chocolate chip cookies baking filled the kitchen.

Rakel glanced at her children. The younger girls, four and six, were making paper shoes to put in the windowsill. That was where each Yule Lad would leave a little Christmas present in turn.

The following night, the first of the thirteen Yule Lads would descend from his mountain home and venture among humans. Sheep-cote Clod arrived every year on the night of 11 December. Driven by instinct, the Yule Lad who lusted after sheep's milk would head for the nearest sheepfold. But to his misfortune and that of the sheep, his long legs were made of wood, so he couldn't bend down to reach the udders. The frustrated Sheep-cote Clod would get his revenge by tormenting the sheep all night.

After the lights were hung, Rakel fetched a broom and dustpan from the corner cupboard. The messiest stage of the girls' project was underway: the gluing of little wooden beads and colourful shredded paper to the edges of the shoes. Hildur had cut the cardboard and stapled her shoe and those of the younger girls into the proper shape. Rakel caught a knowing smile flash several times across her eldest daughter's face as she helped her sisters. Hildur no longer believed in thirteen Yule Lads, but even so, she had the glue stick in her hand and was decorating her shoe with shredded paper too.

Rúnar had woken early that morning and headed outside to work in the yard. Yesterday's storm had left a corner of the horses' shelter sagging. It had needed immediate repairing, before the wind carried off the whole roof. Rakel glanced at the clock ticking on the wall. The last of the afternoon's glow would soon make way for the long night. She turned on the stove. Rúnar would come in before long, and they were having meat soup for supper.

Just now Rakel felt happy. The children were occupied with their crafts, and their home would soon be decorated for the holiday. It was important to her that the girls be left with good memories of Christmas. She already had hers. She smiled when she thought back to the previous week. It had been exceptionally lovely.

It had also been exceptionally dangerous. Which she, of course, understood.

Rakel was confused. Alternating feelings of shame and delight swelled within her. She never would have believed herself capable of such behaviour. How had she been so bold? Something in her life was changing; there was no doubt. The watcher no longer terrified her the way he used to. Maybe she'd put him in his place someday. Defend herself and her family.

She felt a warmth in her fingertips as she flipped over the postcard that had come in the mail today. Stars shining against a dark sky over a snowy landscape, a little red house with a Christmas candle twinkling in its window. *Merry Christmas* had been printed in gold letters at the bottom of the drawing.

Rakel turned the card over and read it again for the umpteenth time today.

Warm wishes for a Merry Christmas and a Happy New Year.
With love,
Your neighbours

Through the kitchen window, Rakel spotted a dark figure approaching the house. She opened the junk drawer and was on the verge of hiding the postcard there among the other scraps of paper, opened packs of playing cards, and rubber bands, when she reconsidered and set the card out on the sideboard. She laid it on top of the stack of Christmas cards that had arrived over the past few days.

'Hi, Daddy,' Hildur said in a bright voice. She was still at the kitchen table, cutting stars from a sheet of yellow craft paper. She then showed her sisters how to glue a star to the tip of their shoe by pressing the paper in place until the glue hardened.

Rúnar answered his daughter's greeting and glanced at the shredded paper strewn across the table.

'The girls have been making Christmas decorations all day,' Rakel said, bending over to take the cookies from the oven. Rúnar walked over and snatched one from the baking sheet. He flipped the hot cookie in his hands, blew on it, and scrutinised it evaluatively.

He appeared to be getting upset. He blurted something about the mess the girls had made, but Rakel pretended not to hear and let it pass. She reached for a wooden spoon and started stirring the soup. It was already steaming. Rúnar patted her tenderly on the shoulder and whispered something softly in her ear.

The pain in Rakel's head intensified again. It got the better of her, and her thoughts turned hazy. But she still conjured up a carefree smile and slowly turned around. The floor creaked. The younger girls were attentively drawing patterns on the sides of their Christmas shoes in marker. Hildur had set down her craft-making supplies, and her dark eyes were fixed on her mother.

'Why don't you guys go out and play a little before dinner? You could take the horses some hay.'

Giving the horses hay was one of the girls' favourite activities. The younger two squealed in delight as they rose from the table and ran for the door.

But Hildur didn't move a muscle. 'I don't want to go,' she said in a solemn voice.

Rakel sighed. 'Go on now, sweetheart. I'll set the table in the meantime. We'll go down to the basement later to look for the figurines,' she added calmly, tucking a lock of hair that had escaped her bun behind her ear. The movement made her head hurt twice as hard. Rúnar stood at her side, nodding approvingly.

Hildur gave in. She reluctantly rose from the table, slipped the craft scissors into the pencil case, put the pencil case on the wooden shelf in the kitchen, and shuffled to the door. She shot her mother one last look as if asking for permission.

Rakel smiled encouragingly and promised to call her and her sisters in soon.

The door clunked as Hildur pulled it shut behind her.

Rakel felt nauseous, but she still managed to look at the postcard on the sideboard. Sometimes a secret was safest when it was put on display for all to see.

Chapter 33

Ísafjörður, February 2020

Hildur had never owned a proper bookshelf. She kept her books in old banana boxes in the corner of her living room. The edges of the dog-eared boxes were held together with duct tape. The selection was pretty minimal: map books and photography books. The title on top was a photography book about surfing in Iceland's Arctic waters. Hildur had shown the American adventure photographer her favourite spots, and they'd gone surfing together a couple of times. As thanks, Hildur had received a signed copy of the book from the author. She touched the cover photo: a surfer standing with her board while the northern lights danced in the background. Hildur grunted. She was probably the only one aside from the photographer who knew the surfer in the picture was her.

At the bottom of the box there were two Icelandic sagas. Hildur had received *The Saga of Egil Skallagrímsson* as a prize for a short story about the sea she'd submitted to a writing contest in high school. Hildur had never been particularly fascinated by Egil's life story; she found the grim, violent Egil who'd begun drinking and murdering as a child a dull character. Hildur's favourite saga was *The Laxdæla Saga*, which she'd bought from the local bookshop. Written eight hundred years ago, the book told the story of a family that had moved from Norway to western Iceland. The tedious genealogical trees and overblown depictions of adventures didn't interest her so much.

But she felt an affinity for the saga's protagonist Guðrún, a strong-willed Viking woman who fought for and took power in a male-dominated society. There'd been room for happiness and sorrow in Guðrún's life. She'd seen in dreams that she'd marry four men, three of whom would die. The prediction came true. Guðrún schemed to divorce her first husband because he was such a bore. The next three died, some due to Guðrún's plotting. At the end of the story, when her son asked which of her husbands she'd loved best, Guðrún had answered: 'To him I was worst whom I loved most.'

The Viking woman's words had come back to Hildur because of Little Kata. Hildur didn't know what had pushed Little Kata down the road to destruction. What had happened to her? When had she made such poor choices that turning back became impossible? Yes, she'd caused a scene at the daycare centre and resisted arrest, but Hildur had seen a profound sorrow in the woman's eyes. Little Kata no doubt loved her children and she'd still caused them pain. Hopefully she'd get back on her feet and get her life in order this time. Hildur wasn't expecting miracles. As a police officer, she'd seen people plummet to the bottom in no time at all, and climbing out of the depths was incredibly hard. Most folks didn't succeed, despite numerous attempts.

Hildur emerged from her reverie. Why had she started going through her books just now? She glanced at the photo album on the table and knew the answer. She had the time now to go through the photographs she'd carried home from Tinna's, so she'd turned to the books as a diversion. She dug through other people's pasts for a living but avoided her own.

The photo album opened with a creak. Fear slunk into Hildur's breast, but she decided to press on. Yellowed photos of Fishermen's Day celebrations, Christmas trees, snowy landscapes. Summery pictures where eyes squinted into crescents in the sun. The rhubarb photo Jakob had spotted the sweater in. Hildur turned the pages. Tinna had taken a lot of pictures of her, and she had a serious look on her face in nearly every one. Her gaze wasn't angry, but there was something unusual about it. Hildur wondered whether she still looked the same way. She engrossed herself in the pictures, focusing on every detail. When she reached the last page, Hildur glanced at her watch and realised time had flown by. She was about to be late for a date she'd made with her friend Hlín.

As she closed the album, Hildur noticed the back cover bulging oddly. She flipped to the last spread. A paper pocket had been tacked inside the back cover, and there was something in it. She pulled out a small stack of square photographs. The pictures had stuck together, and she had to be careful as she pulled them apart.

Six photos. Although they'd yellowed, and the surfaces of some had cracked, it was clear they'd been taken at the same event.

She stopped to stare at the best-preserved photo in the bunch. Three young women stood next to the old harbour building. In the background, a group of older women were cleaning a catch of cod. No year was marked on the photo, but Hildur could tell it was several decades old. Some of the women in the picture were familiar.

There was no mistaking Tinna's features. She was looking straight into the camera with the cheerful expression she still wore. Tinna was the youngest person in the photo; with her thin, long legs, she looked about ten years old.

The other two women were already grown. They were both a head taller than Tinna, with full figures and breasts. Hildur immediately recognised the woman in the middle. Hildur had consciously avoided any photographs of her parents since their funeral. She'd wanted to excise everything she'd lost from her mind. But there in the photo was her mother, Rakel. She was looking down and to the side, a shy smile on her face. That was exactly the way her mother had stood, one leg slightly bent, foot resting on the toes. Hildur felt her body tingling. Fear mingled with curiosity. She felt like she'd opened a door she'd no longer be able to close.

Hildur had never seen the third young woman, but the resemblance to Rakel was so plain they had to be sisters. It suddenly registered she was seeing Hulda, Rakel's and Tinna's older sister, for the first time. Tinna didn't display photographs in her home, so Hildur had never seen any pictures of her oldest aunt.

A strange sensation formed in Hildur's throat. It felt hard to breathe. All three sisters were wearing the same sweater: a white one with thin black lines topped by irregular dots like stars.

Hildur closed her eyes and focused. So many thoughts were bouncing around her head that she was having difficulty keeping them straight. She'd seen something that called to her. Something she hadn't been able to resist despite wanting to.

Just then her phone rang. Hildur reached for it and answered without checking to see who the caller was. At first she only heard wheezing at the other end.

'Hi, I'm calling from the Safety Investigation Authority. This is Róbert.'

Hildur was instantly on the alert, and at the same time wondered at the strange timing of the call. It was Saturday. Róbert said something about the terrible pressure at work and having too much to do. Hildur expressed sympathy. Quite a few people worked longer hours than officially stipulated in their contracts.

There wasn't the tiniest hint of flirtation in Róbert's tone this time. He sounded like he had something serious on his mind.

'So listen, I'm calling in an unofficial capacity because you were so interested in that plane that dropped. The official report will come out early next week. The whole thing is pretty strange. There was nothing wrong in the engine or the cockpit. Everything was shipshape, just as it should have been.'

Hildur felt a slight disappointment. Everything had been in order after all.

Róbert continued: 'The plane dropped because it ran out of fuel.'

'How is that possible?' Hildur marvelled. An experienced pilot would never take off on an empty tank.

'The weird thing is the fuel cap was missing.'

'Did it come off in the crash?' Hildur asked.

There was a stifled sneeze at the other end of the line. 'It wouldn't just come off on its own. Someone must have taken it off.'

Hildur shivered. What exactly had happened to Gunnar's plane? And what was the nature of his involvement in Hermann's business affairs?

Chapter 34

'Don't start getting nervous now. She'll be able to sense the tiniest tremble up there,' Hlín said, climbing on the back of her own horse.

Hildur's friend Hlín Jónsdóttir worked the Westfjords for Icelandic public radio. She was the only employee on the desk. She conducted interviews, took pictures, shot video, and edited everything herself. When something newsworthy happened anywhere in the Westfjords, petite Hlín was on the scene with her huge camera bag.

Hlín had a few horses stabled with a local horse tour company located at the base of the fjord. Her horses pastured there. The company could use Hlín's horses for tours and in exchange Hlín didn't have to pay for the animals' upkeep, aside from their winter hay. The tourist season didn't begin until June, so she mostly rode her horses herself in the winter.

Hildur somewhat awkwardly straddled the back of her small, barrel-bellied horse. The helmet felt odd on her head. Hildur hadn't been riding in years, but she'd agreed to join Hlín for a slow, steady walk.

'What happens if she can tell?'

'She won't obey you,' Hlín said matter-of-factly, then urged her long-maned horse into motion.

Hildur accepted this information: it was the same with some people. If you gave them too much slack in the wrong place, they took advantage of it. Hildur brought her plump, light-brown horse up next to its friend, and both of them started toward the slope rising above them.

'So what did you want to talk about?' Hlín asked.

Hildur had called her journalist friend to discuss Hermann. Journalists knew all sorts of things – including things they couldn't print. And Hlín had reported on Hermann's death, so she was at least superficially familiar with the case.

'About our deceased Sheriff. A lot of people knew about his unscrupulous business practices. It seems strange that no journalists ever wrote about his shady schemes.'

A crooked smile formed on Hlín's lips. She urged her horse into a brisker clip. 'It's not for lack of trying.'

Hildur shot her friend a querying look and tried to keep up. Between her tightly pursed lips, Hlín said there weren't the resources to look into everything.

Hildur knew what Hlín was implying: there were only a few investigative journalists in the entire country who'd be allowed to dedicate working hours to digging into complex cases of fraudulent activity. Bigshots like Hermann existed in every village; there simply wasn't time to comb out all the burrs. She asked Hlín to go on.

'One time I ran into such a strange case involving Hermann's family that I did some investigating in my free time. But it didn't end well.'

Hlín seemed frustrated. Hildur knew her friend had reported on the Westfjords for a long time. Hlín knew the ins and outs of decision-making in the region, was acquainted with the key players, and had made the rounds of every village in pursuit of stories.

'He was so damn good at what he did. Always taking people to court. For slander, illegally spreading private information, or what have you.'

Hlín sounded bitter, and Hildur understood why. Hermann had the money to pay lawyers; journalists, not so much. If you worked as a freelancer, as many journalists did these days, any court costs came out of your own pocket. When one of Hermann's lawyers called and threatened a journalist with an expensive court case, the journalist generally gave in. The financial risk prevented completion of any investigative reporting.

The horses clopped side by side up a pair of sheep trails. The paths were narrow, but Icelandic horses were used to navigating difficult terrain. Hildur's initial jitters had vanished, and riding almost felt pleasant. Her horse's ears were turned out to the sides and its gait was steady. Hildur had ridden her parents' horses as a child, but there had been a break of a few decades after she moved in with Tinna. *Maybe I could pick riding back up someday*, Hildur mused as she gazed at the springtime valley.

There was still snow on the upper slopes. The metre-wide mountain streams burbled as they carried meltwater to the river down below. They were running high and fast. The horses' hooves sent up splashes as they struck the rocky streambeds.

Hlín told Hildur about the old case. She'd heard a rumour about Hermann's son and had started collecting documents and asking questions.

'That lasted a couple of weeks. And then the process server brought me a letter. Hermann had applied for a court-ordered prohibition on disclosure of information.'

A court-ordered prohibition? That's a pretty intense measure, Hildur thought to herself. The court-ordered decision forbade the discussion of certain topics under threat of punishment.

'The order came so fast that he had to have influential connections in the courts.'

'Unbelievable bullshit,' Hildur huffed with a shake of her head.

Hlín explained that she'd heard stories about the son's violence from multiple sources. She hadn't even got off to a proper start when the process server knocked on her door.

Hlín turned around and suggested they ride home a bit more briskly. She still had two horses to exercise and an interview scheduled at noon. Hildur would have preferred a slow walk back to the stable, but she didn't have the nerve to refuse. She would just have to grab hold of her horse's mane and hope for the best. The animals knew they were going home, so there was no need to urge them on; they broke into a speedy trot on their own. Hlín went ahead; Hildur followed, rocking from side to side in her saddle with her eyes closed. When they reached the stream, the horses jumped it in a single leap that felt long to Hildur. As the beasts' feet hit the ground, she slammed into her horse's neck. Her helmet slipped but didn't come off.

Hlín reined in, and Hildur's horse followed the example of the lead animal. Hildur straightened her helmet and slipped her feet back into the stirrups.

'*Jæjja*, was I going too fast?'

'I'm fine, my foot just fell out of the stirrup,' Hildur said, wishing the ride would end soon.

'I started getting upset about that old case again. It really got to me. Hermann's son is a thoroughly unpleasant guy.'

According to Registers Iceland, Hermann's son Ari lived abroad. Hermann's ex-wife had moved from Iceland years before and remarried. Beta had informed both of them about Hermann's death. Hildur remembered Beta having said they were crushed when they heard the news. They would presumably both be travelling to Iceland for the funeral. Hermann's fellow party members had promised to handle the funeral arrangements.

'Do you know what Hermann's son is up to these days?'

Hlín snorted and bitterly said: 'Playing soccer somewhere in Europe. A beloved star and so on.'

Hildur nodded and took a moment to process what she'd heard. 'So you don't remember the nature of the rumours about Hermann's son?'

Hlín's gaze sought out the horizon. Her horse snorted enthusiastically when the fork in the road came into view; the animal knew home wasn't far off.

'It's been so many years . . . I asked Ari's teammates about his behaviour, but no one would talk. That was strange. No one was surprised or shocked by my questions. They just clamped their mouths shut and refused to talk no matter what I tried.'

At the end of the ride, the horses broke into a faster trot again. The speed sent their manes swaying. For the last kilometre, Hildur almost enjoyed herself. She was no longer rocking as much, and since she was sitting straighter, her feet stayed in the stirrups. By the time they reached the pasture, Hildur felt good. She'd survived the ride without falling off and got important inspiration from what Hlín had told her.

As soon as she got back to Brenda, Hildur called Jakob. 'Could you get us contact information on everyone who played soccer in Ísafjörður between 2000 and 2015? The Sports Association secretary can probably help you.' Then she told him how to get in touch with the secretary.

If Ari's teammates knew something and refused to talk back then, it's high time they talk now, Hildur reflected as she waved to Hlín.

And then she set out for Tinna's place. There were a couple of things Hildur needed her aunt to clarify for her.

Chapter 35

The grass-skirted doll attached to the dash swung in time to the 4x4's movements. Brenda the hula dancer was a souvenir from a hitchhiker Hildur had picked up at the side of the road one day. She'd become Hildur's car's mascot and given it her name. The trusty Land Cruiser was a little rusty around the edges but otherwise in good shape.

Hildur reached for her phone and brought up Aunt Tinna's number. Tinna couldn't see who was calling, but her mobile phone had been customised with sound alerts and personalised ringtones. Tinna had chosen Nancy Sinatra's song 'Bang Bang' for Hildur's ringtone. It made Hildur laugh. Tinna liked to listen to soundtracks and had a particular fondness for the music of Quentin Tarantino films.

'Hey, Auntie. I'm in the area. Can I drop by?'

Twenty years before, blood clots had blocked major arteries supplying Tinna's retinas, and she'd lost her vision. First from the right eye, then the left. The doctor said having the condition in both eyes was incredibly rare, but that was what had happened to Tinna. No one could say why. But her nieces' disappearance and her sister's death had been incredibly stressful, and it's possible stress played a role in the formation of the embolisms.

'I'll make us coffee. Would you mind dropping by the shop on the way and buying some of their *kleinur*?'

Tinna sounded happy about the visit. She generally passed her days listening to the news, music, and audiobooks and going for short walks.

'I'm guessing you've been around horses,' Tinna said, wrapping Hildur in an embrace in her entryway. Hildur had been outside the whole time, but horses had a pervasive smell. Hildur told Tinna about the ride.

'As a child, the only thing you did all summer was ride the slopes of Kotsdalur,' Tinna reminisced as she put the donuts Hildur had brought on a plate. Hildur thought it was cute that the discount store's in-house donut brand was Tinna's favourite.

It had been ages since Hildur had heard the name of the valley where she'd spent her childhood spoken out loud. *Kotsdalur.* It was the place Hildur had lived for the first ten or so years of her life. There had been only one other farm in the valley, Kotsdalur Efri's sheep farm. She could still hear the animals' loud bleats. She remembered long, quiet hours sitting on the bench in the barn's back room while Mum helped with the lambing. The images were hazy, but there was something off-putting about them: the strange, sour smell of newborn lambs.

'So what did you want to know?' Tinna asked, dipping her donut in her coffee and taking a bite.

Hildur placed both palms on the table as if seeking strength for what she was about to say. 'I want to know about Hulda.'

Tinna looked in Hildur's direction in puzzlement and rose from the table. She turned on the tap and poured herself a glass of cold water. 'What do you want to know about her?'

Hildur took a moment to refill her coffee cup. Tinna drained the glass, rinsed it and dried it with a dish towel, and returned it to the cupboard.

Hildur described the photos she'd found. 'The third woman in the picture was Hulda, right?'

After a brief pause, Tinna responded in the affirmative. 'Photographers used to travel around the countryside in the summer taking pictures, around Independence Day. Those photos were probably from the early 1970s. I remember it, because the fish-processing plant paid generous bonuses to the workers. There was a record cod catch that year.'

Hildur found it strange that she'd never seen a picture of Hulda. She had no childhood memories of her elder aunt, and Tinna had never spoken much about her other sister.

'Why all the silence?' Hildur asked.

Maybe Hulda's name had been an omen? *Hulda* meant 'secret, hidden'. The *huldufólk*, the hidden people, featured prominently in Icelandic folktales. Hildur could remember countless stories about them; all Icelanders could. Every village had a rock or mound inhabited by the hidden folk, who watched over their surroundings. They helped well-meaning individuals and punished those who mistreated nature or other people. The hidden folk had existed since the day God told Adam and Eve he'd be visiting to see how well they'd succeeded at their mission of replenishing the earth. Eve hadn't managed to bathe all her children before God's arrival and only presented the children she'd had time to wash and dress properly. The rest she'd hidden for the duration of the visit. When God asked if all the children were present, Eve lied. God grew angry and punished Eve, turning all the hidden children invisible and sending them to live in rocky mounds above ground or caves below.

Hildur emerged from her reverie. Her aunt still hadn't answered her question. 'Was Hulda even her real name?'

'Of course.' Tinna paused. 'I was pretty young when she moved away.'

Tinna said she and Hulda had lived under the same roof but hadn't known each other very well. There was a big age difference. Rakel was almost ten years older than Tinna, and the eldest sister,

Hulda, was a couple of years older than Rakel. Rakel and Hulda had been close, but Tinna had never found the same intimacy with her older sisters, especially Hulda.

'Hulda felt a little like an outsider in the family. That might have been because there wasn't complete certainty as to who her father was.'

Tinna's parents, Hrafnhildur and Helgi, had met young and married quickly. Hulda had been born soon after – a little too soon. The rumour in town had been that Hrafnhildur had lured Helgi into being father to another man's child. The story had lived on.

'That's how it's always been here. People talk all sorts of nonsense for the sheer pleasure of talking.' Tinna wiped up the donut crumbs from around the coffee cup and shook them into the saucer in front of her. She took a couple of calm, deep breaths with a thoughtful look on her face.

'The kids at school would sometimes ask me about Hulda's father. It was strange, because my father was Rakel and Hulda's father too. Our parents treated us exactly the same. I know I didn't take the stories very seriously. But maybe Hulda felt differently.'

Hildur saw a golden plover outside the window. The golden-brown bird with black speckles was a sure sign the long winter had officially come to an end. The arrival of the first golden plover was always reported on the news, usually in mid-April. It wasn't even March yet. *They sure are early these days*, Hildur thought to herself.

The stout, short-beaked bird – the size of a thrush – strutted across the backyard, looking around. Hildur opened the window. The plover's call rang out in a wistful minor key. *Chuu-it. Chuu-it.* As if it were mourning something. Perhaps summer, which was still too far away.

'It's possible Helgi wasn't Hulda's biological father, but what difference does that make? We were all one family.'

Hildur knew what her aunt meant. There were former and current spouses, there were one's own children, the children of others, shared children, and children who'd been taken under one's roof to live. The same word was used in Icelandic to refer to female and male relatives. Cousins, second cousins, half-cousins, aunts, and uncles were all equal. Family ties weren't born out of biology but experience.

Tinna began to recite from memory: 'If a man wants to win a woman's love, he must give her gifts and sweet-talk her. The one with the sweetest speech will win her affection.'

'Excuse me, what did you say?'

Tinna started to laugh. 'It's Viking love advice from old books.'

'Got it,' Hildur replied, browsing through the newspaper left open on the table.

'Hrafnhildur was an incredibly beautiful and charismatic woman. When she entered the room, everyone noticed. I think Helgi was so in love with Mum that he wanted her even though she was pregnant by another man. That would have been a big gift to a woman in those days.' Tinna seemed to have sunk into decades-old memories.

Hildur took the newspaper and brought it close enough to read. More of the back-page crossword had been filled in since her last visit. 'It looks like you've had a sweet-talker here too.'

'Don't be silly. Ívar came by to bleed the radiators, and I'm not going to let a visitor leave without serving him coffee, am I?'

Hildur saw Tinna pointedly purse her lips. Hildur was happy her aunt, who lived alone, had visitors. 'Is he a nice man?'

'I wouldn't let him in if he weren't, now, would I?' Tinna said, with a private smile.

Hildur folded the paper and set it down next the junk mail. A little sign by the front door said NO JUNK MAIL, but the people whose job it was to deliver flyers paid no attention.

'Do you know why Hulda moved from Iceland?'

Tinna said she wasn't sure. There hadn't been any major arguments or disagreements, at least to her knowledge. In Tinna's memories, Hulda was quiet and withdrawn in big groups but bold in small ones.

'She was the bravest of us.' Tinna guessed Hulda had wanted to build a life for herself somewhere else, not here at this fjord. She'd gone off to Denmark to work for wealthy families. A lot of other Icelanders over the decades made a similar choice, went off to seek a better life elsewhere. Many crossed the sea to America; some ended up in Europe.

'At first we got a postcard once a month. Hulda always addressed the cards to Rakel, but the rest of us read them too. She saw the world. The cards came from Denmark, then Norway, the Faroe Islands, even England. But they gradually grew less and less frequent. Then it was just a Christmas card, and in the end not even that. I haven't heard from her at all since Rakel's death.'

Hildur glanced at Tinna. Her aunt didn't seem particularly sad as she reminisced about the past.

People came and went. Some of their own free will, others under duress. A blood tie wasn't necessarily lasting, and family didn't always stick together. That's just how life was sometimes.

Chapter 36

Westfjords, 1994

Six months before Rósa and Björk's disappearance

A warm breeze was blowing off the water, bending the tall green grass into soft, swaying arcs. The entire meadow appeared to be in motion, like the sea's waves. The dandelions hummed with the low drone of honeybees. The sky was bright blue with not a cloud in sight.

Rakel held the picnic basket in one hand and used the other to balance so she wouldn't step off the narrow path. The girls were bounding up ahead. Hildur was running up the hill, chasing her little sisters. The girls advanced fearlessly and nimbly, giving little thought to their next step.

Rakel advanced more slowly. She had to focus on her feet and the children at the same time. She simply couldn't let them out of her sight. She was tormented by malevolent thoughts, but there was nothing she could do about them. Rakel was sure they were being watched. The hot, oppressive feeling wouldn't leave her in peace. Her headaches were more and more frequent.

Rakel had told the girls they'd have their afternoon coffee outside. The weather had been so beautiful that morning. They'd decided to walk to the top of the nearest mountain and have a picnic there. Rakel glanced up. It wasn't as if this mound of a few hundred metres was a proper mountain, more of a hill. But climbing a mountain sounded like an adventure.

Just a few more dozen metres of gently rising path before they reached the summit. Rakel looked past the girls and realised they weren't alone. A searing sensation like the sun's rays permeated her body. Her premonition had been accurate. There the neighbour stood, waving at them. Rakel politely returned the greeting.

Rósa and Björk held dandelion blooms in their fists and hurled them at each other. Hildur didn't join in the game. She was standing on the path, back straight and arms hanging at her sides, staring so intently at her mother that Rakel could feel her daughter's gaze on her skin.

'The neighbour's here too,' Hildur stated in a quiet voice.

Mother's and daughter's eyes met. Rakel's heart took a couple of extra beats. She did everything in her power to remain calm and forced a small smile to her face.

Rakel spread the wool blanket on the ground next to the picnic basket and started passing out the food. Flatbread stuffed with lamb, tomatoes, nuts, and crowberry juice. She'd brought a Thermos of coffee for the adults.

Rakel handed her girls their sandwiches. First the younger two, then Hildur, who looked back and forth between the adults as she munched on her lunch. The keys to many secrets were hidden behind the girl's eyes. Whether that was a good thing or a bad thing, Rakel wasn't sure. But she did know the girl's life wouldn't be easy, no matter how her own life turned out.

Chapter 37

Ísafjörður, March 2020

'I took anyone who was dead off the list,' Jakob said, tossing the yellow plastic sleeve filled with documents onto Hildur's desk. 'And I made copies for myself.'

Hildur nodded in satisfaction. She and Jakob had a telephone marathon ahead of them. Jakob had done as Hildur had asked and obtained the list of soccer players from the secretary of the Westfjords Sports Association over the weekend. The two of them would start their round of calls from Hermann's son's teammates. Teams spent a lot of time practising together. There were training camps, tournament trips, and strength training. One of the teammates must have heard something. But Hildur knew that wouldn't be enough. She and Jakob would have to call everyone who'd played soccer during the years Ari lived in the Westfjords. If they were unlucky, the tele-marathon could last days.

Jakob said he'd start from the end of the stack. Hildur brought up the number for the first name on the list. Her call was answered immediately. Judging by the background noise, Atli Helgason was at an airport somewhere abroad. Hildur couldn't identify the language being spoken in the background. She introduced herself and explained why she was calling.

'Ari . . . who?' a gruff male voice asked.

'Ari Hermannsson. You played soccer together in the Westfjords. Do you remember him?'

For a moment, the only sound at the other end of the line was an automated announcement. It was probably a warning that the gate was closing.

'Of course I remember him!' Atli said. It sounded to Hildur as if he were scratching his beard. After a brief pause, he continued: 'Ari Hermannsson had all the makings of a star player back them. I'm not at all surprised he's made it as far as he has in soccer. Great player.'

Hildur doodled spirals in the margins of her notebook and eyed her notes about the clarifications she was hoping to get. She would ask everyone the same questions.

'Do you remember there ever being any talk outside of games of him being violent?'

'I never heard anything like that. But . . . I didn't really know him that well.' Atli seemed genuinely ignorant. 'I'm sorry, but I have to go. They're closing the gate and there are rumours they'll be closing the borders here in Spain because of that damn virus. I can't miss this flight.'

Hildur thanked Atli and ended the call, then crossed him off the list.

She didn't have as much luck with the next five names. She couldn't find a current telephone number for one, and the rest didn't pick up. Hildur stood up and glanced at the list Jakob had in front of him. He'd already called twenty numbers.

Jakob answered Hildur's look with a shake of his head: 'Nothing.'

Then he was introducing himself again and launching into the same initial question.

Hildur sighed, sat cross-legged on her office chair, and picked up her phone. It was going to be a long day.

After the fourth ring, an out-of-breath male voice brusquely answered: 'What?'

Hildur explained why she was calling and was met with silence at the other end of the line.

'Are you still there? I was asking if—'

'I heard what you asked. I'm down here at the soccer pitch coaching the juniors right now. Do you have time to come down? I'd rather talk face to face once practice is over. In half an hour or so?'

The guy was in Ísafjörður. That was a stroke of luck. Hildur ended the call and returned her dirty cup to the kitchen. She'd set out for the soccer field in a moment. It was about a fifteen-minute walk from the police station. In the meantime, Jakob could continue going through the list.

She turned to the window; the weather looked nice. The sun was shining so brightly it might even be radiating a little warmth. But reality struck at the station doors: a glance out the windows never told you how hard the wind was blowing, because there were no trees in the vicinity.

Hildur pulled up the collar of her winter coat and dug her hands into her pockets. She had left her gloves in the car and didn't have the energy to go back and get them. She took the crossing at the petrol station and thought back a few months, to the time her colleague from Reykjavík slipped in the icy car park and broke a hip. The guy in question, Jónas, was Hildur's least favourite police officer, a big mouth and a boor who rumour had it used his wife as a punching bag. When she was subbing in Reykjavík, Hildur had heard Jónas had gone on sick leave due to chronic pain and his wife had found a workplace romance and left him.

There's still justice in the world, Hildur reflected as she trudged toward the playing field.

The players were wrapping up their post-practice stretches when Hildur stepped onto the pitch. The tall man who had introduced himself as Arnar on the phone walked up to shake hands with her.

'Thanks for taking the time to meet,' Hildur said.

Arnar eyed her probingly. 'Of course. Can I ask: you're the Hildur who knew Freysi, aren't you?'

Hildur nodded curtly. She instantly knew where the conversation was headed, she'd had it so often over the winter. The first few times, hearing Freysi's name had hurt. The pain hadn't dissipated since, but she'd managed it a bit better with every passing week.

'I'm sorry he's gone. We practised together sometimes, and he talked about you a lot.'

Hildur nodded again and expressed her thanks. Then she got down to the matter at hand. 'You said on the phone that you knew Ari Hermannsson?'

Arnar let out a long whistle. 'Unfortunately.'

'What do you mean?' Hildur asked, immediately following up with: 'How would you describe him?'

Arnar gave her a look presumably intended to indicate they were on the same side. 'The guy was a total asshole. A good player, but a complete jerk. Was a better actor on the pitch than the southern Europeans. Whined if a fingertip happened to graze him.' Arnar continued in the same breath that he didn't think it would be at all out of character for Ari to assault someone off the pitch.

'He was always getting into fights, especially when he was drunk. Apparently those are the traits that help you push your way into the spotlight.'

Hildur said she'd heard rumours that Ari might have been party to a violent act that happened over a decade before and that had never been officially investigated.

'So why is it being investigated now?'

Hildur grunted and looked Arnar stonily in the eye. 'Let me ask the questions. You just answer.'

Arnar started gathering up the cones. Hildur followed him.

'It's been such a long time; there's no way to remember stuff like that very precisely,' Arnar said as he stalked the sideline, stacking the cones into a tower on his left arm. He walked so fast and his stride was so long Hildur almost had to run to keep up.

Arnar stopped and looked at the houses rising to the west of the field. 'There was usually a pretty good vibe in the locker room after a game. We'd high-five each other and process what had happened. But one time the mood was totally different.'

Hildur listened to Arnar's story. The Ísafjörður team had beaten Keflavík that day. Their opponents had had a lot of strong players, so the win ought to have been a big deal for the whole team. But the key players were somehow subdued. Arnar had been a reserve and hadn't had a lot of playing time. The team's best players, including Ari, had just sat huddled in a group engaged in a heated debate.

Arnar explained the players used to have to take turns cleaning the locker rooms. That night cleaning had fallen to him. 'When I left the locker room, Ari was waiting for me outside. He said he wanted to talk.'

Arnar carried the stack of cones over to the storage box next to the sports centre building, shut the lid, and bolted it so the wind wouldn't blow it open.

'What did he want to talk about?'

Arnar briefly looked Hildur in the eye and told the rest of the story. Ari had made Arnar swear not to say anything about what he'd heard in the locker room to outsiders or he'd regret it. 'I hadn't heard anything! And I told him so, but he didn't believe me.'

Arnar started walking toward the main doors of the sports centre. Hildur followed and waited for him to continue. Arnar seemed to speak more freely when he was on the move.

Arnar related how Ari had pushed him up against the wall and threatened him. 'I don't remember what he said word for word. Something about if I didn't do what he said, I'd get the same treatment "as that pathetic slut".'

Hildur gave no sign as to the relevance of this information. 'Do you know who Ari was referring to?'

Arnar shook his head apologetically. 'I didn't want to ask. Ari was so hot-tempered that no one wanted to argue with him about anything. That's all I know, unfortunately.'

Arnar said the feeling on the team had gradually returned to normal over the next few weeks, and the topic had never been revisited. Hildur was sure there were others on the team who knew what had happened.

She thanked Arnar and gave him her number so he could call if anything else came to mind. She was eager to get back to her list and keep calling, this time focusing on the former teammates Arnar had mentioned by name.

Just then she heard a shout behind her. 'Hey, wait a sec! There's one more thing!'

Arnar ran lightly on long strides and quickly caught up to Hildur. 'Or actually two things.' He shifted his weight to his other foot. 'Would you be interested in catching a film with me sometime?'

Hildur couldn't believe her ears. She'd just questioned this coach regarding a murder investigation, and here he was asking her out on a date. She blew into her hands and rubbed them together to get some sensation back into her frozen fingers. Arnar wasn't her type, and catching a film was the last thing she was interested in just now.

She forced a friendly smile to her face. 'I don't think that's a good idea.'

Arnar had looked hopeful. His bright expression instantly melted into disappointment. 'I understand. It was stupid of me to ask. It hasn't been long since Freysi died—'

Hildur cut him off mid-sentence. 'What about the other thing?'

Arnar stared at the toes of his running shoes. 'I just remembered one more thing Ari said to me. It was so weird that it stuck in my mind.'

The wind began to blow even more coldly now. It had picked up speed at sea and slipped into the fjord, making the bare branches of the low bushes lining the road lurch. Arnar pulled down his sponsor-brand beanie and looked up from his shoes at Hildur.

'He said there was no point trying to say anything or tell anyone, because even Hippocrates was on his side.'

'Hippocrates?'

Then Hildur understood. Sometimes a completely ordinary event or statement felt uncanny because there was something too familiar about it. Something you sensed having experienced before. The pieces suddenly fell into place, and she saw the big picture. She quickly thanked Arnar, left him standing at the sidelines, and took off running for the station. She had to confer with Jakob immediately.

Chapter 38

Reykjavík, March 2020

The seatbelt light came on. The pilot, who'd just given her name as Jónína Axelsdóttir, welcomed the passengers onto the flight to Reykjavík. The estimated flight time was thirty-five minutes, and flying conditions were excellent.

Hildur turned to Jakob, who was sitting at her side. 'You heard the pilot. It's going to be a smooth ride.'

Knowing the conditions were good did nothing to lift Jakob's spirits. His forehead had broken out in a clammy sweat. His legs felt heavy.

He'd already decided he'd never travel domestically by air again in Iceland. His first flight on a small prop plane from Reykjavík to the Westfjords had been an awful experience, and he had no interest in being shaken around like that again. But here he was, sitting on a plane, in a narrow seat with ten other passengers.

Hildur had burst into the police station in a sweat and announced she'd booked them seats on the afternoon flight to the capital. She and Jakob had to head to Reykjavík immediately. Driving would have gobbled up half a workday, which left flying as the only alternative.

The rush was precipitated by the doctor who'd died in the plane crash. When Arnar mentioned Hippocrates, Hildur was sure she'd found one more strand in the thread linking Hermann and Gunnar. Hermann's son Ari had done something dubious, and a doctor had sided with him. That doctor must have been Gunnar, an acquaintance Hermann had known for decades. Now both Hermann and Gunnar had died within a couple of weeks of each other. Hildur had shared what she'd heard from Arnar as well as the information she'd been given by the accident investigator, who'd said the fuel tank cap had come off so cleanly there was no way it happened in a violent crash.

Jakob had allowed himself to be convinced by Hildur's arguments and tended to agree now: the deaths were somehow related.

Hildur pulled her phone from her pocket, glanced at it, and turned it off. Jakob was still thinking about the small aircraft's empty fuel tank.

'But there must be some automatic warning that lets the pilot know the tank isn't shut?'

The little prop plane taxied to the south end of the runway, turned, and accelerated into the wind. Hildur had lowered her voice so the people sitting around them couldn't hear what she and Jakob were discussing. 'The guy from Safety Investigation thought the missing cap wouldn't necessarily set off an alarm in a small plane like that. If the tank runs low, lights start flashing, but the warning probably came too late.'

Jakob shuddered. The prop plane was rolling down the town's sole runway and shaking like the devil in a deep freeze. Speculating about the potential causes of plane crashes wasn't exactly doing anything to ease his fear of flying.

'OK, goddammit. Let's not talk about this right now.'

Hildur mumbled something signalling she understood and turned to the window.

Jakob knew flying was safe. Planes didn't take off from Ísafjörður if conditions were too unfavourable. The runway ran between two mountains, and a wind blowing from the west or east made landing and taking off dangerous, which meant all flights were cancelled. But fear of flying wasn't about knowledge; it was about feelings. Jakob couldn't help it that soaring through the stratosphere in an aircraft the size of a taxi van felt crazy to him.

He closed his eyes and gripped the sweater in his lap. He'd packed along his unfinished knitting to have something to focus on during the flight aside from compulsive monitoring of the aircraft's movements and glancing at his wristwatch.

After a few minutes, the plane reached flying altitude and the seatbelt light went off. Jakob opened his eyes and reached for his knitting needles. He'd finished the hem the night before, and now came the most boring part: half a metre of smooth knit in a single light-coloured yarn.

Hildur eyed the handicraft in his lap with curiosity. 'I thought you already finished that one?'

Jakob glanced at his colleague and kept knitting: 'Yeah, I did. I'm making two of the same kind.'

'It's that serious, huh?'

Jakob smiled to himself and pulled more yarn from the bag stowed under his seat.

Hildur started quizzing him about Guðrún. What were her friends like? Had he met them yet? Did they usually spend the night at his place or hers? Was Guðrún teaching Jakob Icelandic?

Jakob was happy to answer his curious friend's questions. He'd met Guðrún's co-workers at a dinner party. Most of the time they spent the night at Jakob's, because his bed was bigger. Guðrún had been teaching him the language, first individual words, then short sentences. She'd taken him to the convenience store to order ice cream and the bakery to practise. Jakob had made Guðrún laugh at the hardware store, when he wanted to buy her a new coatrack for her entryway and the glue needed to assemble it. Jakob had made a minor mistake in pronouncing the letter 'i' and ended up asking the old fellow manning the shop if he had a coatrack and 'a big tube of strong penis.'

Hildur erupted into loud laughter. 'Who makes a mistake like that?'

Just as Jakob was recounting how he'd tried to explain his gaffe to the flustered salesman, he felt a powerful jerk. The plane's wheels had touched down. They'd landed, and he hadn't noticed a thing.

Hildur jabbed Jakob lightly in the arm: 'I did a pretty good job of keeping your mind off flying, didn't I?'

Chapter 39

Keflavík, March 2020

Dísa

The line was crawling, because only two security checkpoints were open. No more than a handful of employees were around between the busy morning and afternoon shifts. Most of the morning flights to Europe had already departed, and there were hours to go before the afternoon flights to the US took off. Dísa looked around and shifted her weight nervously from foot to foot. Was it always this quiet at Keflavík International Airport this time of day? She had no idea. She'd never been here before. She'd never travelled abroad. She remembered childhood camping trips in Iceland. Mum and Dad would pack the car full of stuff, stop at viewpoints to make camp-stove coffee, and they'd spend the night in camping grounds they happened to come across. They'd travelled around Iceland multiple times.

Her most vivid memories were of the southern shores: black lava-sand beaches, tall waterfalls, gleaming white glaciers. One time her father had got a gift card for a glacier trek from his boss for Christmas, and they'd used it during their summer vacation. Led by a guide, they'd hiked across Vatnajökull. The ice had crunched beneath the spikes attached to their shoes as they climbed up and down its slopes.

Dísa's memories of childhood were positive. It wasn't until she was a little older that things had gone awry. Mum had complained of persistent chest pains. By the time the doctors took her seriously, it was too late. Mum died of heart disease when Dísa turned eighteen. At that point Dad changed, grown quiet and withdrawn, but the two of them had still managed just fine on their own.

Then came that one summer and that awful night ... Dísa wished she couldn't remember it anymore, but she did. For years afterward, her life had consisted of wandering around in a black fog.

But that was in the past. She'd got her life together. A lot of people Dísa had met on the streets of Reykjavík would be surprised if they could see her now. She didn't keep in touch with her old Reykjavík crowd anymore. Not that many were still alive. A lot of them had overdosed; some had committed suicide. The rest were in prison or had moved abroad. And she'd cut ties with everyone she'd known from childhood and adolescence right after the terrible summer.

But she'd survived. She'd never go back to where she'd come from. She'd never be anyone's doormat again; she'd fight back. She'd recently learned that the only way to survive was to hit. Hit or be hit. There might be other methods, too, but she couldn't be bothered to ponder them. She didn't want to overcomplicate her life now that she was happier than she'd ever been.

Dísa was nearly at the head of the line. She started taking off her belt, the way she'd seen the people in front of her do. The elderly couple placing the contents of their bag in a plastic tub looked at her suspiciously. *They must be afraid of catching Covid*, Dísa thought to herself.

She was travelling abroad for the first time in her life. The newspapers had warned of mandatory mask requirements and potential travel restrictions; that was why she'd hurried her departure. The end-of-the-world news didn't faze her as long as she got off this island while planes were still flying. She'd be back someday. Or not.

Dísa had got her first passport a couple of months ago. She'd been saving up for it for years. Every time she got paid, she set aside a little money and hid it in her dresser drawer. She earned her cleaning salary under the table, in cash. She didn't pay any taxes on it, which made it faster to save.

Based on stories Dísa had read in travel-themed discussion forums, she knew the money she had with her would keep her going for a while, maybe a few months. Iceland was incredibly expensive, but in southern Europe everything was cheaper and the sun shone more warmly.

A security officer in a blue uniform gestured for Dísa to approach the conveyer belt. Dísa placed her backpack and belt in the plastic tub. She removed her phone and old laptop and charger from the backpack.

Following the security agent's instructions, Dísa passed through the light-grey gateway and waited at the end of the conveyer belt for her backpack. A bald security agent was staring intently at the screen. He stopped the conveyer belt and reversed it to send Dísa's plastic tub through the x-ray machine again. Dísa saw him gesture at a colleague to come over, then showed the colleague something on the screen. She started getting nervous. Was there a problem?

'Is that backpack yours?'

Dísa nodded. She looked at the bald man's nametag: PAWEL. He had a distinct Polish accent, speaking fast and pronouncing the consonants with a conspicuous hardness. Almost all of Dísa's co-workers were from Poland or the Baltic countries. She was the only Icelander at her workplace.

Or had been, that is.

She'd called the shift lead at the cleaning company yesterday and said she wouldn't be coming back. Her manager had cursed Dísa for the short notice and squawked that she'd never work there again. Dísa didn't care. She'd find work quickly at any cleaning company, because there was a shortage of good workers – the kind who'd show up when they were supposed to.

'It needs to be checked. May I open it?'

I'm assuming the only correct answer is yes, Dísa thought to herself and gave Pawel permission to open the backpack. He rummaged through her belongings. Dísa's heart nearly leaped into her throat when she saw what had caught his attention. Pawel pulled her green notebook from the side pocket. He flipped it over and opened it at several places. He knocked the hard cover and stared insistently at Dísa: 'Metal covers?'

'Yes, they're metal.'

Pawel turned around and walked off with the notebook. Dísa's heart was pounding. She hadn't thought about the metal covers. Would they be a problem? There was no way she could leave the notebook behind. If the covers were a problem, could she take them off? Dísa did everything in her power to remain calm. Now was not the time to draw attention to herself.

'I'm going to send it through again,' Pawel said, offering the notebook to the black mouth of the x-ray machine.

When the belt finally conveyed the notebook out of the machine, Pawel handed it to Dísa politely and smiled.

'Have a nice trip, ma'am.'

Dísa stammered her thanks, took the notebook, and returned it to her backpack. That was close. This notebook was her most precious treasure. She'd written all her thoughts, including her darkest secrets, on its pages. That was where she'd described in detail all the things she'd done recently. No one must ever find out about them.

Dísa tossed the backpack over her shoulder and set out to find the departure gate. She was almost there. Just a little longer, and she'd be far away from here. All the necessary preparations were complete.

Chapter 40

Reykjavík, March 2020

Hildur had rented a car at the airport. She turned right out of the car park and drove past the university campus and the Nordic House. She and Jakob saw Reykjavík's old downtown area and the skyscraping Hallgrímur church up ahead, but they wouldn't be heading that way. Hildur got into the right lane and curved onto Hringbraut, one of the city's major thoroughfares.

Luck was with her. She didn't hit any red lights until the big intersection at Skeifan.

No further clues had turned up at Hermann's office or his home in Ísafjörður, but the Gunnar inquiry might be a different story. Hildur had contacted Gunnar's only child, Katrín. Katrín had sounded coherent and energetic considering her father had died in an aeroplane crash just two weeks before, but Hildur knew people reacted to loss and grief in different ways. She'd called to ask Katrín about her father's belongings. Despite having lived abroad the past few years, Gunnar might have left personal effects in Iceland. Katrín's response had been a pleasant surprise: Gunnar had boxes in storage.

'Katrín lives in Grafarholt; we still have a few kilometres to go,' Hildur said, accelerating to eighty. Ironic that they were going to go rummage through the belongings of a dead person in a district named after a burial mound.

Hildur drove into a prosperous-looking residential area. The white signage gleamed and the wide streets were smooth.

'Looks like a pretty new neighbourhood,' Jakob said.

'Yup. Construction began when I was at the police academy in Reykjavík.'

They walked up to the correct house, Hildur leading, Jakob a couple of steps behind. There was a buzzer next to the wooden door. Katrín must have heard them coming, because she opened it right away.

The woman in the doorway was wearing a black blouse and red jeans. She was a bit older than Hildur, just over forty. Blonde bob, groomed eyebrows. Small silver earrings. Probably a high-status job somewhere, a corner office with glass walls, Hildur guessed.

'You called this morning?' Katrín asked. She extended a firm hand, and introductions were made. Katrín assessed the police officers standing on her front steps but didn't give any indication of wanting to invite them in.

It doesn't matter, Hildur thought to herself. They could just as easily handle their business out here.

'We're investigating the murder of Hermann Hermannsson, who died in the Westfjords,' she explained, then continued with a rough sketch of the investigation's progress.

Katrín nodded and said she'd been following the case on the news. She said she'd known Hermann; he and Katrín's father had been friends for ages.

Hildur then offered her condolences on Katrín's father's death. 'I understand this information may come as a shock, but it's so fresh we haven't made it public yet. We think there might be something suspicious about the plane crash that killed your father. There's a slight chance it wasn't an accident after all.'

Katrín's face turned stony. But within seconds she'd swept away the emotion and gave a slight nod, as if to signal that she'd heard and understood.

'I see. Well, I'm sure you'll inform me when you have confirmation.'

Hildur registered Katrín's stiff reaction. 'News like this can come as a shock. Would you like to speak with a crisis worker? I can call and book a time for you,' she said, pulling a business card from her coat pocket.

Katrín rejected the card and tossed back her head with a dry laugh. 'There's nothing to offer condolences about. I didn't even really know my father. I haven't seen him since he moved to Cyprus for work.'

A car sped past behind Hildur's back. She glanced in the direction of the sound.

'They need to put speed bumps on this street,' Katrín said sharply, glaring at Hildur as if it were her responsibility. The car had barely been speeding over the legal limit so Hildur didn't think chasing after it was necessary.

'We'd like to confirm a couple of things and have a look at the communications between your father and Hermann.' Katrín had told Hildur her father had stored some belongings at her place when he moved abroad, and they were still in her possession.

Katrín looked past Hildur at Jakob, and Hildur noted the way her eyes lingered on him. Hildur found it funny. She'd seen that reaction so many times.

'It's mostly files and documents from his companies,' Katrín said, adding that documents had to be saved for a certain length of time for legal reasons. There weren't many bookkeepers who wanted to store them for clients, so sole proprietors usually kept their receipts at home.

'My father's investments will presumably come to me, seeing as I'm his only child. But I think I'm going to refuse the inheritance.

My father wasn't the most reputable guy, and the less I have to be involved in his affairs, the better.'

Hildur nodded. Katrín seemed to have plenty of money of her own. The house looked big, and a Tesla and a gleaming new Ford F-series pick-up stood in the carport.

Hildur hoped Katrín wouldn't ask for a warrant, because she didn't have one to present. She hadn't had time to get one. All she and Jakob were doing was having a quick look through the belongings of a man who'd died in an accident, if the next of kin gave them permission to do so.

Katrín turned her back to them and opened the top drawer of a console in the entry hall. She clattered around in it until she found what she was looking for: a black plastic fob attached to a plastic strawberry.

'The garages are there to the left. It's the middle door. Gunnar's things are in yellow boxes at the very back, against the wall. Take all the time you need. I have a video call with Germany, so unfortunately I'm not going to be able to help.'

That suited Hildur. The less they had to discuss the reasons for their visit with outsiders, the better. She thanked Katrín and took the key. Katrín spun around in her ballet flats and pushed the door shut behind her.

Hildur swiped the fob against the reader. The door to the flat-roofed garage unlocked with a click.

Jakob looked near the door for a light switch, and a moment later fluorescent tubes bathed the space in a bright glare.

The garage was like a sporting goods store. Three new-looking full-suspension mountain bikes, a bike trailer, and camping gear. Down coats and snow pants hung neatly on racks. Hildur spotted a few pairs of adult and children's cross-country and downhill skis.

'Pretty athletic bunch,' Jakob mused as he wove his way through the excess to the back wall.

About a dozen yellow moving boxes stood in three tidy stacks. Jakob set aside the junk that had accumulated on top of one and handed the box to Hildur. 'You start from this; I'll take this one in the very back.'

There were a lot of boxes; they would have to work quickly if they wanted to finish before evening. They wouldn't be able to come back in the morning, because their return flight to the Westfjords took off at ten. Storm-strength winds had been promised the following afternoon, which presumably meant changes to domestic flight schedules. And Hildur had promised Beta they'd be back at the station tomorrow.

Hildur started to go through the papers. Invoices, receipts, tender templates. Maybe all the folders contained were similar documents, which were meaningless to them, but Hildur still meant to go through each one individually. If the doctor had left anything of interest behind, they might stumble across it here.

'Does it bother you when women stare?'

Jakob was pulling books and magazines from his box. He looked surprised.

'Well, of course some men do too,' Hildur added quickly. 'The ballerina we just met couldn't take her eyes off you, even though she was talking to me.'

Jakob laughed, flustered. 'I didn't notice anything. But I guess it doesn't bother me. Or I don't know. What kind of question is that anyway?'

Hildur was amused. Jakob could be so out of it when it came to such things.

'Your internship ends this summer. What are you going to do afterwards?'

The answer came so quickly that the issue must have been on Jakob's mind: 'I think I'll stay here.'

Hildur had sensed as much, but hearing it from Jakob was nice. Jakob told her about his plans to take Icelandic lessons. He was going to try to get citizenship as quickly as possible and apply for a job with the police. Hildur thought it was a solid plan. They were constantly understaffed on the force, and some officers, especially in rural areas, hadn't even received formal police training. It was enough for one of the partners to have met the legal competency requirements.

'Guðrún and I have also been talking a little about ... how pointless it is to pay rent for two places.'

Hildur had the urge to rush over and hug her colleague, but there were a few boxes and several teetering piles of paper between them. She settled for a thumbs up.

Jakob lifted his final stack from the box. There at the bottom, beneath issues of *Science*, was a stash of Danish porn magazines.

'You don't have a homegrown industry here in Iceland?' Jakob joked.

'I'm sure you can find all sorts of things online these days,' Hildur replied.

Jakob packed the old magazines back in the box and reached for the next one.

Within a little over an hour, they'd been through half the boxes. Hildur raised her hands over her head against the wall and stretched her upper body. The awkward position she'd been working in was making itself known in a budding shoulder stiffness.

They hadn't come across anything of interest yet, but they wouldn't stop until they'd gone through all the material.

'By the way, have I told you? I have a lawyer now, and he said my only option is probably to take the custody case to court. So we may apply to the court for enforcement of my right to see my son.'

'What does that mean in practice?'

'Lena might be fined if she keeps stopping us from seeing each other. I could also ask the courts to assign someone to pick Matias up and bring him to our meetings, but I don't want him to suffer any more than he already has.'

Hildur nodded. She understood Jakob's concern. Leaving your child at a stranger's mercy felt bad. Even thinking about it cut deep. A murmur swelled somewhere behind her ears. She sensed an oncoming pressure as a painful sensation in her chest. She had to get out of the garage.

'I'll be right back. I have to get some fresh air,' she said to Jakob as she hurried out.

Hildur leaned against the building and shut her eyes. It felt as if everything around her were cooling off. Warm air was lighter than cold air. When warm air rose, cooler, heavier air flowed in and took its place. She was the cold air.

Hildur took a few deep breaths and clenched her fists. *Concentrate, concentrate, concentrate.* She tried to convince herself she'd feel better soon. What was happening to her? Were these panic attacks? She didn't know what to do or what might help. Even the thought of the sea's waves didn't calm her.

Just then Jakob yanked open the garage door and urged Hildur to come back in. He'd found something that might be of interest. Hildur still felt ill, but she managed to set aside the sensation for now. Jakob's enthusiasm was contagious.

He thrust a small cash box into Hildur's hands. There was a tiny key in the lock.

'The Holy Grail meets the Panama Papers,' Jakob said, pulling out the box's contents for Hildur to see. 'Statements from Swiss bank accounts, incorporation records from Bermuda, Cyprus, and Gibraltar . . . And then these documents in Icelandic.'

Hildur browsed through the stack of papers. The doctor's name appeared over and over as a beneficiary and the holder of bank accounts. Bank statements flashed before her eyes. All the withdrawals and deposits were sizeable sums: tens of thousands of euros, minimum. Hildur had never heard of any of the companies sending or receiving the money. She immediately thought the papers might be related to tax planning or even worse, proof of financial misdoings, but Hildur wasn't particularly interested in either. She knew people who worked in white-collar crime in Reykjavík. She could bring the papers to them, but it was unlikely they'd do anything with them. At least the documents she had here in her hands were dated over a decade ago, so if something criminal had taken place, the statute of limitations had presumably passed.

'But what's this?' Hildur mumbled to herself as she pulled a clear plastic folder from the box. She dangled it between her forefinger and thumb and squinted at the topmost document inside the transparent sleeve.

Hildur understood what she had in her hand. A physician's statement.

'Holy hell.' She pulled on a pair of disposable gloves, removed the sheaf of papers from the plastic, and started translating their contents for Jakob.

'Twenty-one-year-old Dísa Önnudóttir was brought into urgent care on 25 July 2008 with serious injuries. - - - Torn perineum, severe damage to external genitalia, damaged sphincter and mucus membranes. - - - Acute procedures were performed, further care in Reykjavík mandatory. - - - Patient spoke of being raped - - - Samples were taken, to be sent to Reykjavík for analysis - - - Patient means to

report the crime to the police. (Patient claimed to know the perpetrator, Ari Hermannsson?)'

'Ari Hermannsson,' Jakob repeated.

Hildur nodded victoriously. The famous soccer star had raped a young woman and got off scot-free because his daddy happened to know the doctor who examined the victim. The corrupt doctor had never delivered the statement to the police and had hidden it instead. It was the police's good fortune that Gunnar had kept the document instead of destroying it. The crime repulsed Hildur, but she was also pleased. One crook's mistrust of another had delivered them a critical clue.

Jakob leaned his elbows on the stack of boxes and shook his head in disbelief: 'So that's the sort of good ol' boys' club we're dealing with.'

Hildur noted the doctor had taken DNA samples from the victim's skin. She meant to check with Reykjavík, but she was almost positive they'd never been sent anywhere.

Chapter 41

The hotel's wide doors slid aside as Hildur and Jakob strode in. A long brown mat absorbed the mud and water from their shoes. The green-and-white exterior looked like a monument to the 1980s, but the ambiance was cosier inside. Situated near Reykjavík Airport, Hotel Loftleiðir was a local landmark. The hotel's official name was Natura, but locals still referred to it by its former name. Many Icelanders had memories of the Loftleiðir. Christmas lunches were enjoyed in the hotel's restaurant, meetings were scheduled in its conference rooms, and many who lived in the countryside stayed in its guest rooms when visiting the capital. The big hotel's affordable prices lured guests for weekend getaways.

Hildur had booked herself and Jakob rooms for one night. It was only a five-minute drive to the airport, so they could take their time eating breakfast before catching their flight.

The heavily made-up desk agent flashed them a quick smile, then turned toward her computer. Her long red nails started tapping at the keyboard. 'Would you like a room with a shower or a bath?'

Hildur studied the woman's hands. Her fingers didn't even reach the keys; she was typing with her nails. It looked like a lot of work.

'We have two separate reservations. Two rooms.'

The woman lifted her fingers from the keyboard and gave Hildur a querying look. Then she glanced at Jakob. 'I see. So you're not together?'

Hildur was getting frustrated. What the hell was this cross-examination?

'Separate rooms. We're travelling for work.' She felt like she was explaining to a three-year-old.

'Of course. One moment, please.'

The agent activated a keycard and handed it to Hildur. She curtly informed Hildur that breakfast began at seven in the hotel restaurant and Wi-Fi didn't require a password.

Then she turned to Jakob, and a broad smile spread across her face. She cheerfully launched into a description of the hotel's gym, massage services, and nice walks in the neighbourhood. She asked if this was his first time in Iceland and if he needed any tourist tips about Reykjavík. Then she glanced at her watch, and her smile broadened even more: 'I'm off in an hour.'

Shaking her head, Hildur walked away from the reception desk, found a plump armchair, and sat down to wait. She pulled her phone from her pocket and called Beta. After giving a lengthy monologue, Hildur heard a sigh at the other end of the call.

'Goddammit, Hildur, this sounds really messy.'

'I checked LÖKE before we flew down. Ari's name doesn't appear in it. If a crime took place, the police never learned about it.'

'Meanwhile Dísa's record is so long it could be knitted into a scarf,' Beta said, after tapping at her computer for a moment.

Beta read the list of fines Dísa had accumulated. Drugs, shoplifting, assault. She'd been to jail plenty of times over the years for causing disturbances on the streets of Reykjavík. Beta paused. The radio was clearly on in her office, because Hildur could hear the afternoon weather forecast promising sunshine in southern Iceland.

Hildur knew they now both understood how things stood: someone had murdered Ari's protectors.

'You two need to talk to Dísa Önnudóttir right away,' Beta said, inhaling sharply as if in response to a sudden, stabbing pain.

Hildur heard Beta open a drawer, followed by a rustling. Some people headed out for a smoke when their nerves got the better of them; Beta had her packages of cookies.

After a couple of crunches, Beta asked sharply: 'This Ari ... don't tell me he's ...'

Hildur knew what her boss was about to ask. She assured Beta that she'd already checked. Hildur had spent the drive from Katrín's house to the hotel on the phone while Jakob drove. Ari's soccer team had played a match the day before. He'd posted a picture on Instagram that morning of him sitting under a palm tree at a pool and tagged it #aftergame.

'He's alive and sweaty.'

Before Beta could respond, Hildur reported the next steps she'd already taken: 'I got in touch with an old colleague in Reykjavík. A patrol is on its way to Dísa's home. I'll keep you up to date.' Hildur ended the call and slipped the phone back into her pocket.

Jakob was waiting for her at the lifts: he jubilantly waved the keycard he held in his hand. Hildur tossed the backpack containing a change of clothes and a toothbrush over her shoulder and joined him.

'Did she use that keycard to extort a date out of you?' she asked as she stepped in through the opening elevator doors.

Jakob followed, shaking his head in bewilderment but visibly pleased. 'These Icelandic women, Jesus Christ.'

Chapter 42

Westfjords, 1994

Three months before Rósa and Björk's disappearance

Rakel was raking the yard. There wasn't much to rake, because there weren't many trees. Four stunted spruces leaned behind the house. The alders planted out front ages ago had survived the severe conditions in the fjord, and it was the leaves they'd dropped that Rakel was now trying to collect in a pile.

She glanced at her watch. One thirty. She'd have to leave in an hour to make it to town on time. The younger girls would go to Tinna's after school while Rakel went to her doctor's appointment. The day before, she'd been clumsy with the potato pot and spilled boiling water on herself. The big blister that had formed on her arm looked inflamed.

Her hand hurt, but even so she kept raking, because it felt good. The tool's tines sank easily into the soft soil. The pull dragged along dirt and odds and ends and left a beautiful trace behind. Rakel raked again, a long, slow pull. As soon as the leaves were in a neat, compact pile, she bagged them before the wind gusted and ruined everything.

Rakel left the rake leaning against the house, grabbed the bag by the mouth, and started walking toward the compost pile.

The wet yard made squelching sounds underfoot. Water as deep as a child's boot had collected at a spot where the ground sank a little. Rakel stepped into the puddle, and the brown silt from the bottom clung to the soles of her knee-high boots. Muck rose to the surface with every step she took. Then she caught a whiff of a sweet, rotten smell.

I should have dug a deeper hole, she thought to herself.

She'd raked the other half of the front yard that morning and carried the twigs and leaves to the compost pile, where she'd spotted something white amid the food scraps. It was their white-nosed cat, Rjómi, lying there. Rakel had nudged the animal. It had been soft but hadn't reacted. It was dead, of course. Rakel had moved the potato peelings and coffee grounds aside and found more white fur. The tiny three-week-old kittens lay beneath their mother.

Rakel had acted quickly. She couldn't leave the cats there for the girls to find. She'd briskly fetched a sharp spade, dug a hole in the backyard, and dropped in the cat carcasses. A dense layer of soil on top, and she'd figured the matter was settled.

But she'd failed again. The hole was visible, and the dead cats stank.

It was getting late. She didn't have time to dig another hole. She emptied the bag of leaves over the pit and carried over some rocks. She already had a story ready for the girls. She'd developed an allergy to the cats, and the kittens and their mother had gone back to their former home, the farm owned by Helga and Hallgrímur. That's what must have happened.

Rest in peace, mother and children, she thought to herself as she dropped the last rock in place.

Chapter 43

Reykjavík, March 2020

'It's March, and you're suggesting we go to the beach,' Jakob said doubtfully.

Hildur laughed and turned from the hotel toward the pedestrian path leading to Reykjavík University and the public beach beyond. The temperature was only seven degrees Celsius, and the wind was blowing at ten metres per second.

A moment ago, Hildur had received a phone call from the patrol that had knocked on Dísa's front door. No one had answered, and the place looked dark. The police hadn't been able to locate any records indicating student status or a workplace. Hildur had called Beta, and together they'd decided to immediately release a photograph of Dísa to the general public and ask for tips regarding her whereabouts. Beta had promised to call the harbours and airports.

The Reykjavík police and forensic investigators would head over and conduct a search of Dísa's apartment as soon as they wrapped up a more urgent assignment. Hildur wondered what could be more urgent than searching the home of a potential double murderer, but she'd been told that since no one else's life was in immediate danger, she would have to wait her turn. And while waiting, Hildur wanted to show her colleague the heated beach.

They continued to the beach in silence. Hildur knew the area well. She used to come swimming here all the time when she lived in Reykjavík.

'I've never heard of anything weirder than a heated beach,' Jakob said.

The hot-water pool at the waterline was packed with people. A few swimmers were splashing in the shallows. Steam was rising from the sea. It was considerably warmer than the surrounding air.

'Icelanders love package holidays to the Canary Islands and Florida,' Hildur said. Those who'd developed a taste for them started demanding a sandy beach in Reykjavík that was warm enough to swim in. Tons of white sand were spread along an undeveloped stretch of shoreline, and the output of a hot spring was pumped into the sea there. Two grey-haired people walked calmly along the beach as the Atlantic washed over the rocks. Seabirds arced over the bay. The pair of retirees dipped their feet in the warm water.

'Weird and probably really damn expensive,' Jakob said.

Hildur swatted away the notion. The volcanic island had more than enough hot water for several heated beach resorts.

After observing the Arctic beachgoers for a while, Hildur and Jakob decided to walk back to the hotel and see if, despite the early hour, they could get dinner at the restaurant there. They were both hungry.

'Hey, your Rósa and Björk investigation: did you have a chance to go through those photos Tinna gave you?' Jakob asked as they strolled along. A pair of little brown rabbits hopped across their path and into the trees. The rabbit population had increased in recent years. Some pets had escaped by accident, but there were also people who'd grown tired of their little friends and intentionally released them. The Öskjuhlíð woods were full of urban bunnies these days.

Hildur told Jakob about the pictures she'd found of the sisters and how all three of them were wearing matching sweaters: the sister sweater. She then related everything she knew about Hulda and the uncertainty about Hulda's father's identity.

'Do you think Jón was related to them, since he was wearing a matching sweater too?'

Hildur shook her head. There was no way that was possible. Her family and Jón no doubt had relatives in common if one went back a few centuries, but they weren't close kin. Jón was linked to her family some other way. And he'd got his sweater from either Rakel or Hulda. Tinna had told them she'd tossed hers out when it got too threadbare.

The wind picked up again. Jakob pulled up his hood to shield his head.

'I don't understand why Hulda moved away so young. I haven't found any logical reason for it,' Hildur said.

Jakob thrust his hands into his coat pocket and glanced at Hildur from under his brows. 'Does there always have to be some big reason? Maybe she just wanted to see the world and left.'

I suppose, Hildur reflected. *That's possible too.*

She and Jakob had been walking for a good hour now, and evening was falling. They could see the hotel's lights. Just as they were about to enter the building, Hildur's phone rang. The call was from an unknown number. The timid female voice at the other end asked whether she was speaking with Hildur.

'Yes. How can I help you? Or I mean, who's calling?'

There was something vaguely familiar about the voice, but Hildur couldn't place it. The wind swirling outside the hotel and the traffic noise prevented her from hearing properly. She pressed the phone to her ear and stepped into the lobby to hear better.

'It's me, Little Kata.'

Little Kata? Why is she calling? Hildur didn't respond; she just waited.

'Listen... I just saw this weird thing on the *DV* website. It's about Dísa, even though Dísa doesn't look anything like that picture.'

Hildur's interest was immediately piqued. *DV* was Iceland's sole daily tabloid, and its news site was constantly updated. She knew the photo from the police archives was old, but it was all they had. 'How do you know her?'

There was a mournful chuckle on the line. 'We all knew each other, us women. Besides, Dísa is the only one except me who's still alive.'

Of course, Hildur thought. Networks were small on the street too.

Little Kata wanted something; otherwise she wouldn't have called. 'Why are you sharing this information with the police?'

The answer came as fast as a slap to the face: 'I'm not snitching. You know we don't talk to the cops.'

For a moment, the only sound at the other end of the call was a quick-tempoed breathing punctuated by a couple of false starts. Little Kata had more to say. The hotel lobby was filling with tourists returning from day trips. People were streaming into the restaurant, and red-cheeked, good-natured guests at the bar were sipping their first beers of the evening. The night was still young, and dreams were waiting to be fulfilled. Hildur waited patiently.

'I wanted to tell you because you've been fair to me. And when I get myself back on my feet, you could help me with social services. I want to see my kids.'

Hildur felt a tingling in the vicinity of her chest. The people at the bar began to fade into the back wall of the restaurant. For some reason, Little Kata's words had touched her.

'Dísa looks totally different these days. She has a job and everything.'

'A job?' Hildur asked. She'd looked up Dísa's information, and there had been no indication of income in recent years.

Little Kata laughed and told Hildur about an ex-boyfriend who had a basement apartment near Reykjavík Airport. When he'd ended up in prison, Little Kata had been forced to look for a new place to stay.

'I used to see Dísa smoking outside the airport all the time. She always had her cleaning cart with her. I don't get why. I guess she was really proud of her job or something...'

Hildur listened to the subsequent monologue for a few minutes, uttering one-word responses at what she considered were appropriate intervals. Then suddenly Little Kata was in a hurry to end the call.

'I have to go. My NA meeting starts in half an hour, and I don't want to be late. I'm going to give it a shot again...'

So Little Kata really was trying to get off drugs. That was an important step.

'Cool. That's really cool how you keep trying. Maybe things will still turn out well.'

Hildur heard Little Kata grunt drily. She thought she caught a hint of satisfaction in the chuckle.

'Maybe,' Little Kata said, and hung up.

Chapter 44

Hildur was annoyed. Beta had just called and reported that passenger data indicated Dísa had flown to Málaga the previous afternoon. Her identity had been confirmed from the airport security cameras and the airline's passenger manifest. Further efforts to locate Dísa would be hampered by the fact that it was possible to travel within the Schengen area without any passport checks. Hildur and Jakob had stumbled across her trail a day too late.

Hildur tried to shift her frustration to the back burner as she pushed open the door to the cleaning company's break room. The place was a mess. An ancient coffee maker burbled on a small shelf in the corner of the cramped space. A bag of rolls and half pack of cheese slices were out on the table. The floor felt sticky underfoot.

Thanks to Little Kata's tip, Hildur had found out the name and address of the company that handled cleaning services at Reykjavík Airport. Hopefully she and Jakob would find someone here who'd be able to tell them something new about Dísa.

A young man – who looked barely twenty – took a roll from the bag, broke it in half, and set a slice of cheese between the halves. The other person sitting at the table was woman a little older than Hildur. She was scrolling through her phone and muttering something in English about basketball practice.

'Checking these Facebook groups is driving me crazy! I have three kids, and they all play basketball. There are posts every day in every group about changed practice times, tournaments, and frozen-fish fundraisers. I can't even do my work I'm so busy trying to keep up with who has to be where when . . .'

She took a swig from her water bottle and continued her tirade. The boy just sat there, looking bored and carefully chewing his roll. He didn't contribute to the woman's outburst; he looked like he'd heard the same complaints plenty of times before.

Hildur knocked on the door frame again. The woman looked up from her phone and peered over her glasses at Hildur and Jakob, then switched into fluent Icelandic.

'Aha. The new shift leads, I assume? Or are you here to make sure we're wearing our masks? I'll tell you right now I'm not putting one of those nappies over my mouth. You try cleaning up other people's messes, dripping sweat with a scarf around your face. No thanks. Call the police if you have to, but I'm not wearing that mask. So you can just get the hell out of here.'

Hildur asked the woman to calm down. She explained they were police officers but the reason for their visit had nothing to do with the use of face masks.

The woman didn't respond; she just stared first at Hildur and then at Jakob further back. Hildur introduced herself and Jakob and took down the names of the woman and the boy. His name was Peti; the woman introduced herself as Agata. Peti was from Lithuania, Agata from Poland. Because the two of them communicated with each other in English, Hildur switched languages too.

Hildur explained she and Jakob were looking for Dísa. 'I heard she worked here from . . .' She paused to check the name of the shift lead from her notes.

The shift lead had been a difficult case. At first she claimed she'd never heard of Dísa and no one by that name had ever worked for the company. Not officially; Hildur knew that. When

Hildur explained they weren't investigating off-the-books employment and just wanted to find Dísa, the woman had given in and told what she knew, then added Dísa was gone.

'Your boss said Dísa wouldn't be coming back to work. We need to talk to her. Did either one of you know her?'

Peti raised the coffee pot toward the police officers. Hildur and Jakob thanked him and declined the offer. Peti dribbled ultra-pasteurised milk into his coffee and set two cups on the table. At the same time, he said he'd never had any dealings with Dísa outside the workplace.

Hildur looked at Agata. She folded her arms across her chest and leaned back in her chair, looking thoughtful. 'I don't know anything about that girl's life. But I liked working with her. She was always on time and never complained about anything: conditions, salary, or how gross the work is.' Agata cast a long, pointed look at Jakob and Hildur over her readers and continued: 'What I'm saying is, she was a very unusual Icelander. I don't get why she was wasting her time with people like us. She even has an Icelandic name. I'm sure she could have found work elsewhere.'

Hildur nodded. She recognised the local prejudice against foreigners. Icelanders liked tourists, and people from Nordic countries were considered somehow harmless. But the more complicated one's name and the less one looked like the native population, the more difficult it was to get a foothold in society. Hildur remembered a study where applicants had sent in similar applications for advertised jobs. The only difference had been the applicant's name. The applications sent with an Icelandic name were more likely to be chosen for interviews than the applicants whose name suggested a foreign origin. An educated Pole lost out to an Icelander with no training in almost every instance. That was unfair.

Jakob interjected: 'Did you work together often?'

Agata looked delighted. 'Judging by the way you talk, you're not from here either!'

So Jakob had an opportunity to explain his background again. Agata nodded enthusiastically and said she was very happy foreigners were gradually being hired as police officers too. Then she fell silent and thought for a moment before answering Jakob's question.

'About half my shifts. We cleaned the airport together. I would handle the cargo offices; Dísa always wanted to do the passenger terminal.'

Hildur's curiosity was sparked: 'Why, do you think?'

Agata grabbed her coffee cup from the table and loudly cleared her throat. 'I have no idea, but it was fine with me. Cleaning the cargo side is a lot easier. The passenger terminal sees a lot more traffic.'

Peti closed the bag of rolls with a rubber band and put the cheese in the fridge. He glanced at his watch and said it was time to get back to his broom. Then he seemed to remember something.

'One time at the end of the day Dísa and I were outside the main doors at the airport, having a smoke. Or she didn't smoke; she'd just keep me company. Dísa told me she loved the feeling at the airport. She liked watching people coming and going and the planes landing and taking off from the runway.'

So Dísa had been interested in aeroplanes. Hildur wasn't sure that was the whole story. Hopefully the officers conducting the search of her home would find something that would be of use.

Hildur thanked Peti and Agata and left them her contact information. Agata was leaving the break room when she stopped in the doorway and turned around.

'Why are the police asking about her? Or wait...' Her face took on a knowing expression. She looked as if she'd solved a mystery. 'Do you guys work for the tax office? I can tell you I pay my taxes and my retirement contribution from my wages. Some of my pay goes to the union every month too. You can't take any risks when you have little children.'

Agata would have continued babbling if Hildur hadn't interrupted her. 'We don't care about tax cards.' She had to give a non-answer, because they hadn't found Dísa yet and hadn't decided on next steps. 'Dísa is connected to a case we're investigating. We just want to talk to her.'

Agata nodded but looked as if she didn't believe a word of it. 'She's not in trouble, is she? Like I said, a nice girl and a hard worker, but she wasn't exactly normal. She would haul this big notebook around everywhere she went and write things in it, even when she was on the clock. People her age are usually glued to their phones every waking moment, but not Dísa. She was always taking notes to make sure she remembered things.'

After Agata and Peti exited, Hildur walked over and turned off the coffee maker. The old coffee ended up down the drain. She reached for a sponge and squeezed a generous dollop of dish soap on it. There was nothing they could do right now but wait. Beta was preparing a SIS alert. SIS was the database shared by the Schengen area police, border patrol, and customs officials. Local law enforcement could use SIS to report someone missing or track down stolen vehicles, firearms, or passports. If Dísa ended up in dealings with the law or tried to leave the Schengen area, the system would indicate there was an order to detain her.

Many of Iceland's bigger crooks and more harmless small-time criminals had tried to wriggle out of the law's reach by travelling to warmer countries, but their escape had often ended in arrest. Hildur remembered at least a couple of recent cases of Icelanders charged with narcotics offences who'd managed to travel to the Costa del Sol on a one-way ticket. But thanks to international cooperation, the Spanish authorities had returned them to Iceland within a few months. Finding a suspect was possible but could take far too long.

Hildur turned on the hot water, and a moment later an eggy smell filled the room. The water was heated by a slightly sulfurous hot spring. After rinsing away the soap, Hildur slowly rubbed the glass pot with a dish cloth and tried to keep her cool.

'Dísa has a head start of almost two days. In a murder investigation that's an eternity.'

Chapter 45

Hildur stood in her hotel room in the pre-dawn gloom. In a couple of hours, sunlight would lift Reykjavík out of darkness. She'd been woken by a nightmare, so she decided to go to the hotel gym. She'd have time for a workout before the morning flight. The hotel staff wouldn't hit the gym for another hour. Morning was a good time to train. She could work out in peace and wouldn't have to worry about safety distances or the limits on numbers of people that gyms had begun enforcing.

Shoes on the shelf, sweater on the rack, gym bag on the bench. Hildur glanced at herself in the locker room mirror. She had fat bags under her eyes and her skin looked greyer than it had yesterday. No surprise there. It wasn't even five in the morning.

Hildur had had nightmares before, but this dream had been different. She'd been in the sea and heard someone calling her name. She'd begun swimming toward the voice when a big wave came and swallowed her. The wave had looked like the one that had crashed down on her the last time she'd been surfing. After being tossed around by the wave, she'd swum to the surface, heard the voice again, swum toward it, and another wave had come. The dream had felt particularly distressing because something familiar had turned on her.

Over the last few days, she'd spent a lot of time reliving the past. The stories about Hulda, the words of Bjarni the sheep farmer... It was all churning up too fast, and she couldn't get a proper grip on any of it. It felt like the more steps she took forward, the hazier everything grew. None of it seemed to make sense.

Hildur tied her thick hair in a bun at the nape of her neck. She grabbed a jump rope and set her alarm to go off on repeat every sixty seconds. Slow, simple jumps to start. Then fast hops, switching feet the whole time. For the next minute she did double-unders, with the rope passing under her feet twice during each jump. Her muscles warmed, and her blood began to pump.

Once her body was ready, Hildur adjusted the squat stand to the right height. She took a fifteen-kilogram bar from the rack; it was easier for her to grip it than the thicker twenty-kilogram bar. After a couple of sets of quick reps, she started slapping weights on the bar. As she squatted, she pushed her hips back a little and spread her knees outward. Her legs began to burn deliciously during the long sets.

The previous night's dream about drowning had felt so real. She'd heard the rush of the water and tasted the sea's salt on her lips. Or maybe they'd been tears.

When there were eighty-five kilograms on the barbell, Hildur drew her lungs full of air and held her breath. Using the breath to create pressure in her core supported the lower back in particular. For most people, that was the first thing to give. One, two, three... She held a brief pause and took an especially deep breath. She had two more reps in her. When she rose to her feet for the last time, she didn't have the strength to walk back to the stand, so she let the barbell drop from her upper back to the floor. As it fell, it scraped her skin. Hildur lifted her shirt and looked at herself in the mirror. There was a small abrasion on her upper back. The bleeding stung and brought relief at the same time.

After her workout, Hildur lay on her back on the floor and stretched her legs. She closed her eyes to relax, but the nocturnal wave instantly returned. Hildur didn't understand where the wave was coming from or why. Her fear was surfacing nearby, but it kept escaping her grasp.

Chapter 46

Westfjords, 1994

Two months before Rósa and Björk's disappearance

Rakel leaned against the wall and tried to relax. She looked out the entryway window: the dismal, dingy clouds hung so low they'd soon touch the bottom of the valley. The heavy greyness lent the landscape a blurred quality. The mountains blended with the sky; the road broke off at the wrong place. Rakel held her aching head in her left hand as she dialled the number from memory with her right.

'Hi, it's Rakel. I'm sorry, I forgot to call on the right day. Happy birthday.'

'Don't be silly. I didn't do much to celebrate. We went for a long walk and made pancakes.'

'I'm glad you had a nice day. But listen ... things have got a little complicated over here. Things aren't as they should be. I'm sure we're being watched.' Rakel paused to swallow down her tears. 'I found the cat and kittens in the compost. All dead. I'm pretty sure who did it, but I don't know if I'm thinking straight right now.'

'Maybe you should talk to an outsider about it. Isn't there anyone at the health centre who could give you some resources?'

'I don't think that would change anything. But I do have a different idea.'

Rakel pressed the phone to her chest and clenched her fists. She pulled herself together, continued in a steady voice, and explained what she was thinking. She said what was necessary. Her breath started to spasm, like that of a fish flung to dry ground. She spoke in rapid-fire simple sentences, as if afraid she'd run out of time.

'Please do it for my sake,' Rakel said, and ended the call.

Chapter 47

Ísafjörður, March 2020

Hildur smelled the yellow-brown goop and decided it was edible. She put the big Tupperware bowl in the microwave and tapped in four minutes. At full power, that should be enough to heat up the healthy serving of lamb stew. After Hildur's last visit, her Aunt Tinna had pressed a box of food on her to take home.

There's plenty here for the three of us, Hildur thought to herself as she took the mash of potatoes and ground lamb from the microwave. Luckily Beta and Jakob hadn't had lunch yet. Hildur set the table: the Tupperware bowl, three plates, three forks, and a roll of paper towels.

Beta praised the table setting for its practicality.

'Tell your aunt thank you; this is delicious,' she said after the first forkful. 'Does she use rib meat?'

Hildur's mouth was full, so she settled for a nod.

They were supposed to have met before noon, as soon as Jakob and Hildur returned from Reykjavík. But a staff planning meeting at the daycare centre meant it hadn't opened until the afternoon. Beta had had to stay home with the kids. Once again, her husband hadn't been able to take time off work, and she'd been forced to be flexible. So now they were going over the case while they ate.

The day's paper lay open on the table. As Hildur shifted it aside to make room for her plate, her eyes struck on an article. She quickly scanned it.

A Europe-wide SIS alert had been put out on Dísa. The news had immediately spread to the local papers. MURDER SUSPECT ON THE RUN, screamed the headline. The photograph was years old, as Little Kata had claimed over the phone. Dísa's skin was weathered, her overall appearance dishevelled. Two thin, red braids framed a pale, freckled face. Her overgrown bangs concealed some of her penetrating gaze.

'I'm just wondering...' Hildur began, scraping up the last of her mashed potatoes with her fork and shoving the fork in her mouth. She thought back to the crime scene: the exposed, snowy site accessible from all directions. The shortest trip there was from one of the two car parks: the one for the downhill slopes or the cross-country tracks. It was likely the perp had left their car in either and crossed the snow on skis or snowshoes. 'Could Dísa really be the killer? I looked it up, and she's never had a firearm permit. Hitting a moving target from a distance isn't something that happens by chance. You have to know what you're doing.'

Jakob gathered up the empty plates and set them on a stool until it was time to wash up. 'A permit doesn't mean anything. Maybe some of her less sober friends taught her.'

Beta chimed in: 'In Gunnar's case, her involvement seems possible.'

Hildur agreed. Cleaning staff could move around without drawing attention to themselves or their doings. As an airport cleaner, it would have been relatively easy for Dísa to approach a privately owned plane and fiddle with the fuel tank cap.

'But what if she has an alibi for both killings?' Hildur insisted.

Beta looked back down at the newspaper. 'Well, it would have been nice to ask her, but she packed up and cleared out.' She let out a weary sigh and lowered her voice: 'And it may be these two cases have nothing to do with each other. That would mean we're looking for two different perps and we don't have a single credible suspect. Or maybe our friend Gunnar just forgot to replace the cap after refuelling.'

In theory, all alternatives were possible, but Hildur had to admit the signs were pointing at Dísa.

'Did anything come out of that search of Dísa's home?' Jakob asked, reaching for his knitting needles. Hildur registered what he held in his hands: huge, weird-looking safety pins. She couldn't help asking about them, despite their having nothing to do with the case at hand.

'I'm connecting the sleeves to the body; I'm moving the armpit loops aside. These big safety pins are a heck of a lot better for that than normal needles or bits of yarn that easily snap,' Jakob said, pinching the ten-centimetre-long safety pin shut between his thumb and forefinger.

Hildur shook her head. Despite loving sweaters, she understood nothing about knitting. The previous autumn, Jakob had knitted her a beautiful multicoloured brown sweater. It had instantly become her favourite.

Beta had spoken with her colleague in Reykjavík that morning. Hildur figured nothing much must have turned up or Beta would have mentioned it right away.

Dísa's home had been an ordinary little studio apartment reminiscent of a dorm room. A narrow bed, clothes neatly piled on an IKEA shelf, and a minimum of cosmetics in the bathroom. No traces of anything suspicious. Not so much as a beer bottle in the fridge.

'The investigators collected fibre and DNA samples. A few fibres were recovered from the maintenance shed at the ski track, and they're going to compare the samples collected from Dísa's home to them. But we're working with pretty slim pickings,' Beta said.

They just had to hope Dísa ended up in the authorities' clutches as soon as possible.

Hildur's desk phone rang. She walked to her office and lifted the receiver. Before she could even finish saying her name, a deep male voice launched into a loud, rapid-fire harangue. The words came in a single panicked outburst:

'Goddammit! What's wrong with you people? Have you all lost your minds? You'd better slam on the brakes, and fast. I'm sure Dísa hasn't done a thing. A SIS alert? Really? She's done honest work for years cleaning up other people's messes and what do you do? You suspect her of a homicide! Do better.'

The call ended as abruptly as it had begun. It had been a poor connection, but Hildur thought she'd caught it all. She put down the receiver and rejoined Jakob and Beta, who were looking at her questioningly.

'Who was that?'

'Hmm. Some lunatic who saw the article about Dísa in the paper,' Hildur said, pulling her hair tight at the back of her neck, then using an elastic to tie off a ponytail.

Whenever the police made information public, they received not only useful calls but many from lonely individuals who needed someone to talk to or people who'd been estranged from reality for years. But all calls had to be taken and all emails opened, because one never knew beforehand what would be relevant and what wouldn't. Nevertheless, these pointless attempts at contact were irritating, because they stole time from real work.

Hildur was on the verge of lifting the dirty plates from the stool and taking them to the sink when she abruptly stopped. She'd suddenly realised something. Just a minute. What was it the caller just said on the phone? Holy smoke! He'd just given her some critical information.

Chapter 48

Westfjords, 1994

A month before Rósa and Björk's disappearance

There was a knock at the door. Rakel was so startled she splashed her coffee onto the newspaper. She grabbed a dish cloth from the counter, pressed the coffee stains out of the paper, and hurried into the entryway.

Rakel had been reading the news. The girls had just left for school, and Rúnar had been at sea since early September and wouldn't be returning to Ísafjörður until early November. She'd made the most of the quiet morning.

Rakel reached for the handle and pulled open the door. A man in a flannel shirt stood there, looking lost. Rakel started. When she took a second look, she recognised him. He was a little older than her and had a big scar running across his face. *Jón*. Rakel had heard the stories about him, and they weren't very uplifting. She'd occasionally seen him in passing at the petrol station or supermarket, but other than that he seemed to keep to himself. Like her.

Jón rubbed his scarred forehead and coughed apologetically. 'Um, good morning. I ran out of petrol. I left my car over at the side of the road. No one was home at the neighbours' so I walked here. Do you happen to have a canister and some petrol I could borrow that would get me to the nearest service station?' He pulled a wrinkled bill from his pocket and held it out to Rakel. 'I'll pay. I just need to get to work.'

Rakel felt the tension dissipate. A passerby had come for help, not to cause trouble. The guy seemed genuinely worried.

Rakel put on her shoes and took her long autumn coat from the rack. 'Let's go around to the back of the barn. We have petrol, and I'm sure we can find a canister too.'

She gestured for him to put his money back in his pocket. She didn't want to profit from another's misfortune.

Behind the barn, Rakel poured petrol from the large container into a red plastic five-litre canister. When it was full, she screwed on the cap. 'This should get you to the service station.'

Jón seemed delighted. He thanked Rakel effusively.

'I'll walk you to your car, so you don't have to make another trip to bring back the empty canister,' Rakel suggested.

Jón's expression changed. He instantly closed up. 'No, I'll walk by myself. I'll bring it right back. I'll drive back this way.'

Rakel didn't give in. 'But I love to walk. I need some fresh air and it will give me a chance to stretch my legs. Besides, you're shivering. Don't you have something warmer to wear? It's almost winter.' She grabbed an off-white sweater from the hook next to the door and handed it to Jón. 'Here; you'll warm up faster. That north wind is really cold today.'

And with that, she stalked off decisively toward Jón's car.

He let the sweater dangle from his hand and took a couple of quicker steps to catch up to Rakel. 'Please don't come.'

Rakel stopped and turned. She eyed Jón probingly. He'd shown up at her door asking for help, said his car had died on the outskirts of her farm. She had a right to know. Her resolve caught her off guard. She stared at Jón until he gave in.

'I have stuff in my car no one is supposed to know about,' he said.

A fencer of stolen goods. No surprise there. Ísafjörður was rife with rumours about Jón's shady businesses.

'I'm not interested in your stuff. I just want the canister back. It belongs to my husband, and I don't want it to be misplaced. You can return the sweater later.' Rakel turned and continued walking to the car.

For a moment, they made their way in silence.

'Can you make a living selling stuff that way?' Rakel asked, startling herself with her directness.

Jón rubbed the scar on his forehead with his free hand and mumbled something Rakel couldn't make out. She interpreted it as an affirmative response.

'Do you do a lot of jobs like that?' Rakel continued. She didn't want to judge; she was merely curious. If there was anyone who knew everyone had their personal cross to bear, it was Rakel. Out here, beyond the reach of God, the tax authorities, and medical services, people did what they had to to survive.

Jón shot Rakel a cagey, surprised glance. But he still answered. 'Now and again. When someone pays me to. I don't really have a lot of other options.'

Rakel nodded and took a moment to process this information.

They arrived at Jón's car. It was a few years old and parked roadside at the turn-off. Jón opened the fuel hatch, twisted off the cap, and started pouring the petrol into the tank.

Rakel watched Jón as he went about his business. Everyone knew who he was, but no one seemed to know him very well. Jón behaved oddly, and the scar made him scary. People gave him a wide berth. Even the nosiest gossips never sought out his company.

Jón tipped in the last of the petrol, closed the fuel hatch, and handed the empty canister back to Rakel. 'Are you sure you don't want me to pay?'

Rakel nodded firmly. 'I don't want your money. But I have a proposal for you.'

Chapter 49

Ísafjörður, March 2020

Hildur cracked the conference room window. She, Beta, and Jakob had been sitting in the closed space for too long. Breathing instantly felt easier.

Hildur strained to remember and did the best she could to repeat word for word what the irrational-sounding man had just said on the phone. 'And then I realised something.'

Beta and Jakob looked at Hildur expectantly.

'How did the caller know Dísa has been working as a cleaner for years? There's no mention of a job in the press release.'

'What are you getting at?' Beta asked, then sneezed three times. She looked unusually tired. Her skin was grey and her eyes were bloodshot.

Hildur tossed the ponytail that had fallen to her torso over her shoulder and sniffled. Hopefully she wasn't coming down with something too. Now was not the time to get sick.

'Whoever that caller is knows Dísa. It's someone who knows her well and is clearly convinced of her innocence.'

Beta blew her nose and tossed the tissue into the rubbish. 'A coworker or friend, maybe?'

Hildur was sceptical. 'She didn't really have Icelandic co-workers. This guy spoke Icelandic without an accent. And do you remember what her co-workers said? Dísa kept to herself. She didn't seem to have a very wide circle of friends. But you never know . . .'

Hildur consulted her notes. Even though the numbers she called were stored in her phone's memory, she always wrote them down, too, just to be sure. She checked to see who the number was registered to. An address came up immediately:

Axel Jónasson, Nesgata 4, Hafnir.

'In the middle of nowhere,' Hildur explained to Jakob.

Hafnir was a small, poor cluster of homes near Keflavík International Airport. The village on the flat, windy expanse was home to no more than a hundred or so residents. The houses were derelict. Those who could had moved away – at least to Keflavík, or all the way to Reykjavík. Those who had no choice remained. The police knew a lot of sad stories from Hafnir. Despite its small size, the village required an inordinate number of visits from law enforcement. Drinking and violence.

'Give me the name, and I'll look into his background,' Beta said, snatching the note from Hildur's hand.

Once Beta left, Hildur sat down next to Jakob. He was knitting; Hildur lost herself in staring at his hands. Observing the monotonous motion was relaxing. There was something meditative about the steady clink of the needles and the slithering movement of the yarn.

She considered the motive of the man who'd just called. Why had he been so sure of Dísa's innocence? Had Dísa been with him at the time of the murders? Had Axel known the real murderer? Or was it possible that he himself was the killer?

Hildur heard a clank as Jakob lowered his knitting to the table. He took a deep breath, as if considering what he was about to say. 'Listen, this has nothing to do with the current investigation, but there's something I have to ask you.'

Hildur turned to her colleague. She could tell from the look in his eyes that he was serious. The intensity of his gaze was unsettling. She pushed back her chair so she could get up from the table. But Jakob grabbed her arm and stopped her.

'You've driven me around the Westfjords,' he said. 'We've been to a lot of beaches and several villages. But you've never shown me where you've lived as a child.'

Jakob seemingly registered Hildur's distress, because he released her arm. 'I can go there with you if you want. Maybe visiting the scene would allow memories to surface?'

Hildur didn't respond. She'd be lying if she claimed the idea hadn't occurred to her. The sense that she was approaching something like a turning point felt encouraging and frightening at the same time. The Hermann and Gunnar investigations had consumed all her attention recently, but even so, images of Tinna and her mother and her father had started to bubble up. And somewhere beyond reach of her memories, there was Hulda. Hulda, who for the most part remained invisible.

Jakob looked like he wouldn't give up until Hildur answered him. She didn't feel like discussing the matter just now, when she had so many things going through her head.

'We'll see,' she eventually sighed.

Just then Beta approached the door to the conference room. She didn't step inside. She looked even paler, and had a doubtful look on her face. 'The infectious disease clinic just called Óliver. He tested positive for Covid. We have to quarantine at home. You two will have to get tested too.'

The chair clunked as Hildur popped to her feet. 'Goddammit.'

They'd be losing a third of their manpower just as the investigation was reaching a critical stage. The timing was catastrophic.

Beta looked miserable. She'd been advised to leave work immediately.

Nevertheless, she'd spoken with someone she knew at the Keflavík police station about Axel. The address in Hafnir fell within the station's remit. 'He promised to handle it right away. Apparently things are quiet there; the travel restrictions mean the airport is pretty dead. We'll continue coordinating online or by phone.'

Beta fetched her belongings from her office and waved at Hildur and Jakob before shuffling down the dim corridor and disappearing.

The room was cool now. Hildur stood to close the window. Looking out, she saw Beta's receding, vaguely hunched figure melt into the grey townscape and vanish around the corner.

Hildur glanced at Jakob, who was rapping the tabletop with his needles. 'Two murders, two police officers. Hopefully there won't be any more bodies.'

'There's only one thing that really worries me right now,' Jakob said, tapping his nose with a needle. 'How deep are they going to insert the swab?'

Chapter 50

Jakob rubbed his neck and plopped down on the couch.

After Beta's departure, he and Hildur had exchanged thoughts about Dísa. They'd agreed it was unlikely she'd be apprehended in Spain in the near future. The SIS alert included a request for automatic extradition, but Spain was five times the size of Iceland and home to forty-seven million people. Dísa had flown to Málaga and could have travelled on to just about anywhere from there. Finding one young Icelandic woman would take some time. No social media accounts had been found in Dísa's name, and her Icelandic phone number hadn't been in use for several days now. They'd called all Dísa's co-workers and neighbours again, but no one had been able to tell them anything except she'd come to work in the mornings and gone home in the evenings. She seemed to have been alone in the world.

After work, Jakob and Hildur had gone to the local hospital to be tested for Covid. Then Jakob had gone home. The test results had been promised by the following morning.

Jakob set two glasses of beer on the coffee table. Guðrún had come to his place straight from work and now sat on the couch, wrapped in a blanket. They hadn't seen each other for a couple of days, and it felt like a long time. Airline employees had been calling in sick, so Guðrún had taken some extra shifts and spent the past couple days traversing the airspace between Reykjavík and Akureyri.

Theoretically Jakob wasn't supposed to see anyone before he got his test results, but Guðrún was an exception. If she got sick, they could quarantine together. That didn't sound half-bad.

Guðrún reached for one of the glasses of beer. 'I'm so glad I don't have to go to the airport tomorrow. I'm going to sleep in until nine if not later, then go into the shop to place orders.'

Just now Jakob was so happy he had a hard time accepting it. He knew he and Guðrún had only known each other a few months. The initial infatuation had been amazing and intense. It was like being swallowed up in a new space where nothing felt the way it usually did. There was more to it, though. Guðrún was so sincere about everything. He never had to wonder what kind of mood she'd be in or whether she might like something or not. She was always direct with him. That put him at ease.

'Listen, there's something I'd like to ask you. Promise me you'll say no if it feels awkward.'

Guðrún set her glass back down on the table and sat up straighter: 'I promise. What do you need?'

'I turned to the Finnish Ministry of Justice for help. They're asking the Norwegian authorities to step in and request mediation with Lena.'

Guðrún looked delighted.

'Don't get too excited,' Jakob said. Talking with the expert at the Ministry of Justice was merely the first step. Chances were there would be no mediation process and Jakob would have to take the matter to the Norwegian courts.

'I've made a list of all the meetings and calls Lena has sabotaged. There are dozens of them,' Jakob continued. And then he explained his plan.

If he had to turn to the courts to seek enforcement of his visitation rights, it might be useful to have evidence of Lena's attempts at sabotage. The lawyer had told Jakob his own notes might not suffice. The unfortunate fact was a foreigner was inevitably in a weaker position due to language skills alone.

'I have a videocall scheduled with Matias today. Could you film the call with your phone?'

Guðrún took hold of her wavy blonde hair and gathered it into a bunch over her left shoulder. Jakob had noticed she did it whenever concentration was required. But there was something about Guðrún's expression that made him regret having asked for her help. She looked a little uncertain.

'Argh, I shouldn't have got you mixed up in this. I apologise. Please forget what I just asked. It was stupid of me . . .' Jakob found himself stumbling over his words and lowered his face into his hands.

Guðrún reached for his wrist. 'Come on, don't start being silly now, since you haven't been before. Of course I'll film the call.' She paused as she searched for the words. 'I just choked because we haven't done anything like this before. You know what I mean?'

'Filmed a crazy ex's calls?'

There wasn't much they could do but laugh. Besides, laughter lightened the fraught moment. It made it easier to breathe.

'OK, man-bun,' Guðrún said, nudging Jakob in the shoulder. 'Time to get dressed and whip out our phones.'

The blue-and-white Skype logo appeared on the screen of Jakob's phone. He was at the kitchen table, and he selected Lena's number to place the call. Guðrún was sitting at an angle behind him, recording the moment. She wouldn't be able to see Lena, and Lena wouldn't be able to see her.

The videocall connected. Once again, Jakob had decided to start off with a good-natured but not overly familiar approach. He didn't want to annoy Lena.

'Hi, Lena, how are you?' he began casually. Lena had wanted to make Jakob dance to her tune, and that's exactly what he'd done. He tried to please her so he'd be able to talk with his son. It made him feel cheap.

Lena gave a noncommittal response. Jakob decided the Norwegian authorities hadn't reached out to her, at least not yet. She would have no doubt made some snarky comment if they had. The bureaucrat at the Ministry of Justice had urged Jakob to not discuss the issue directly with the child's mother. He'd advised Jakob to leave the matter to the authorities.

'Are you guys at home?' Jakob asked.

'You don't need to know where we are,' Lena retorted.

Jakob reflected: about twenty seconds had passed before the first punch. He decided to cut to the chase.

'Could I speak with Matias, please? We have a videocall scheduled for today.' He did everything in his power to keep his voice as calm as possible.

He heard Lena call out to Matias, who was apparently in the other room. 'Could you come to the phone? There's a man here who wants to talk to you.'

'Lena, I'm Matias's father. Not some man.'

Lena turned to the screen in evident frustration. 'You tried to control me the whole time we were together. What I looked like, what I ate, what I said. You can't do that anymore. I can call you whatever I want!'

Jakob shut his eyes and silently counted to five. He was on the verge of losing his cool and strained to maintain it. 'What you just said isn't true. I've never controlled you. I'm Matias's father, and you have to let him see me, *his father*. I'm not some man; I'm his dad.'

Matias appeared on the screen. He climbed into his mother's lap, stuffed dinosaur held tightly at his side. Jakob saw it was the one he'd given Matias during the Christmas vacation. That instantly made him feel good.

'Who's on the iPad?' Matias asked his mother, taking a closer look at the screen.

Lena held the boy in her lap, cast a bored look at Jakob, and eventually said the F word: '*Far*. Your father.'

Matias looked at the screen in confusion. His grip on the green dinosaur tightened, and he turned to his mother. 'No, it's not. That's not *far*. *Far*'s over there,' Matias whispered to Lena, pointing somewhere off-screen.

'Matias, what have you been up to today?' Jakob's voice had started to quiver. He wanted to forget what his son had just said. *That's not far*. He tried to breathe steadily but his breaths grew shallower and shallower. Suddenly he felt incredibly tired.

'Filip. Filip is *far*, Filip is *far*,' Matias started repeating. When he realised the power of his words, he continued chanting and squirmed down from his mother's lap. 'Filip is *far*, Filip is *far* . . . *Faaaar* . . .'

'Who's Filip?' Jakob asked Lena.

Lena behaved the way she had in similar situations in the past; she expressed her discomfort in malice. Jakob saw her glance pointedly over the screen. Jakob guessed she was looking at Filip.

'Who is he? And what does he mean, father? I'm the father.'

'That's absolutely none of your business.'

'I'd like to talk to Matias some more. Could you please bring him the iPad in his room so we could talk privately? Could you please do that, Lena?'

Jakob hated himself right now. He hated himself for begging.

'You saw yourself that he doesn't want to talk anymore. Stop harassing us. Goodbye.' Lena ended the call, and the screen went dark.

Jakob's head went dark too. As if a hood had been pulled over it. A fearful thought flashed through his mind: he was losing something that would be hard to get back.

He lowered his phone to the kitchen table, stood, and clenched his right fist. He shouted something unintelligible and punched the door between the living room and the kitchen. There was a loud crack as the wood split. He slowly turned around, knuckles dripping blood.

Guðrún was still holding her phone. Her eyes were moist, and her cheeks were flushed.

When their eyes met, neither of them could hold back the tears.

Chapter 51

Westfjords, November 1994

Two days after Rósa and Björk's disappearance

It was November, and the time was 8 p.m. The fridge was humming. If the clock hadn't been ticking on the wall, one might have thought time had stopped. The sun had set hours ago, and no one had remembered to turn on the outdoor lights. All that could be seen beyond the window was darkness.

Rakel was crying. She'd been crying almost non-stop for two days. She'd dozed off and on for a few hours, but the quality of the sleep was such that she'd woken even more tired. Exhaustion and grief were slicing through her layer by layer, like a sharp knife into soft fruit.

She shifted her blurry eyes from the window and glanced at the kitchen table: a Thermos half-filled with coffee, a few cups, a carton of milk that had been left standing for hours. The police officers and two search party members seated there stared silently at their hands. Only one person, the neighbour sitting at the end of the bench, would look at her. There was empathy in the gaze.

Rakel tried to establish eye contact with the policemen and the searchers, but they refused to look back. Lips pinched, they shifted uneasily in their seats and rubbed their thumbs. Eventually the younger one gave in under the pressure and sighed deeply:

'Our dog disappeared once. We found it a week later in the mountains. It was starving.'

The older police officer shot his colleague a cautioning look and kicked him under the table.

'I'm sor ... I mean, I'm sorry, I didn't ...' the young man stammered, uttering the remainder of his sentence in such a soft voice that his words were drowned out by the hum of the refrigerator.

According to the clock, they'd been sitting at this table for almost three hours. Rakel felt curiously tranquil. Her movements were stiff and slow. Her headache had intensified. Her insides hurt.

Rakel reached for the Thermos, untwisted the cap, and refilled her cup. The coffee had been sitting so long it was only lukewarm, but it would have to do. The old-fashioned tablecloth squeaked as she set the Thermos back down. She encouraged the men to help themselves.

Then: 'Have you heard from the search party?'

The grey-haired man in a light-blue sweater looked relieved at having been asked a precise, concrete question. He was a volunteer with the local rescue patrol and been assigned to wait at the home of the missing children.

'I spoke to them half an hour ago. No update. The dog went back and followed the trail again, but it ended at the tunnel's mouth. A driver saw the girls walking along the side of the road. There haven't been any sightings of them since. But they're still searching. Let's just try to stay calm.'

Rakel thanked him with a slight nod. She wrapped her palm around her cup and lowered her gaze to its contents. She stared at the coffee in silence, rocking herself back and forth.

*

After her visitors left, Rakel went into the bathroom. She washed her hands and looked at herself in the mirror. Her skin was grey, her hair a mess, her cheeks bright red. She spread a soothing lotion on her face. Then she took a comb from the bathroom counter and began unsnarling her hair. She winced. Her head felt tender, but she kept combing. Tiny red drops dripped to the sink. She'd pressed too hard. As it struck the white porcelain, the drops formed uneven, comet-shaped splotches. Rakel damped the corner of a hand towel and pressed it to her scalp, then wiped her forehead. She ran water from the tap and tried to clean the bloodstained sink with her other hand. Then she reached for the tap and turned it off.

When she looked back up, she jumped. Hildur was standing there in the hallway, staring mutely at Rakel's reflection. The girl's eyes were wide and questioning but she didn't speak. Hildur hadn't said a word since the evening before last. She'd been lying in her dark room under the covers. She hadn't even reacted when Rakel told her the police had arrived to help with the search.

'Hildur,' Rakel whispered, turning around.

But Hildur was gone. Rakel heard a door thunk shut at the end of the hall. Silence fell over the house.

Rakel carefully set the comb back down next to the sink. She took an elastic band from the medicine cabinet, collected her smooth, combed hair into a loose ponytail at her nape, and thought about her firstborn daughter. The morning of the day before yesterday, Hildur had said she felt sick. She'd had a headache, and her stomach had hurt. The illness meant she'd stayed home in bed. She hadn't spoken since.

Rakel sighed and took another glance in the mirror. A weary woman looked back at her. Her swollen eyelids and pulled-back hair aged her. She parted her dry, pinched lips and whispered so softly she could barely hear herself: 'I suppose this is all for a reason.'

These are the lies we tell ourselves, and Rakel wanted to believe them.

Chapter 52

Kotsdalur, March 2020

Hildur had just returned from a run. Her sweaty running jacket was hanging from the doorknob, airing out. The insoles from her running shoes were drying on the entryway radiator.

She'd meant to go surfing as soon as she'd woken. But when she smelled the sea-stink on her neoprene suit she'd immediately changed her mind. She'd understood she still wasn't ready to venture back into the waves. That made her sad.

To shake off the unpleasant feeling, Hildur had gone for a run in the woods. There was a small coniferous forest at the base of the fjord, near the golf range, summer cabins and camping area. The area was full of life in the summer, but it was still so early in the year she hadn't come across a single soul.

It took half an hour to run from the centre of Ísafjörður to the trees. A rarity in the area, they were what made the place special. When Norwegians had colonised the island over a thousand years before, over a quarter of its land area had been covered by birch woods. Within a hundred years, they'd all been chopped down. Iceland's forests had yet to recover. Erosion depleted the soil, and the treeless tundra spread. As a result of reforestation efforts, small clusters of trees had been successfully planted in places around the country, including here on the slopes of Ísafjörður's mountains.

Hildur had done a few maxi-sprints on the forested paths, then jogged home. The fifteen-kilometre run had taken her an hour and a half. That was a good time, when you considered half the trip was uphill.

Hildur was sitting on the living room floor, stretching her glutes, when there was a knock at the door. A moment later, she heard Jakob's voice in the entryway.

'Let's make some coffee to celebrate. My results came back negative too,' he said, swinging the bagged pastry in his hand. Hildur had texted him about her negative Covid test results before heading out to exercise.

'You want to put the coffee on while I jump in the shower?' Hildur didn't usually care for uninvited guests suddenly appearing in her living room, but Jakob was an exception.

Through the rush of the shower, she heard comforting sounds from the kitchen. It felt surprisingly nice to have someone bustling around in her home. At the same time, Hildur was perfectly clear she had no interest in a steady boyfriend. Even with Freysi, she hadn't been completely sure what she'd wanted. She'd been a loner since childhood. That's why it was odd the presence of another person in her kitchen didn't feel so impossible after all.

Hildur stepped out of the shower and realised all her bath towels were in the laundry. She'd have to make time to wash clothes tomorrow. She grabbed a hand towel from the shelf and used it to dry herself.

Maybe she'd eventually find someone to share more than the occasional evening with. Someone who'd do the laundry with her now and again.

To save time, Hildur had moved some of the contents of her wardrobe from the bedroom into the bathroom. It was handy having clothes within reach when she stepped out of the shower. She took a pair of high-waisted underwear and a sports bra from the basket, then pulled on a pair of old blue jeans and a T-shirt emblazoned with Ísafjörður's coat of arms.

The kitchen smelled of baked goods. Jakob took two red mugs from the cupboard and filled them with coffee.

Hildur and Jakob seated themselves at the table and cut themselves thick slices of danish. After devouring his, Jakob wiped his mouth, placed the crumpled paper towel on his plate, and pushed the plate aside.

'So what do you think? Why did your mum know someone known around town as a criminal?'

'I'm going to have another cup of coffee,' Hildur instantly interjected. 'You want one?' She stood and reached for the coffeepot. Without waiting for an answer, she refilled both cups and took a long sip of her own.

'Bjarni knew your family,' Jakob continued. 'He remembered your mother in particular; he said she seemed unhappy to him. I know this sounds awful, but we have to consider this scenario too. Has it ever occurred to you things might not have been the way they should have been in your home? Is it possible your mother did something to your sisters?'

Hildur fell silent. She felt the revolting taste of bile rise into her mouth. The thought of familicide was horrific and incomprehensible to her, but in the darkest hours of the night, she'd wondered the same thing.

'If she did something to my sisters, why was I left alive?'

Jakob twirled the coffee cup in his hands and eyed Hildur at length. He didn't know what to say. Who would, after being asked a question like that?

Hildur had always believed her childhood had been completely ordinary – until her little sisters had disappeared on the way home from school, that is. She'd never suspected anything. Their day-to-day life had been completely normal.

Jakob deposited the empty plates in the sink and stood there leaning against the counter. 'You and I are going to drive out to your childhood home. You said you haven't been back since your parents died.'

Hildur could see the insistence in Jakob's eyes. He held out his upturned palm to her: 'Brenda's keys. We're driving there now.'

Hildur shook her head. 'No way. We have to get to work!'

Jakob thrust his hand closer. 'No one needs anything from us right now. We haven't heard from Beta yet. She promised to call as soon as she found out anything from Keflavík. There's nothing for us to do.' He wiggled his fingers impatiently, demanding the keys.

Hildur shook her head. But it was pointless, because she knew she'd already given in. She took the keys from the hook and placed them in Jakob's palm.

Half an hour later, they emerged from the dark, narrow tunnel Hildur feared and hated. Luckily they'd only come upon two passenger vehicles inside. Jakob had driven steadily and surely, pulling over at the turnouts to let the oncoming cars pass.

A view of a fog-enshrouded valley opened up outside Brenda's windows. The murk made the surroundings boundless and soft. Contours vanished.

Hildur told Jakob about the fog. It spoke of the presence of the hidden people. These invisible nature-dwellers only showed themselves to humans when they wanted to. Countless stories told of shepherds who wandered off in the mountains after losing their sense of direction in a dense fog. If the shepherd was a good person, the hidden folk helped him find his way back home. If the hidden folk considered him immoral, they lured him further and further and led him to a cliff to die.

'Mist is a blurry boundary between our world and theirs,' she concluded.

Jakob didn't reply; he just kept his eyes glued to the road. They drove in silence. Hildur kept pointing him in the right direction until they came to a fork in the road.

'Where to now?'

Hildur closed her eyes and felt the grief swell in her breast. She hadn't been here since the police had come knocking on Tinna's door.

Are you related to Rakel Helgadóttir? the officers had asked. There had been two of them. The older man had held his hands behind his back and handled the talking. The younger officer, probably a trainee, had stood quietly on a lower step, staring at the door frame. Hildur had been barely a teenager at the time. She'd peered at the visitors from behind her aunt's back. It had struck her as strange that the younger police officer hadn't so much as looked at her or Tinna.

Could we come in and sit down? We have some unpleasant news. There was a serious car accident in a fjord a hundred kilometres away. Rakel and Rúnar were in the car and ... well ... and well, neither one survived.

Hildur remembered how her aunt had gasped and started to scream.

The poor little girl doesn't have anyone anymore. Anyone. The poor little girl doesn't ...

That's what Tinna had said over and over for two days. Rocked herself at the edge of couch and kept repeating herself. The police had sent a county social worker to visit them the next day. The quiet, grey-haired woman had let her eyes wander the walls and said everything seemed fine and they could call this number if things got too hard. They could always go to the emergency room at the hospital too.

After that, it had just been the two of them, Hildur and Tinna. Not much later, the embolisms had robbed Tinna of her eyesight, but even so she'd always looked after Hildur. Hildur's aunt had cared so deeply that she'd never taken Hildur back to her old house. The two of them had started a new life together.

Jakob lowered a hand to Hildur's back. 'You have to visit at least once.'

Hildur tossed her head to the right. One of the Kotsdalur valley farms stood at the end of that road. The other was to the left. Both farms were uninhabited these days. Hildur's parents' land had been left to her when they died, but she hadn't done anything with it. She paid the property tax and the road maintenance fee every year, but she'd never even been as far as the crossing to have a look.

Brenda rocked from side to side on the bumpy road. Empty for decades, the house up ahead looked like a mockery of a home. The windowpanes were shattered, and the paint was peeling. The front door's hinges had given way, leaving the door hanging half-open. The partially melted snow revealed patches of mouldering brown earth.

Jakob pulled up next to a crooked, half-collapsed stone wall. Everything seemed hazy to Hildur. Maybe it was because of the thick mist that had settled in the valley. Jakob was standing at her side in the muddy yard of her former home. A little further away, she saw an old barn-like structure that had collapsed in one corner. Even though she couldn't see it from this angle, Hildur remembered there was a pen behind the barn.

'That was the stable. The horses were taken ... That's right, the neighbours came and took them,' she managed to say.

They were only a couple of hundred metres from the sea. Hildur deduced from the crash of the waves that they were medium sized, even though she couldn't see the water through the curtain of fog.

'What was your special spot here?' Jakob asked, as if reading Hildur's mind.

Hildur pointed toward the sea with her right hand. She couldn't move the left one, because Jakob was holding onto it. 'I liked being down by the water. Especially when Mum made us play outside. I'd go down to the shore, while my sisters would go to the pen to be with the horses.'

Jakob nodded and started slowly walking toward the house. He pushed on the peeling front door. It complained loudly but opened.

Jakob stepped in first and pressed the light switch. The ceiling light didn't come on, of course. The buildings in Kotsdalur hadn't had power for years. The day was so grey that very little light penetrated the small windows. Jakob stuck his free hand into his coat pocket for the torch and turned it on.

'Did she make you go outside because she had visitors?'

Hildur shook her head and lowered her gaze. 'Maybe. I don't know.'

Jakob led Hildur into the entryway, which had a view of the kitchen. Almost everything had disappeared over the years. Hildur knew there were gangs who made the rounds of abandoned homes looking for objects and furniture to sell. It was unlikely they'd found anything of value here.

Hildur recognised the three-legged stool in the corner and the little table attached to the wall. Its surface was dotted with the desiccated carcasses of dead flies. A red-and-white cross-stitch of snowflakes hung above the table. Hildur touched the handicraft; it had grown sticky with time.

'I'm guessing you remember more than you think. You weren't that young, after all.'

The pressure inside Hildur swelled. The crooked door swung in the wind. The sea crashed more and more loudly in her ears.

'Who used to visit your mum? Who was it who visited when she made you go outside?'

The waves' crash swelled to a roar. It felt as if she and the sea were drawing closer to each other.

Hildur tried to stumble out of the house, but Jakob refused to let go. The room began to spin. She wanted out. The sea was growing louder. Hildur could feel the wave bearing down. The cold, vertical wall approached at high pressure, and she didn't have time to get out of the way. It swallowed her in a black eddy.

'I remember you telling me your father was out at sea fishing when your sisters disappeared. He didn't participate in the search. Do you remember anyone who participated more than the others? Was there anyone who spent an extraordinary amount of time here with your mother?'

By now the room was spinning so fast that Hildur almost lost her balance. She saw the snowflake cross-stitch on the entryway wall. And suddenly she remembered who'd given it to them.

Chapter 53

Ísafjörður, March 2020

Beta shut her eyes more tightly and tried to calm herself. The plump pillow supporting her upper body did a little to ease her laboured breathing. The burning sensation in her lungs and pulsing pain in her muscles had kicked in along with her positive test result. She was the only member of the family suffering from strong symptoms.

Beta heard sounds from the kitchen. A minute later, the electric kettle started to burble. Judging by the rustling, Óliver was making ramen for the kids.

Beta was furious. She lowered her head to the pillow and struggled to restrain her temper. When she felt this bad, the last thing she needed was any extra palpitations or throbbing veins.

Óliver was the one who'd wanted to move to the Westfjords in the first place. His family was from the area. Initially the notion of moving to the countryside had seemed like a good idea. She'd wanted to work at a small police station, close to the people she was serving and further from the power struggles that plagued big units. But now everything was going to hell.

Óliver had grown more distant over the winter. At first Beta hadn't paid much mind to the change. They were coming up on fifteen years of marriage. There had been a lot of good moments interspersed with some periods that were less good. But Beta had assumed their partnership was permanent. Evidently she'd been mistaken.

Óliver had had to confess where he'd caught Covid. During a business trip to Reykjavík, he'd seen Sofía, who'd just returned from skiing in Austria. From that infamous village of Ischgl, where Europeans on their winter vacations had picked up the virus to bring back home. Sofía and Óliver didn't work at the same company, so it hadn't been hard for Beta to guess what was going on. The worst thing was Óliver hadn't even tried to deny the affair. He simply hadn't said anything. He'd refused to discuss the matter and retreated into his shell, treated Beta as if she didn't exist.

Beta turned over on her belly and dangled her head over the edge of the bed. The position offered her lungs momentary relief. It was hard to get any rest when the whole of your life to date was falling apart. She and Óliver had a mortgage and two small children.

A coughing fit racked her body. The dry hacking scoured her throat and brought tears to her eyes.

If they divorced, she wouldn't be staying in Ísafjörður, that was for sure. If she did, she'd run into Óliver every day. It would be easier to disappear in Reykjavík. On the other hand, Óliver was unlikely to stay either, because his job and the red-headed Sofía were in the capital. Red-headed. After finding out Sofía's surname, Beta had googled a picture of her. Smooth face, big eyes, small mouth. No dark bags under her eyes from lack of sleep.

Should she have made more of an effort? Gone to the salon more often, got more sleep, worn saucier underwear instead of woollen long johns?

Before long, she'd be looking for a new job and a smaller home, a rental.

The stupid thoughts surged into Beta's head, and there was nothing she could do about it. She massaged her temples and tried to cheer herself up. She'd definitely had better days, but she'd live.

Suddenly she remembered she'd received an email from Keflavík about Axel Jónasson. She was the station chief; she ought to remember everything. No one could take on all her duties even if she was ill. Now she'd forgotten something critical.

Beta groped for her phone, opened her email, and saw the much-anticipated message had arrived yesterday afternoon. She cursed her mistake and brought up Hildur's number. The phone rang for a long time but there was no answer.

Beta rolled over onto her back and hauled herself up into a semi-sitting position. Luckily Jakob answered right away.

'Where the hell is Hildur?'

Jakob said Hildur had left a moment ago to pay a visit to the nursing home. Beta wondered what that might have to do with the murder investigation, but she swallowed her words.

'I got an email from Keflavík. I'll forward it to you. Have a look at it with Hildur as soon as she gets back from her excursion, OK?'

Chapter 54

Hildur's family had had a very small circle of friends. There was nothing unusual about that. They'd lived in the countryside. In the 1980s, Iceland had only been home to 220,000 people, 140,000 fewer than today. Even though a greater proportion of the population had lived in rural areas back then, homesteads had been few and far between. There'd been no tourists in rental cars, group sports activities, or annual holidays to sunny places. In the countryside people lived on their farms. Coming across a car on the local road was news, and other people were seen mostly on holidays and when someone needed help.

The only people Hildur remembered aside from her schoolmates, sisters, Aunt Tinna, mother, and distant father were the neighbours, Hallgrímur and Helga. They'd taken over the Efri sheep farm. The two households were the sole residents of Kotsdalur valley.

Hildur had only one clear memory of these neighbours. They'd given her and her sisters a cat, and the cat had spent winter nights sleeping at Hildur's feet.

She remembered the husband having died a few years ago. She'd read an article in the local paper noting that Hallgrímur's death signalled the end of an era. With his passing, the last farm in her home valley, remote Kotsdalur, had been abandoned. The widowed Helga had moved into the county nursing home; there was no way she could have managed the big house on her own.

Hildur closed her office door behind her and glanced at her sports watch. A few minutes to four. Board game hour at the nursing home would be over soon. She had to hurry. She wanted to be there before six, when dinner service began. Hildur had just spoken with a nursing home employee and asked if Helga from Kotsdalur still lived there. She'd used her status as a police officer to get the answers she wanted. Hildur didn't have any reason to see Helga in her role as an officer of the law, but introducing herself as a police officer made it easier to find things out. The nursing home wasn't supposed to release information on its residents to outsiders, but the bright-voiced young woman at reception had blithely told Hildur what unit she'd find Helga in.

The county nursing home was located in a series of three-storey apartment buildings, and Helga's apartment was in the last one. Hildur walked in through the sliding doors and stepped into a pale-yellow stairwell. She started climbing up to the second floor. There was a lift, but Hildur preferred to walk. The stairs were carpeted in a brown rug that muffled sound, ensuring residents weren't bothered by the noise of people moving around the building.

A red wreath hung on the door, wishing visitors 'Merry Christmas'. Hildur knocked. She heard shuffling footfalls inside, and then the door opened. Hildur saw a woman leaning on a rollator, a couple of centimetres of grey at the roots of her black hair.

The woman registered Hildur's glance. 'My hair looks awful. The hairdresser isn't scheduled to come in for colouring for another two weeks. I just hope those darned Covid restrictions don't come into force before then . . .'

Helga moved labouriously and slowly, but she spoke a lot and fast. She gestured for Hildur to enter and backed her rollator toward the living room. 'Whose daughter are you?' she asked, eyeing Hildur.

Helga was hunched, but her eyes twinkled. Hildur made a note of the older woman's surprisingly smooth skin. If she hadn't known how old Helga was, Hildur might have mistaken her for a much younger woman.

Helga's gaze slid from Hildur's eyes to her toes and back up again. Then they stopped. Leaning on her rollator, she took a couple of steps closer and stared Hildur dead in the face.

'Good God. You're Rakel's daughter, aren't you? You have the same eyes. Dark green and sea blue.'

Helga was standing so close that Hildur caught a whiff of just-drunk coffee and some sort of chocolate pastry.

Hildur felt like she was closing in on something important. No words emerged from her lips. Her eyes grew moist, and something heavy rose into her throat. All she could do was nod.

'Dear girl, please sit. Would you like some coffee? I just had some at our board game club, but I'd be happy to make you a cup if you'd like.'

Hildur declined the coffee and seated herself on the couch. The green corduroy upholstery was soft and comfortable. Her eyes sought out the wooden bookcase. It was the exact kind you saw in old people's homes: one shelf was filled with books, another with cross-stitches and silver dishes. Two of the shelves displayed old photographs in wooden frames that had darkened with age. Hildur scanned the pictures. She recognised the people in the wedding photo as Hallgrímur and Helga. They stood side by side, looking seriously into the camera. There were pictures of them working together on the farm and a couple of confirmation portraits, which Hildur deduced were of younger relatives, as in her recollection Helga didn't have children of her own.

One picture sent shivers up Hildur's spine. All the other photos were in wooden frames, but this had been placed in a silver one.

And the silver didn't show any signs characteristic of tarnishing, which meant the frame had been cleaned regularly.

Hildur stood and walked over to the bookcase. She reached for the photo and took a closer look at it. It was of her mother. Rakel was wearing overalls and leaning against a wooden fence. The were sheep in the round pen behind. The picture had been taken in the autumn, when the sheep were brought down from the mountains.

'Rakel was a hard worker,' Helga remarked. Hildur noticed the old woman's eyes glisten as she travelled back into her memories: 'She took care of you girls and the horses and still helped us every autumn getting the sheep ready for slaughter; helped us shear the spring wool and the autumn wool. You used to help too. You'd bag the wool. You were this tall,' Helga said, lowering her trembling hand to hip-height.

'I . . . I'm so late,' Hildur said, searching for the words as she returned the picture to the shelf.

Helga's gaze was full of warmth, and she nodded a couple of times. Her jaw dropped slightly. Hildur realised the old woman was no longer in complete control of her movements.

'I've been trying to figure out what happened to my little sisters that November day. You're the only person who knew my family who I haven't spoken with yet. And I, I . . . I only came now.'

Hildur could no longer hold back the tears. Big, hot trickles streamed down either side of her nose. When the tears made it to her jawbone, she wiped them away.

'Shall we sit?' Helga suggested, pushing her rollator over to the armchair. She groaned as she lowered herself into it. Hildur sat on the couch next to her.

'It was a terrible time. Utterly incomprehensible. No one could understand how two little girls could just disappear like that. Nothing like that had ever happened here in the countryside before.'

'I remember you sitting in our kitchen a lot after my sisters went missing. You brought us a red-and-white cross-stitch and hung it in the entryway.'

Helga nodded and fixed her gaze firmly on Hildur. A beautiful smile had spread across her face. 'I tried to be what help I could . . . That cross-stitch. I brought it, but your mother's the one who hung it up. I remember her pounding a horseshoe nail into the wall.'

They sat there in silence, staring at the photographs on the bookcase. The wall clock ticked on. The faint murmur of cars driving past carried in from outside.

'Is there anything in particular you remember about that period?'

Helga turned from the bookcase to Hildur. 'Dear girl, there's nothing wrong with my memory. But even so, it was almost thirty years ago.'

Hildur understood. What had she been thinking? That a neighbour who'd lived three kilometres up the road would be able to tell her something after all these years?

Helga's hand trembled as she touched her hair. Hildur heard her lungs rattle as she took a deep breath. 'There is one thing I do remember. I don't think it's of any consequence, but it's bothered me ever since. I behaved like such a coward back then . . .'

Hildur pricked up her ears.

'It was autumn. The same year your sisters disappeared. I hid in the entryway and pretended no one was home.' Helga seemed distressed. She turned away from Hildur and hung her head.

Hildur didn't say anything. She waited patiently for the other woman to go on.

Helga looked at the hands in her lap before continuing in a soft voice. She explained how she'd heard the crunch of someone walking outside; they'd just had fresh gravel laid. Helga had looked out the entryway window and seen a car had stopped on the road. Even though it was some distance away, she'd instantly recognised it. There was only one person in the area who had a red Suzuki: Jón.

Helga lowered her voice to a whisper and patted the fat arm of her chair as if to underscore her words. 'Jón was a real good-for-nothing. A believer shouldn't say this, of course, but I wasn't the least bit sorry when he died last autumn.'

Hildur settled for nodding. It was all she could do. Her body felt as immobile as a pillar of salt. Her insides were tingling. It was the same sensation she felt whenever she was approaching some significant clue in a criminal investigation.

'He kept knocking on the door and calling out. But I didn't answer. Hallgrímur wasn't home, and I didn't dare be alone with Jón. I pretended like I wasn't home. He shouted for a while then walked away.'

After a long pause, Helga began sobbing. 'Jón . . . I saw Jón turn onto the road leading to your place. I knew Rakel was home alone. I've never forgiven myself for not having had the sense to call and warn her.'

'Did you and my mother talk about it afterward?'

Helga nodded and said softly: 'Your mother was reluctant to talk about it, but she did tell me Jón had run out of petrol. When I tried to ask more questions, she completely shut down. She and I talked about absolutely everything, or at least I thought we did, until that day. But the only thing she would say about Jón was she'd given him petrol.'

Helga reached into her sleeve for her folded handkerchief and dabbed at her eyes.

She and Hildur sat in silence again, staring at the bookcase. Two women of different ages for whom the smiling Rakel in her silver frame had meant a lot.

Hildur thought about what Helga had told her. Helga had Rakel's picture front and centre on her bookcase. 'I'm guessing you and my mother were very close?'

A fresh warmth radiated from Helga's eyes. Hildur saw the old woman's hands grip the arms of her chair as she nodded, chin trembling. 'Yes, we were. But we were both married too.'

Hildur understood. For the first time, she got the sense she truly comprehended something about her mother she hadn't grasped in the past.

Suddenly memories started surging into her head. She remembered long visits at the neighbours'. How she and her sisters had been allowed to play with the kittens while their mother had helped with the sheep. It was only now that Hildur grasped the visits always took place when Hallgrímur was away.

'My father was away a lot because of his work,' Hildur said. She wouldn't probe for any more information unless Helga volunteered.

Helga nodded and smiled a little through her tears. 'Yes. Your mother was a rather unusual fisherman's wife. She was happiest when Rúnar was at sea. Whenever your father came home, she would get these terrible headaches.'

Helga raised her arm and coughed into her elbow. Then she took hold of her rollator and stood. Its wheels squeaked against the floor. She slowly crossed the room, leaning on it. She stopped at the big window and looked out. A few violets grew in pots on the windowsill.

'I have only one regret in life,' Helga said, plucking dried blooms from the houseplants.

Hildur moved over to the edge of the sofa and leaned all the way forward, as if trying to get closer to the past.

'That I didn't have the courage to leave. If I had, things might have turned out differently.'

'What do you mean?'

Helga said she and Rakel had toyed with the idea of leaving. Rakel would have taken the girls, and the five of them would have moved away together. Somewhere far from Kotsdalur. Preferably abroad. But they hadn't had the money or the courage. Helga said that ultimately she hadn't been able to leave Hallgrímur. He'd been so good to her.

Hildur couldn't believe her ears. Had her mother actually planned on leaving her father and moving away with the girls? Why? For love? It struck her as such a strange notion. How little we really knew about each other in the end.

'After your sisters disappeared, I tried to support Rakel as best I could. We spent a lot of time together that winter. Rakel knew I would never leave the farm, so she stopped talking to me about leaving for good. But now and again she would plan some short trip so we could spend some time together alone.'

'One day she surprised me. She'd already booked us an inn and bought the tickets. But then... Just before we were supposed to leave, that horrible car accident happened, and I never saw my Rakel again.'

Helga's voice had softened to a whisper. She pinched a dry leaf from the nearest violet between her forefinger and thumb and gave it a gentle tug.

Hildur felt her breath catch. 'Where had you two planned on going?'

Helga slowly turned around and looked right at Hildur. Tears welled up in her eyes again. Hildur noticed the old woman's fist unclench, and the dead blossoms fall to the floor.

'To the Faroe Islands. That's where we were supposed to go.'

Chapter 55

Westfjords, 1995

Three months after Rósa and Björk's disappearance

Rakel was tired. The past three months had felt like a news broadcast that kept breaking up. She listened to the beginnings, ends and middles of conversations but couldn't process everything she heard. A film had formed between her and the outside world, keeping life at bay.

The dwindling of her energies hadn't come as a surprise. Her strength had been ebbing for some time. The knowledge that she would have to go through this alone was like a heavy sack. It dragged her back into a hunch and made her heart tire at the slightest exertion.

Rakel walked up the stone stairs and knocked. The front door of the seaside house was flaking. As a matter of fact, the entire exterior could badly use a fresh coat of paint. Tinna had talked about giving it one and replacing the windows this upcoming summer. *That would be a good idea*, Rakel reflected. If the paint were allowed to peel, the rain and wind would do their work and damp would get into the property's structures.

Rakel's sister Tinna lived alone and spent all her time at the music school. She had no time for renovations; she taught at the school during the day and piano and singing for adults at night and directed the local children's choir.

The same choir Björk and Rósa had sung in. Rakel thought mournfully about her younger daughters. Rósa's curling pigtails and Björk's dimpled, winning smile that was short of two baby teeth.

In weaker moments, she ruminated on the terrible state she'd allowed things to get into. Life had slipped through her fingers, despite her best efforts to do things right. But the harder she'd tried, the more everything had snarled into a knot.

She knocked a second time, stepped inside, and called out to her sister.

'I'm down here folding the clothes, wait a sec,' came the faint reply from the basement.

Rakel took off her trainers and set them on the shoe shelf in the entryway. She stepped into the kitchen and stood there, gazing at the view outside the window. The cold Atlantic before her; the steep, snow-covered slopes rising on either side.

As the coffee percolated, the sisters stared out at the sea. Of the pair of them, Tinna had always been more direct. And so the baby of the family started the conversation by plunging straight into the most painful topic.

'How are you doing?'

Rakel kept her eyes nailed on the sea. 'Getting out of bed every day is a battle. The afternoons are easier than the mornings.'

Tinna hugged her sister and began to tenderly stroke her head. Rakel shrank from the touch. Her scalp was still tender. 'A horse bit me when I was feeding it; it's still a little sore,' she blurted, folding her arms across her chest.

'A horse?' Tinna wondered. She looked closely at Rakel.

Rakel nodded and kept her eyes fixed on the vista outside the window. 'Is the coffee ready yet?'

Tinna sighed and shrugged. She looked like she wanted to say something, but she settled on silence.

Rakel swirled her teaspoon around her cup. 'There's something that's been on my mind.'

Tinna took a sip of her coffee, looked her sister in the eye, and urged her to continue.

'I should probably talk to someone ... a professional. The insomnia isn't getting any better. I'm really exhausted.'

'This has been so hard on you,' Tinna said in an encouraging tone.

Rakel said she'd spoken with a therapist. The therapist had suggested they begin with a series of visits. 'Her practice is in the south; I'd have to go there for a while.'

Tinna seemed to instantly grasp what Rakel had come to ask of her. She reached across the table and gently patted her sister's hand. 'Of course Hildur can stay with me while you're in Reykjavík. She can sleep in the guest room, and it's only a couple of minutes' walk to school from here.'

Rakel looked gratefully at her sister.

'Do we need to go by and feed the horses?' Tinna asked.

Rakel told her sister that wasn't necessary. The neighbours had promised to look after the animals as if they were their own.

She gulped down the lump that had formed in her throat. Her eyes were glistening. She dried the corner of one with her sleeve.

'Hildur can stay with me any time,' Tinna said. 'It probably won't hurt for her to be in a different environment for a while anyway.'

Rakel nodded, sniffling. Things would work out. Soon everything would be better.

Chapter 56

Ísafjörður, March 2020

After saying goodbye to Helga and exiting the nursing home, Hildur unsilenced her phone. She had five missed calls: two from Beta, three from Jakob.

Just then her phone rang again. It was Jakob. He sounded hurried and stressed. 'Beta just called. She sent us the information she got from Keflavík. Come to the station as soon as you can; there's something I have to show you.'

Hildur shaved a couple of hundred metres off the walk by cutting between the hospital and the nursing home. When she stepped into the office, short of breath, she found Jakob at his laptop, looking impatient.

Hildur pulled up a chair and focused on the screen. Axel's professions had been listed in the phone book as fisherman and salesman. He owned a company with two small homes registered to it. One was in Selfoss, in southern Iceland, and the other one... Hildur paused and gave Jakob a pointed look: '... is here in the Westfjords.'

Jakob nodded. 'That much I understood. He has a cabin in Knife Valley.'

Hildur browsed through the data collected on Axel. Suddenly she realised she'd just read the most important piece of information contained in the email. 'And someone else has resided at that address.'

Jakob nodded again. 'Yup. Dísa Önnudóttir.'

Hildur took a couple of deep breaths and pulled her chair right up alongside Jakob's. She leaned her elbows on her knees and looked at Jakob, then the laptop screen, then back at Jakob. She kept reading. The local police in Keflavík had run the names of all individuals who'd been registered as living in the same household as Axel at any given time.

'This Anna Hilmarsdóttir... Anna and Axel lived at the same address until her death.'

Jakob nodded a third time. He seemed to have realised the same thing as Hildur. 'Our mystery caller Axel is Dísa's father.'

Hildur felt drained. When she'd looked into Dísa's identity during the trip to Reykjavík, the only information she'd found in the register was Dísa's mother's name and that she'd died when Dísa was eighteen. Now Hildur realised why the information on Dísa's father had been missing. Her mother and father had never been married. Only one parent had been named at birth. When a child was born out of wedlock, the father had to claim paternity.

'For some reason, Axel never did,' she huffed.

Hildur wrote down the address of Axel's cabin on a piece of paper. They needed to drive straight out there. Hildur made a brief call to Beta and asked for permission to bring a firearm from the locked cabinet. Under ordinary circumstances, Icelandic police officers weren't allowed to carry firearms without their superior's permission.

Hildur and Jakob started gearing up. Hildur thought it would be wise if everyone at the scene wore a bulletproof vest. Axel had at least one moose-hunting rifle and presumably plenty of ammunition. Better to be cautious and alive than careless and dead. Hildur remembered one assignment she'd imagined would be a routine visit to an address where a group of drunks were squatting. The neighbours had complained about noise, and Hildur had been among those who went to check things out. Suddenly one of the squatters had started threatening her and her partner with a weapon. The gun had gone off, but the shooter had been so drunk the bullet had missed by several metres.

Axel didn't have a criminal record, but that didn't mean much. They might find anything at all waiting for them when they showed up. Just to be sure, Hildur asked a police patrol to accompany them. Since he hadn't completed his police training, Jakob wasn't allowed to carry a weapon. Hildur got him some pepper spray from the supply room.

As they were walking up to the car, Hildur's phone rang. She glanced at the screen. It was Gylfi, one of the patrol officers she'd just spoken with.

'Did you guys make it out there already?' Hildur asked, then sighed at the response. 'OK, wait there. I'll call back in a sec. Thanks.'

She ended the call and returned the phone to her pocket. 'That was Gylfi. He and his partner just went by the house. There was no one home. The place was empty.'

Jakob threw back his head and rapped his knuckles against the car's roof in frustration. 'Dammit. So he got away too?'

Hildur shook her head. Things didn't actually look that bad. Gylfi had found a note taped to the front door that was apparently meant for the water meter reader: *Gone fishing, key under the mat, water meter in the basement. Back tomorrow morning. Axel*

Hildur pulled out her phone again. She wanted to make sure Axel was telling the truth. In fishing villages, the harbourmasters knew everything worth knowing.

Apparently Axel actually had gone fishing. The harbourmaster had seen him checking his nets before heading out. Axel had said he'd be spending the night at sea and returning early the next day. The location of Axel's little boat was visible on the harbour's monitoring system.

Hildur and Jakob could have had the coastguard take them out and bring Axel in, but they had no reason to. He hadn't run off; he'd clearly indicated when he'd be coming home.

'We'll give it another shot tomorrow morning,' Hildur said, letting her eyes slide from the car park to the shore. The rising tide would soon reach the top of the wall that protected the road from the sea.

All they could do now was wait.

Chapter 57

Atlantic Ocean, 1995

Three and a half months after Rósa and Björk's disappearance

Rakel felt bad about having lied to Tinna. But sometimes life forced you into situations where the ends justified the means. This had been one such situation.

Rakel had never intended to go to Reykjavík.

A couple of weeks after the visit with her sister, Rakel stood on the upper deck of the passenger ferry *MS Norröna*. The closer to harbour the boat got, the louder the seagulls' shrieks and the stronger the smell of fish. She took off her beanie, folded it up, slipped it in her pocket, and let the sea breeze tousle her hair.

She was smiling. She was finally smiling.

Rakel had slept in a four-woman berth and exchanged a few words with her cabin mates, three Danish university students on their way home to Århus. They'd been studying geology in Iceland for half a year and hitchhiked to the boat from Reykjavík. They drank the inexpensive cans of Danish beer they'd bought in the duty-free store and told stories about the creepy sheep farmers who'd offered them rides when they were hitchhiking. Rakel had listened to their tales and smiled at their self-confident chatter.

At the same time, she'd felt a little sad. She could have been one of them once upon a time. If she'd been more independent at their age and done something she wanted instead of simply doing what she was told, her life might have taken a different path.

Rakel grabbed hold of the white railing and gripped it hard. Once again she found herself sinking into the past, into choices that couldn't be unmade. She reminded herself that ruminating over what-ifs was pointless. From now on she was going to do everything right. From now on she'd be the one making decisions about her life.

After getting a solid night's sleep, Rakel had said goodbye to her cabin mates, packed her gym bag, made her way to the ferry's little restaurant for a cup of coffee, then came up on deck. She wanted to watch land approach. She wanted to feel the vessel gliding up Skopunar fjord.

Fjallið, the mountain rising behind the city, welcomed those arriving by ship to the main island. Fjallið meant 'mountain'. It wasn't visible if there was fog, but today the weather was clear. The morning sun shone from a blue sky as the giant white ship pulled into the small harbour at Tórshavn.

Rakel first saw the red waterfront buildings and the line of cars waiting to board the ferry. The closer to land the boat got, the more real her new life became.

Rakel allowed her gaze to slide up to the crowd at the harbour. She knew where to look: she knew her sister Hulda would be standing at the back.

Despite living on an island, Hulda was afraid of water. Especially near piers, where it was a long way from the edge to the bottom. She avoided boats and never went swimming in the sea. Hulda was still the same person she'd been as a child: extraordinarily cautious, very quiet, and distinctly aloof – totally unlike her sisters. Tinna was loud and sociable, Rakel less so but talkative in company. Meanwhile, even as a child Hulda hadn't spoken to anyone if she could avoid it.

Hulda had moved to Denmark as a young woman. She'd wanted to see the world. Life had later brought her to the Faroe Islands. Years had passed since Hulda had been in contact with her family back home. But they were still family. Deep down, Rakel had known she could trust Hulda.

Once Rakel had got in touch with her sister, Hulda had listened attentively and promised to keep Rakel's secrets. Arrangements had been made quickly. First Rakel had seen her children out of danger and to safety. Her sister had promised to handle the paperwork and get the girls registered so they could attend school. Hildur had fallen ill the morning of the escape, forcing Rakel to make a slight adjustment to her plans. She'd sent Rósa and Björk on ahead. She and Hildur would follow later.

Rakel had meant to make the trip with Hildur and Helga not long after the younger girls' disappearance and subsequent search, but Helga had started having doubts about a permanent move. She wasn't prepared to leave after all. Rakel had been sad, but only for a moment. She didn't mean to give up that easily. Once she sold the horses and got money for a new life, she'd be able to change Helga's mind.

Rakel had asked Helga to join her for a short vacation instead. When her beloved saw what a shared life could be like, she might see things differently. They could live together. After that there'd be no more secrets.

Never again would Rúnar drag her across the floor by her hair. Never again would she have to fear for herself or her children. She would no longer have to listen to Rúnar's sick threats about how easy it would be for her and the girls to experience the same fate as the family's cat and her kittens.

In a few weeks, Rakel could tell Tinna the truth too. Family, especially Hildur, was incredibly important to Tinna. Rakel knew their departure would be hard on her younger sister. Letting Tinna look after Hildur for the duration of this trip had been a good decision. Because Rakel and the girls would never be returning to Iceland.

Rúnar had been terrorising her life for as long as she could remember. As soon as they were married, he turned jealous, controlling, and violent. Rakel blamed herself for not having had the sense to leave earlier.

And then she spotted them.

Near the path leading up to the red-and-white lighthouse, a familiar figure stood a little apart from the others. Her apricot sweater with the black collar was visible from a distance. Blonde, wrist-thick braids fell past her powerful shoulders to below the breasts.

And there in front of Hulda stood two girls watching the boat pull into harbour: Rósa and Björk.

Rakel felt her eyes well up with hot tears. The sea wind carried them off, blew her skin dry. She'd done it. She'd finally left.

Chapter 58

Ísafjörður, March 2020

Hildur pulled the police vehicle into the service station car wash and started scrubbing the windscreen. She rinsed and scrubbed, rinsed and scrubbed. The minute she stopped moving, the recurring nightmare she'd had for the last few nights started spinning through her head. The dream-waves seemed to invade her consciousness even when she was awake. It was unsettling.

Hildur rinsed the sponge, turned off the water, and spooled the hose back on its stand. Out of the corner of her eye, she saw a male figure approaching. It was Jakob.

Hildur climbed in the driver's seat and gestured for Jakob to climb in next to her. They fastened their seatbelts and checked one last time to make sure they had all the gear they needed. And then Hildur turned right out of the service station forecourt.

The daycare children were walking over the pedestrian crossing in a double line. The teachers at the front and back made sure the group stayed together. Hildur recognised Little Kata's daughter among the children. She seemed to be engrossed in conversation with her partner and smiling. That made Hildur feel especially good. Some people had bad things happen to them and still managed to carry on with their lives. Hopefully that five-year-old was one of those individuals for whom things turned out in the end.

'You look a little tired,' Jakob said.

Hildur grunted and muttered something vague about not having slept well, then added: 'You don't exactly look perky yourself.'

'I tried to talk with Matias a couple of days ago, but it was a mess. Things just keep getting crazier and crazier with Lena ... I stay up at night worrying about it.'

Hildur nodded. She could see how anxious talking about Matias made Jakob. Would the situation ever grow any clearer? They reached the open highway, and she punched it up to eighty.

'I'm not leaving things like this. I've already started taking steps,' Jakob said, explaining about his conversation with the representative from the Finnish Ministry of Justice. Hildur thought Jakob's suspicions were accurate: Lena would never agree to mediation, and the matter would go to court.

'Now that I have a lawyer, I'm going to be shelling out a lot of cash. Tell me if you have any good, legal ideas for making money fast.'

'Become an influencer,' Hildur replied laconically. 'Or start mining bitcoin.'

The morning workout started coming from the radio. A twenty-minute coffee-break workout was part of the regular weekday morning programming on Icelandic public radio. An older female voice instructed listeners to breathe deeply and get into a comfortable position, to raise their arms into a 'T' and squeeze their glutes.

'Hey, I understood that butt thing!'

It took Hildur a moment to grasp what Jakob was talking about.

'What she was just saying on the radio: squeeze your butt muscles together.'

Hildur was delighted. Her colleague was gradually picking up the language.

'Some students start from *Introduction to Icelandic*,' Jakob said. 'I start from the butt cheeks.'

Hildur congratulated him with a thumbs up.

At the former fish-processing plant, Hildur flicked her indicator left. She turned onto a narrow road running past a two-storey apartment building and a few homes. Further up on the right stood the rarely used town hall and a couple of workshops. They drove past the former daycare centre.

As with many other villages, fishing had been a major employer here ten years ago. The place had been flourishing. Now almost half the houses were either empty or served as summer cottages. Only a handful of people remained. The store had shut its doors; the daycare centre was closed. The dilapidated homes with their broken windowpanes added to the ghostly feeling. Hildur sighed. This was only one village among the many that had fallen on hard times as fishing quotas were sold to the big harbours.

'What an eerie place,' Jakob said as they got out of the car. They scanned the yard. A couple of black ravens glided across the sky; a dog barked in the distance. The wind was wailing further up the valley, but it wasn't blowing here. Hildur assumed the nearby mountains offered some protection from it. No doubt the village had originally been built in this exact spot because it was sheltered from the wind. The sea was right there, so it wasn't hard to get to the harbour, even in winter.

The house looked like a lot of the other houses in the village: a two-storey home fortified against the elements by a corrugated metal roof. Unlike many others, this roof looked new. Its bright red colour glowed in the morning sun. The windows had been recently replaced too. The stout planters on the front steps had been planted with heather.

The patrol car pulled up behind them in the drive.

'We can probably go in, can't we?' Jakob asked.

Hildur nodded and began approaching the house. The patrolmen would cover them. One of them circled around to the back of the house in case Axel tried to escape that way. Hildur glanced at the heather; the plants looked well-tended. She was just setting her foot on the first tread when the front door suddenly jerked open.

'Watch out! He has a gun,' Jakob cried out.

A grey-haired, broad-shouldered man was staring at them from the doorway. His red plaid shirt was neat and his expression was calm, but there was a determined look in his eyes. Hildur could hear him breathing heavily. Her eyes fixed on the moose-hunting rifle in his hands. She recognised it instantly: an interchangeable-barrel Sako with a telescopic sight.

The seconds stretched out as the rifle moved. Hildur could tell the situation was over. She knew what was about to happen.

Axel gripped the rifle by its barrel and held it out butt-first toward Hildur. A fully packed gym bag lay at his feet.

'It's not loaded. The cartridges are over there in the drawer,' he said, nodding at the shelves in the entryway.

Hildur slowly climbed the two stairs. She kept her eyes on Axel and reached for the rifle. She handed it to Jakob and asked Axel if there were any other firearms in the house.

He shook his head. 'That hunting rifle is the only one. I didn't need anything else. It's such a fine weapon. That's what I used to shoot that bastard when he was skiing. From a hundred metres and straight through the heart.'

After saying these words, he took the gym bag, tossed it over his shoulder, stepped out, and pulled the door shut behind him.

'Shall we go?'

Chapter 59

Hildur entered the station's conference room with Axel. She was wearing jeans and a burgundy rollneck with a white cardigan over it. Axel's flannel shirt was informally untucked. A police officer and a murder suspect wouldn't be the first guess to come to a casual observer's mind.

Hildur had decided she would handle the Axel interrogation with the patrol officer Gylfi. Gylfi had slipped on the job that morning, and the resulting sprain meant he wouldn't be able to do his harbour rounds with his partner, so Jakob had been sent in his stead.

Hildur set three paper containers and spoons in the middle of the table. She'd promised to get them something to eat before the interrogation, and Axel had asked for ice cream. It wasn't a particularly unusual request. Some wanted pizza; others, a cigarette. Then there were those who wished for ice cream. Gylfi had brought three big bowls from the grill.

Hildur looked at the printout Jakob had left on her desk that morning.

'This is the information we've received from the firearms manufacturer Sako. The company has a few retailers here in Iceland who receive new products to test before their official release. Are you aware your name is on this list?' Hildur asked, nodding at Axel.

He answered in the affirmative without a moment's hesitation.

Hildur was sure Axel wouldn't be changing his story. He'd already confessed everything in the car on the way to the station.

Now it was time for the official interrogation. Axel hadn't wanted legal representation or an interrogation witness. There seemed to be no need.

Hildur opened her laptop, read Axel the caution, and prepared to type up everything she heard. She asked Axel to explain what had happened in his own words.

'I shot Hermann from the window of the maintenance shed at the cross-country ski tracks.'

'How did you know he was there?'

Axel said Hermann had used the fitness app Strava when he exercised. His profile had been public, making it ridiculously easy to monitor his athletic activities.

'I posted up in the shed several evenings waiting for Hermann, but sometimes he'd be skiing with other people. I didn't want to risk hurting anyone else. I waited for a night when he was alone. I aimed and fired. I left the body there, and apparently you found the bullet and the casing. I just gave you the weapon.'

Hildur nodded. Axel's confession notwithstanding, the Sako would be sent to Reykjavík for closer analysis.

She moved on. 'Why did you plan and carry out the murder of Hermann Hermannsson?'

For the first time during their conversation, Hildur saw crack appear in Axel's calm, almost carefree manner. The skin around his eyes tightened, and his jaw thrust forward a little. Hildur had no intention of rushing Axel; she gave him time to think. She reached for her ice cream and ate a couple of quick spoonfuls. The frozen chocolate-rice crunched pleasantly in her mouth.

'I assume by now you're aware I have a child. My spouse Anna died of heart disease several years ago, and Dísa and I were left alone together. At the time, Dísa was a young adult at a delicate stage of her life. Anna's death was hard on both of us, but I felt like we'd done OK.'

Axel related how hard he'd worked to support himself and Dísa. He'd fished, sold cookery sets from door to door, and taken cleaning gigs.

'I was always at work, which meant I was away from home a lot. I admit I could have been more present in Dísa's life, but it wasn't possible. I had a big mortgage and I wanted Dísa to continue playing music. Violins are expensive instruments. I wanted her to be able to study wherever she wanted after high school. To make sure money, at least, wouldn't be an issue.'

What Hildur saw before her was a father who worshipped his child. His eyes gleamed when he explained what an excellent student and gifted violin player Dísa had been.

'We'd had a good life until that one night in July.'

Hildur encouraged Axel to continue. She already knew what he was going to say. She just needed to get it down for the official transcript.

'The soccer association's summer party was held in a tent next to the sports centre.'

Everyone in Ísafjörður knew about the local soccer association's annual party. It was the highlight of the holiday season, and everyone was invited. During the day there were balloons, bouncy castles, and cotton candy machines. As day turned to evening, the families with young children excused themselves and an unofficial bar opened. Beer, wine and hard liquor were retrieved from car boots. The celebrations continued until early in the morning.

'Dísa went to the party. She was wearing a new blue-and-white-striped dress she'd been admiring in the shop window all spring. I finally bought it for her for the summer.'

Axel paused. He rubbed his face with his palms and pushed the half-eaten bowl of ice cream away from him. Then he continued in a soft voice: 'Sometime after midnight her friends noticed she wasn't there.'

They'd found Dísa in a stand of trees a couple of hundred metres away. She was covered in blood and had bruises on her face. Apparently she'd taken a blow to the head and lost consciousness for a moment. Dísa's friends had carried her the short distance to the hospital emergency room.

Axel had a tough time talking about what happened. Hildur and Gylfi knew the nature of Dísa's injuries from the physician's statement, but as detailed in Axel's own words they sounded even more horrific. He recounted in a calm voice how Dísa had been sexually assaulted so violently that the doctor on call literally had to sew her back together.

Then his voice rose. Hildur saw the hatred within him straining to get out. 'Dísa told me she'd told the doctor what happened. She'd even told him she recognised the rapist. It was Ari Hermannsson, a soccer player a little younger than her.'

Axel buried his face in his hands.

Hildur shot Gylfi a quick glance and read there on her colleague's face what she herself was thinking: this was incredibly hard on Axel, but it made no sense to call it off now.

After a couple of minutes, Axel lowered his hands to the table, let out a deep, determined sigh, and continued. 'Then that damned doctor destroyed the statement. The rapist got off like a stallion in a brood of mares.'

Hildur asked about samples. In cases of suspected rape, semen samples are collected for DNA analysis.

Axel grunted sadly and said the sample had disappeared too. 'Ultimately it came down to Dísa's word against that of the hometown soccer star. You don't have to be Sherlock Holmes to deduce what happened. Dísa never reported the rape to the police.'

Hildur typed quickly on her computer to get it everything down, although, of course, the interrogation was being videorecorded too.

She pitied this man; he and his daughter had tried to seek justice through official channels, but the system had betrayed them. Now he was sitting here in this cramped conference room eating ice cream and confessing the crimes he'd committed.

'After that summer, everything changed.'

Axel said Dísa couldn't stand the familiar surroundings anymore and moved to Reykjavík. He explained he'd lost his daughter to the streets. He wasn't surprised that was what happened, but it had still been horrendous. Dísa started numbing herself with drugs and cut off all contact with family and friends. She didn't want to see anyone who reminded her of what had happened in Ísafjörður.

'What did you do after that summer?' Hildur asked.

'I moved to Hafnir for a sales job. Lousy place, but close to the airport. Goods moved faster when I could handle business with the cargo companies and customs in person.'

Axel said he'd run into Dísa from time to time in Reykjavík, but his daughter had almost always been in such bad shape that she hadn't even recognised him.

'And then a couple of years ago I ran into her at the airport. Something miraculous had happened. She looked like she'd got a grip on life again. It felt amazing.'

'Have you two been in touch since?'

Hildur and her team had requested Dísa's phone records, and they indicated Dísa hadn't called or texted anyone much. There had been no evidence of contact between father and daughter. Maybe Axel would be able to shed some light on this.

Hildur registered Axel tensing a little. Losing contact with one's child must have been incredibly painful.

Axel settled for a shake of his head.

Hildur looked up from her laptop and out the window. The clouds had dropped; she couldn't see the peaks anymore. It would be raining again soon. The weather was constantly changing, sometimes every fifteen minutes.

Hildur coughed once and moved on. 'What about this other case, Gunnar?'

Axel said he'd been taking a shipment to the airport the way he had countless times before. He was a familiar face to the airport staff and was able to move around the area with relative freedom.

'I knew Gunnar had temporarily returned to Iceland from Cyprus. He was going to be speaking at some innovation event. There was some mention of it in one of the business newspapers. That's when I knew I had to do it now. I'd never be able to get my hands on that bastard of a soccer player who lived abroad, but I knew I'd be able to give those two crooks the punishment they deserved.'

Axel said he'd attended the innovation event, claiming to be a blogger who wrote about start-ups. He'd chatted with Gunnar and learned in a roundabout way about his flying pastime. He made sure he was at the airport with his packages the next time Gunnar was scheduled to take a plane up. Axel described how Gunnar had fuelled the aircraft and climbed in the cockpit.

Hildur typed furiously. After finishing a sentence, she looked questioningly at Axel.

'I walked up to the cockpit and knocked on the window. I said I'd noticed the cap on the fuel tank was loose and offered to tighten it. Gunnar thanked me for the help.'

It was almost as if a small smile flashed across Axel's face. His plan had worked. A few minutes later, the plane had taken off and the fuel had spilled from the tank.

Hildur looked Axel sharply in the eye. 'Weren't Gunnar's suspicions aroused when he saw you?'

She didn't see Axel's face so much as quiver. His expression was like stone.

A moment later, he relaxed a little, chuckled, and reached for his ice cream. 'Clowns like Gunnar talk to hundreds of people at business events like that. He'd never remember an ordinary guy like me.'

Then he finished his ice cream.

'There's one thing here that bothers me,' Hildur said, shifting slightly in her seat.

Axel's guard appeared to go up. He lowered his elbows to the table and leaned onto his hands. He looked inquiringly across the table at Hildur.

She stood and walked to the far end of the room. 'You executed the murders with forethought. You took everything into consideration except . . . except your own arrest. Using those new cartridges and calling here . . . It was almost as if you didn't care if you were caught.'

Gylfi turned slightly toward the window. The old office chair creaked beneath him. Presumably he'd been wondering the same thing.

'Lung cancer, T4 M1.'

'Excuse me?' Hildur asked, returning to her laptop.

'Metastasised lung cancer. It's already in my brain, so I'm a goner in a few months at the latest.'

Hildur looked at the aged man sitting in front of her. Life had dug deep furrows in his face. Even so, there were no external signs of fast-approaching death. He looked so ordinary somehow, not at all terminally ill.

Axel seemed to notice her scepticism: 'I'm having a good day today, but I don't have them very often anymore. Cancer makes your whole body ache. But I'm lucky; I can sleep. On good days I'm still able to function pretty well.'

Axel took a sip of water from his cup and glanced at the newspaper open on the smaller table next to the wall. It happened to be open to the obituaries. Icelanders wrote lengthy epistles about their deceased loved ones and had them printed in the paper's multi-page obituary section.

'I wonder what they'll write about me when I'm dead? Fisherman from the Westfjords who was found guilty of murder and died of cancer in prison. Missed by . . . no one,' Axel mused. His words weren't directed at anyone in particular. 'Tell me, do you think I'm a bad person?'

'It doesn't matter what we think,' Hildur said. 'We'll finish this up according to protocol, then you'll be transferred to jail down south to await trial.'

Axel nodded in acceptance. 'I don't think I have anything else to say. I killed both men and I'm glad I did. My only regret is I wasn't able to get my hands on that animal. I hope someday he gets what's coming to him.'

He drained his glass and gulped loudly. 'Could I have more water and my pain medications?'

'Of course. Gylfi will go get them for you in a moment. First I want to print these documents for you to sign.'

Hildur finalised the transcript, saved it, and walked into Beta's office. Standing there at the printer, she reflected on Axel. He'd been forced to watch his child's suffering without being able to do anything about it.

The nearly soundless printer pushed out smooth sheets of paper, black on white. It irritated Hildur when she heard people say everyone had a chance to choose success and happiness. If the greatest personal setback you'd experienced was your pet dog dying of old age, it was easy to live in a bubble where you thought everything was possible.

But sometimes nothing was possible, no matter how hard you tried.

Chapter 60

Westfjords, 1995

Three months and three weeks after Rósa and Björk's disappearance

The week had gone by far too fast. They'd spent seven lovely days together on the main island. The girls had shown her the neighbours' sheep farm. The four of them had gone hiking in the mountains next to Hulda's village. In the evening, after the girls had gone to bed, she and Hulda had had plenty of time to talk and plan for the future. Hulda had thought everything through. Rakel had been surprised at how much Hulda knew and how well she'd managed to arrange things.

The girls had started school, and Hulda had got them into the local girls' choir. They'd already made a couple of friends who lived nearby to play with after school. The children didn't share a language, but it wasn't hard to playing together. Icelandic and Faroese were surprisingly close to each other.

Rakel tapped her fingers against the steering wheel and turned up the radio. She only had a couple of more hours to go and then she'd be home. The drive from the eastern fjords crossed all of northern Iceland before reaching the road leading to the Westfjords. The heavy fog typical of eastern Iceland had slowed Rakel down, and she'd been forced to stop at an inn in Laugar for the night. But she'd still make it home on time, since Rúnar wouldn't be coming back until tomorrow.

Rakel loved how free she felt at the wheel. She practically had the road to herself. Icelandic public radio Channel One was playing oldies, which added to her sense of joy and liberation. The landscape outside the car was wintry, snowy.

When Rúnar headed back to sea after his week-long break, Rakel would pack her and Hildur's most important belongings and clothes into two suitcases. Helga would join them. The three of them would drive to the ferry terminal in eastern Iceland, board the boat to the Faroes, and when the ferry arrived at Tórshavn she'd tell Helga and Hildur everything. That Rósa and Björk were alive and staying with their aunt and they'd all moved here for good.

She didn't dare tell them any sooner. She didn't dare so much as whisper about her plans to anyone. Word of them could not make its way to Rúnar's ears. Rúnar had ears everywhere, even among the rocks that had rolled down from the mountains. Rúnar never took his eyes off her.

Hulda had promised settling in the Faroes would be easy. Even if Rúnar found out one day that Rakel had taken their children there without his permission, there wasn't a thing he could do about it. Hulda had told her about the Hague Abduction Convention. The purpose of the agreement was to secure the return of children who'd illegally been taken abroad. For instance, if a father illegally brought a child from Iceland to Denmark and the mother requested the child's return, the Danish authorities would have to send the child back to Iceland. But children weren't sent back from the Faroe Islands, because the Faroe Islands had never ratified the agreement.

Rakel marvelled at how much Hulda knew about everything and what an incredible help she'd been.

The shoreline road reached the base of a fjord. Three more fjords and one long tunnel. Then Rakel would be home.

The sun caressing the sea's surface made the water look warm. The sea might be shimmering, but it was treacherously cold. The mass of water billowed back and forth leisurely. The swells were mementoes of distant storms.

The shoreline road began to rise. Rakel stepped on the clutch and moved down a gear. The road entered a straight climb of a couple of hundred metres long. Halfway up the hill, a sign warned of a steep curve and a blind summit ahead. Blind summits were dangerous, because the oncoming traffic couldn't see anything beyond the crest of the hill.

Rakel changed down again and let the speed drop to thirty. She'd never come across anyone at the crest of the hill, but she knew that didn't mean it could never happen. And so she kept the car firmly to the right side of the road and passed the blue sign at the summit.

Rakel had a special fondness for this spot. Immediately after the crest of the hill, the road veered sharply to the left. On the right, a lava-rock formation a few metres high separated the road from the sea. According to old folk tales, the formation depicted a troll who'd gone fishing. Trolls ventured forth in darkness and couldn't tolerate sunlight. This troll's nocturnal fishing trip had gone on too long, and the creature had been caught in the rays of the morning sun. There it remained, a few dozen metres from the shore. Rakel passed the troll, smiled to herself at the old story, and continued on her way.

An hour later, Rakel arrived at a familiar fjord. The dark, single-lane tunnel felt endless. It always had. Ever since . . . ever since the girls had vanished in it. She knew the truth, but she didn't know how to best process the traumatic event with her daughters. After picking them up, Jón had driven directly to his farmhouse, where Rakel had been waiting outside. Before hurrying home, she'd told the girls about the surprise trip to Aunt Hulda's. On the surface, things had gone smoothly, but she knew feelings had been roiling beneath. The girls had no doubt found the rapid change distressing.

The past months had been incredibly difficult for Rakel too. She knew she'd done the right thing, but she'd nonetheless caused her children and her sister Tinna great suffering. The guilt had weighed heavily on her, at times intolerably so. Somehow she was going to have to process the move to the Faroe Islands and all the other changes more deeply. But she trusted things would work out.

The tunnel ended, and Rakel drove from the mountain's blackness into the valley. It was late afternoon, but the sun's rays still reached the south-facing slope. Soon she'd be home.

Then she felt herself freezing. Her car slid dangerously close to the right shoulder. With one swift movement, Rakel managed to correct and steer the car back into the middle of the road. But her fear didn't dissipate.

At first Rakel thought her sunglasses had been dirty. But the grimy smear on them was Rúnar.

Rakel saw her husband standing outside their house. She hadn't been mistaken. Broad-shouldered, vaguely hunched Rúnar was thrusting out his chin the way he had all these years. The more upset he was, the further his head pushed forward. Rakel groaned audibly. What was he doing home already? The fishing boat hadn't been scheduled to come back until tomorrow.

Rakel had the urge to turn around, but she couldn't. Rúnar had seen her. It was too late. She'd have to drive up to the house and take whatever was coming to her.

She slowed down and parked carefully next to the fence. She locked her face into a neutral expression, opened the door, and climbed out of the car as casually as she could.

'Hi. You're home already.'

Rúnar shook his head and scratched his protruding jaw with one hand. He had a spade in the other. He leaned against it, trying to project a relaxed demeanour, but Rakel could tell he was seething with rage.

'Where the hell have you been?'

Rakel hung back next to the car and tried to remain calm. *Everything's fine. I have nothing to hide*, she told herself. Out loud she said:

'At therapy. In Reykjavík. The neighbours fed the horses while I was gone.'

Rúnar tossed the spade to the ground and took a couple of brisk strides toward Rakel.

'Stop lying. You're dressed up. A silk scarf and everything. You've been with Hallgrímur. I just dropped by their place. Funny, there was no one home there either. Are the two of you trying to trick me by coming home at different times?'

Rakel's hand touched the light-blue silk scarf she'd wrapped around her throat that morning. *It sets off my chestnut hair*, she'd thought. She'd felt beautiful.

Rúnar took another step toward her, and Rakel felt her breath catch. His strong hands squeezed around her throat. His distorted, hatred-filled face was close to hers, and his stale breath surged into her nose.

'Reykjavík, huh? I can tell from your miserable face that you don't even know how to lie. When our fishing boat pulled out of harbour, you followed Hallgrímur to some shitty motel. You fucking whore!'

Rakel could smell liquor on Rúnar's breath. Despite being steaming drunk, he managed to fling her aside with such force that she fell to a semi-sitting position on the ground. Rúnar's words hurt, and she couldn't fathom his rage. Where had he learned to talk like that?

'Let's have a look in your bag and find out what you've been up to,' Rúnar hissed. He opened the back door of the car, yanked out his wife's gym bag, and unzipped it. He pulled out the clothes one at a time, eyed each article with contempt, then flung them to the ground. White socks, sweater, two pairs of trousers, dirty laundry stuffed in a plastic bag. The polka-dotted beauty bag where Rakel kept her shampoo and hand cream.

Rakel saw the disappointment in Rúnar's eyes. It wouldn't be long before the disappointment turned to rage, and Rakel knew it. She waited, because there was nothing else she could do. She'd never be able to outrun Rúnar. She wouldn't make it into the house to call for help. It would take the police at least half an hour to get to the valley. That would be plenty of time for Rúnar to break a window and get at her.

Rakel coughed. She tried to keep her voice steady and turn the conversation toward something as mundane as possible: 'Why don't we go inside so I can make us some coffee?'

Rúnar snapped something unintelligible. He looked disdainfully at Rakel and returned his attention to the bag. After rummaging through the side pockets for a moment, his face broke out in a victorious smile.

Rakel saw a small piece of paper in his hand. Her heart skipped a few beats when she realised what he was holding. The ferry ticket. Rakel felt like crying. How could she have been so careless as to leave the ferry ticket in the side pocket? She'd destroyed everything else: receipts, foreign-language wrappers, addresses jotted in a notebook.

'Goddammit, you're smarter than I thought. Smyril Line. You've been to the Faroe Islands.'

And then Rúnar went totally quiet. He stared at the ticket crumpling in his hand. Rakel saw his stomach rise and fall in time to his breathing. He bent down to pick up the spade, took it in both hands, lifted it into the air to build momentum, and brought it down. Rakel heard a thud and felt a broad, dull pain spread from her shoulder to her ribs and feet.

One, two, three . . . She started counting. By the time she got to seven, she couldn't feel any more pain. Rakel saw the concentration on Rúnar's face as he battered her. She felt the small rocks from the gravel-strewn yard, saw her hands shielding her head. She lay there on the ground, counted the seconds, and tried to think what to do.

One thing she did understand was she had no good alternatives. She couldn't let Rúnar find the girls. She had to think of something.

Rakel heard the spade fall against the wall of the house and felt Rúnar's legs straddle her body. He bent down, tore Rakel's hands from her face, and forced her to look him in the eye. A low growl erupted from his chapped lips:

'Who were you screwing in the Faroes?'

Rakel pressed as far into the ground as she could. She felt the rocks dig nastily into her back and the thin skin at the nape of her neck. She probed her teeth with her tongue and discovered one of her front teeth had chipped. She felt a warm trickle on her forehead. Rakel figured it was blood. She softly whispered back:

'Rúnar, now I see what I've done to you. Please forgive me. I haven't been a good wife.'

For a moment Rúnar looked like a child who'd been caught doing something naughty. Rakel had confused him. She had to take advantage of the situation.

'I see now that you had to teach me. And I deserved it.'

There was a stabbing pain at Rakel's side, and her lungs felt strange. She'd probably broken some ribs.

'Please forgive me. I want to fix everything. There's something I want to tell you about the Faroe Islands. There's something I want to show you.'

Rúnar straightened his back and stood up. He looked at her with an oddly complacent gaze. He looked lost.

'The girls are there. I brought them there to safety. But now I see how stupid that was. You just wanted to help. Please forgive me, Rúnar. I haven't deserved you. I want to make it up to you. I want you to come with me to fix this. If we start driving right now, we'll make it in time to catch tomorrow's boat.'

There was no boat the next day, but there was no way Rúnar would know that.

Rúnar stood there staring at her. Rakel didn't know what was going through his head, but he looked atypically calm. He was somehow out of it.

'Why don't you and I go on a little trip, and we'll come back with a surprise,' Rakel said. She reached for the sunglasses Rúnar had smashed and twisted and slowly rose to her feet. Her ribs hurt, but she didn't want to show it. She wiped away the blood from her forehead with her coat sleeve and tried to imagine she looked like an ordinary woman heading off to run ordinary errands. She wiped the dirt from her trouser legs and started dragging herself toward the car.

She decided to keep moving until Rúnar attacked her again and stopped her.

But he didn't. As Rakel reached for the door handle, she glanced back and saw Rúnar just standing there staring at her, arms dangling at his sides.

'Well, shake a leg then,' he finally hissed, opened the passenger door, and collapsed in the seat.

Rakel climbed in at the wheel. She pressed the accelerator and turned up the radio. Rúnar slumped at her side, half-asleep and stinking of booze. Now and again he'd comment on something, but he spent most of the drive staring out the window looking bewildered and taking sips from his pocket flask.

'You're not fooling me. You have some guy there,' Rúnar slurred, punching the dash.

Rakel ran her tongue across her chipped tooth and sighed: 'No, I don't. You'll see. This will be over soon.'

Rakel glanced at Rúnar out of the corner of her eye. Those hands. All the times they'd dragged her around the floors of their home. All the times he'd pulled her by the hair through doorways. Rakel had never shouted, because she hadn't wanted the girls to know their father was a monster. She'd chosen the worst possible spouse for herself. It was the biggest mistake of her life. He'd killed their cat and threatened to do the same to their children because he'd got it into his head somehow that they weren't his, that they were the neighbour's.

Rakel was done giving in and being on the receiving end of the insane violence she'd never confessed to anyone, not even Helga. She was too tired to play along anymore. She would fight back, even though she would pay a high price for doing so. Lying there on the ground outside her house, Rakel had decided she would no longer bend to Rúnar's will.

She was overcome with sorrow. Just an hour ago, everything had been different. She'd been feeling profound happiness, because her plan had almost succeeded.

As she sat at the wheel and glanced at the human monster slouching semi-awake at her side, she realised the truth was she only had one option left.

And then the tender notes of her favourite song filled the car. Óðinn Valdimarsson's soft voice sang about returning home after a journey.

He began with a depiction of green summer meadows and sunshine. Treacherous winter had been left behind; summer was just beginning. He sang how he'd soon see his love, who was waiting for him in the countryside. They'd build a house together in a sunny spot and live there happily.

The winding road began to climb. Halfway up the hill, a sign warned of a sharp curve ahead and an approaching blind summit. Rakel kept her eyes firmly on the road.

The familiar lava formation rose to her left. The troll that had been caught by dawn. The moss shone bright green in the sun.

Rakel accelerated, depressed the clutch, and changed gear. The engine wailed loudly.

She inched her right hand over to the man sitting at her side and unbuckled his seatbelt. Rúnar was so focused on his flask he didn't notice.

'Rúnar,' Rakel said loudly and gave him a hard push in the shoulder.

Now it was her time. She would get her revenge. For everything. She'd do it now. She spoke in as tender a voice as possible.

'You always suspected me and Hallgrímur. You claimed Hallgrímur was our children's father.'

Rúnar stared at Rakel without speaking. His breath was rattling.

'But you know what? You're wrong. I never wanted anything from Hallgrímur.'

Her voice was honey soft. She stroked her husband's cheek with her right hand and smiled broadly. Her broken tooth must have turned the smile into a grimace. Rúnar seemed to be perplexed by her tenderness.

'You were also right,' Rakel whispered and stepped on the gas. 'The children are yours, but I never was. I loved her. She secretly fixed everything you kept breaking. We didn't want to hurt Hallgrímur; that's why we kept it a secret.'

Rakel looked at her husband. His bewildered expression revealed that the words had sunk into his consciousness. Rakel relished the moment.

'Helga was for me what you never were. I truly loved her.'

Rakel heard the song coming from the speakers. It was as if fate had looked on her with favour one last time and played the song just now. She loved it. The gentle male voice soothed her. Warm and steady, it ushered her on like a guardian angel.

'When my journey ends I'll find you.

You, my greatest love.

I've come home.

I've come home.'

Rakel floored it and didn't turn at the curve.

Chapter 61

Ísafjörður, March 2020

Brenda the hula doll swished her hips on the dash as Brenda the Land Cruiser rocked down the bumpy road. The spring rains had picked up, and the temperature had risen above freezing for a couple of days in a row. The dirt roads that had suffered during the winter wouldn't be repaired until mid-May. Until then, one just had to make do. It was only in May that spring's arrival seemed more likely. Those who thought two sunny days in a row in March meant spring were in for a rude awakening. The transition from winter to spring was brutal on all optimists.

It was all the same to Hildur. She'd seen enough springs to know the sky could throw out a snowstorm and bring back winter. She wasn't an optimist, but she wasn't particularly morose either. Questions of happiness and satisfaction simply didn't interest her. She found them a waste of time. She lived and did things. Sometimes life felt bad, sometimes life felt good. The weather had nothing to do with it, that was for sure.

Waves are an exception, she reflected. The wave forecast had indicated surfing would be fantastic today. Hildur had promised to fill in for an officer who'd fallen ill and handle the evening patrol shift after her working day. She'd taken the liberty of not going in until noon.

She'd decided today was the day she'd brave the waves for the first time since the accident.

Axel was awaiting trial at the largest prison in southern Iceland, Litla-Hraun. Beta had announced she'd be moving back to Reykjavík after the summer and suggested Hildur be named acting chief of police until a successor was found. Hildur had absolutely no interest in the role. The thought of having a supervisory position felt unpleasant; she didn't want to take responsibility for the doings of others. She just wanted to do her own work.

She'd strapped her surfboard to Brenda's roof and packed her neoprene suit in the cargo space. But before she ventured into the sea, she needed to drop by and say hello to Hlín. It was only seven, so her friend would be feeding her horses their morning hay right now. Hildur got that the horses were important to Hlín, but even those that stayed outside year-round took an enormous amount of work.

Hildur parked in the muddy yard near the horses' shelter. She pulled up the hood of her parka to protect her head and grabbed a thick brown envelope from the passenger seat.

The horses were munching on hay under the shelter at the south of the pasture. Hildur opened the gate, being careful not to shock herself on the wire. Hlín raised a hand in greeting.

'You couldn't stay away? Should I get the saddles?' Hlín said with a wink.

Hildur laughed lightly and declined politely but firmly. Then she reached deep into her breast pocket and pulled out the brown envelope she'd rolled up and slipped in it.

'Do you remember when we spoke about Hermann and his son?'

'How could I forget?'

'Well, I need you to forget this,' Hildur said, holding out the envelope. Hlín patted her hands together to shake the hay from her gloves and took it. 'You never got this from me.'

Hlín glanced at her friend. She seemed to understand. 'OK. It was sent to me anonymously in the mail. It happens sometimes,' she said as she opened the envelope.

She pulled out a neat, several-page document. Hlín eyed it from start to finish, then went back to the beginning and read more carefully. A low whistle escaped her lips. She looked questioningly at Hildur.

'I came across it by chance during a murder investigation.'

'This is . . . this is appalling,' Hlín gasped, looking back down at the documents.

'Agreed. It's also your ticket out of those ram-breeding stories.'

Hlín immediately seemed to grasp the papers would cause a huge stink. The resulting story would probably make the news abroad. Hildur knew there wasn't a single sponsor or team owner who could turn a blind eye to it.

Hlín slid the envelope down the bib of her winter coveralls to protect it from the rain. 'Thanks. Nice of you to come by and look at the horses.'

'My pleasure.'

Hildur made her way back to the car. She climbed in, swept off her hood. and buckled her seatbelt. She turned left out of the drive and left again right after the river, toward the mouth of the tunnel gaping in the mountain's wall.

The forecast had promised long, low waves in a certain bay. Superb surfing conditions had been predicted there before, but Hildur had never paid any attention. She'd always skipped it as an alternative that didn't exist. Now she was on her way there, to surf at Kotsdalur, her former backyard. She knew she dared to face the sea today.

Chapter 62

Siurana, Catalonia, May 2020

Dísa

Dísa had set up her camp chair at the base of a big tree. The spreading branches offered shelter from the noonday sun. The birds were singing; a donkey brayed in the distance. The camping ground was quiet at this time of day. The only other people around were a woman and her children sitting on the benches. In an hour or so, the camping ground's little canteen would fill up as the climbers took a break and came to eat lunch.

The village – population a few dozen – was popular among climbers. The nearby limestone cliffs lured thousands of campers from around the world every year. The locals were used to constant comings and goings. No one paid any mind to Dísa. She melded easily into the mixed crowd of families and couples, groups of friends and people who'd come on their own. There was room for all sorts among the climbing hippies who hung out on the rocks and the professional climbers who'd trained to peak condition.

Dísa had come to Siurana by chance. She'd met a couple of globe trotters in Málaga who'd come to Spain when Covid restrictions were tightened in their homeland. The bright-eyed Italian girls in hippie jewellery hadn't had any plans other than making it to Catalonia. They'd told Dísa they knew a few squatters there and would stay with them at first. Dísa had tagged along as far as Tarragona, where she saw an advertisement for the climbing area at Siurana, and hitchhiked inland. The owner of the camping ground had been looking for a helper to handle the grunt work. Dísa had showed up at just the right time. She cleaned the restaurant and the camping ground's common areas for a couple of hours every night and in return was allowed to stay there for free.

She'd been in Siurana for a few weeks now. How long she'd stay, she couldn't say. At some point she'd no doubt want to return home, but the time hadn't come yet. For now she wanted to enjoy the warmth, the nearby hiking trails, and the scents of awakening spring.

Dísa looked at the notebook in her lap and took her pen in hand. She wanted to record this feeling as vividly as possible. Before she began writing down memories of her trip to Spain, she read through what she'd already written. She'd filled the previous pages in Iceland a little before she left.

What you leave behind, a cleaner will find. I don't know when I started getting tired of it. I began returning shitty surprises to their rightful owners. It felt so amazing!

Ha, that arrogant couple at the car rental! They were probably surprised when they finally got to their car and one of the back tyres was flat. Something sharp had accidentally popped it. Such a shame. Ha ha ha.

Or that hussy applying lipstick in the bathroom . . . She'd probably never guess I was the one who tipped off the Financial Supervisory Authority about her schemes. I watch the news, and I know what insider trading is. There was a form on the supervisory authority website that made it easy to submit an anonymous tip. Damn, it felt good when I saw her picture in an article saying she was suspected of insider trading. The special prosecutor had opened an investigation. Boom!

And then that rude pimple-faced kid at the supermarket. The one who humiliated me at the register. I know he found what he'd left behind. I got his address by following him home one day after work. I ordered a couple of hundred kilos of horse manure from a stable and had it delivered to his backyard. The woman selling the manure wondered about the terrace house address, but when I told her I was building a big garden for summer and really needed the nutrient-rich horse manure, she stopped asking and promised to deliver the goods right away.

Dear diary, things work out surprisingly often when you start working them out.

Dísa took a sip of her ice-cold soft drink, turned to a blank page in her diary, and started writing the things that had happened during yesterday's hike. She smiled in satisfaction. Of course she didn't write down absolutely everything on the pages of her diary. It wouldn't be smart to reveal all her secrets.

There were only two people in the world who knew what had really happened that spring. She and her father had planned and carried out everything together. Her father had wanted to give Dísa a chance for a new life and succeeded.

Her new life had begun the moment she untwisted the cap to that fuel tank.

Chapter 63

Faroe Islands, late May 2020

Axel Jónasson was born in Hnífsdalur on 16 August 1962. He died 20 May 2020 at Eyrarbakk after a long battle with a serious illness.

His parents were Jónas Karlsson b. 2 July 1930, d. 10 October 1992, a smith from Ísafjörður, and home economics teacher Anna Jónsdóttir b. 28 September 1942, d. 3 November 2008, from Borgarnes. Their children were Axel Jónasson, Svala Jónasdóttir, and Kristján Jónasson. Kristján, who had had a career as an accountant died 4 April 2018, and Svala, who worked as a cook, died on 17 December 2009.

Axel's life partner was Anna Hilmarsdóttir. Anna died in 2005.

Axel and Anna had one child, Dísa Önnudóttir. Dísa was born 29 January 1987. She lives in Reykjavík.

Axel's funeral will be held 10 June 2020 at 1 p.m. at the church in Eyrarbakk.

My father was a good man. He was helpful and a good friend to his friends. He couldn't stand injustice. My father loved being out in nature and hunting. When I was a child, my father's favourite thing to do was record the movements of migrating birds in his notebook. He and I would often go for nature walks together. I'm sure he continued bird watching after I moved away. Every spring, he said, there were two sounds he loved above all others: the call of a golden plover and the sound of me singing.

My father's life wasn't easy toward the end. He was very ill and had to face injustice and tolerate suffering. But he managed in his own way.

Rest in peace, Daddy. I'll miss you.

Dísa

After reaching the end of the obituary, Hildur folded up the *Morgunblaðið* and left the paper on the table in the coffee shop. The departures terminal at Keflavík was quiet. She'd come to the airport three hours before her flight, just to be sure. The pandemic had eased, and the Faroe Islands had loosened their immigration restrictions. She would finally be able to make the trip she'd been planning since March.

A lot had happened over the spring. The article Hlín had written had proved explosive. Ari Hermannsson lost sponsors and wasn't getting any playing time. His team had cancelled his contract. And after the article was published, similar stories began to bubble up about other Icelandic soccer stars. Suspected rapes, suspected crimes against minors, assaults. Hildur got the impression the nation's soccer circles would be washing their dirty laundry for a long time. Hlín would begin working as an investigative journalist at Iceland's most prestigious newspaper that autumn.

The flight time from Keflavík to Vágar Airport was under two hours. Vágar was located on an island of the same name. As the plane made its approach, Hildur saw a familiar-looking landscape out the window. Sea, green islands, steep cliffs, a smattering of small villages. Hildur had looked into practical arrangements well in advance. She knew where to go. She caught a taxi at the airport and gave the baseball-capped taxi driver the address.

The drive to the outskirts of the capital, Tórshavn, would take about forty minutes.

She leaned her head against the car window and gazed out. Wherever she looked, she saw rolling green hills, some steep, some less so. The morning light was pitilessly bright. The landscape reminded her of her childhood fjord. The world was brilliant; the sky was high. A gushing waterfall next to the road splashed so wildly the driver had to turn on the windscreen wipers.

Grass-roofed houses, sheep, an endless green vista. When the taxi crossed the bridge connecting Vágar to the main island, Hildur finally saw the sea up close. It roiled a deep blue beneath the bridge. Waves pummelled the island's shore. Some water was left swirling in small caves inside the cliffs.

Hildur emerged from her reverie when the taxi stopped. She glanced at the house: black roof, white exterior. Flowers next to the front door. A large flock of sheep in the meadow. This had to be it.

After a lot of tracking down, she'd finally found Hulda. Hulda had had a big sheep farm and substantial pastureland but didn't live at the farm anymore. For a few years now, she'd lived in the Alzheimer's unit at Tórshavn municipal hospital. Her caregivers hadn't been able to provide Hildur with any information, because Hildur's wasn't listed in their records as a family member. And so Hildur had called the local police station and asked about Hulda's farm. Who was looking after the animals while Hulda was in the hospital? The friendly policeman had told her about Björk, who had stayed on at her mother's farm.

The sun emerged from behind the clouds, setting the scene aglow again. Hildur had to shut her eyes against the brightness. She heard the taxi pull out of the drive. A bird twittered from its perch on the gutter.

Hildur stopped on the top step, took a deep breath, and knocked on the door.

Silence.

A cloud slid in front of the sun, darkening the landscape. Somewhere in the distance a sheep bleated. Hildur shifted her weight and knocked again.

The handle pressed down, and the door opened. The woman who answered said something in Faroese. Hildur interpreted it as a greeting. She was on the verge of responding but suddenly didn't know what to say. She just stared at the dark-haired, freckled woman standing in the doorway. The woman was holding a bag of dry cat food and looking queryingly at Hildur.

Hildur began in English: 'Hulda . . . Um, is this Hulda's house? Do you live here?'

The woman raised her hand to her mouth, and her eyes widened in fright. 'Mum! What is it? Did something happen at the nursing home? Why didn't you call right away instead of coming here like this—'

Hildur raised her palms reassuringly: 'No, no. Hulda should be fine.'

The worry on the woman's face faded into curiosity.

'I'm not from the nursing home. I hope to be going there later. Hulda is, well . . . I mean, she's . . . She's my aunt.'

The woman took a closer look at Hildur. She tilted her head to the left and squinted. Hildur felt a pang in her breast. She'd seen that look before. Sometime long ago.

'Aunt? Now I don't understand . . .'

The woman was speaking more quickly now. Hildur saw her eyes take in the details. She felt the woman's gaze caress her hair, her eyes, the sides of her nose. All sorts of questions were going through Hildur's mind, but none of them seemed to make any sense. And none of them seemed to suit the moment.

Hildur looked at the head gently tilted to the side and the eyes that were simultaneously appraising and curious. Hildur remembered having seen exactly the same look when they'd made Christmas decorations at the kitchen table.

'You're Björk, aren't you?'

It took the woman a moment to register the question. She stared at Hildur. Her head tilted a bit further to the left, and the muscles around her eyes tensed even more. Hildur stood there on the stairs and tried to imagine what was going through the other woman's head just then.

'You might not remember; it was all so long ago. But I'm Hildur. I'm your sister. Does Rósa live here with you too?'

The freckled woman shook her head. Her hands dropped to her sides. Dry brown nuggets rolled across the floor. A longhaired grey cat leaped out from behind the door. It had seen its moment had come and began gobbling up the tidbits.

Hildur looked at her little sister as if she were a distorted mirror image. Familiar yet totally foreign. Which is what they were, in a way. From different ends of the same reality, one wooden threshold between them.

Björk took an unsteady step backward and made room for Hildur to enter.

'Would you like to come in?' she asked in a soft voice.

A Word from the Author

Hildur could be my friend, but she's fiction. Most places mentioned in *The Grave in the Ice* exist, but the events and characters are invented.

Any possible similarities between the story and reality are completely coincidental. But that's what life's like: coincidental! We wander around and bump into each other. Sometimes those collisions have consequences, and no one can accurately predict them beforehand.

My warm and sincere thanks to all those helpful people who supported me through the writing process.

Thank you, Ingibjörg Elín Magnúsdóttir and Aldís Hilmarsdóttir, for patiently answering my questions about police work.

Thank you, my Instagram followers who helped me with questions regarding soccer and other matters.

Thank you to knitwear designer and coworking space friend Sigríður Sif Gylfadóttir for helping me with the details of knitting – and helping Jakob knit Hildur a sweater! It turned out beautifully.

If any errors have made their way into the text, they are mine alone.

A big thanks to my publisher, WSOY. Publishing manager Anna-Riikka Carlson: thank you for your trust and sharing in my enthusiasm for Hildur, Rósa and Björk.

Executive editor Hanna Pudas – my deepest thanks! I don't know where I'd be without you. Not here, that's for sure. Thank you, editor Lea Peuronpuro, for your unstinting expertise in the final stages of the manuscript. Thank you, WSOY brand manager and fellow Satu Satu Sirkiä for your fantastic work marketing the Hildur series – and helping me look after my wellbeing.

A thank you to Bonnier Rights literary agent Eleonoora Kirk for introducing the Hildur series to an international readership. Thank you, Lippo Luukkonen, for the legal assistance.

Lastly and most importantly: Thank you family, relatives, and friends. I'm happy you're the ones I've bumped into.

Satu Rämö

February 2023

Don't miss out on Hildur Rúnarsdottir's next case . . .

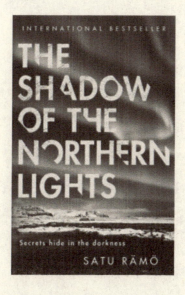

As Christmas comes to the west cost of Iceland, a corpse is found in a fish farming pond. Detective Hildur Rúnarsdóttir and trainee Jakob Johanson barely have time to start their investigation before another body is discovered. And soon a third.

While investigating the case, Hildur's lost sister weighs heavy on her mind. Meanwhile, Jakob travels to Finland for the hearing of his fraught custody battle, that leaves him facing dire consequences. As the number of deaths continues to grow, Hildur and Jakob are desperate to catch the killer before they strike again.

COMING AUTUMN 2025
AVAILABLE FOR PRE-ORDER NOW